SANDIE SHAW AND THE MILLIONTH MARVELL COOKER

Heady times in the summer of 1965...

In the summer of 1965, when rock and roll fills the dance halls, the Marvell factory in Grafton is buzzing. Could it be because singing sensation Sandie Shaw is coming to town? Or maybe it's because, for some workers, even bigger events are taking place off the clock... There's the general manager and his naïve young mistress, Evelyn the elegant secretary carrying a hidden burden and the immigrant workers making a new life in a new land. For innocent student Cassandra, her summer on the production line teaches her far more than she ever imagined. Their lives unfold to the sound of the sixties.

SANDIE SHAW AND THE MILLIONTH MARVELL COOKER

Sandie Shaw And The Millionth Marvell Cooker

by

Wendy Robertson

Magna Large Print Books
Long Preston, North Yorkshire,
BD23 4ND, England.

British Library Cataloguing in Publication Data.

Robertson, Wendy
   Sandie Shaw and the millionth Marvell cooker.

   A catalogue record of this book is
   available from the British Library

   ISBN   978-0-7505-3100-9

First published in Great Britain in 2008 by Headline Review

Cover illustration courtesy of Headline Publishing Group

Published in Large Print 2009 by arrangement with
Headline Publishing Group Ltd.

Magna Large Print is an imprint of Library Magna Books Ltd.

Printed and bound in Great Britain by
T.J. (International) Ltd., Cornwall, PL28 8RW

For Bryan and Susan,
and in memory of Barbara and Tom.
They all knew factory life.

Acknowledgements

This story is a celebration of the unique quality, humour and energy of the people who worked at a particular factory in the North in the 1960s. I am pleased that heavy industries like mining and shipbuilding continue to respect their justified working-class heroes. However, I have to admit to a twinge of regret that the present day legacy of light engineering is the emptying factories, production by computer terminal, and a bizarre TV programme where the prize for some young blood, who doesn't know what he doesn't know, could be his own production project. How Patsy and Karen would have mocked! How Charlie, Tamás and Stan would have laughed! This novel is for the heroines and heroes of factory life just like them.

I would especially like to thank my editor Harriet Evans for encouraging me to write another quirky story that reflects the truth of its time. And thank you to Celine Kelly for shepherding Sandie safely onto the printed page; Yvonne Holland for her special attention to detail; Juliet Burton for her wit and her friendly support, and Gillian Wales for her friendship, sensitive advice and unique access to crucial sources.

After I had finished writing this story I met and

talked with Dean Torok, who told me of the time his father came from Hungary to work in the factory in the sixties. Weirdly, it seemed to me that here was Tamás, come to life. Thank you for that feeling, Dean.

Notes on a Time and a Place

I will tell you a story of a factory, a very special place. It was a long time ago but for me it's just as though it were yesterday. We're in the mid-1960s. The last age of post-war innocence: the dawn of the age of celebrity.

We are coming out of our post-war shell. We'd been told that we had never had it so good, and now Mr Harold Wilson tells us Labour will make it even better. There is even talk of us counting our currency in the French way. Further afield, Africa is throwing off our colonial yoke and ordinary Americans are getting a better deal from Lyndon B. Johnson, even if they are being sucked into the escalating war in Vietnam.

These world-changing affairs seem very far away in Grafton, a small ex-mining and iron-working town studded with woodlands and set in green hills. Despite the sixties swinging elsewhere, Grafton is an old-fashioned kind of place. Some boys still join their fathers to watch football, race dogs and keep pigeons. Men still drink in clubs where women are banned. Labour-intensive Sunday dinners still keep the women-folk out of mischief on Sundays.

At the Gaiety Dance Hall they play Beatles songs but remember times when dancing rock'n'roll was only permitted if you confined your excesses behind the sateen rope that divided you from the 'proper' dancers. The memory of bopping in the cinema aisles to Bill Haley's 'Rock Around the Clock' is the new nostalgia.

The contraceptive pill is nudging Grafton women into a new way of looking at things. Even so, the dynamism of the 'sexual revolution' centres more around the rootless universities in the North, than here at its working-class core. On the bright side, more working-class children than ever before are climbing the new rickety ladders into higher education, to new-build colleges and polytechnics, now working-class Meccas.

The town of Grafton, once built around coal, now relies on Marvell Domestic Appliances for its income and prosperity. This big factory employs two and a half thousand workers – mostly women – who support eighty per cent of the households in the town. Some of these women are third-generation workers, their mothers and grandmothers having worked on the Marvell site in the Second World War to assist in the making of bombs to drop on Hitler.

My name is Cassandra Fox and in the summer of 1965 I am one of these workers. My own mother works at Marvell's, so for this summer it is allegedly my good fortune to work here on the production lines in the week when Sandie Shaw – that thrillingly iconic singer – is flown in at great expense to present the millionth Marvell cooker to their millionth lucky customer.

In Marvell's factory popular music – a weird echo of the wartime *Workers' Playtime* – blares out from the factory Tannoy, punctuating and sometimes overlaying the industrial clamour. These days, rather than the old swing bands we have Bill Haley, Buddy Holly, Chuck Berry, Elvis Presley, the Everly Brothers. And now the Beatles. The women and girls sing along from time to time as a favourite track catches their ear.

The week I start at Marvell's the Tannoy is blaring out Sandie Shaw's '(There's) Always Something there to Remind Me' instead of 'Can't Buy Me Love' and 'I want to Hold your Hand' – much to the disgust of younger workers who think their taste is far more sophisticated than this. After all, the Beatles, the Rolling Stones are where it's at these days.

My tale of Sandie Shaw's visit to Marvell's is only one of many stories, told and untold, that fuse together to make that ten days in the mid-sixties so very extraordinary.

Early Start

Monday

On the day I started at Marvell's I sat beside my mother on the early bus, which smelled of soap and freshly lit cigarettes as it swayed and bumped through a morning that seemed bruised and battered from the night before. The bus was packed to an illegal level: too many bodies crowded together. Faces shone out and receded in the pallid, early glow of streetlights. There was no talk, no eye contact at this time of day. People just smoked and coughed, scanned the papers, picked horses, read horoscopes, and checked on last night's football score. Some girls, cigarettes in mouths, were taking out their big rollers and putting on full make-up. One girl was clipping on large daisy earrings.

At the factory gates the streams of workers, flowing from the dozens of buses, merged into a river of people pouring down the walkway towards the flat grey hangar-like buildings that encompassed the great Marvell enterprise. I had to stop to take it all in. Of course I had heard about this place from my mother. And I had seen it many times from the bus on the main road. But up close it was another thing: bigger and dustier, kind of seething with some life of its own.

Straight ahead this long, high loading bay

fronted the big cooker building: a large wagon was already parked there, its rear doors wide open. Two boys in warehouse coats over their drainpipe trousers were sitting with their legs dangling over the edge of the bay, having a last cigarette before they started, and whistling appreciatively at the best-looking girls as they passed.

'Come on, Cassie!' My mother nudged my arm and led me through a door at the side. While we stood in the queue waiting for her to clock in, I blinked around at the inside of the building and caught my breath. The building was twice as big as it seemed outside. The long production lines stretched into the distance; overhead wires looping down like so many spider-webs. No machine sounds. Just the echo of voices, as hundreds of people trickled towards their stations, muttering, laughing, dumping out their cigarettes.

My mother grabbed my arm again and marched me down the line till we came to a crossroads. 'This is me!' she said. 'And that's you.' She pointed towards a kind of watchtower of offices at the centre of the building overlooking the lines. An iron staircase led up to a gantry with doors leading off it. 'Up those stairs, love. There he is. You can't miss Charlie Priest. The smooth bloke that's wearing a suit. Tell him I sent you. He knows you're coming.'

She strode off then, like she owned the place.

I ran up the stairs under the eyes of Mr Priest. He had shaving cuts on his face and smelled strongly of aftershave.

'I'm Cassandra Fox,' I said. 'I was told to come here.'

'Linda's gal? Good worker, our Linda.'

He had this funny voice, not quite American. He looked me over. I saw myself reflected in his eyes: a girl of nineteen, nearly as tall as he was. Neat figure, nice legs. Mousy hair swept back too hard in a ponytail, making the face longer and thinner. Even then I knew my good points and my bad.

I stared back at him defiantly.

'Let's get you started then.' He led the way through an outer office where two women were already typing. One, a fair slender woman, really good looking, looked up and smiled with faint sympathy. In the corner a man in a ragged spotless white coat was staring up at a notice board, and beside him a youngish man in shirt and tie squeezed his eyes against the smoke of his cigarette as he ticked off columns in a ledger in front of him. He raised his head and his eyes flickered over me just like Mr Priest's had. But I was not offended this time. This one was good looking, not in a film-star-ish way, but in a tight, pale-skinned, high-cheekboned, grey-eyed kind of way.

I have to tell you my heart lurched. But I was only nineteen then, still a virgin and unspoken for, so my heart tended to lurch with alarming regularity.

In his office Mr Priest sat down behind a desk piled with papers and files and bristling with offcuts of metal. He nodded at the chair opposite and I sat down. Then he lit a cigar, took a good drag and filled in some forms.

'Here, sign this, Cassandra Fox,' he said. He signed a time card and pushed it across to me. 'I've marked it up for you this morning. But don't you forget to clock out tonight on the machine. The girls'll show you how. And don't forget to clock in tomorrow. Remember!' he drawled. 'Not clocked on, not clocked off, not paid.'

And that was it. No palaver about getting a job in those days. He led the way back out onto the gantry, his hand just touching my elbow. I could feel the glances of those people in the office. Perhaps it was unusual for him to take this trouble. I imagined the general manager had minions to do all this. Perhaps the blonde woman. Or the fair man. Maybe my privileged position was something about what my mother told me yesterday, about her and Charlie going back a long way. She'd seen my look and smiled slightly. 'Not that, Cassie. He was a simple progress man there when I started and we got on pretty well. That's all.'

On the gantry, we looked down at the long production lines and the sheer noise hit my ears. The women were working away, some of them shouting over the noise of the Tannoy blaring out 'Summertime Blues', their raucous tones counterpointing the smooth tones of Eddie Cochran. The penetrating voices and straining music were underpinned by the humming grind of the conveyor belt. I wondered if you ever got used to the noise. I thought that it must turn some people deaf. But then how would they know?

'I'm sending you down on the wiring jackets,

Cassandra. Nice little job. There are good workers there'll show you the job,' said Priest. He leaned over the railing of the gantry and bawled, 'Steve!'

A young man looked up from the box of wires he was loading onto the end of the line from a trolley. He was a little too fat but had smooth mushroom-coloured hair and was very neat, wearing a shirt and tie and pressed slacks, not overalls like some of the other boys I'd seen as I came in.

'Yes, Mr Priest?' he said.

'Take this young woman down the wiring and set her on with Patsy O'Hare. I'll let Stan Laverick know I want her there. Name of Cassandra Fox. Linda's girl.'

The boy's keen glance moved to me and he grinned. His eyes stayed on my face. At least he didn't look me up and down.

'Yeah, boss,' he said.

I looked down from the gantry, glued to the spot. The place had this funny smell; of dust and powdering concrete; of burned paint and industrial grease; of bodies and cigarette smoke.

Priest laughed. 'Daniel into the lion's den, eh?' He gave my shoulder a push. 'Get on then, young lady. You gotta start sometime, somewhere. Linda tells me you're a clever sort, but down there is the real world where clever counts different. Down there, we work. We know how many beans make five. Another kind of education, you could say.'

I took a deep breath and made my way down the iron stairs. I'd said nine words to Priest and

21

now it seemed I was in the machine, part of his operation.

'Now, Cassandra!' The boy called Steve winked at me and we walked shoulder to shoulder down the line under the sharp eyes of the operators, whose hands never stopped moving as they followed their progress. This was it. *Do or Die.* This was it.

'Ouch!' I licked my finger, and dropped the wires. Again.

The woman called Patsy O'Hare – narrow face, grey-blond hair piled high on her head, pouchy cheeks, too much lipstick – didn't stop working. 'Not doing too well, are we? Cassandra, was it?' There was no sympathy in her voice. 'From where I sit, looks like you've two left hands.' Her voice was as deep as a man's, but resonant, not hard to listen to.

I stared at the bench in front of me. The boy called Steve had showed me the job: screw two small screw holders into a kind of wiring harness with small screws. Once you'd done that, the slowly moving line took it to the next girl, who bunched dozens of wires and, hands flying, screwed them into the harness.

Steve introduced this girl to me as Karen. Her glossy black hair fell onto her shoulders and she wore her long fringe set in two maxi-rollers. Her eyes were lined in kohl. Even with rollers she had glamour.

''S easy!' Karen went over it again after Steve had left. 'You just do this, this, this and this.'

That word *just!* The job wasn't easy. It cut your

fingers till they bled, and my fingers, quick as they were with pen and paper, were very slow.

I struggled on for half an hour under the eyes of these two women and at last Karen sighed, jumped off her stool and came to stand by me. 'You want a bit of help, love?' Her words were friendlier than her tone. 'You're stopping the line here.'

I rubbed my eyes with my sore hands and said a humble thank you.

Karen slipped into my seat and demolished my backlog of work, her hands whirring to the point of invisibility. Watching her steady machine-like movements, my eyes swam and my body dropped to a machine-like throb that fell into rhythm with the music on the Tannoy: 'Bye Bye Love'.

Talk about dated...

Karen jumped up again and I thanked her too enthusiastically. Patsy O'Hare looked up, not stopping her wiring. 'No need to say thank you, flower. Our Karen just doesn't want you to stop the line and lose us all our bonus. Looking after number one, like we all have to.'

I picked up the wires and screwdriver. 'It's not fair to expect me to be quick straight away. It's not my real job.' God, what a whiner I sounded.

'Not a real job! Ooh, I forgot! Student, aren't you? Should'a known. Fancy name you got. No job at all, this, for someone called Cassandra,' said Patsy.

I'd had grief – even fights – about my name at school as well. Can't count the number of times I'd wished my name was Jane. Now things were not so bad. There was even another girl at my college called Cassandra.

'You're lucky to get a job at all just here for the summer,' said Karen. 'Must know somebody.'

I nodded. 'My mother works down on circuit breakers.'

'What's she called?'

'Linda. Linda Fox.'

'I know her. Marvell's bloody marvellous family policy,' growled Patsy. 'Landed us with more duck eggs than a NAAFI omelette.'

'I can't help it if ... ouch ... this wire's like knives. Doesn't half cut you.' I got down to scrabble on the floor for the dropped wires.

When I got back on my stool Karen lifted her open hand in the air, her fingers splayed. 'What you need is plasters, love. One for every finger. Prevention better than cure.'

I put down my screwdriver and looked round. 'Where do you get plasters...'

'Woah! Matter of fact you can get plasters from the woman who takes care of the lavs,' said Patsy. 'But stop where you are for now, flower. Don't want you stopping the line all together.'

So, ignoring my stinging fingers, I picked up my screwdriver, got my head down and worked on, avoiding the gaze of the other two women and only half listening to their talk about Elvis and Priscilla and the wonderful romance of it all. Every so often Karen would come round silently to help me with my backlog but nothing was said.

After what seemed like many hours the nine o' clock buzzer went. First break. I could have cried with gratitude. This time last week I had been rolling in for my first lecture, already sleepy from

24

my college breakfast.

As the conveyor ground to a halt the rippling sound of talk filled the workshop like the twittering of starlings in the hangar-like space. I knew from my mother that in this ten-minute breathing space in the factory, secrets were spread, reputations and marriages were made and ruined. Her cynical view was that some of the women exaggerated their experiences to tell a good story, others invented tales – told outright lies – so as not to be left out. Confidences and revelations were good currency at break-time.

Patsy brought her stool round to sit beside Karen, who smiled and lounged back, her flask of coffee in one hand and a cucumber in the other. She took a bite of the cucumber as though it were an apple.

She looked at me. 'Don't you like it here, then?' she asked. 'Cassandra?' She said my name like it was a joke.

I shrugged. 'I've just started. What do I know?'

Patsy laughed. 'Doesn't need to bother to like it. Cassandra here will be back away, shot of us all in a few weeks' time. Nice name, that. Where might it come from?'

'I was called after that man that writes in the *Daily Mirror*.'

'I read his stuff,' said Patsy. 'He said they shouldn't hang Ruth Ellis. Years ago. Right too. He was talking sense. Bloody men!'

Karen bit into her cucumber. 'It's a man's name, then?'

'No, it's after a Greek goddess who foretold the future.'

'I'll tell you my future,' said Patsy. 'Work, work and more bloody work.'

That seemed unanswerable.

'You got a boyfriend, then?' said Karen, closing her sandwich box and putting it back in her bag.

'Well, I know some boys.' One of the nice things about college is the possibility of being friends not just with the girls there but with the boys from the university down the road. Equality and independence is the thing these days. Everyone seems to keep their options open. Only a few of the girls have begun to pair off. Just now, that suits me.

'Aye, them college lads,' said Patsy. 'I heard about them. Get up to all sorts, don't you? Sex and drugs, and rock and roll, isn't it?'

'Not for all of us,' I said primly. Not all the time, I added in my head. Nearly choking yourself on a joint or two doesn't really count as drugs. One of the boys had taken LSD and said it was amazing but he had none the day we met him, so we couldn't try it.

Patsy folded her arms, pressing her breasts high, like a pouter pigeon. 'Don't get me wrong, flower. Me, I like a good time. Don't we all? You're a short time on this earth, I say.'

Then suddenly the Tannoy blared out with Sandie Shaw singing '(There's) Always Something There to Remind Me'. A cheer went down the line and a few of the women started to sing along. Karen jumped down from the stool and started to sway and dance to the music. The boy called Steve brought his coffee and leaned on the end of the line to get a better view. Then the

26

record finished and she stopped dancing. Another cheer erupted from the line opposite and Steve put his fingers to his mouth and whistled.

Karen jumped back on her stool, breathing hard. 'I tell you what! I can't believe she's really coming here to this place. To Marvell's. That Sandie. Just think! It says in the paper she's just waiting for another big hit like that one.' She took out her rollers and combed her fringe down over her eyes with her fingers. She took a mirror from her pocket and peered at herself.

Steve grinned at her. 'A blind man on a fleeing horse might think you look like Sandie, Karen. Except for one thing.'

She pouted. 'And what might that be?'

He pointed downwards, grinning. 'You got your shoes on.'

'Oh, very funny. D'you think anybody'd leave their shoes off on this filthy floor?'

'*She* might. Charlie Priest's ordering this big clean-up for when she comes, so they say.'

Then the buzzer went again and the conveyor started to whine. Steve gathered his empty trolley and went off whistling '(There's) Always Something There to Remind Me'. Patsy went back round to her side of the line and Karen rewound the two giant rollers.

'Be good to see Sandie in the flesh, though,' she said. 'I can't believe she really is coming, you know. It was in the papers. What about that, Patsy? Sandie really coming here! I can't believe it.'

Patsy glanced at me and rolled her eyes. I picked up my wires and my screwdriver, my heart heavy again. I had forgotten about the

27

plasters. No time to get them now.

Patsy picked up a bunch of wires and her hands started to fly.

'I tell you what, Karen. When that Sandie sees you she'll think you're making game. You really *are* her spitting image.'

Karen tossed back her hair, not displeased.

Patsy's hands dropped into their rhythm. 'How about it, though? Millionth cooker? Millionth bloody cooker? Who're they kidding? I might have turned a million wires for them, but I've never seen parts for a million cookers going down this line, I'm telling you.'

Karen's hands were flying over the wires. 'Don't you think we've made a million, then, Patsy?'

'You! You're out of the egg, lass. Have you any idea what a million is?'

'It's a lot.'

'You go out on the darkest clearest night, flower, and look at all those bloody stars. See them? A million's twice, thrice as many as the stars you see there. Have we made that many cookers? That's a joke.'

As at last I began to drop into a rhythm of my own, screwing in those wires, it occurred to me that Patsy O'Hare was not so stupid. Not stupid at all.

Karen's hands stopped for a second, then they started again. 'Anyway, Sandie Shaw's coming and that's that. Fancy seeing her in the flesh! A star!'

Patsy shrugged. 'Can't see what you're getting so rosy about, Karen. She's just a young kid. I

28

saw her on the telly. Has as much flesh as a starved cat. Just a string of chewy gum that forgot to put its shoes on.'

'You can't say that, Patsy. Sandie Shaw's famous. She's top of the pops. Earns hundreds of thousands. They say she gets a hundred letters a day, half of them asking to marry her.'

Patsy grinned. 'Ah! Now I see why you want to look like her, Karen! All those men asking you...'

A man stopped by the line then, bright and sparrow faced, wielding a clipboard, wearing a spotless white coat that was hanging in rags at the hem. I recognised him. He was the man from the production office.

'Who we got here, then, Patsy?' he said, genially enough. 'I think we saw this young lady up in the office.'

'Summer worker, Stan, here to play. Steve looked for you but couldn't find you. Brought the lass here himself,' said Patsy. 'It's Linda Fox's daughter, name of Cassandra.' She nodded at me. 'This is Stan Laverick, love. Thinks he's God Almighty, but really he's our beloved foreman.'

'No need to be sarky, Patsy.' He ticked something on his clipboard. 'You all right, kid? Young Steve told us he'd put you down here.'

I looked down at my bloody fingers. 'Yes. I'm fine.'

'I know your ma. Linda's a good worker.'

'I'll tell her you said that.'

'Do that. She's all right, is Linda.' He turned his attention back to Patsy. 'Get on to the girls, Patsy. Big clean-up's called for this week, getting ready for this big Sandie event. This line needs a

29

clean – on it, in it and under it. Mr Priest says *Mr Owen himself* has sent the message down.' He breathed the name of Mr Owen as though it were the name of the Almighty. He went on, 'Good housekeeping! Everything's gotta be spick and span for this visit. Not just Sandie Shaw but Mr Owen'll be here. Maybe even – even – Mr Abrahams from London. We'll stop the line ten minutes before finish today, Patsy. Steve'll sort you for dusters and brushes. That'll make a start.'

Patsy stared at him for a minute. 'You're joking, ain't you? We're not paid to clean, *Mister* Laverick. We'll lose time, man. You'd better adjust our bonus. We're not losing bonus, Stan, Sandie Shaw or no Sandie Shaw.'

'It'll be adjusted, Patsy. Charlie Priest has said the bonus would be adjusted. Don't make waves. Oh, look!' He gestured towards the gantry. 'Mr Priest wants me.' He moved off swiftly, half walking half running on his slightly bent legs.

'Run away, why don't you?' Patsy called after him. 'Bloody Stan Laverick. Bloody Sandie Shaw. Our bonus'll be down. You can bet on that.' Her painted face was suddenly grim. 'I'll tell you what! If I'm down on bonus this week I'll flay that Stan Laverick.'

A True Miracle of These Times

My hands move. My hands move. Pick up, screw in, check, move on.

This whole place smells. It smells of solder, burned wire and the ghost of cordite from the war. It smells of women and blood. It smells of old dust and new paint. It smells of the egg sandwiches the women bring to eat in the dust at the end of the line.

So many women. Of course there are men too, in the press shop and the tool room. But here on the lines it's all women, with a few men to lord it over them, such as that bow-legged foreman, and a few men in battered suits. You've got to say that Mr Priest wears a better suit than most. He seemed nice enough when he interviewed me. He must have a sense of humour, giving me this job down here with these two women who are brilliant at it. They have the hands of angels, hands that blur as they work, they're so fast. Steve told me that Mr Priest brings visitors to watch them, like they were prize turkey or pigs in a show.

My hands move, my fingers tipped with blood.

I'll never, never keep up with them. Never in a thousand years.

I suppose, like my mother says, I should count myself lucky. At least now I know what it's like to work in a place like this. So I know more about

31

life, more about *her* life, I suppose. In our lives up to now, her being at work – at the factory – was just her being out of the house and coming home dog-tired. Now I know more. All this couldn't be further away from school, or college. As she says, it's educational in its own way.

My hands move. Pick up, screw in, check, move on.

I really liked school. It was orderly, graduating from one class to the next, reading prescribed texts for predictable teachers. At the very least it was a change from the unkempt house, the wretched unmade bed and the dead-ash fire. School and library were my refuge. Quite a pet of the librarians, I was. They kept me the snuggest corner, found me the best books. They quite took care of my sex education with Alex Comfort and Simone de Beauvoir. But each day the comfort came to an end when I was thrown out of the library at closing time, to go back to the cold house, my mother's perplexing, cold rage. She's so much better now, but she was very depressed in those days: easy to see why, my father dying so inconveniently young, leaving her with me and all their debt.

That house and the library were all I knew until – one of the true miracles of these times – I went off to this college that has big coal fires, three meals a day, bread and jam left out at eight, your laundry done and, at last, some true friends. When I'm there I live up to my name and tell fortunes by candlelight, before coming down clanking stairs to my own little room at midnight. And in the carved wood library there are books and books. And in the rooms there is talking

32

about Chaucer and Andrew Marvell on someone's bed till three o'clock in the morning.

Andrew *Marvell*. That's ironic.

Like my mother says, I should count myself
lucky, getting this summer job at Marvell's at all.
Like Patsy says, they have this family policy,
which means I only got this job because my
mother works down on circuit breakers and she
and Mr Priest 'go way back'. I wonder if they
really were an item, whatever she says. Hard to
think that about your mother. Forty seems pretty
ancient, really. Patsy here must be at least that.

My hands move. Pick up, screw in, check, move on.

My fingers feel like frozen sausages as I try to
bunch wires and screw them into the harness. I
drop the wires, I drop the screwdriver, I screw
the eye into the wrong hole. And these women
grunt and scowl at me because I'm losing them
their bonus. Maybe Charlie Priest is playing a
joke on *them*.

I have to tell you, this Patsy O'Hare frightens
me. She reminds me of the principal of our
college, this large looming woman who smells of
violets and can make a whisper resound across an
auditorium. This Patsy, with her foul mouth and
her quick hands, makes me feel like Gulliver in
Lilliput. She's a funny one, Patsy, pushing and
pushing until she finds your weak spot, then
ramming in hard. The other one, Karen, just
follows her lead. She's Patsy's pet: just that bit
gormless, peering through that long fringe with
her painted eyes. But she's quick, nearly as quick
as Patsy.

My hands move. Pick up, screw in, check, move on.

33

But I'm beginning to think now there's a lot more to Patsy than meets the eye. She reminds me of my mother in some ways: hard as nails on top, hard as diamonds underneath. And, as it is with my mother, I do want Patsy to like me. If I'm quicker at this job maybe Patsy will like me and let me glimpse the diamonds underneath. Corny, that, but true.

Patsy's going on again about this Sandie Shaw visit – all this extra cleaning, and being worried about losing her bonus – obsessed with money, that woman.

Karen laughs at her. 'You'll be there cracking the whip, Patsy, flattering us all to clean and dust like it's your own living room. You'll see.'

'One day they'll get more than they bargain for, that lot. Asking us to do extra for no more pay,' says Patsy darkly.

My relief is boundless when the buzzer finally goes for lunchtime. I gulp my egg sandwiches and go down to see my mother in her block. There's hardly time to do that but the fresh air will be good after the hot burned air of the line. And I'll get away from Karen going on about Sandie Shaw.

My mother is sitting up at her bench doing the *Daily Mirror* crossword. She pushes it away reluctantly when she sees me but her smile is warm enough.

'Cassie! What're you doing down here? Did you clock out?'

'No. I–'

'Should have, you know.'

34

The other women on her line are watching and listening with interest.

'I didn't know...' I lean against the bench beside her. She takes my hand in hers and looks at the women beside her. 'See that? Cut her fingers to ribbons. This job of hers is gunna cost me her wage in plasters.'

Sympathetic smiles and murmurs patter down the line.

I pull my hand away. See? I'm back in Lilliput again, among giant women. Or is that Brobdignag?

'It doesn't matter,' I say. 'I'm getting used to it.' I put my fingers behind my back. 'Karen, this girl I work with, says it'll get better.'

She smiles. When she smiles my mother's face lights up: it's thin and gloomy in repose. 'A lesson learned. It can only get better. It'll come, Cass. Don't worry. Here, I didn't eat this.' She pushes a Penguin biscuit towards me. 'You can have it.'

'Thanks.' I push it in my overall pocket.

She looks at the clock at the end of the line. 'You'd better be getting back, love. Stan Laverick'll have his eye open for you, seeing as you didn't clock out down there. Can't besmirch the family name, you know!' She exchanges smiles with the woman beside her.

I turn slowly and make my way towards the big double doors at the end of her line. Patsy said it. *Marvell's bloody marvellous family policy.* Getting their pound of flesh out of me, and my mother too.

I take out the Penguin and start to munch at it. It's peppery and sweet at the same time.

Suddenly I am thinking of my friends Emma and Jeanette out in France, picking grapes in the sunshine. I should be there with them now. Picking grapes in the sunshine. I glance at my watch and start to run towards my block, trying to ignore the shame of the tears that are falling from my eyes.

Birthday Girl

Monday

The general manager of Marvell's, Charles Priest BSc., (known as Charlie to everyone except his wife, Millie) had just moved into Elm Rise, to a large detached house with double gates, on the prime site in Grafton, at the far end of a new estate by the bluebell woods. Millie always said she knew they had really made it when they moved from a semi in the centre of the estate to this detached house that overlooked the Bluebell Beck. The week before she had felt so pleased with the new house that she said to Charlie she intended to combine her birthday with a house-warming party.

Her Charles was not so sure. 'It'll be a Monday, lover,' he said easily. 'A work night.'

She pouted. 'My birthday's on that Monday, Charles. It doesn't have to be an all-nighter. We can have a cocktail party, seven till nine, like they do on the American pictures.' She knew Charlie liked all things American.

'Well, put it like that, honey...'

'You can invite that lot from work. And Mr Owen and his wife as well.'

'Mr Owen won't come.'

She bristled. 'They're only flesh and blood, Charles. Mr Owen is not God Almighty.'

That's the trouble, Charlie thought. Mr Owen *is* God Almighty. At least at Marvell's he is. For the group of men who ran Marvell's, who ate, slept, dreamed of the place, the factory was their church, their chapel, their Palace of Varieties, and Mr Owen was their God, their master of ceremonies. And Charlie was their high priest. He smiled to himself. The thought pleased him. Priest by name, priest by calling.

She stroked his face. 'Go on, Charles. It is my birthday, after all. Plea-ease!'

So he gave the party the nod.

In the end Millie had circumvented Charlie's nervousness by sending Mr Owen his invitation through the post. It was a very tasteful invitation, one of a set she had bought specially at W.H. Smith. She didn't waste postage on the rest of the Marvell men, just gave Charlie a pile to put into the internal post.

She was vindicated by the gracious handwritten reply she received from Mrs Owen. As for the rest of them, she had to make do with word-of-mouth responses via Charlie.

Anticipating the party had been part of the fun. Millie glowed with the thought of how the lesser wives would gasp at the size of her L-shaped lounge, her two bathrooms and her covered patio, its borders now ablaze with bedding plants. And, being in the trade, even the men would be interested in her new German dishwasher and her Italian tumble dryer.

'It just shows who we are, Charles! Not one of them has a house like this. Just off the council estate, most of them.' She had even persuaded Charlie that a cocktail cabinet in oiled teak would make the perfect birthday present. That would show them.

Millie Priest had always had a little bit of edge. That was one of the things that Charlie liked about her. She had always felt herself rather better than those around her. Growing up in a flat over a shop with quite a bit of ready money sloshing about, she had been brought up to feel privileged in comparison to the mere wage-earning, sometimes unemployed, people around her. After all, didn't she speak properly and own six pairs of shoes in different colours? Hadn't her grandfather been a member of Grafton Chamber of Commerce? The fact that the shop was open all hours, seven days a week, in order that her family could make their rather elaborate ends meet, went unremarked.

Charlie Priest had been the first young un-attached car-owning lounge-suit-wearing man Millie had encountered in her shop-bound life, and before long she had a succession of Charlie's rings on her finger and a succession of houses that reflected Charlie's ever-increasing status at Marvell's.

And now at last, for Millie Priest, Elm Rise was worth all the work she had put into her Charles.

Her devotion to him was such that she failed to see that there was not much about him except his suits, his car, his slight American accent (acquired in a six-month work attachment in San Diego) and his ferocious devotion to Marvell's. He had risen through the company by craft, intelligence and sheer grasp of the process. And, it had to be said, he had never lost his committed, working-class attitude to the job, his only pretension being the slight American accent.

On the Monday of the party Millie cleaned all morning and baked all afternoon. She made three different kinds of quiche, tiny sausages on sticks stuck into two half pineapples, a huge carrot cake and a chocolate cake, all jostling for space on her linen-covered teak table. Her new cocktail cabinet was fully stocked with liquor of every kind and her fridge door was full of bottled beer. (Charlie had acquired his taste for chilled beer in the States.)

And now tonight, in that moment before people arrived, with the house at its best and Charlie standing in front of the marble fireplace smoking a cheroot, Millie experienced a rare moment of unalloyed bliss. Then, as people trickled in with birthday presents, flowers and wine she felt like queen of all she surveyed.

As the evening unrolled, the cocktail cabinet unfortunately failed to impress with Mr Owen, who was teetotal. And Mrs Owen kept dropping her sausages off the sticks. She was heard to murmur in her warm Scottish accent, 'Och, look at me! A nice shortbread biscuit or a sausage roll I can handle, but sausages on sticks! I'm all

39

fingers and thumbs.'

Fortunately the other wives loved Millie's cocktail cabinet, sipped their martini cocktails with delicate appreciation and had no problems at all dealing with the sausages on sticks. They hovered near the drinks cabinet and talked of their families, of fortune-tellers, and of the particular delights of shopping in Northallerton, which had a wonderful Saturday market. Their menfolk, generous whiskies in hand, wandered back to the blind side of the L-shaped lounge and hovered around Mr Owen. They talked about the Americans tumbling helter-skelter into Vietnam, about the cunning of Harold Wilson and the delights of village cricket, before getting down to various tales and legends about Marvell's in time gone by, and speculating whether Mr Abrahams, their greatly honoured founder and owner, would come north for this momentous presentation of the millionth cooker.

Stan Laverick, the foreman, stood at the edge of the crowd, glass of cold beer in hand, feeling uncomfortable. He experienced a trickle of envy at the ease of Alan Cartwright, who was standing at Mr Owen's elbow and wearing, as befits a sales manager, the best suit in the room. Stan himself would have been happier at the end of the bar at Marvell's club, drinking the keg beer, which was – as beer should be – slightly warm. Cold beer was another of those American things that had been creeping in since the war.

At the other end of the room the production secretary, Evelyn Laing – childless, husbandless – felt equally at odds with the women round the cocktail cabinet. Evelyn had been dragged reluctantly to the party by Tamás Kovacs, the young production controller from her office. Tamás had been desperate. 'It says *and partner*, Evie. You wouldn't want me to turn up alone, would you?'

Tamás could charm the birds off the trees.

Evelyn was less charmed when, once he'd settled her on a chair by the wall with a vodka and orange, Tamás had deserted her to join the circle around Mr Owen and Charlie Priest. She made a mental note not to let herself be charmed by him ever again.

From her throne-like seat in the wide bay window Millie Priest eyed Evelyn coolly, really annoyed at the younger woman for having what looked like natural blond hair, long legs, a neat figure and a quiet black dress that had a London look about it. The woman was only a secretary, after all! She wasn't even married. And at her age too. She must be at least thirty, despite that clever make-up. Still, Millie worked up a smile and held up her drink towards her.

'You all right, Evelyn?' She spoke in her kindest tone. 'You're very quiet.'

All the women looked at Evelyn, who found herself blushing. 'I'm fine, thank you, Mrs Priest...'

Two of the women giggled.

'Millie, please!' said Millie, arching her brows. 'No formalities here, are there, girls?'

More giggles.

Millie stood up. 'Can I get you a top-up, Evelyn?'

Evelyn put her hand over her glass. 'I'm fine,'

she repeated.

'Good.' Millie sat down again and turned to Joanie, Stan Laverick's wife. A pale, drained woman in discreet beige, Joanie was no competition. 'Like I said, we had the lobster with the sauce. What a mess we made! The plate looked like the aftermath of the Somme.'

'I never had lobster,' said Joanie. 'Never in all my life.'

'You've missed nothing,' said Millie. 'Believe me.'

'You can never tell with seafood,' said Lynne Cartwright, who had come as some kind of yellow meringue. 'I always say to my Alan that seafood and me will always be strangers. My sister-in-law had it on holiday in Portugal. She had to get home by ambulance plane! They were very good, the insurance people.'

The other women murmured in sympathy.

Millie turned to Evelyn. 'You'd have to eat foreign food when you worked abroad, I suppose? Didn't Charlie tell me you had worked abroad?'

Now all eyes were upon Evelyn. Mrs Owen smiled slightly.

'Yes, I did,' said Evelyn. 'But mostly I liked the food. Very much, in fact.'

'You were an *air hostess?*' said Lynne. She might as well have said 'prostitute'. 'I bet you went all over the place.'

'Well, Paris...'

'Paris?' said Lynne. 'I think that's overrated. I went there on the train once. It was wet and cold. Springtime in Paris! That's a laugh.'

Evelyn was stung. 'Paris is the perfect city, I think. Beautiful even when it's cold. I was in South Africa too. That was warm. And Australia, that was warm. And New York, that was freezing. Liked them all.'

Lynne glanced at her from head to toe. 'And were you always just an air hostess?'

They were all staring at her with a kind of chill eagerness.

'*Just* an air hostess?' Evelyn shook her head. 'Well, no, actually. I met this family on a flight to New York. They took a shine to me and I became their nanny. Took care of their children. They travelled a lot. Me too.'

A nanny! Joanie and Lynne exchanged glances. 'I could never do that, *nannying*,' said Millie. The other women relaxed. Envy was not required.

Mrs Owen sat up straight in her chair. 'Och, I imagine it was quite a hard life, my dear, taking care of other people's children. It's never easy, even with your own.'

Evelyn smiled at the older woman, grateful for the implied respect. 'It could be. But they were really nice kids. And it did have its compensations. We met a lot of famous people. Travelled a lot. The father was based in New York. Holidays in France.'

'Not holidays for you, though,' said Millie sharply. 'Minding kids. That's no picnic.'

Joanie Laverick shook her head. 'You're right, it isn't. My boys were murder in Blackpool last year. On and on for money for the slot machines.' She turned to Evelyn. 'I bet you were coining it,

43

like. Not even your keep to pay for.'

Mrs Owen frowned at her and glanced at Evelyn.

Evelyn shook her head. 'It wasn't like that, Mrs Laverick. You had to pay your way, to keep up your own standards. Nice clothes and stuff. And there were so many things to do on your days off. You had to take the opportunity of where you were and what there was to do, and that cost money, I can tell you.'

'Did you ever see the Statue of Liberty?' Mrs Owen shifted the gear. 'We saw that once from the ship. A wonderful sight. You'd not believe how tall it is. My husband was thrilled to see it. Called it the eighth wonder of the world.'

The other women turned to look at her, contemplating the thought of the phlegmatic Mr Owen being thrilled about anything.

'My Charles likes America.' Millie sat back in her chair. 'But me, I think travel's overrated. You can see all those places better on the telly. There are plenty of good places in England. Look at Torquay. The English Riviera. Give me that, any time.'

That's me put in my place, thought Evelyn, downing the last of her vodka. She observed Mrs Owen sending a look down the room to her husband, who caught it neatly, obviously from years of practice.

He put down his coffee cup, stood up and shook Charlie's hand. 'Well, Charlie, thank you for a wonderful evening but we'll have to get ourselves away. Work tomorrow, then I'm preaching tomorrow night at the Fellowship...'

44

Alan caught Stan's gaze and raised his brows, sharing the paradox of their forceful MD being not only teetotal but a lay preacher as well. They had both grown up in factories where the sport was to tease any number of blokes for such eccentricities. But Mr Owen could flaunt both these things because he was a great boss and, along with Mr Abrahams, the reason why nearly three thousand Grafton people had work.

Mr Owen followed Millie to retrieve their coats and the others could hear his deep Welsh voice thanking Millie and Charlie again for their kind hospitality. The women in the bay window watched as he put an affectionate hand through his wife's arm and led her down the drive to his car, a burly, reliable Humber, a bit like the man himself.

Evelyn took the opportunity to raise her eyebrows in Tamás's direction. He looked at his watch and stood up. 'Me too, Charlie. I've gotta go.'

'You preaching too, Tam?' Stan slapped him on the back. 'I'd never have thought it of you, son!'

'I'm no preacher,' said Tamás. 'But, like the boss said, there's work tomorrow and I've got to get Evelyn back home. I'll not get home till eleven.'

Charlie permitted himself a knowing smile. 'Night is young, eh, lad?'

Tamás caught Evelyn's frown. 'Nothing like that, Mr Priest. Me and Evelyn are just good friends.'

Charlie nodded. 'I believe you, thousands wouldn't.'

Suddenly the rather small hallway was brimming with arms, legs, coats, with Charlie's cigar and Millie's Miss Arden perfume. Evelyn slipped on her coat and made her way outside, but not before Millie Priest had treated her to a thin smile and an invitation to come again, 'Er ... sometime.'

Millie watched Evelyn go to stand beside Tamás's Riley Elf and wait for him to unlock the door. She and Charlie watched the little car roar down the cul-d-sac.

'We made a mistake there,' she said. 'Inviting her.'

Charlie clicked the door shut. 'What's that?'

'We should have said wives only. Fancy that boy bringing a *secretary*.'

'Couldn't do that, lover. Couldn't expect the lad to come on his own.'

'Maybe we shouldn't've invited him. He must be fifteen years younger than the rest of you.'

'Couldn't do that, like I said. He's one of the team, is young Tam. Mr Owen's keeping a watching brief there. Wouldn't be surprised if we're all working for Tamás in ten years' time.' He lit another cheroot and took a drag. 'Anyway...'

'Anyway what?'

'What's wrong with a secretary? Not good enough for a shopkeeper?'

This made Millie charge back into the lounge to join the women. She allowed Joanie to pour her another drink while Charlie settled down at the other end of the room for a game of cards with the remaining Marvell men.

Millie downed her drink, poured herself an-

46

other, and said, 'Now then, girls, why don't I show you round the whole house? You haven't seen half of it yet. Did I tell you there are two bathrooms? Just bring your drinks with you.'

Backfire

As they drove away Evelyn said, 'Never again, Tamás. I knew it was a mistake. Those women thought I was a freak.'

'No one thinks you're a freak, Evie. Honest. No one in their right mind, anyway. And it looked very cosy, all you girls down that end of the room.'

Evelyn lit a cigarette. 'Girls! Are you blind, Tam? I was the youngest there and I'm thirty-one.'

He shrugged. 'All girls together. That's what it looked like.'

She let smoke drift from her mouth. 'Listen, Tamás. Me, I know about *all girls together!* Didn't I travel the world for six years, *all girls together?* I admit that wasn't all plain sailing but it was a laugh. There in that house with its two bathrooms and its cocktail cabinet, believe me, it *wasn't* all girls together, it was all mummy vipers together. And that Millie Priest is queen viper – all forked tongue and lashing tail.'

He clicked on the Riley's full beam as they turned off the main road and left the town lights behind. He laughed. 'Honest, Evie, these women, they can't have been that bad.'

Instantly he felt her long nails digging into his arm.

'My name's Evelyn, not Evie. And those women *were* that bad. They sniggered at me. You'd think I was the Creature from the Black Lagoon.'

He drove on in silence for a while, then he said, 'Well, Evelyn, I'm really sorry you didn't enjoy yourself.' It was said in his throat, his accent more apparent. He was clearly disappointed. She chuckled, touched his arm gently now as he changed gear to make it up the long hill outside her village. 'Not your fault, Tamás. I shouldn't have agreed to go with you. My fault. I should've known better than to go to the birthday party of someone I've never met, who doesn't know me from Adam. Or Eve! I should have said no.'

He groaned. 'Heck, what a wonderful first date was this!'

'It wasn't a date, Tamás. I told you I'd come because you seemed so desperate to have someone to go with. I went with you as your friend. You know that.'

He steered the car into her narrow back lane and drew up beside her gate. He turned off the lights. They sat in silence for a moment. He turned and put an arm across the back of her seat. 'Evie, I–'

She sat forward so his arm couldn't touch her. 'Like I said, my fault. Don't worry, Tamás. It was an interesting experience. I've been to a few parties but this was my first time here in Grafton. The Marvell men at play! Nice, really. It was touching to see Mr Owen out of the office. And at least that Mrs Owen didn't qualify as a viper.' She turned away from him and peered through the car window. 'Oh. There's my dad watching out for me.'

'Evie,' he said desperately, 'you are a grown woman. Your father...'

She laughed out loud. 'Well, Tamás, I tell you what. I'm grown up enough not to be a worry for my dad, who's not in a good state just now.' She squeezed his arm, kissed the very edge of his cheek and got out of the car.

He watched her stride gracefully up the path, then turned on the engine and backed out of the narrow back lane. He thought how strange it was to think of elegant Evie with her high heels and London clothes living in one of these old pit streets.

As he drove back to the main road he thought of the pleasure that Evelyn had brought to his job. Like all the other men he'd sat up and taken notice when Evelyn Laing joined the office.

Among her given tasks was some typing for him. In the beginning they had merely passed the time of day. The weather was always a useful topic here in England. (His father had taught him that when they first came to England – always *begin* with the weather.) In time he and she had more interesting topics than the rain.

Within a month he was bringing his sandwiches and newspaper to sit through lunch at her desk. At first she would read her glossy magazine, he would read his newspaper (always the *Guardian:* he and his father had read the *Guardian* together when they were first perfecting their English).

Before long he and Evelyn would talk right through lunchtime. He told her about himself and how much he loved working at Marvell's. He could have gone to Edinburgh to be with his father but he stayed. 'I felt at home here,' he told Evelyn. 'Edinburgh was my father's adventure.' He saw himself as lucky at being promoted so quickly at Marvell's, picked out to be moved to the next level. 'Look, I started on the lines at fifteen, speaking very little English. They nurtured me here. I think this is an amazing place.'

She told him about returning home after her mother died, exchanging a privileged international lifestyle for life in a pit village, so she could take care of her father and work at Marvell's to keep them both. No, she hadn't saved any money from working all those years up in the air and abroad. It was not her way. What she'd earned she'd spent on clothes, which she loved; and on enjoying her time off, travelling alone to satisfy her curiosity about the world. That was how she ended up at home just about broke, her only profit a trunk of fine clothes, some rather good jewellery and some great memories.

From the first Tamás had been surprised at how content Evelyn was about this, how tranquil. She seemed to like Marvell's as much as he did. She was like no girl he had ever met. Oh, he'd had girlfriends, picked up at the Gaiety Dance Hall or from the blossoming avenues of the factory lines. With his natural manners and Hungarian charm he was never short of a girlfriend. With this girl and that, he'd had some great times. But he'd never wanted so badly to talk to a girl, to spend time with her, as he did with Evelyn. Of course she was not so much a girl as a woman and this made a whole lot of difference.

He'd wanted to get closer to her for months. And tonight Charlie Priest's party had finally provided the excuse to get beyond lunchtime sandwiches. But that had backfired with a vengeance.

Tamás sighed. With a bit of luck he'd be in time for a pint at the Oak Tree with his friend Mick. At least that would be more relaxing than keeping up with the competitive chatter of his bosses, who always seemed to change character when Mr Owen was around. He loved his job and he loved Marvell's, but sometimes you really needed to get away from it all.

He didn't feel like going straight home to Maria, his landlady. Maria was a compatriot of his father, who had come over in '56 with a husband. Within a year he had upped and run off with a Grafton factory girl, leaving Maria with two babies in a house so chaotic that the social services kept a check that the children weren't being neglected. One particularly nice woman, despairing of her failure to encourage her client to sort herself out, rolled up her sleeves and spent a whole day cleaning the house alongside Maria. When Tamás came home that day, he thought some kind of miracle had happened. As she left, the social worker had a word with him on the doorstep. He had to explain to her that he was not a brother or a cousin, just a lodger. Maria let him have the front bedroom. His wage kept the house going and that was that.

'I saw the padlock on that bedroom door,' said the social woman drily.

'That was Maria's suggestion,' he said. 'The kids got in there one day and poured flour and soot on my suits and pee'd in my shoes. She said would I stay if she got a padlock for my door?' He looked down at the woman. 'Maria's a bit down, do you know? Her brothers and her father ate some Russian bullets in '56. Then she came here with Stefan and he ran away from her. The kids run wild and she doesn't notice too much. But she can be very good with them; she wouldn't do them any harm. She tells Hungarian fairy stories to them every night.'

The woman shook her head. 'Keep your eye on her and them, will you? I've put the office number on the table.' She looked him up and down. 'At least you're here. That's something.'

After that day, with Tamás's help and Maria's astonishment at the kindness of the English social worker, the house was never quite as bad. But still it wasn't a restful place, and for Tamás the Oak Tree and a pint with Mick, or a session with Stan at Marvell's social club, was often the better option.

Back at Elm Rise Millie carefully folded her silver lamé jacket back in its tissue before putting her hair into big sponge rollers. 'I still can't think why that woman was here.'

'Who?' said Charlie innocently, pulling on his

silk pyjamas.

'You know who. That secretary. It wasn't right, her being here, Charles. She might have heard something confidential. Dangerous and demeaning.'

Charlie smothered his derisive laugh by kissing Millie on the back of her neck, where there was always an appealing little triangle of baby hair. 'Weren't you serving behind the counter of a corner shop when I met you, lover? Didn't I fall in love with you on that "enchanted evening", the minute I saw you across a crowded shop?'

She shot him a murderous look through the mirror. 'That was different, Charles, and you know it.'

He moved across to sit on the bed, leaning against the Dralon headboard, his long legs straight in front of him. He chose a safer topic. 'Anyway, did you get a new frock for this thing with Sandie Shaw?'

Her face softened at the thought of the blue shantung suit she had finally hunted down after days of searching. Fenwick's French Salon had finally come up trumps. 'I have, and I'm not showing you,' she said. 'It's a surprise.'

'I'm sure you'll surprise us all, lover – Mr Owen, Sandie Shaw, the mayor, every last one of us.' He opened his arms. 'Come on, you, it's cold across here.' As she moved across the room, that certain smile on her face, Charlie thought you could say what you like about his Millie – she was small minded, snobbish and full of herself – but she was fantastic in bed, even with her rollers in.

'Happy birthday, lover,' he said, dodging a roller as he buried his face in her soft neck. 'Happy birthday to you.'

Cassandra Fox Learns About Love

Having said that thing about being a virgin – not such a rare thing for a nineteen-year-old in 1965 – I suppose I should come clean here about my love life, such as it is, or has been.

I have to admit I wasn't overwhelmed with friends when I was young. At grammar school I beached up with Moira. She was long and lanky and, like me, was always on the edge of things. I would have loved to be popular, to be at the centre of things, but she had this cynical view of the hurly-burly of school life that really appealed to me. She saw herself as keeping us both safe in a hard school. (I think she might have taken too much notice of *Tom Brown's Schooldays*. No roasting of small children happened here in Grafton.) Moira agreed with me that at school boys were not really an issue. They were either noisy, rude and unkempt, or earnest and studious. And as Moira was very tall, they were all too short. But she lived a long bus-ride away from me so our friendship was a school thing more than anything else.

It was later on, in the bedrooms and common rooms of Dukes', my small old-fashioned girls' college, that I learned about the nature of intense friendships. And about boys, about feminism and the Pill, the psychedelic revolution and the unique magnetism of the ground-breaking music of new groups such as the Rolling Stones. Of course, up there in that Northern female fastness this was all rather more theory than anything else. The opportunity to practise what we preached was sadly limited.

One person who had actually practised was this girl who was a kind of friend, Jeanette. She had slipped down the scale to come to our college when she was 'sent down' (curious term, that!) from university for bopping when she should have been swotting. She claimed that at her university *every* girl she knew had been having sex with boys! The sound of breaking taboos cracked falsely in our young ears. Jeanette was surely exaggerating! This assumption was merely her personal experience. We knew she probably was: she was loud mouthed and promiscuous in her speech and allusions, so probably her sleeping habits reflected that. Surely she was wrong?

So, you see that we were an innocent lot at Dukes' College. One of my friends was a Plymouth Brethren whose hair had never been cut and had never drunk alcohol nor worn make-up. And she didn't seem all that strange to us. One girl on my corridor would get down on her knees morning and night, and pray in very personal terms to Jesus. We didn't do that ourselves but we thought she was rather sweet.

During the week the great gates of the college were shut at nine thirty in the evening; on a weekend it was ten thirty. The latecomers had to report to the principal's room. Her lamp was always burning. No men, even brothers, were allowed in the rooms. After all – as she said many times – could not one claim any man for a brother?

There was this time at Dukes' when a woman in a severe suit came to lecture us on personal hygiene. She had the neutral tone of a hospital matron but her main aim was commercial: to introduce us to the benefits and delights of Tampax. On a show of hands she discovered that only four out of eighty girls had ever used such strange objects (I was one of the seventy-six). An air of disbelief pervaded the room as, with the aid of a wall chart, she demonstrated how one used Tampax. Afterwards I said to the others I couldn't see how on earth one could get the thing *in!*

The sophisticated Jeanette could not speak for laughing at our naïvety. (Of course she was one of the four who had used them for years.)

Two days after the Tampax revelation Jeanette declared loudly that the college was some kind of a bizarre throwback, but my closest friend Emma retorted that this *throwback of a college* had given Jeanette sanctuary when the university had unkindly spat her out. Jeanette declared that you'd think it was the 1860s, not the 1960s up here in the backwoods, then sulked for a whole afternoon.

Emma was my first great friend at Dukes'. When I got there I was a nervous wreck – not sure what I was doing, but relieved to get away from home, even to this time-warp institution. In those days I was shy and introverted. My

56

mother's generally depressed outlook on life rubbed off on to me. My life to that point had been home-school-library, home-school-library: a kind of counterpoint to my mother's home-factory-home routine. It was her idea, though, for me to go to college after doing quite well at school. We'd managed on a pittance so far, she said, and could do so for another few years with the help of the grants that were around then. And anyway, what ordinary job would there be in Grafton for someone like me who could do nothing but read?

When my mother and I looked at the college brochures the places all seemed so magisterial and male. Then I saw a picture of the wonderful Arts and Crafts library in the Dukes' brochure and I was sold. My mother shrugged and said if that was what I wanted then she would not object.

On my first night at Dukes' I was hiding in one of the deep window seats when the girl I would come to know as Emma scooped me up.

'What are you doing? Reading? Put that down and come and have a cup of tea.'

In Emma's room I met Justine, Joy and Elaine, who were halfway down their first cups of tea. (They also were picking grapes with Emma and Jeanette in France while I toiled through that summer at Marvell's.) Jeanette usually hovered on the edges of this group but never quite belonged.

I ended up spending all my spare time with this crew. We walked together, read together, did assignments together, had coffee in village cafés together. Simple stuff. We talked about ourselves, our dreams, our ideas, our families and our fears. Elaine and Justine talked about their boyfriends. These were innocent relationships: more Jane Austen than Harold Robbins. Jeanette muttered something about people never having lived.

Emma was a year older than us, charismatic and rather worldly wise. She wrote letters to several boys who were friends but did not see the point of tying herself to any one man. It was from her I learned that it was OK to link another person's arm, to put your arm around them when they were upset, to kiss their cheek in greeting. This was all new to me, a person who could not remember her mother even touching her. Learning that there was comfort in touch, that touch could convey much subtler things than words, was a much greater part of my education than learning how to use tampons.

I did not realise then – did not even notice – that there might be erotic undertones to all this. Years afterwards I was astonished when Justine told me that two of our tutors had been clearly 'of the Sapphic persuasion'. That had all gone over my head.

But most of all in that little college, as well as learning to think logically and love language, I finally learned to know myself, to relish friendship for its own sake, and to value my own feelings. It was at Dukes' that my frozen self-absorption began to melt and I began to look outward on the world.

I began to write more freely to my chilly, enclosed mother, and talk to her more in the vacs. The Dukes'-melt even reached the edges of her garment. And now at Marvell's the new confidence I had acquired at Dukes' allowed me to manage to talk to Patsy and Karen on the line and to tolerate with equanimity the teasing from Stevie and the yelling of Stan Laverick.

Don't get me wrong. Dukes' wasn't a nunnery. There were some boys around. They would come up from the university in droves, quite keen on the quaint charm of Emma and her crew. We entertained them to tea and walks on the nearby beach. Perhaps they too fancied a bit of Jane Austen, having supped the delights of Harold Robbins in the steamy corridors of the university.

To my surprise one or two of these boys quite liked me. They enjoyed my speculative talk and what one boy called my 'odd charm'. (Charm? What was he talking about? I asked Emma later. She just laughed and said that having charm and knowing it was kind of contradictory.)

I enjoyed a few hand-in-hand walks, a sprinkling of cheek-kisses, one or two clutching lip-kisses. I can't say now whether it was these boys' mannerly restraint, or my armour-plated inaccessibility, but none of this went any further.

Of course, back in our rooms we discussed this 'lack of action'. The consensus was that one's armour plating would fall off when one was *ready*. And now, with the prospect of the Pill, we knew that it was only one's own *readiness* that was the issue, not some puritanical throwback obligation. This, in a way, made it harder.

'Of course,' Emma said once, 'these boys'll tell you otherwise. Well, they would, wouldn't they?

They'll talk to you about this being the age of "choice", "freedom". But it's their choice, not yours they're advocating.'

Jeanette pouted. 'You lot just don't know what you don't know. You really don't!'

Emma grinned. 'So you keep telling us, love.'

Apart from all this, the other great thing I learned in that first year at Dukes' was how to *dance!* We danced in the common room to LPs some of the girls had brought from home. Those of us who couldn't bop learned from those who could. The best dancer was Elaine from Liverpool, who had been to the Cavern dozens of times and had actually spoken once to John Lennon! She was a galvanic, stunning mover and was in great demand as a partner. She showed us the basic moves, told us we were free to improvise and we were away. The exhilaration – much of it sexual, I'm now sure – of moving to that heavy beat was the last fire that freed me from my frozen tower.

At the end of term I was naïve enough to think that the crowning of this great year would have been to join Emma and the others in France. We would enhance our unique bond by picking grapes under blue skies in the hot sun. But this wasn't to be. Even a cheap student trip to France cost money. In the end I didn't even tell my mother of the trip. She had other plans and had already seen Charlie Priest. My place was taken by Jeanette, who was more solvent. And by the time I started work at Marvell's I had rather angrily accepted that picking grapes in France was not for me.

When I think about those days at Dukes' I realise that Emma was probably the only one who knew the extent of the changes inside me. I had lived with my mother too long to show her, even now, how deeply all these things affected me. But I know the Cassandra Fox who sat there with Patsy and Karen on the line, the Cassandra who exchanged words with Stevie Hunter, the Cassandra who was to walk the gangway with Tamás Kovacs, was very different from the guarded chilly creature who dragged her heavy cases through the gates of Dukes' College on that first day of term, knowing nothing at all about love.

Marvell's Social Club

Tuesday

The day after Millie Priest's birthday party Stan Laverick was pleased to get back to routine. Privately he had thought it very odd to have a party on a Monday, but everyone knew that Charlie Priest let Millie have her way in a lot of things. Stan supposed it kept her happy and allowed Charlie a bit of leeway for other things he rather relished.

That night, Stan was late home for tea, having stayed back for a particularly rigorous production meeting, where he'd hammered Tam Kovacs to get on to the buying department about a crucial shortages of time switches, and Alan Cartwright had droned on too long yet again about the coming Sandie Shaw bonanza – 'Sure to offset the cost of her fee and her flight up from London.' He had primed the Marvell southern sales director to pick her up from her house and get her to Luton, and he himself would meet her at Newcastle to be here on the dot at two o'clock on Wednesday next week. 'It'll go like clockwork,' he purred.

Then, while Stan looked gloomily at his watch, Charlie Priest took up the theme and talked about the Marvell demonstrators coming from the south to cook the spread on their own Marvell cookers. 'And the mayor and deputy mayor'll be here for certain, as well as this bloke called Wellington, who runs the nightclub here and is used to celebrities. He should be able to take up the social slack,' he said, lighting another of his small cigars.

Whatever that means, thought Stan gloomily, standing up to go at last.

When he finally got home he took his dinner out of the oven and sat at the kitchen table to gulp it down. His Joanie had already left for her twilight shift at the factory and he had passed his sons, Clyde and Joe, out on the street, kicking a ball about with the boy next door. Joanie's mother would be in to baby-sit at eight so Stan could go for his nightly recreation at the Marvell social club, which was just on the corner.

This place, a converted church hall, which Mr Abrahams had bought once on a flying visit North, was a leisure club for Marvell workers.

Subsidised by the company, the club provided cheap beer and snooker for a steady group of Marvell employees – all men – who liked to get together after work.

Stan liked the club. It was a democratic place, where shop-floor workers and bosses met as equals and relaxed in the trusted company of men they knew. Stan regularly played snooker here with young Stevie Hunter (the progress chaser on the wiring line), and always drank with an old boy called Henry, who swept up in the machine shop. The higher-ups sometimes came. Charlie dropped in now and then for a beer, always complaining it was too warm. Even Mr Owen came to show fellowship but, of course, he only drank orange juice.

In fact, most of the bosses who turned up at Marvell's club had started on the lines. Marvell's was famous for growing and promoting its own talent. Just look at Tamás Kovacs, standing across there now, by the bar. Tamás could barely speak English when he started as a progress lad on the lines, and had never had an interview for any of the important jobs he'd secured on his way up the ladder. Now he spoke near-perfect English, and Stan once overheard Mr Owen saying young Tamás made as good a fist of being production control manager as anyone in the Marvell companies across the country.

'Hey, Stan! Game of snooker?' Tamás called across.

'I'll take half a crown off you.' Stan drank off his pint, and reached in his pocket. Tamás took off his denim jacket and picked up a cue. As they moved round the table making their pots they talked about Middlesbrough's last match, about Cassius Clay beating Sonny Liston and the new knockout rules in the World Championships.

Pocketing his winnings after triumphing easily, Stan went with Tamás back to the bar where Jack the barman had set up two more pints.

Stan picked up his glass and treated Tamás to a sideways glance. 'That Evelyn seems like a nice enough lass, Tam. Didn't know you were really, well ... been seeing her long, have you?' He took a gulp of beer and wiped his mouth. 'You bloody Hungarians always take the cream of the crop.'

Tamás sipped his pint calmly enough. 'It's not like that, Stan. I needed somebody to take to Charlie Priest's party and Evie said she'd come. That's it, I'm telling you.'

'I suppose you'll have lots of lasses, you. Tied to nobody's apron strings, you!' Envy dissolved into joviality in Stan's voice. 'Only a landlady to worry about.' He laughed. 'Some landlady. I heard she was quite a character.'

'Maria's OK said Tamás briefly. Then, 'I gotta be honest with you, Stan. Girls are not on the agenda for me just now. No time, d'you see? Six days down at Marvell's and Sunday at church. No time.'

Stan nearly choked on his beer. 'Church?' He spat out foam. 'You?'

Tamás grinned. 'Do not bust a gut, Stan. I meant to say "bed" not "church". Sleeping off my week at Marvell's.'

'And drinking off your days down here,' said Stan, looking at Tamás's reflection through the steamed-up mirror behind the bar. 'Bloody Marvell's! I can see why you live for our old place, seeing as we rescued you from the bloody Russians. At least you've got no wife, no kids, no mother-in-law to tie you down. Plenty time to get tied down, eh? Play the field?' He was suddenly uncharacteristically hungry for details of a life more colourful than his own.

Tamás drank off his beer. 'Just as you say, my friend. Plenty of time.' He looked at his watch. 'Gotta go.'

'No need,' said Stan. 'Jack here's not averse to a stoppy-back, are you, Jack?' He nodded towards the barman.

Tamás shrugged himself into his denim jacket. 'I need my beauty sleep, my friend. Up bright and early for a meeting with Charlie and Mr Owen, then more of this Sandie Shaw thing. Everything's gotta be organised. No hitches.'

'You'd think they'd give that thing a break, just for a day or two, wouldn't you? Ain't happening till next week. Things'll get done. They always do at Marvell's.'

'Charlie might ease off. But about Mr Owen, I do not know. The newspapers, television cameras'll be there. It is his beloved factory, don't forget.'

Stan scowled. 'That Patsy O'Hare's been on to me again about lost time on the big day. A few of the women'll miss their bonus, and they don't like it.'

Tamás sipped his beer. 'We've been talking about guaranteed bonuses if production numbers are met by that day lunchtime and the lines are clean and tidy. Then they can work at a steady pace just for show. It's the working factory that Mr Owen wants the visitors to see. Just jig Patsy and the others up about that; tell them that I said so.'

'Why don't you tell them yourself? Patsy and the others have a soft spot for you.'

'I have a soft spot for them. I started running for Patsy's line when I was a kid. Her and the others taught me everything about factories. A lot about this country too.'

'It'll be a bloody funny country if you only know it through the eyes of Patsy O'Hare,' Stan growled. 'But like I say, son, women are putty in your hands.'

'Lay off, Stan. If I were you I'd see if I could inspire those girls to clean up the line whatever happens. Or Mr Owen'll be a little upset and nobody wants that, do they?' Tamás turned to go.

Stan signalled to Jack for another pint. 'You can only hope,' he said to Tam's back. 'They can be awkward buggers, women.' Then, when Tamás had reached the swing doors he called out to him, 'You should get yourself down the Gaiety, son! Lots of nice lasses down there. Not snooty like that Miss Fancy-pants Evelyn. Remember, all work and no play makes our Tam a very dull boy.'

'Man, you're obsessed!' Tamás grinned, shook his head, then pointed his fingers like a gun and mimed shooting Stan. He blew the tips of his fingers and pretended to holster his gun. He was smiling as he made his way along the street. He was fond of Stan, even if the older man relished

66

sleaziness more than was comfortable. And he was grateful to Stan. He had been as much an inspiration as Patsy in the early days. He had been Tamás's first line leader and had knocked him into shape with a combination of bullying and praise. The very best thing about Stan was that he'd shown no resentment at all when his protégé had overtaken him in the career stakes. The only inequality between them now was Stan assuming the role of sexual mentor, which could, of course, be embarrassing at times.

Wishing now he'd brought his car, Tamás turned up his collar against the drizzle and set off home through the dark, half-deserted streets of Grafton. His thoughts turned yet again to Evelyn Laing. That woman really was something special. She had a kind of classy quality missing from the home-grown beauties on the lines or down at the Gaiety Dance Hall. She glowed but she did not sparkle. In the office she worked away quietly. She was polite and willing but always somehow detached. It had been a real surprise when she'd said yes when he had asked her to Charlie's wife's birthday party.

He'd felt proud, handing her into his car and walking into Charlie Priest's fancy house with her at his side. Evelyn was older than him and that added to her fascination. She had travelled further than him, been to places he had just read about in books, met people whose names were in the papers. Not that she talked about it too much: Evelyn wasn't showy, but she was sophisticated.

From the first it had seemed impossible that

she should be interested. What would she see in him, who (apart from the journey with his dad from Budapest), had never been further than London for a top match, or York for the races? Marvell's was his world. It was where he began and where he ended. It had been his refuge, his A levels and his university, his hobby, and his passion. He was happy to stay put.

Then it started to rain in earnest and Tamás increased his step. He really had to face up to it. Evelyn Laing was not on his horizon. No hope there. Perhaps he should make his way back to the Gaiety and the girls there, like Stan said. Check it out. What was it that Stan said? 'All work and no play.' Had he really become such a dull boy?

He started to run.

A Sophisticated Life

Tuesday

'That you, Evie?'

As she let herself in Evelyn noticed again that the paint on the front door was down to the grain. She really would have to see to that.

'I saw you coming down the street, smart as a carrot.' Her father's voice, once deep and rich, had become plaintive and feminised, just as the flesh on his face had become softer, more like that of an old woman than an old man. Still, somewhere inside there was the ghost of the good-looking man he had been.

She paused by the hall stand in the tiny vestibule to slip out of her shoes and into the red velvet mules acquired years ago in a little Maori shop in Wellington, New Zealand.

'Course it's me, Daddy,' she said, summoning up her brightest voice, not the easiest thing after an eight-hour shift at Marvell's. 'Who else?' She peered into the oval hall mirror to renew her lipstick and pat on some Coty pressed powder.

He was sitting by the window in his usual spot, his newspapers and medicines on the small table beside him, his radio to hand: just as she'd left him at seven thirty this morning. But his sticks were beside him and she knew that at some times in the day he would have made his way to the downstairs bathroom or into the kitchen to eat the sandwich lunch she had left for him on a tray covered by the linen cloth, hand embroidered by her mother for her own bottom drawer fifty years ago.

Now he was eyeing her blankly. 'What are you doing here?' His pale face under his luxuriant thatch of grey hair was strained.

Here we go. 'I'm just in from work, Daddy.'

'But you just left! I saw you go.'

'No, darling. You're mistaken, I've been to work at the factory all day, and now I'm back.' She went and brought the sandwich tray. 'Look! You've eaten your sandwiches. You heard the alarm go at lunchtime and you went to the kitchen to get your sandwich. So I must have been away all day, mustn't I?'

69

He beamed then and looked more like his old handsome self. 'Of course. Silly me. Must have slipped my mind.' He leaned sideways to see around her. 'Is your mum with you?'

She sat down beside him and took his hand. 'No, Daddy, Mum's not here now. She's not here now. You remember, don't you? She left us three years ago. Just before I got home.'

He frowned. 'Left? My Caroline wouldn't leave me. Never.'

'She did, Daddy. But she didn't want to leave you. You're right about that.'

It had been a shock to everyone, including Evelyn, that it was her mother who went first. Everyone thought that her father would be first to die; it was he who had suffered the stroke and had these terrible islands of complete forgetfulness where he seemed more like some plaintive child than a man. But no, it had been her mother, Caroline – brisk efficient Caroline – who had dropped dead in a supermarket queue. Caroline's best friend, Tizzy, told Evelyn that she had died of a broken heart, having lost her beloved Matt in all but body.

Now her father was looking at her blankly.

'Remember?' she said desperately. 'We take flowers for Mum, don't we? We take a taxi up to Grafton Old Cemetery, remember? We take flowers. Caroline died, Daddy. We take flowers every week. Every time we read her name on the stone. "Caroline Laing, beloved wife of Matt and mother of Evelyn?" Remember?'

He sat slackly back in his chair. 'Oh, my dear Lord,' he said. 'Oh. Oh, my Caroline!' And the tears came flowing down.

She put her arms round him and rocked him backwards and forwards. He smelled of the salmon sandwiches she had made for his lunch. 'Don't cry, Daddy, Don't worry. She's safe now, safe with Jesus.'

In those early days it gave her comfort to be able to say those words to him because her father, who had once sang in the choir at his chapel, believed in such things. But his innate faith had dissolved from his mind like many other things: the street-corner post office that had left him bankrupt; his close knowledge of the landscape and history of Grafton; his old friends from chapel and the bowling club. So now, his faith dissolved into nothing: all he could cry for was *his Caroline,* who was not so much in his memory as imprinted on his soul. In the days after her mother's death Evelyn cried alongside him but these days her heart was dry, bereft of tears. In a weird way the words about Jesus were now more a comfort to her – who had no faith – than her father, who had once radiated his instinctive and distinctive belief in Jesus and God the Father.

This poor man in her arms was a different creature from the one she'd left to go on her travels. That Matt Laing had been sturdy, handsome, protective over his beautiful wife, perpetually amazed even after thirty years that she had chosen him. He had kept Caroline to himself for nearly twenty years until, at forty, she'd had Evelyn. He used to tease them both, that until that day his marriage had been one

71

long honeymoon. But in truth when Evelyn came on the scene he had shared his passion between them, calling them his twin sweethearts.

Matt Laing had always relished the fact that his daughter, Evelyn, was more genteel than the girls in the streets around the post office. He was proud of her going to the grammar school and learning the piano. And he went with her to London when she had interviews for her first job as an air hostess. It was a great thing in those days, being an air hostess, and he was proud of her. Even so, he didn't moan when she exchanged the glamour of aeroplanes to take up her first job as a nanny; he respected her that she'd rather nanny children in private than nanny adults in public, as you did as an air hostess. Even when the post office went bankrupt and he and Caroline had to move into the tiny street house, he took vicarious pleasure in Evelyn's life with her employers, the Leavises, who were older parents with young children. He was pleased to tell his friends in chapel and at the bowling club that Mr Leavis was some kind of theatrical impresario and his picture was often in the papers.

His greatest memory – gone now – was the time he and Caroline visited Evelyn in the Leavises' grand house in St John's Wood and Mr Leavis took them all out to dinner at his favourite restaurant in the West End. The next day Mrs Leavis said to Evelyn how gracious her parents were. Mr Leavis said they were like Burt Lancaster and Hedy Lamarr, both of them 'real lookers'.

At Caroline's funeral Matt had been calm, apparently unmoved, but as the weeks went by

Evelyn witnessed what her mother had called his 'forgetfulness' at first hand. She suffered his unexpected flares of anger and groans of unsuppressed grief. Sometimes he didn't know her at all; other times he called her Caroline. Sometimes he looked past her and talked to Caroline as though she were there in the room. In these months Evelyn realised just how much her mother had kept from her. In her letters she had presented the stroke as a physical thing that she could manage. There had been no mention of this behaviour that the doctor called 'dementia'. At the funeral the doctor told Evelyn that without Caroline's loving, watchful care an institution was the only option for Matt. 'Unless, Evelyn...' he almost swallowed the words, '...you yourself would take it on?' He knew about her from her mother. He knew all about her colourful life. Not a life one would give up, he thought.

That night Evelyn rang a disappointed Mrs Leavis to say she would be staying at home and not returning to work. And that was that, as far as her sophisticated life was concerned. She knew she'd need to work to keep them both but she had no skills apart from nannying. There were plenty of jobs around these days but who needed a nanny in Grafton?

But Marvell's did need workers. And Evelyn Laing ended up working in the progress office at Marvell's and – as it turned out – enjoying every minute of it. The people were down-to-earth, witty. The work was easy if you had a logical mind. There was a bustle and urgency about the place; a sense of importance and consequence regarding the world out there. Things were looking up in England, and everyone from Land's End to John o' Groats wanted flash new cookers in their newly fitted kitchens.

And for Evelyn, Marvell's was a timely sanctuary, a crucial resource for her new and less sophisticated life with her father.

Hungarian Rhapsody

Tamás Kovacs lived in a pre-war prefab on the Oak Tree Estate overlooking St Agatha's Church at the top end of Grafton. None of the graves in the churchyard were dated before 1856, the year when three lucrative mines were sunk on the straggly Grafton moor.

Tamás had met his landlady when he and his father first got to England, at their first resettlement centre. When Maria Vargha's husband left her, she had needed some protection even inside the Hungarian community, so Constantin and Tamás provided it.

The prefab estate, unlike the old pit streets, was laid out on a grid, its Toytown appearance enhanced by neat gardens and neat houses with lace at the windows. Despite its neatness, Oak Tree Estate was the lowest step on the Grafton housing ladder and in time its original residents had been decanted into new well-appointed council houses. When the Hungarians came from the resettlement centre many of them started

74

their British experience in these prefabs. After a period they too, like Constantin, Tamás's father, went off to better houses, or other towns. Maria Vargha and Tamás were two of the few Hungarians left on Oak Tree Estate.

Maria's prefab front garden overflowed with luxuriant grasses and the windows were draped with dust-magnet curtains in elaborate lace. Inside the house, curtains in thick plum velvet covered doors as well as windows, and curtained off the cooking from the eating area in the kitchen. The furniture was too heavy, the shelves too overflowing for Spartan post-war English tastes. And the familiar smell of garlic overlaid by paprika that greeted Tamás as he opened the door – that too was alien here in Grafton.

It was hard for Maria – in Grafton or any town nearby – to get the three different kinds of paprika that she preferred to use for her goulash. So she had to travel on the bus to Newcastle to get that, and olive oil in quantities larger than the diminutive bottles only obtainable at chemists'. She grew her own garlic and salad vegetables in her orderly back garden. Constantin had built her a small lean-to glass house at the back of the prefab, where in good years she grew tomatoes, cucumbers and peppers.

Even after the intervention of the social worker the house was often a mess, but when she was on form Maria was a great cook. Constantin Kovacs told his son that his own mother –Tamás's grandmother – could not have improved on Maria's goulash, her potato *latkes,* and the seven-layer vanilla and chocolate cake that she called *Dobostorte.*

When she was off form (still mourning her lost family and still stewing in her sense of foreignness), all she could manage was a goulash that was added to, sprinkled with more paprika and reheated every day.

Today Tamás had to push the door hard to open it against the pile of newspaper behind it. Maria had piles of these all around the little vestibule, having saved one every day since she moved into the prefab in 1958. She had starting buying the newspapers to spot the repeated pictures of the Russian tanks in Budapest facing the euphoric militiamen, bewildered by their early, albeit short-lived, victory over the occupiers. She would describe to Tamás – as though she had never said it before – how her brother had got a tank to stop and had talked amiably enough with a Russian soldier, only to be shot the next day by a more vengeful Russian in another tank.

Her sizeable living room was cluttered with magazines and carrier bags, with pushchairs and baby toys, obsolete now that Maria's children were at junior school. The shelves were heaped with books bought at random from junk shops and church sales, 'for their education. They must speak the best English.'

Today the house was empty. On Tuesday nights Maria visited her friend Monika, who had married an Englishman and graduated from the prefabs to an upside-down house on the high-rise estate. On Tuesdays the two women would have a single cigarette and a glass of Tokay that Monika's husband had brought from an army stint in Vienna. At nine o'clock Maria would return home to listen to the BBC World Service for reports on the Cold War in German, which she understood better than English. In the house she was sad and silent, spoke little English. At bedtime she sang to the children in Hungarian.

In the early days she would not join Constantin and Tamás in their nightly visit to the cinema to learn English. She could not tolerate the very wall of words that was to furnish Tamás and Constantin's conversation, and be the key to their get-out from floor-sweeping and shelf-stacking, their first step on the arcane English ladder.

When finally Constantin got his opportunity with the Edinburgh job he had tried to get Tamás to come with him. 'Chances, my darling boy, great chances up there with me in the capital of Scotland,' he said to Tamás in their old language, which by then was not much spoken between them.

'I'll stay here, Papa,' Tamás had replied in English. 'Mr Laverick says I am a very quick learner and I've a good chance to move up the ladder at Marvell's. I like it there. They are friendly people.'

Constantin stared at him for a while, then reverted to English.

'So be it. You must write to me every week and come to Edinburgh for the holiday.'

'Holidays,' corrected Tamás absently.

'Holidays.' His father laughed and ruffled his son's hair. He rubbed his own moustache and smoothed it again. '*Holidays* only it *is*, my little Englishman.'

Tamás liked Maria. He had always felt at one with her in her intense, buried grief. As a boy he had grieved silently for the loss of his mother and brother. In the early days he learned from his father to put his grief way in a dark place somewhere behind his heart, and get on with things. This made him quiet and too watchful, even in the safe harbour of Grafton. Then, when he started working at Marvell's, the women in the factory laughed and teased him, called him 'bonny lad', made him blush, and told him to call them 'auntie'. At Marvell's, the mothering that had stopped with the Russian guns was taken up by these marvellous women on the line.

Linda Fox, mother to the new girl, Cassandra, was not loud and jolly like these women. She was quieter, more reserved. But still she had been very kind to him and his father. Constantin had sought her out to practise his English, talking to her about his own life and the nature of life and politics in the modern world.

The last thing his father said before he left for Edinburgh was that Tamás should look out for Maria. 'Keep your eye on the poor woman. She's still in the wilderness.'

And that was what Tamás had done. His wage kept the household going and provided clothes and shoes for the children, who knew no Hungarian except for the fairy tales and songs. They spoke perfect Northern English and came to love watching *Doctor Who* on the TV he had bought for Maria with his Christmas bonus in 1962.

Tonight Tamás went into the kitchen and stirred the big pan of goulash, allowing the intoxicating wave of garlic and paprika to attack his senses. He ladled out a bowlful, took it to the table and sat down to read the newspaper while he ate. He read a commentary about the *Mariner IV* spacecraft, which was now sending back the first close-up pictures of Mars. Mars! He made a mental note to talk to Judith, Maria's oldest, about it. Who needed *Doctor Who?* Who needed bombs and tanks? This was the real future, out in the wide arena of Heaven. Wasn't it?

Cassandra's Evening In

On the Tuesday night, after a second whole day on the lines, I walk home after work with my mother. We take the path that leads from the factory site, through the new estate that the council have built over a derelict ironworks. The estate is very modern, kind of startling at first, in this town of cosy streets and long back lanes. This development is called low rise but it's high rise to us earthbound Graftonians: an interlocking grid of new homes that houses hundreds of families. It's ribbed by these fenced-in landings and they say in some of the maisonettes (nice word!) you actually go *down* a flight of stairs to the front hall. Weird. On the plus side they say the bathrooms on this estate are brilliant and central heating means no dirty fireplaces. The women are delighted with them. It's a long way different from our own little street house, with a bog out the back. But at least we do have our own back yards. The man in the house next door to us has filled his back yard with geraniums. It's very pretty.

As a matter of fact that bog out the back is one reason I never invite anyone here from college. Emma and the others are reasonable human beings, but they wouldn't get the way we live, not at all.

My mother and I walk along separately as usual. We rarely touch. But tonight she's in a better mood than usual. Her piecework rate is up and there's a chance that her bonus will be bigger than her 'friend' Marje's. 'Not that I care about that,' she lies to me. 'But I know that Marje does.'

I take a punt on her good mood and ask about that Hungarian who's been on my mind all day. I've caught sight of him twice, charging around with a clipboard in his hand. Once he caught my gaze and a smile flickered across his face.

'Young Tamás?' says my mother, her voice lilting into a rare laugh. 'Oh, yes, I know Tamás Kovacs. His dad, Constantin, worked on our shopfloor when he first came from Hungary. Clever sort of man, Constantin. He could be funny. Ironic. Even though he was a foreigner.' There was a note in her voice like the echo of laughter.

I say, 'How did they do that? Learn English so fast?'

'Well, Constantin would talk to me a lot, ask me questions about how it worked, the English language. But the thing that really did the trick for them was listening to the BBC and going to the pictures every night, the two of them: sitting through two houses, every single night. I said to him, why not just learn off the people around them, like me and the others at the factory?

Constantin apologised very carefully then, and said he really wanted to speak – well – *English* that would work in other parts of the country. Like London. Or Edinburgh, where he thought he might go because he knew someone there. He did apologise gracefully, though. They were very polite, those Hungarians.' She smiles slightly. 'Known for it.'

Without thinking, I push it further. 'Seems like you liked him, this Constantin?'

She stops on the pavement and frowns up at me. (I am three inches taller than she is. It is funny, looking down on your own mother.) 'Well, I've got to say Constantin was a change from the other people I meet,' she says slowly. 'Interesting to talk to. Those things happening in Hungary were world events, Cassandra. On the television, on the radio. Those tanks in the street ... people like us...' She pauses. 'I was fascinated by him, well, by his life, to be honest. But then he got this chance in Edinburgh and that was that.'

I hold my breath. It's rare to see past the humdrum day-by-day depression that seems to define my mother. But here I am doing just that, seeing her as I might see any woman. She's not yet forty, and here she is standing there, luxuriating in something that might have been.

But now she's striding on and I have to increase my pace to catch up with her. I know better than to try to continue the conversation. She has ways of cutting you out, cutting you off, and leaving you stranded. Despite living with her for nineteen years it really does leave you with a sense that you don't know her at all.

81

When we get to the High Street she thrusts five shillings into my hand. 'Here. Get us some fish and chips for tea, love. I'll go on and light the fire and put the kettle on.'

I stand and watch her hurry on to the sanctuary of our little house. In all my life I've never known her pay attention to any man. Since I was two there has only ever been her and me and the present ghost of my boy-father, killed at twenty-two the first time he rode on a motor-bike pillion on the Great North Road. It said in the telegram, which is still behind the clock, that the driver was unhurt.

Inside the fish shop I bump into Steve Hunter, who grins at me from the queue. 'Teatime, eh?' He takes his fish and chips and waits at the door until I move up the queue and get my 'fish and chips twice, wrapped'. His packet is open and he's eating fish with his fingers. 'Teatime, eh?' he repeats. He thrusts his packet at me, 'Have a chip.'

'No, thanks. I'll eat mine when I get home. Off a plate.'

He looks along the street. 'You live round here?'

'Along there and round the corner.'

'Can I walk you there?'

'You can if you like.'

As we walk along he shortens his stride to keep pace with me. 'You enjoying it across at Marvell's, then?'

'It's OK. I like Patsy and Karen.'

'That Patsy's the queen of the line.'

'Looks like that. She's funny. Deep, though.'

'She's all right if you're on the right side of her.'

'So are we all.'

He looks down at me. His nose is slightly big for his face but there is this very attractive spark about him. 'I was wondering, like, if you'd fancy going to the pictures? With me, like?'

We turned the corner onto my street. 'The pictures? When would that be?' I said.

'Tonight. We could make the second house.'

I think of my own cold house and am tempted. 'No can do. I've got to have my tea and ... well ... I have things to do.' Really, I have nothing to do.

'What things?'

'I've got jobs to do for my mother.' It's a lie but it will do. I stop at my narrow door. 'This is me.'

He looks at the single windows, up and down. 'You live here?'

'I just said.'

'I'd have thought ... the way you talk...'

'You'd have thought what?'

'Well, you'd have lived in one of those new houses on Elm Rise...'

'Well, you thought wrong.' No wonder I feel I can't bring my college friends here. Even Steve is surprised at the way I live. I put my key in the lock. He puts a hand over mine. 'Ever been to the Gaiety?'

'I went when I was still at school.'

'You should get there, Saturday night.' He stands back. 'Right then. I'll see you there. Save me a dance, will you?'

I have to smile. 'I might.'

'Good. Right. See you!' And he walks back down the street whistling 'That'll Be the Day'.

'Who was that?' says my mother taking the

packet of fish and chips from me. (The window is right on the pavement so it's easy enough to see what's going on outside.)

'His name's Steve. He's a progress chaser on our line.'

'Good-looking boy.' There's a question in her flat statement.

'I just met him at the fish shop and he walked along with me.' I try not to sound defensive. 'Just somebody from work.'

'Good. You need friends round here.' She tips the fish and chips onto the waiting plates. 'You never seem to make friends.'

Oh yes I do, I think. But they are in another, sunnier place, picking grapes. But you neither, I accuse her silently. You have no friends. You keep yourself apart. 'I'm all right.' I say out loud. For a second I have an image of my real friends out there under the sun, picking grapes or drinking coffee in some French café.

She looks at me, her eyes narrowed, as though she's really noticing me for once. 'Are you all right, Cassandra?'

'Course I am.' I pull my gaze away from hers and look across at the kitchen cabinet. 'Is there any vinegar? I'm starving.'

The Other Woman

Wednesday

Walking down the lines, Stan Laverick, was pleased to see that student Cassandra Fox getting on with Patsy and Karen. You could always rely on Patsy O'Hare. Patsy was a bit of a tartar, but she was a good worker and wouldn't see the work go amiss. Production wouldn't suffer just because they had drafted in a student worker, and that was all that counted here.

Stan liked these women on the lines. They took his roaring in good part and knew how to make and take a laugh. Not so snooty and look-down-your-nose as the girls in the offices. (The exception that proved that rule was that air hostess girl, Evelyn, who had a mild way of looking at you that was as old as time: spoke of worlds of experience. Young Tam Kovacs was in for a treat there.) For Stan the women on the lines were the best of women. There was a lively, honest, sexual buzz down there. The women were better than the flouncing office girls in their straight skirts. And they were better looking, especially the young ones, even when they left their rollers in for work. Couldn't blame them for that, leaving them in to look their best on a night. Of course the rash of rollers in the factory was always more widespread on days when there was to be a dance at the Gaiety.

Stan paused to sort out a dispute between the progress lad, Steve, and a line leader. The matter settled, he took Steve to one side and asked if he had asked that young Cassandra out yet. She was OK in a Miss Mouse kind of way.

Steve shook his head, 'I'm working on it. But I see what you mean, Stan. She's not half bad.'

'Bet you a tenner you don't make it to five with that one,' he said.

Steve put both his hands up in fists and flicked his fingers one to ten. 'You're on, Stan.'

Stan strolled on down the gangway, thinking about love. He himself had experienced one great love in his life. Unfortunately he met her twelve years after he had married his Joanie and settled down to a life that echoed that of his father and his grandfather: work, the club, the dogs, kicking a ball about with his lads, making love to Joanie on Saturday night after the dance at the Gaiety. They didn't make love after the Thursday dance as Joanie was always too tired.

He had actually met this woman – this love of his life – at the Gaiety Thursday Special. He always got up in the barn dance, when you started with your own partner and then danced with every woman in the room. (Funnily enough it was in the barn dance that – just out of his National Service – he had met his Joanie in the first place...)

That particular Thursday night he had just danced with a stout girl with a fat ponytail, moved on, when this woman slid into his arms. Instantly the air crackled between them. She was no young thing, perhaps even older than Joanie. But she had green eyes, spring-wired hair, and a dimpled grin, and he could feel his heart tip this way and that as they did their single barn dance turn.

That would have been that, but the next week Joanie was on an extra twilight shift at Marvell's. She'd said for Stan to go on to the dance. She would rush home, get changed and meet him at the Gaiety later.

The green-eyed woman was the first person he saw as he came through the double doors. When the band struck up a foxtrot he went across and asked her to dance. By the time he had steered her expertly round the floor she had told him that her name was Leila and she was widowed, that she came from a village out near the coast, that she had her own little MG and that she loved to dance.

He was too well trained to go and sit out with her but he did come back and ask her for five dances in succession. He explained that he was expecting his wife any minute, that he had two sons, the elder in an upper set at the new comprehensive, that he was in management at Marvell's Cookers, and that he had never met anyone like her. And he had a car too, a Ford that he had bought second-hand from his boss, Charlie Priest. And, he repeated, he had never met anyone quite like her.

Halfway through their fifth dance, she slipped a note into the top pocket of his best Burton suit. 'My number. If ever...'

He swept her into a well-executed dip, his heart

singing. Then, over her shoulder he saw Joanie bustling through the double doors and his heart-singing stopped. The music stopped as well just then, and he and Leila were marooned in the crowd in the middle of the floor.

'The wife's here,' he said. 'I'll have to love you and leave you, Leila.'

She shrugged. 'See you, then.'

'See you,' he said.

She held his glance for another second, then turned and walked away through the dissolving crowd of dancers.

'Who was that?' said Joanie when he joined her.

He shrugged. 'Some woman,' he said. 'She got me up in the Lady's Choice. Good dancer.'

Joanie laughed and said, 'Some women! Can't keep their mitts off other women's lads! Especially when they look like the original lost sheep, like you do.'

Since that night he had got into the habit of visiting Leila once a fortnight at her bungalow at the coast, where they played Frank Sinatra records and made awkward love on her green Dralon couch. Stan had never got as far as her bedroom, but apart from his fortnightly visits he rang her every other day and they told each other what they were up to and what they would be doing with each other if they could.

Then the presentation of the millionth cooker was mooted and Alan Cartwright announced at the big production meeting that they calculated that the millionth would be sold at a specific best-selling store on the coast. Stan was inspired by the thought that this lucky person might be his special friend Leila. He fantasised about exchanging secret smiles with her at the presentation and perhaps slipping off afterwards somewhere quiet for a drink.

He rang her to tell her of his plan. 'So you could get it, Leila. Be there at the right time and you could have it.'

She laughed. 'You're quite something, Stan. Won't it break the rules?'

'Nobody's to know, are they?'

She laughed again, that gurgling sound that always made his heart tip. 'All right then. I could do with a new cooker. I'll be there.'

The designated store, when she arrived at the time Stan said, had quite a buzz about it. There were more people than usual at the counters and a man in a very smart lounge suit looked down from the top of the staircase that dominated the store. Behind him stood two men hung around with cameras and two other men in tweed jackets.

Leila looked at the Marvell cookers and chose one – gleaming and not over sized – that took her fancy. She was second in the queue at the counter. In front of her were a younger man and an older woman. The man asked to see the big Marvell cooker that was standing at the end of a line of cookers. She watched as the assistant grinned his delight and signaled to the man in the lounge suit standing on the stairs. He bustled across to the couple, pulling the photographers and reporters in his wake.

A crowd of assistants and shoppers clustered around the couple. People started clapping and the woman and her son looked bewildered. The manager shook the man's hand. 'Your luck's certainly in today, sir.' He turned then, and shook the old woman's hand. 'And you, madam.'

She looked up at him. 'It's me wants the cooker,' she said. 'And me that's paying for it.' Leila smiled to herself at the neat way the old woman had put the man in his place.

He was unperturbed. 'Well, madam, not only will you get your cooker free,' he beamed, 'you will be presented with it at the Marvell factory by no less a personage than Miss Sandie Shaw.'

There was a patter of applause and the flash of a camera.

The manager went on, 'And not only that, but the generous Marvell management is going to give you a week's holiday in Majorca.'

'Well, that's something,' the old woman said. 'I haven't ever been to Majorca.'

At that point a young woman arrived and handed out champagne to everyone, including Leila, the assistants and various passers-by drawn in by their own curiosity, as well as the reporters and photographers from the *Northern Echo* and the Middlesbrough *Evening Gazette*.

The photographs were all in the next day's papers. So, although he was disappointed that his plan had misfired, Stan did have the compensation of two photographs (one pinned up now on the progress office notice board and one lodged in his wallet next to his heart), of the crowd toasting Mrs McLochlan and (it turned out) her nephew with champagne in round Babycham glasses. Leila was standing there in front, to the left of the lucky winners.

Stan's wife, Joanie, didn't even twig what it meant when she came across the photo in Stan's wallet while she has raiding it for money for the milkman. She just said to Stan, 'Keeping that picture in your wallet? Marvell's! That place'll come between you and your wits, Stan. Like I always say to my mother, sometimes I think I'm married to Marvell's cookers, not Stan Laverick.'

Leila phoned Stan at work and told him all about it.

'You should have seen the old woman put the snooty manager down, Stan,' she giggled.

'It's not right, Leila. You should have that cooker.'

'Don't go on, Stan. I had my glass of champagne. I had a laugh.'

All of this made Stan love her even more. He did manage to get Leila a cheap cooker from Staff Sales. It had a small chip, back left. He bought it with snooker winnings hoarded away from Joanie's eagle eye and prying fingers.

'You shouldn't waste your money on me,' Leila protested when he turned up one night with the cooker in an unmarked Marvell van. 'I have money left me by my husband. I can buy my own cookers. It's company I lack, love, not money. That's what you give me, you give me time.'

She let him fit the cooker, but she insisted on paying him for it. Then she opened her own champagne and they had their own private celebration of a very particular Marvell cooker, which now belonged to her.

Stan's greatest joy was that he could manage to

see her every other week. His lifetime habit of going to Grafton dogs twice a week provided some cover. If he was missing a couple of times a month no one at the dogs really noticed.

Since Stan had met Leila, his mates at work – even Joanie herself – noticed how cheerful he had become. These days there was a spring in his step, an occasional grin on his usually lugubrious face. Even so, in his heart of hearts, Stan knew this whole thing with Leila just couldn't last. But while he could see Leila every other week and ring her every other day, he was content.

Scrapbooks

Wednesday

On the winding bus journey home from work Evelyn Laing's wandering mind fixed suddenly on Mr Priest bustling through the office on Monday, with that new young girl. Cassandra Fox! That was the name. Mr Priest was making a familiar fuss of her. Evelyn's mind went back to her own induction at Marvell's. Mr Priest had made sure it was *he* who interviewed her. (She had heard, since, the men in the office laugh at this. *Charlie Priest and all the pretty girls...*)

When she first met him she thought Mr Priest made a good impression on her. A very smooth man, brown skinned, he always wore suits in light fabrics, even in winter. On her first day, he looked at Evelyn over the half-moon glasses he affected then. 'On the *lines?*' he drawled in that strange accent. His eyes moved over her, top to toe. His tone rather suggested she proposed working on the plains of Sodom.

She had tried to be patient. 'I really need a job, Mr Priest. My father's just been widowed and he is very ill. I have to stay at home now. I need a job.'

'So you said. But why not an office job?'

'I have no skills. I told you that.'

'Not from what I *heard*. Not from what I *see*. I can *see* you have skills.' This was said just this side of a leer.

She had glared at him and he had the grace to go red. She left it a second then she let him off the hook. 'Taking care of passengers, Mr Priest? Taking care of children?' She laughed. 'Not much use in an office. Unless you're a bit keen on fantasy.'

His eyes brightened.

That was a mistake. She rushed on. 'But any job will do, Mr Priest. I always was a quick learner. I pick up new things in no time.'

He shuffled the papers on his desk and coughed. 'Two vacancies in the typing pool. One outside here, in the progress office. Filing. Invoicing. Plenty of shop-floor jobs, of course. But there's no point in you going down there. Those women can be aggressive, chasing bonuses, watching each other like hawks. They'd eat you for breakfast, that lot. You'd be like a diamond in the dust. The offices are easy compared with that.'

So that was that. He set her on that day in the

progress office just outside his door. Typing was easy enough, once she'd learned to trust her fingers and stop thinking. She never did learn shorthand, but made up for it with accurate scribble and a good memory. As Mr Priest said, the work wasn't hard.

Rather to her own surprise she loved working at Marvell's. She liked the job; the work was easy and the people were generally kind and funny in a salty kind of way. The factory was as dramatic as any of Mr Leavis's theatres; at the beginning of a shift it buzzed with energy and tension, just like backstage before the curtain goes up.

Her introduction to the special kind of life on the shop floor was the daily task of taking post to the various offices around the different blocks. The women on the lines would often look up from their work, hands still busy, and watch her. On the first day they called across and asked her what her name was, and where she was working. As they got to know her they would make a direct comment about how she looked or what she was wearing. 'Canny dress, that, Evelyn.'

Passing the tool room – a male preserve – she was always treated to wolf whistles and occasional invitations to meet one of the toolmakers down at the Gaiety or the Oak Tree pub. Now and then on the shop floor she witnessed rows and angry voices, and endured the bellowing of Mr Laverick, the foreman, who had a huge voice for such a small man. As she came to know them all better she got to appreciate the teasing and laughter, the jokes based on nicknames and unfathomable comic allusions based on long mutual acquaintance. Comedy was the lubricant in this big machine.

Of course, Mr Priest tried his luck with her but was quite gallant when she turned him down. The other men in the office could be flirtatious but they were wary of her. Like Mr Priest they were sensitive to the different signals she sent out. Marvell's had its own subtleties.

In the year Evelyn started Tamás Kovacs had not long been in this, his first senior management job. She liked Tamás. She liked it when he brought his sandwiches and shared her lunch-times. He was quiet but not shy. His interest in her life and travels was open and quite bold. And he was different from the others with his fair sculptured face and faint accent. She admired his efficiency and saw just why he was popular with the managers and the progress men. The women on the shop floor really liked him, proud of the fact that he started at Marvell's working along-side them. He might be a boss now but he had been one of their own.

From that first long day at the factory, Evelyn found that just being there constituted a kind of social life. When she got home to her father she was content to make their meal, watch a bit of news on the television or – her father's favourite thing – get out the photo albums of his life with Caroline when they were young, or his scrap-books filled with photographs and postcards of Evelyn's travelling life. The contrast between those glamorous images and their living here now in this tiny house with its tiny yard and down-stairs bathroom was lost on him but not on Evelyn. The scrapbooks did not make her nostalgic but they added some colour to her monochrome life at home.

It was the scrapbooks that gave Evelyn and Tamás Kovacs the idea about Sandie Shaw.

They had worked together for quite a long time when, a month before, having kept her back to do some overtime, Tamás gave her a lift home and came into the house for a cup of tea. They had been working on his minutes of the big monthly meeting with Mr Owen. He had stayed back with Evelyn while she transcribed his notes from his big ledger. Always the perfectionist, he had been anxious that the facts were absolutely right.

That night, once Evelyn got her father settled before the television in the little front parlour, she sat with Tam in the kitchen talking about this forthcoming production of the millionth Marvell cooker: the main topic of discussion in the minutes. A million cookers! She could not believe it. Tamás assured her that the calculations had been done and this was correct. He would know.

They went through the plan for this really big headlining event. The civic heads of Grafton were keen to take part.

'So they should be,' said Tamás. 'Everyone knows Marvell's is the mainstay of this town.'

'Provides a lot of work,' she agreed.

'But like I just said at the meeting, it shouldn't be just showing off to the mayor. It should be something for all the people on the lines. Those women. The workers, you know? Some kind of show. Something glamorous. The women would like that. Not just the mayor with his chain.'

That was when Evelyn got her inspiration. She put her hand on the open scrapbook sitting on the kitchen table in front of them. 'I tell you what!' she said. 'Look! Here's Sandie Shaw! See this photo of her with Mr Leavis? See, that's him, right on the end? A film premiere, I think. Why don't you get Sandie Shaw to come and present your millionth cooker to somebody? A kind of prize for buying it!'

'Sandie Shaw? Someone like that?' he frowned. 'They wouldn't let her come here just to give someone a cooker. Not here.'

'Well, I did read in the paper about a pop star opening some shopping mall in Hemel Hempstead or somewhere. Presenting the millionth Marvell cooker would be much more fun for her than that.'

'How could we get somebody like her? D'you know her?'

Evelyn laughed. 'I don't actually *know* her, Tam. But I'll ring Mr Leavis. He'll have her number. He has this little black book with all kinds of contact numbers. Calls it his Bible.'

'If you think...'

She picked up the telephone and rang the Leavises' number. Mr Leavis answered and instantly asked if she were coming out of her hasty retirement to get his family in order again.

'We always miss you, Evie.'

'And I miss you, and Aaron and Sophie. But my life's here now. I tell you what I'm after, Mr Leavis. I'm after a number for Sandie Shaw's agent.' She explained the situation.

Mr Leavis was tickled by the idea. 'Ring her,

Evie! Her name's Eve too. She's a bit of a gorgon, but very businesslike. The idea might have some mileage for her. I did hear that she was looking for something new, something big for Miss Shaw. A new song, a new career boost. She might find this entertaining.'

'Not really a career boost, though!'

'As I said, she might find it entertaining. And she has fans up there as well as down here.' He paused. 'I imagine there will be money in it?'

Evelyn glanced at Tamás, who nodded vigorously. 'Yes, very good money, I think.'

So the day after that, Tamás put forward Evelyn's suggestion to the daily meeting. After due discussion, Alan Cartwright, the sales manager – 'who did all the fancy stuff' – rang Sandie Shaw's agent and had a long and businesslike conversation.

And that, Evelyn reflected as her bus trundled to her village stop, was how this whole Sandie Shaw carnival had begun. She had known from the beginning that it would be fun, more like old times. She was looking forward to it.

War of the Worlds

Wednesday

I am halfway through my first long week at Marvell's, working alongside Patsy and Karen. Lots of the younger women on the line have their rollers in today, some bound up in chiffon scarves, some with their rollers naked to the world.

Steve Hunter and the other progress lads – all in overalls – are wheeling their trolleys along the lines, filling plastic boxes with detritus from under and around the machinery. Steve starts raking out the difficult bits of rubbish with a long brush. Patsy nods across at him, her second chin wobbling. 'Nice to see a bloke wielding a brush and shovel, Stevie.'

He scowls at her and then glances uneasily across at me. 'Put a sock in it, Patsy.'

'Ah, diddums! Do we have to wear overalls to keep ourselves clean, pet? Just like the common workers? Thought we had a collar and tie job, did we?'

'I said leave it.' He moves ten yards down and starts to poke away under the line with his brush.

Patsy turns her razor beam on me. 'And I bet you think it's a right come-down having to flog a living in a godforsaken place like this, flower.'

I keep my eye on my wires, I'm getting better and I don't want to arrest the flow. But, finally able to talk and screw in wires at the same time, I say, 'Like you said before, Patsy, I'm lucky to get a job anywhere. My own mother flogs a living here. And I know plenty about flogging for a living. I worked in shops when I was still at school, and at the dog track, tipping it all up to help my mother. I sometimes think it kills her, working here.'

Patsy's hands are flying. 'It kills us all, flower. But then, when you think of it, it doesn't. We're still here, ain't we?'

'It gets her down. Sometimes she talks about this place like it was the War of the Worlds here. The end of civilisation as we know it. She goes to sleep the minute she gets in the house. Can't lift a hand even to light the fire. I've made my own tea since I was ten.' Cripes. Where has all this self-pity come from? My mother's not that bad.

'War of the Worlds? Great film, that?' Karen glances across at me, her eyes bright. Pretty as she is, she's looking a bit strange today with those big rollers in the front of her hair and the long hair at the back wound around big wodges of cotton wool. She says, 'Me, I wouldn't go for all that tipping-up and making your own tea. Our mam has my dinner ready the second I'm in. She does all my washing and makes all my clothes. She can copy anything from a magazine. Anything.'

Lucky her. My hands are slowing down. My work is piling up.

Patsy laughs. 'Takes care of you like a baby, your mother. You're a spoiled baby, Karen, that's what!'

100

Karen comes round to help me with my waiting pile. 'If you say so, Patsy. Doesn't always feel like that.' She sounds quite gloomy, for her.

Gratefully I watch her demolish my backlog. 'I'd say you were lucky, Karen. Sometimes I wish my mother did all of that. Or wanted to.'

Uniquely, Karen stops working and stares at me. 'Well, I always thought I was lucky but I'm not sure about that now. You're the lucky one. You don't really have to work in this place. You're playing at this. And soon you'll get out, away.'

Patsy stops work a second, looks hard at Karen, then carries on. 'That's for sure,' she said. 'You'll bugger off for good.'

I get back up on my stool and start again. 'Playing?' I say. 'I'm here because I need the money. Just like you. Just like those other lasses on the line. Just like little Stan, strutting down there with his clipboard. I need to get some money to tip up for my mother so I can get back to college in September. And when I get there I've gotta work hard too, but with no pay, because if I don't pass my exams all this'll have been a waste.'

Patsy nods. 'Aye, pet, you're not wrong. We're all in it for the money. Just like Charlie Priest up there.' Charlie and Stan are up on the gantry, talking. 'Our Charlie likes his nice car and his house and his holidays in Majorca, doesn't he?' She glances at Karen, now on her own side of the line. 'Don't he, Karen? Anything he can get his hands on. That Charlie Priest is a greedy man.'

The Tannoy crackles and Karen starts to sing along with Eddie Cochran, reflecting on his

'Summertime Blues'. I laugh and join in with her. All those lyrics about trying to take time off and being stopped by your boss seems to fit here and now.

I put down my head over my wiring. I feel guilty now about blabbing all that about my mother. Word will soon get round that Linda Fox is a slut about the house and neglects her kid. But really that's not true. It takes every part of her to come here and work a shift. This is as much as she can do, to bring in the money to run the house. When I was thirteen (having been studying some biology) I had this dream of a great leech sucking blood out of my mother and when the leech rolled over, fat with blood, you could see the name 'Marvell' on its side. It was the same as the lettering on the side of the vans that rolled through the factory gates every day.

Three years ago the doctor told my mother she was clinically depressed and gave her stuff called Valium but she threw them away when she was too sleepy to get up to go to work in the morning. I now see how good she is at hiding all this black home self here at work. She's known here as a good worker and is always immaculate in herself. No one but me ever sees the Herculean effort it takes for her to get to Marvell's at half-past seven in the morning, fifty weeks a year. And then there is taking care of the house or me. Sitting here trying to keep up with Karen I realise my mother is a Marvell herself, battling her depression to get here every day. To this!

The buzzer for lunchtime. Great. I put down my screwdriver and run my hands, one against the other, to get the cutting feel of the wire off them. Patsy and Karen drag their stools to the end of the line and get out their food and flasks. Karen takes out her rollers and cotton wool and combs her hair down.

'Why do you do that?' I ask, feeling bold. 'Take your rollers out in the middle of the day?'

Karen stares at me, a bit like a marmoset with those black lines round her eyes. 'To give my hair a rest. Not good for it to be screwed into rollers all day long.' Her tone says, *Do you know nothing about hair as well as nothing about other most important things?*

'You staying here for your bait, or going walkabout, flower?' says Patsy.

Yesterday I ran to the canteen and bought a cup of tea to go with my meagre sandwiches. 'Well, I...' I hesitate. 'My mother said to go down to circuit breakers and have my sandwiches with her.'

'Did she now?' She unscrews her flask and sniffs her coffee.

Karen sets out her food on a copy of the *Daily Mirror*. Pies. Cakes.

I say, 'I could stay here, I don't have to...'

'Suit yourself,' said Patsy.

I draw my stool nearer the end of the line and reach into my bag for my sandwiches and bottle of Coca-Cola. Suddenly Steve Hunter is there, brown sandwich bag in hand.

Patsy grins at him. 'Haway, honey! Come and have a spot of bait with your Auntie Patsy. Not that you have to wait for any invitation.'

He folds himself up onto the floor with his back

to the console and opens his bag. He glances at me, takes a bite out of his bun and looks up at Karen. 'No doubt about it, Karen. Looks like Sandie Shaw's come early, your hair down like that. You've got the image, kiddo.'

Karen nibbles at one of her cakes. 'People are saying that all the time. But just you watch. Bloody Stan Laverick'll be along and tell us to tie it back.'

'It's not him who says you have to take out your rollers and pin back your hair,' says Steve.

'It's not who that doesn't say that?'

'It's not Stan Laverick that says the lasses should tie their hair back.'

'It is. He comes down the line and–'

'Just a mouthpiece,' says Stevie. 'It's Charlie Priest. I heard him say it. Tell those girls to tie their hair back. He's always saying it.'

Patsy slurps her coffee.

Karen goes red. 'Mr Priest? He wouldn't. He...'

'He what?' said Patsy.

'Mr Priest likes it, my hair out. He told me.'

'Told you?' says Patsy quickly. 'Told you when?'

'One night. He gave me a lift. It was raining.'

'You never told us that,' says Patsy.

Karen pouts. 'I don't have to tell you everything, do I?'

'Neither do you, pet. Neither do you.' Patsy takes a big bite out of her tuna and salad cream sandwich.

Now we are all busy eating. I finish my paste sandwiches and pick up my Coca-Cola.

Patsy finishes her sandwiches, smoothes out

her sandwich paper, folds it into a small square and tucks it back into her bag. Then she breaks the silence. 'They say there's this feller on development that's got three lasses from A Shop up the stick.'

Steve winks at me and ducks his head down over his third bun.

'Up the...?' I'm puzzled.

Patsy smirks. 'Where've you been, love? Inside some egg or other?'

'She means pregnant. Expecting,' said Karen. She has cake crumbs on her full lips.

'*Enceinte,*' I say.

'What?' says Patsy.

I blush beetroot red. 'That's how the French say it.'

'Ooh *là* bloody *là!* Proper Mary Poppins, aren't we?'

'Good film, that,' says Karen. 'I took our little 'uns to it.'

Patsy drives on. 'Those three girls up A Shop won't care how you say it, pet. Up the stick is up the stick. They'll be running around like mice on a wheel finding some way to *get rid*. Talk about *War of the Worlds*. They should'a taken this Pill thingy, or crossed their legs or sommat.'

'They'll legalise that soon,' I venture. 'The girls talk about it at college. My friend Emma had a sister who had an abortion.'

Steve is looking uncomfortable.

'What?' says Karen.

I borrow Patsy's phrase. 'She *got rid*.'

Patsy nods. 'You read about it in the Sunday paper. Campaigns and that. Not before time, if

105

you ask me. Just now they'll have to find some old witch up an alley and... What's this, Stevie? Blushing? Red as a pay-night fire.'

I'm blushing myself. 'Patsy, it's not–'

'Nice? *Decent?* Not nice to talk like this where the lads are? But lads like our Steve here have got to know where their high jinks lead to, an't they? They've got to know who carries the can. Or the bairn, as the case may be.'

Karen laughs very loudly. 'Oh, Patsy, leave off, will you? You're embarrassing the lot of us. Here, have a fairy cake. My mam just made it last night. You too, Cassandra. You as well, Stevie.' Steve and I take one, then Karen holds the bag up for Patsy, who hesitates, shrugs, and takes her cake delicately, little finger in the air.

Stevie eats his cake fast, then coughs on the crumbs. He eyes me. 'I bet you lot are going down the Gaiety Saturday. Heard you're a big dancer, Karen. It's a prize on Saturday. You got prizes already, an't you?'

Karen flicks back her hair. 'Five prizes so far, Stevie. And I'm going for another one Saturday. Patsy's going too. She always goes for the competitions. Never misses one.'

'You dance, Patsy?' I say, trying to keep the surprise from my voice.

'Nah,' says Patsy. 'I watch. I'll say this for our Karen here. She's a bloody good little dancer even if she does make it look like some bloody tom-tom war dance.'

Karen giggles. 'We all know you'd rather see Fred Astaire do his soft-shoe shuffle, Patsy.' She turns to me. 'Honest, though, I don't know whether I could win if Pats wasn't there. She's my lucky pixie.'

Patsy scowls. 'Pixie be buggered.'

Stevie stands up and brushes the crumbs from his shirt. He looks me right in the eye. 'You going down the Gaiety Saturday then?'

'The Gaiety? I don't know...'

Karen laughs. 'Cassandra don't do downtown dances, Steve. She's a college girl.'

'Yeah, that's it,' says Patsy. 'All sex and drugs, no rock and roll.'

I manage a smile that I hope is enigmatic. 'You don't know half of it, Patsy.' I turn to Steve. 'You know what, Steve? I think I'll go to the Gaiety. And did you say there was a competition? Maybe I'll enter it.' I put my things in my bag.

'That'd be sommat to see.' Steve smiles. He stands up and shakes out his long legs. 'I'll see you down there, then, girls.' And he walks back down the line, whistling.

'He can be a cheeky little bugger, that Stevie,' says Patsy fondly.

Now the buzzer goes and the line starts to hum. My heart sinks and I push my bag under the line, pull my chair back into its place on the line, ready to start the afternoon shift.

Patsy laughs. 'Hey ho, girls! Here we go!'

On the Gantry

Stan Laverick and Charlie Priest leaned over the rail of the gantry and watched the shop floor wind up for the afternoon shift. As some people put away their packed lunches and settled down to work, and others trickled in from the canteen, things began to stir: like the winding up of a clock that would tick away and keep perfect time until five o'clock.

Charlie (only half listening to some club joke Stan was telling him that involved a butcher and some sausages) was relishing this moment. This whole machine was working. Parts went on the line, products rolled off and all this was down to him and the few chosen men around him. Charlie was good at what he did and he knew it. More importantly, his mentor, Mr Owen, in charge of all the factories in the North, knew it. And even down at his London base Mr Abrahams – whose energy had set up Marvell's after the war – knew it. Mr Abrahams' particular genius had been to predict the post-war demand for high-class appliances not just here, but all over the world. Now Marvell's even exported to the USA, where domestic appliances were an integral part of the American dream.

The last time Mr Abrahams came up North he actually shook Charlie warmly by the hand twice. 'You are the hub of this factory, Mr Priest. The very hub.'

Charlie didn't kid himself. He knew how much of all this was down to the men around him, the team that had emerged in the last ten years, nurtured by Mr Owen. He kept them all in line – even Charlie – so they produced the goods on time and to spec. But here in this factory, he, Charlie Priest, was king. He was the one who wound up the clock so it would tick away, efficiently powered by the workers, who were this odd combination of anarchy and stoicism, energy and idleness. And humour. There was always laughter. Handling them was no easy option but he could do it. Charlie wouldn't have admitted it to a soul but there was no buzz in the world like the one he got with his job: not even sex, and he was quite partial to that.

His wandering attention returned to Stan Laverick, beside him, who was almost doubled up laughing. 'Thought you'd like that one, Mr Priest! This feller had them shouting for more down the club last Saturday. You should get down there sometime, Mr Priest. Lads'd appreciate it. You used to get down there at one time.'

'You could just say life's a bit too hectic these days for that, Stan. I've obligations. Commitments.'

'Aye. Entertaining customers. I know. It'll be nightclubs, gambling clubs and things. I went to a nightclub once in Stockton. Saw Frankie Vaughan. It was a glitzy place. Just like the pictures. You'll have been there, I suppose.'

'So I have, Stan,' said Charlie. 'So I have.'

Down below, the shop floor had now got into its

rhythm. Stan knew this was the point where the manager would return to his office but he wanted to keep him a few moments more. 'So it's really gunna happen next week, Mr Priest? Sandie Shaw?'

'Signed and sealed. A thousand quid and well worth it. It'll put a bit of a sparkle into the proceedings, Stan. Papers. Television. All paying attention.'

'Will she sing?'

'Afraid not. Alan Cartwright signed the deal. It's in the contract that she wouldn't be pressurised to perform. Pity, that. She has this bright, perky voice. More partial to a bit of jazz myself. Cleo Laine, Johnny Dankworth. But they say Sandie's top of the pops.'

'So when she comes she'll just ... like ... say that ... like sommat like "Here's the millionth cooker"?'

'No. Not even that, Stan. The contract says she doesn't have to say anything.'

Stan frowned. 'Sorry to say this, Mr Priest, but it sounds like money for old rope.'

Charlie sighed. 'You don't get it, do you, Stan? It's not what she *does*, it's who she *is*. Like the Queen. You know.'

'Right. That's one way of looking at it.' He paused. 'Will she be wearing shoes, Mr Priest?'

Charlie laughed. 'Well, Stan, I'm not entirely daft. I stood my ground so that she would stand hers, so to speak. It's in the contract. The feet will be on view, so to speak.' He lit a small cigar. 'Confidentially, Stan, I have a certain weakness for women's feet.'

Stan clutched his clipboard very hard. 'It's arses with me, Mr Priest. That Marilyn Monroe. Pity about her. What a loss that was. She had a lovely...'

They both stared down at the lines a moment and meditated on the particular charms of Marilyn Monroe. Stan, seeing a woman cross the floor to go to the toilet, scribbled her name on his clipboard.

Charlie came back from his dream of a white skirt and underground air ducts. 'Now, Stan, this woman who's getting the prize? Is she presentable?'

Stan thought she would have been even more presentable if it had been Leila. 'Absolutely, Mr Priest. Alan Cartwright and I've spoken to her on the phone about the model she wants. And I'm going across to the coast to see her tonight. I'll make sure she knows the drill.'

'Good man. Over and above the call of duty. I like that.'

Charlie leaned over and stared intently at the line.

Stan coughed. 'Sometimes, Mr Priest, I really envy you.'

'How's that, Stan?'

Stan waved his open hand towards the shop floor. 'All these wom – workers, sir. Power of life and death. Job or no job. Look at that kid of Linda Fox's. Cassandra – queer name, that; I bet she was grateful. Look at her. You give her a job.'

Charlie laughed. 'You have some strange ideas, Stan. But I do my best for this lot. If I do my best for them the whole place works. That's what I'm here for. You know that.' He glanced back down at the lines. 'Is that new girl settling in? That Cassandra Whatsit? I see you put her on Line Two. Doing all right, is she? With Patsy and that dark girl? The one with the hair.'

'Karen. I might be mistaken, Mr Priest, but young Steve said it was you that told him to put her down there. With Karen and Patsy. You said to put her with Patsy O'Hare, who might have a loud mouth but is a good trainer. Of course she's ham fisted, like. But they all are when they start. And this one's a bolter. Been to the lav three times this morning.' He tapped his clipboard. 'I have it here. Then again the lass doesn't have to make a career of working here, does she? Not like her mother.'

Charlie looked across the shop floor again and frowned.

'What is it, Mr Priest?'

'That girl down there with Cassandra Fox and Patsy O'Hare. That dark one with the ridiculous rollers. Karen, is it?'

'That's Karen. Bloody good worker.' Stan knew that Charlie knew exactly who the girl with the rollers was.

'Tell her to get those rollers out. She looks ridiculous.'

'OK.' Stan put a note on his clipboard, biting back the comment that a quarter of the women were wearing hair armoury of some kind or another. He tried a different tack. 'Canny bit stuff, that Karen,' he said. 'When she takes those rollers out, like. She's the dead spit of Sandie Shaw herself. I thought mebbe you'd noticed that, Mr

Priest.' He spared Charlie a narrow sideways glance.

'Can't say I have, Stan,' drawled Charlie. 'Can't say I have.'

'They say on the rock'n'roll nights at the Gaiety she's the queen of the dance. Best bopper going.'

'Do they now?'

Stan continued on his fishing trip. 'She's only into bopping, mind. They've got bets on it, the lads. No one's ever got past "three" with that Karen. That's what they say, like.'

Stan knew he had hooked his fish when Charlie Priest adjusted his tie and swallowed a little smile. He turned towards his office door. 'Anyway, Stan, make sure that girl takes those rollers out. And the rest too. This place is like one big hairdresser's salon.' Then, with his hand on the doorknob, he turned round. 'If you think she looks like Sandie Shaw, Stan, maybe she should be the one presenting the flowers.'

The door closed behind him and Stan stared at it. 'Bloody hypocrite.'

'What's that, Stan?'

He turned and nearly bumped into Steve Hunter, leaning on a brush. 'Mr Laverick to you, son,' he scowled.

'I'm done, on Lines One and Two, Mr Laverick.'

'Are they clean?'

'Spotless. But I'm here to make a complaint. I'm not some kid or a cleaner. I'm a progress chaser, not a sweeper-up.' He put the brush into Stan's hand, making him drop his clipboard.

Stan threw the brush back at him and picked

113

up his clipboard. He roared, 'Don't you tell me what you will or won't do, lad!'

A woman on the nearest line looked up, her hands still busy. She noted how this more familiar roaring contrasted with Stan's placatory tone with Mr Priest. She saw a lot from her place on the line.

Stan dusted off his clipboard. 'And don't you tell me what you are and you aren't gunna do, lad, unless you want your cards.'

Steve stood his ground, staring at him. They both knew right-out temper-tantrum sackings were a rare luxury now: the unions were flexing their muscles these days. They could shut the place in a day and knew it.

The Tannoy burst out with the first track of the afternoon. The watching woman on the line started to sing along with Buddy Holly 'That'll Be the Day'.

Stan calmed down. 'I tell you what, lad. You and me'll just go down stores and get you the biggest pot of white paint we can find. And you can start to paint the edge of the gangway with neat white lines, so Miss Sandie Shaw will know the way to come when she visits us. That'll show up our red carpet very nicely. And you can pass this around. I have it on the best authority that Sandie Shaw will not be wearing her shoes. An' we can't let her dirty her lovely tootsies with factory dust, can we?'

'I don't–' protested Steve.

'You don't have no choice,' said Stan.

On the way to stores Stan stopped by Patsy's console to roar at Karen to take out her bloody rollers.

114

'Again?' She looked him in the eye, her hands still moving over the wires. 'Says who?'

'Says Mr Charlie Priest.' He nodded up to the empty gantry.

'He says you and those other women wired up like they're in *Doctor Who* lower the tone of the whole of his shop floor.'

She glanced at Patsy, then Cassandra. 'Well, I'll not take them out, not even for Mr Charlie bloody Priest.'

Stan grinned. 'On your own head be it!' He turned to Steve and winked. 'On your own head, geddit?'

Karen rolled her eyes. 'Very funny!'

Steve shrugged. 'I thought we were getting paint Mr Laverick,' he said sourly.

The three women watched them walk down the line to the double doors.

'Twerp!' said Cassandra. 'The man's a twerp.'

'We know it, pet, Stevie-boy knows it,' said Patsy. 'But lover-boy Stan Laverick has no idea.'

'Lover-boy?'

Karen grimaced. 'Old Stan has this fancy woman across at the coast. Fat face. Dyed red hair. Older than him. They met down at the Gaiety. Everyone knows.'

'Except his Joanie,' grinned Patsy, who had gone to the same school as Stan's wife.

Cassandra thought that knowing people's secrets like this was a neat way of cutting them down to size. It stripped them of any real authority.

'So, will you take out your rollers?' she said to Karen. 'Like they're telling you to?' She glanced up at the empty gantry.

'No she won't,' said Patsy. 'They might think they own us body and soul but for Chrissake they don't own the hair of our heads.'

Karen came round the line. 'Like Patsy says, what I do with my hair is my own business. Now, shift over, Cassandra Fox, while I make up your backlog. Good job I like you or I'd leave you to stew.'

At the Bus Stop

The final buzzer goes and I get this idea that I might go home with my mother, so I walk the length of the factory, against the tide of the exiting workers, to her place on the circuit-breaker section. I picture her in my mind, crouched at her bench in her overalls and the tight peasant kerchief she always wears to protect her pale hair from factory dust.

'She's gone to the lav,' says Marje Finnegan, my mother's friend and old adversary, her hands still busy on the circuit breakers. Marje smirks. 'Bit of overtime. Split it between us. Just the half-hour each. I could have done it myself like, but Linda won't let go of her share.'

I know from our brief night-time conversations how work-greedy Marje is. My mother's always on about it. 'But we all need that work, Cassandra. Overtime and bonuses are what makes the difference. But that greedy Marje, she'd grab

116

it all if she could. You have to fight your corner with types like her, Cassandra, or you'd always be on basic.'

I once had the temerity to say to my mother that it seemed a bit petty to go to battle over a bit of work. She exploded. 'Petty?' she said. 'Petty? Nice for you to be able to say that, Cassandra. I know you've passed your exams and earned your grants but what do you think pays for those clothes and books you need? And not bringing a penny in? I tell you what pays for them. My bonus!'

It was unanswerable. I learned years ago not to question this hunger for work that was the focus of her mother's life. Our house is barely cared for, virtually a tip, my mother is perpetually depressed. Marvell's is her purgatory, her entertainment, the stage on which she performs; her job on circuit breakers and her own hunger for bonuses are what keeps her going. It is her only vehicle for passion.

But then I am an ungrateful wretch. Hasn't she told me that so many times? Told me in her perfunctory way that says she doesn't care whether I'm grateful or not, that she does what she does for herself.

I decide not to wait to have a word with my mother, then walk back through the emptying factory, thinking how it's my mother's reputation as a worker that has nailed this rare holiday job for me. And I know I have to be grateful. It's a fact that this summer I could be miles away, right away from Grafton and Marvell's. I could be earning better money than this in a faraway place: money for myself. But I feel guilty about how hard my mother works so I have to stay at home in the vac, instead of following Emma and the others from college to pick grapes in France to earn money that they'll then use for a cheapo holiday in Spain. I was flattered that they were disappointed that I couldn't join them. Emma urged me to use my factory money to join them on their Spanish spree. 'Tell your mother travel broadens the mind, Cass,' she urged, clutching my arm in that way of hers. I couldn't tell her I have no factory money. My factory money will all end up in my mother's purse.

'Now then. You look lost. It's Cassandra, isn't it?'

It's that Hungarian again, walking alongside me. The one who stopped by the line the other day.

'How d'you know my name?'

'I asked Stan Laverick, the man who knows everything.' He shortens his step to match mine. He smells of lemon and marzipan. Mmm.

I don't know his name. 'I'm not lost. I work on wiring jackets.'

'Then you must be lost. You're in the wrong place.' I'm struck again by his deep smiling voice: accented, softer than any of the harsh male tones I've heard since I've been in this factory.

For some reason I am annoyed with him. 'I told you! I'm not lost. I went down to circuit breakers to see my mother. She's Linda Fox.'

'Oh, I see. Linda. I know Linda! She is a great favourite of my father's and was kind to me when I started here. Marvell's is in your blood, then?'

'Yugch! I hope not.' Watch it, Cassandra, you're sounding truculent. 'I'm not really here, you know. Only for the long vacation.'

'Vacation? Ah, yes, I remember. You're a student. What are you studying?'

'English, mostly.'

'So what will you be at the end?'

'I don't know. I'm just doing English because I like it. I might teach it.'

He laughs. 'That sounds what they call "cushy".' He has this smile in his voice.

'Cushy? It's very hard work, studying.'

'As hard as working at Marvell's?'

'I wouldn't say that. Different. You don't get bloody fingers.'

'I bet.' He stops by the stairway to the gantry. 'I'm off up here now. Nice to talk to you ... Cassandra. That's a nice name. I never knew anyone called Cassandra.'

My heart lurches. I know it's a cliché but I can feel it. Lurching. 'So, what do they call you?'

His hand engulfs mine as he shakes it. 'I'm Tamás Kovacs. They call me Tam here.' He laughs. 'Sometimes they call me Tam O'Shanter. They had to explain that to me!' He starts up the iron stairs to the gantry. 'And perhaps you should not ever look down your nose at Marvell's, Miss Cassandra. It's a great place. No bad thing to have it in your blood even if it does get blood on your fingers.'

He leaps up the stairs two at a time and I watch him with interest. He has long legs and an easy narrow body. He's very attractive. He could very well be the best thing that's happened to me

119

since I arrived here on Monday morning.

It's raining when I get out of the building, too wet to walk home. The fleet of factory buses has gone, so I have to walk up to the road to get a service bus across the town. Patsy and Karen are there, huddled under an umbrella. 'You still here, lass? Thought you'd gone. Stan caught us and kept us back to help clear the line, so we missed the bus. But I thought you were long gone.'

'I went across to find my mother but she was nowhere to be seen.'

'Hard cheese!' Patsy holds the umbrella higher. 'Here, flower, squeeze in. No need for any of us to get a soaking. Lucky Karen here brought her brolly.'

Patsy's head is squashed under a headscarf and she's still wearing her overall under a short coat, but Karen has combed out her hair and repaired her eye-lines. Under her light mac she's wearing a blouse with a Peter Pan collar and a matching soft bow. Honestly, she is quite, quite beautiful. She pulls her coat tighter round her and shivers.

'You all right, Karen?' says Patsy. 'Someone walk over your grave?'

'I'm all right, Patsy. Really I am.'

A long green car passes and draws up ten yards further on. Karen smiles her sweet smile. 'That's a lift for me. Hang on to the brolly, Patsy, will you?'

We watch as she runs along, jumps in and the car eases away.

'Now that's a bloody surprise,' says Patsy sourly, 'or not.'

'That's Mr Priest, isn't it?' I say, fascinated.

120

'Are they friends? Did you know about it?'

I can feel Patsy's shrug. 'Know about it? Everybody on the site knows about it. It's a habit of his. Karen's not his first bit on the side and won't be the last.'

'But you don't say? You don't talk about it?'

'No, flower. We don't say. Not the way we do things, blabbing.'

I am really curious. 'But how—'

Patsy interrupts me. 'Like I said, we don't talk about it.' She leans forward to peer down the road. 'Now where is that bus? You stay back, do a bit of overtime and the bloody bus company goes on strike.'

I lean forward too, trying to maintain my space under the umbrella. 'Overtime?' I say. 'I'm pleased Stan didn't catch me for that. I didn't expect overtime. Me, I'm whacked and I haven't even done any overtime. How do you do it, Patsy? Keep going?'

She laughs. ''S easy when you know how. Stick with me, kiddo, and you'll get lots of overtime. First five years are the worst, flower. After that it's easy.'

'No offence, Patsy, but people like you and my mother, I don't know how you stand it. Honestly.'

'You've got it wrong, flower. I don't know about your ma but me, I like it all down the factory. I'm bloody good at what I do. So much to do in a day and you do it, faster and better than anyone else. Brilliant. The office girls prance around the place and the bosses think they're God's gift to us all, but without people like me and your ma they're nothing. We do it faster and better than anyone else, so we get the best bonus. And bloody hell, Cassandra! Them cookers when they're finished! Bloody shining white and perfect, and you know they're only like that because of us. Marvell, bloody marvellous. Better than sex, I'm telling you. Better than crawling about after some man to get a pat on the head or a quid in your purse to feed the kids. Better than warming your father's slippers and eating second at the table after the men.'

Hallelujah! Why doesn't my mother talk like that? 'Patsy, I...' I want to tell her how great I think she is.

'Aw, shurrup, lass.' She peers along the road again. 'Look! Isn't that an end to a perfect day? The bloody bus has stopped round the corner. We must be bloody invisible. We can't all of us get a lift in a flashy Volvo, can we? Now lass, get your skates on and run!'

So we run and catch the bus and I go home to light the fire in a chilly house, ready for my mother's tirade about just how greedy for work that Marje is. But now I'm looking forward to tomorrow just for the pleasure of working alongside Patsy and Karen. Real life is there, when you think of it.

Half an hour later my mother is coming through the door, clutching a packet of fish and chips. So at least I won't have to make the tea. As we set the table I tell her about meeting Tamás Kovacs in the gangway.

'He said he knew you.'

A rare smile. 'Tam Kovacs? Nice kid. Funny

lot, the Hungarians. They were either very fair or very dark. Tam and his dad were like that. Tam very fair, his dad very dark. He was a beauty, that boy. Willing, like, and really clever .You could tell that, even then when he knew no English.'

'Does his dad still work there?'

She shakes her head. 'Soon as he got his tongue properly round the English he was off. Works for an architect in Edinburgh, drawing buildings. That's what he'd been in Hungary, you know. A captain in the army, then an architect. He told me that.' She tips her fish and chips on the plate. Her eye strays across to the television. 'Put the news on, Cassandra. They say it's likely the Tory leader will resign. What'll they all do now, to save us from ourselves?'

At the White Leas Motel

Charlie Priest loved his job, but even though he was a very driven, highly efficient manager, he still had energy spilling over for other things. He had never heard the term *droit de seigneur,* but there was something feudal in his way of going about things at Marvell's. He was no film-star hero, but he had a sharpness about him, a kind of localised glamour. And he was The Boss.

There were all kinds of women in the factory but Charlie had a kind of Geiger counter for innocence. Now and then he would visit some young worker with his close attention. He enjoyed treating them to three-course dinners in quiet locations, and liked to give them some pocket money to buy a new dress or a pair of high-heeled shoes. He felt that he treated them well. Even when he dropped them he made sure they were never on a bad job and made good bonuses. Fair exchange, he always reflected.

Only once had he been wrong-footed by this young thing who had really fallen for him and not understood the nature of the contract. She started to telephone him at home, even once during *Songs of Praise* on a Sunday night, which was his Millie's favourite. That one time Millie twigged something was up, but he told her it was some young kid from packing who had a crush on him. He couldn't help that, could he, her haunting him? Millie calmed down when he bought her a Ford Capri and he made sure that, within a week, the girl was sacked for bad time-keeping.

He had broken his 'only young' preference that time he suggested a drink with Evelyn Laing, whose understated glamour when they first met had quite knocked him sideways; it was probably a good thing that she turned him down, as there might have been trouble there. She wouldn't have been happy with a weekly tryst in some distant motel. A diamond in the dust was our Evelyn, as well as a bloody good worker. And then there was that new girl, Cassandra, who had drawn his attention that first day, but she had a hard, innocent edge about her that was very unpromising.

But young Karen was, he had to admit, something more his style: a natural beauty with a certain rough-hewn modesty. No matter how much he teased or tempted her he could never get her to take off all her clothes. She always kept her petticoat on. And her high heels. But then he liked that.

Karen loved the wax-polish smell and smooth feel of Charlie's car. She knew, from talking to him after they made love, how Millie washed and polished his car inside and out every Sunday morning before he went to play golf. She knew also that Millie's own Ford Capri was her pride and joy. She had learned about Millie's delight in her new house and its two bathrooms with showers. Karen would imagine herself telling Patsy all about this and Patsy saying to her that for someone who was playing away, Charlie Priest was a man obsessed with his wife.

The day he picked her up at the bus stop Charlie drove fifteen miles on from their usual motel, to a smarter place called the White Leas Motel: an assortment of concrete boxes that boasted Elizabethan beams on its frontage. He left Karen in the car while he checked in and returned with the keys to the room, two bottles of Cherry B for her and two chilled bottles of Newcastle Brown Ale for him. Charlie's American aspirations did not stretch to champagne on ice.

In the square box of a room Karen took off her mac, laid it neatly over the dressing stool and sat on the bed, her knees together. 'This is nice,' she said, even more nervous than usual. 'Better than The Bell, isn't it? I don't think they changed the sheets there, do you? My mam would have been horrified.' She paused. 'If she'd have known, like.'

Charlie had made the need for secrecy on their very first outing. 'More romantic, love, don't you think? Keeping this just for ourselves, telling nobody,' he had said.

Now he handed her the Cherry B in a tooth glass. 'Here, drink up, love. The Bell wasn't too bad, was it? Served its purpose.' He sat beside her and drank from his bottle. 'But I thought you might like a change. A bit of a treat for a good girl. You are a good girl, lover, aren't you?'

She sipped her Cherry B.

He touched her Peter Pan collar. 'This is nice,' he said.

'My mam made it. Copied it off a picture in *Vogue* magazine.'

'Clever woman, your mother. She make this too?' He touched the pussycat bow.

'Yes,' she said. 'It matches.'

He loosened the bow and moved the palm of his hand into the neck of her blouse. 'You've got this really nice skin, lover. Smooth.'

She pulled away, finished off her glass, and put it on the bedside table. He put his bottle on the floor.

'Charlie...' she said.

Then he was kissing her hard and she could smell his aftershave and feel his hands inside her blouse, undoing her bra. His tongue was in her mouth and she felt helpless and excited at the same time. Now she was with him, helping him take off her clothes and pulling at his waistband.

But still in the end, to Charlie's frustration, he had to manage the whole thing without her taking off her slip. After some post-loving laughs and romantic murmuring they went to the hotel restaurant and had steak and chips and Black Forest gâteau. As Charlie ate he told Karen about the holiday he and Millie were planning in Benidorm.

'Exclusive hotel, Karen. Four stars. Can't beat a bit of class. Remember that, Karen. Can't beat a bit of class.' He purred. He always purred in the hour after they had made love. He drank whisky then, and smoked a cigar, as though she were the meal he had just eaten.

Later, when she got home tipsy (two Cherry Bs in the bedroom, two glasses of wine in the restaurant), Karen was pleased that her mother was still at the bingo. She folded her clothes on her bed and ran herself a deep bath. She lay back in the water and thought about Charlie. Tonight, in the stew of passion he had told her that she was beautiful and that he loved her. In those split seconds she thought he meant it. And in that split second she thought she loved him. But later in the restaurant she knew he didn't love her. And she knew she didn't love him – not now, not here. But it *had* been true, she was sure, just in those few scalding moments in the room.

Now at home in the bath, Karen looked down at her body shimmering bone-white under the water. Bodies were funny things. Making love had really hurt that first time with Charlie. He told her it would, and had been very understanding when she shouted. He also said it got to be all right in the end. And it did. It got to be good. Now, somehow, when he kissed her in that way of his, her whole body became hungry for him, raging for him to move to the next stage.

The thing was, she'd had things to tell him after they'd eaten, but he was so busy enjoying his cigar and talking about Millie there was no chance. Tomorrow. It would have to be tomorrow.

Cassandra Puts on the Style

Thursday

The chirpy, whistled notes of 'Wake Up Little Susie' trickled from Steve's lips as he kneeled up from his white-line painting to watch the women filter through the door that led to the toilets. Now he regretted his deal with Stan to paint through lunchtime for extra bonus. He'd had to gulp his sandwiches in three minutes before getting back on his knees with his big pot of paint. After eating their lunches at the benches the women were drifting into the toilets to do whatever women did when they went into toilets. They certainly stayed in there a good time. Steve reflected that the men were in and out of the toilets in a flash. No lingering there. It was not what men did.

I was shocked the first time I saw the women's toilets at Marvell's. The good housekeeping that generally operates on the Marvell factory floor

128

does not seem to extend to the women's toilets. It smells of old perfume, air-freshener and bleach. The walls are covered with inspired scatological aphorisms, sentimental love poems, names connected by hearts, and cartoons of the more explicit kind. Some of the wash basins hang off the wall and the doors have to be propped open or shut.

Now and then when you go in there's a woman sitting and smoking in the corner, who's supposed to keep the place clean and dispense MBE tablets to the women for menstrual pain, and STs and tampons if they are, as they say, 'caught short'. The woman's not there all the time. According to Patsy she's best friends with the nurse and hangs out in the nurse's surgery. I don't blame her. You wouldn't want to spend all day in a place like this.

There's a long bench at the end and a few broken chairs salvaged from the shop floor scattered around on the worn tiles. Today I wash my hands more thoroughly than usual. Through the cracked mirror I can see Patsy O'Hare sitting on the bench smoking and Karen peering into the mirror repairing her eye-lines. Her eyes look a bit red. Her hair is up in a smooth, tight, French pleat. Today she's being Audrey Hepburn, not Sandie Shaw.

Head on one side, Patsy says, 'If I didn't know you better, Karen, I'd say you'd been blubbin'.'

Karen sniffs. 'Must have a cold coming on. Dunno if I'll make the dance on Saturday.'

Patsy lights a new cigarette from the old one. 'Never stopped you before.'

'You're right there. Danced through hell and high water, me...'

Patsy grins. '"...on the beaches, in the fields", you'll be talking about "blood and sweat, toil and tears" next, girl.'

Karen sits down on a broken chair, pulls out her cigarettes and offers the packet to me. 'Cig, Cassandra?'

I look at the door, wonder whether I should try to escape, then sit down beside Patsy. 'No, thanks. I don't,' I say.

Patsy chortled. 'Don't you kid us, Madam Cassandra! Me, I've read about them students. Flowers in their hair, isn't it? Boozing? Drugs? Three on a bed? Fags is mother's milk compared with all that. Students!'

'So you keep telling me, Patsy.' Suddenly I feel a bit embarrassed that my girls' college has not quite reached the Age of Aquarius, even though – like Patsy – we too have read about it in the newspapers. 'Nothing like that in my college, I'm afraid.'

'Pity,' says Karen. 'Too snooty for any of that and too snooty to have a fag with us? Too good for anyone, ain't you?' Her voice is tearful.

Patsy and I exchange glances.

I put a hand on Karen's arm. 'I don't mind trying one if it bothers you, love.' I take one from the packet in her limp hand, put it in my mouth and turn to Patsy so she can light it with her clicking lighter. I screw my eyes against the flair. I take a draw; the burning smoke hits my chest and I start to cough. I cough till the tears come to my eyes, then thrust the lit cigarette back at her. 'Sorry, Karen,' I splutter. 'I would if I could.'

Then Patsy and Karen laugh, and I laugh too, tears in my eyes. Karen pushes the cigarette back towards me. 'Here. Give it another go. Another drag. It's better second time. Like sex, come to think of it.'

I don't want to take another drag. But I do. This time I manage but I'm still breathless and my head is swimming.

Patsy grins. 'Not so bad, is it, flower? At least it gets the stink of the shop floor out of your head.'

The Tannoy starts up with '(There's) Always Something There to Remind Me' for the tenth time today. It's beginning to seem very old fashioned. Karen gets up and leans towards the mirror, smoothing back her hair. Patsy jiggles one way and another to the music. 'Why don't you do Sandie Shaw, Karen? Cassie here's never really seen you do your Sandie Shaw.'

I normally stop people from shortening my name but wouldn't dare do this with Patsy, who anyway is only trying to cheer Karen up. I join in. I stub out my cigarette with some relief. 'Yes, Karen, go on. I'm dying to see you do it.'

Already moving to the music, Karen eyes us both through the mirror then slowly stubs out her own cigarette in a saucer on the windowsill. Moving more energetically now, she takes the pins from her hair, lets it fall, combs her fringe with her fingers and kicks off her shoes. She mimes the song as she dances, then pulls me up off the bench and I dance to the music with her. I may not like to smoke but since that first time at college I've always loved to dance, and now

131

I'm not quite Karen's equal but I'm good enough. It's such a relief to dance and not think. Even here in this sleazy place.

Other women drift into the toilets, and lounge against the washbasins to watch. Then the tempo zips up to 'Rock Around the Clock' and we're rocking the walls down, Karen and me. The women clap and whistle, then one by one they trickle away as the music changes to some ballad.

We collapse into the chairs and Karen slips on her shoes and sits down. She examines her feet. 'They're filthy. Look at me!'

'You're a great dancer!' I say, perhaps too enthusiastically.

Patsy lights another cigarette and takes a draw. 'Not a bad bopper yourself, Cassie!' The smoke trickles from her mouth as she speaks.

I am breathless now – from the dancing, not the cigarette. 'We don't spend all our time with our noses in books you know. One girl at college – she's from Liverpool – has seen the Beatles dozens of time! Knows John to talk to.'

'John? Really?' Karen, standing up again and putting her hair back up in its French pleat, eyes me through the mirror. Then she starts on her eye-lines again, her nose only inches from its surface. She must be quite short sighted. 'You should get down the Gaiety yourself, Cassandra. You'd have as good a chance as anyone in the competition. There are some right cloggers sign up for it, you know. Don't know their left from their right. They saw *Rock Around the Clock* ten years ago and think they're *it!*'

I have to laugh. 'Well, thank you! I'm flattered

to be asked.'

'Get yourself down there, flower,' said Patsy. 'Nothing to lose, have you? I'm going down there myself. Just for the laughs, like.'

Karen sniffs. 'First, but, you need to do sommat about that hair of yours, Cassandra. It's like I had mine when I was eight.' She pulls a chair in front of a mirror. 'Here. Sit here.'

So I have to sit on the chair and let Karen take out my ponytail and run her hand through my hair to loosen it. She takes out her long-tailed comb and combs it through, back-combs it, and then smoothes it over her fingers into fat curls with grips from her overall pocket.

As she is playing hairdresser, keeping her eyes on my hair, she talks to Patsy. 'Oh, Pats, I forgot. I was talking on the bus to Brenda. You know, the ginger-haired lass off Line Ten? You know, she's one of the girls that bloke in Development got ... well...'

'Up the stick, I know,' says Patsy. 'What about her?'

Through the mirror I catch the tense glance she bestows on Karen, who is gazing down at my hair.

'Well,' says Karen, winding my back hair round her finger and pinning it in a kind of *Gone With the Wind* curl. 'She wants to...'

'*Get rid?*'

'Well,' says Karen, manufacturing another *Gone With the Wind* roll (my hair looks really, really terrible), 'she does have these three brothers and two sisters at home. Her dad's always on the beer. Her mother's away with the fairies.'

Patsy's face is grim. 'So, what about her?'

'I told her you knew this woman who could give you something to ... *get rid*. That what she gives you is OK. Oh, you know! Doesn't she have some kind of powder that does the trick? Didn't you tell me once?'

Patsy's face is like thunder. 'Nobody has to let themselves in for that these days. What's this bloody Pill for if not for that?'

'Yes,' I say, too eagerly. 'Women are in charge of their own sexuality now. There's been a revolution...'

'Been no revolution on Line Ten, there hasn't, lass? And when push comes to shove no doctor'll prescribe for girls, only married women,' growls Patsy. She finally gets Karen to meet her gaze through the mirror. 'So she wants to know about the woman in Durham, Karen? This girl?'

Karen's eyes are back on me as she back-combs my fringe. 'I couldn't think where the woman lived. I wanted to tell this Brenda. But I couldn't remember where this woman lived.'

'That's 'cos I didn't tell you.'

Karen fixes the final sausage curl. 'Well, Pats, if you tell me I'll tell Brenda. It'll be a real help. This girl's been ... well, beside herself. Her mother's threatening to kill her.' She's staring at me now through the mirror. My hair is really, really awful. My face is far too small for the over-the-top, Scarlett O'Hara style.

'Has she now?' says Patsy. 'Been beside herself, has she?'

I shake my head at Karen. She gives me a watery smile and starts to unpin my hair. 'This *is*

134

rubbish, isn't it?' she says. Her tone is so heartfelt I know she's talking about far more than my gash hairstyle. She takes the pins out, combs her fingers through my hair and reassembles my ponytail. It's bumpier and softer now: nicer, if I am to be honest.

Finally Patsy says, very slowly. 'The woman's name's Mrs Morrison, flower. She's one of them hippies but is OK really. She lives in those streets by the railway viaduct. Parliament Street. Number fourteen. The door's purple and pink. Must be that hippie thing, Cassie. Maybe she's one of your beatniks. Psychedelic? What do you think?'

I am still staring at the mirror, relieved to have my ponytail back. 'Hippie?' I say. 'I'm no beatnik. And I'm called Cassandra, if you don't mind.'

'Get you!' says Patsy.

'Thanks, Pats,' says Karen quietly. 'I'll tell Brenda. She won't half be relieved.'

Patsy stubs out her cigarette and stands up. 'Yes, flower. I can see that,' she says. She nods at me through the mirror. 'You don't need no fancy-dan hairdos, Cassandra. You're all right as you are.'

The siren rips the air and echoes through the toilet. We are the only ones left.

'No rest for the wicked, kiddos,' says Patsy. 'Come on, you two, or Stan Laverick'll be on our backs.'

Karen grins at me, back to her old self again. 'And you get yourself down the Gaiety for the competition, Cassandra. Even with that ponytail you'll wow the lot of 'm. No question.'

135

I feel like I've come through some kind of door. 'I think I will. Sounds like a laugh.'

On the way back to the line I nearly fall over Steve, the progress boy, who's kneeling down drawing a white line down the edge of the gangway.

'Keep at it, son,' says Patsy as we pass. 'You'll get your reward in heaven.'

He picks up the paintbrush and points it at her like a gun. He mimes shooting. 'Kapow! You're dead.' Then he grins at me. 'What is it you girls get up to, in those toilets?'

I wink. 'You'd be surprised.'

'I tell you what, Steve, we've 'ticed Cassandra here to go to the Gaiety to bop in the competition.' says Karen. 'You should get yourself down there.'

He winks at me. 'Maybe I will. I might just do that. Give you all a treat, that's what.'

Back on the line Patsy is very quiet, working away, her hands almost a blur. I am nothing like as quick, but am at last in a kind of rhythm so can spare a little attention to conversation. I try to jolly Patsy along. 'I can't believe how fast you are, Patsy. Doesn't seem possible the number you do.' Even to my ears I sound ingratiating.

'Aye, lass. Fifty bloody wirings a minute. Four thousand an hour.'

I am frowning down at the job. 'That's three thousand, actually. Ouch!' I suck my finger and when I look up I catch Patsy's scowl as she mutters something about a slip of the tongue.

'*Actually*, Patsy,' says Karen, her hands shimmering over her job, '*actually* you've got your sums wrong! Go to the bottom of the class and do some lines! We've got Mary Poppins here, remember? She knows her Ps and Qs without having to watch them. Got a clever lass here, don't forget that! She's got other fish to fry. Doesn't give a bugger for wiring harnesses, bonuses, or Marvell's bloody marvellous cookers.'

'Oh, for a second I forgot our Cassandra was one of those bloody clever arses,' says Patsy.

So had I. The harmony of our time in the toilets is now shot to pieces. My fingers keep on with their job but I can feel tears rising to my eyes. 'No need for that, Patsy.'

'No need for what?'

'That language.'

'What language was that, Cassandra?'

'Nothing. No bloody language at all. Ask Stan up there on the gantry. No language at all.' Now I am sniffing away my tears. I reflect again how I don't know what the heck's going on here. I might as well be on Jupiter.

Then Karen laughs. 'Take no notice of Patsy, Cassandra. Her bark's worse than her bite. Mine too. No picnic being a student, I bet. All those books! What d'you do to deserve *that?*' She stretches one arm above her head and flexes her fingers, and sets down to work again. 'Could never stand school myself. Teachers were a load of frigid old cows. And that was just the men. Taking it out of you for wrong uniform, wrong shoes, wrong sums, wrong spelling, for dyeing your hair. Fingering, whining on. Not an ounce of spunk in them.' She laughs. '*We* knew how to get at them. They were in tears half the time, men and women. And you wouldn't believe those toilets down the yard with the lads hanging over the wall and you with your knickers down! And all those red bits on the map and Edward the Bloody Confessor. Bloody useless facts, if you ask me.' She flexes her fingers again. 'My best day at school was the day I left.'

Patsy takes up the rant. 'School? Never there much myself. Always playing the nick, me.' She wriggles in her seat, flexing her back. 'Oh, I'd learned plenty of facts, like, by the time I was your age, Cassandra. Like how to make a full Sunday dinner when my mother was in bed with the newest little 'un, or up there giving my dad his little treat before his dinner.' Her hands become still in front of her. 'I knew how to wipe snotty noses and change nappies. I knew how to tip up my pay so my dad could put his bets on and get to the matches when Sunderland were playing away. And I knew how to keep out of his way when he had a skinful and wanted to play "kiss-cuddle-or-torture".' She leans over for another bunch of wires and her hands start to fly again. 'Then here at Marvell's I learned how to fend off the lads with their *Roman hands and Russian fingers*. That was a little joke flying around in them days, Cassandra. D'you get it? *Roaming hands and Rushing fingers.*'

I nod, I am trying to imagine Patsy in a swimsuit. 'I get it.'

'And I learned how to cheek the bosses here so they still liked you and looked after your bonus.' Then her voice drops to a murmur. 'And I knew

138

just how Errol Flynn kissed a woman and how Scarlett O'Hara drank neat perfume to get the stink of booze off her breath when Clark Gable came back to her at Tara, that place that burned down in the end.'

She must have picked up my thoughts about my Scarlett O'Hara curls out of the ether.

Karen grins across at her. 'Patsy! You really are out of the ark. Errol Flynn! You old romantic.'

I'm working faster now and think maybe I won't need Karen to do my backlog. I am grateful now the flare-up is over and my slip-up has been forgiven. But I don't understand them properly any more than they understand me. They've known each other for years and I've just landed on this planet. I can't talk to them properly without seeming like a show-off or some kind of twerp. But I'd really like to talk to them about myself, about me, how I came to be here, now; about my mother and school and college, about my own personal stuff. And I'd like to ask them about their lives, not just pick up things from watching them.

But I can't. And as I've observed, no matter how well Patsy and Karen know each other, they don't tell each other everything either. There are a lot of secrets even on this planet.

You Know Charlie

Thursday

The production office had been as busy as usual. After the eight o'clock daily set-up meeting with all his managers, Charlie Priest had kept back Alan Cartwright to update him about arrangements for the presentation next week, going over with him which of the local officials was attending apart from the mayor, checking that the red carpet would be on site the day before and the bouquet of flowers was actually ordered. That sorted, he sent Alan after Stan Laverick, to check that he had organised himself to visit the winners and brief them properly about the protocols of the visit. One of the secrets of Charlie's success was that, as well as always seeing the broad picture, he was a terrier for detail.

As usual Evelyn Laing, in the outer office, was entertained by this early morning rush. It was just like the winding up of a clock. Tamás had come out of the meeting and had his head down at his desk over stores sheets and notes of shortages. Alan had charged away and left Charlie's door open so when Charlie's phone rang Tamás and Evelyn were forced to eavesdrop on his eager conversation with a very important person.

'That's right, Mr Abrahams,' said Charlie, a thread of excitement creeping into his usual

140

drawl. 'Everything is hunky-dory. Jack Stern down at Enfield is going to pick up Sandie and her agent and take them to Luton Airport...'

Evelyn observed that Charlie was joining the trend now of calling famous people by the first name. The first time she'd experienced that was when one of Mr Leavis's office girls had referred to *Elvis* and she had said, 'Elvis who?', much to the girl's amusement.

'...Then, Mr Abrahams, Alan Cartwright is picking her up at Newcastle and she should be on site here by two. Then there'll be the tour of the factory and she'll meet all the local brass hats. Then she'll present the millionth cooker to the winner. The store at the coast are very excited about it. They've already placed another big order. The telly boys'll be here. And radio. There'll certainly be a clip on the six-thirty news here...'

The liquid harmonies of the Platters singing 'Only You' trickled up the gantry steps into the outer office. Tam glanced up at Evelyn and smiled. She smiled back and put down her head over her typing.

'...The press and radio as well, Mr Abrahams. Yes, *sirree*. And the factory is looking at its best. Spotless. I have an army of cleaners working as we speak... No, no, sir. The spend's not excessive for what we're getting, believe me... No, I'm afraid Sandie won't sing. I couldn't get the manager to agree to that, not for what we're paying. But I'm assured that her feet will be bare... Well, that's kind of her signature, Mr Abrahams. Yes, sir, it *is* odd... Yes, there'll be a red carpet so her tootsies won't get cold, so to speak... No, we were going to buy it, but it turns out the Town Hall have one so we're borrowing it... Thank you, Mr Abrahams. All in a day's work. We're lookin' forward to seeing you here, sir. Must be six months since we saw you.'

Then the phone clicked and they could hear Charlie dialling another number. At that point the door to the gantry opened wide and a girl in an overall came in. Tamás recognised her as Patsy O'Hare's workmate. Evelyn reflected that, like so many of the girls down on the shop floor, this girl had that butterfly beauty that is the preserve of the young. Her skin was flawless, her eyes were outlined in black and her glossy black hair was swept up in an Audrey Hepburn pleat.

Her gaze settled on Evelyn. 'Mr Priest in?' she said.

'Perhaps you could wait?' Evelyn peered at the diary kept next to her desk. 'You'll have an appointment?'

'Nah. I just wanter see him.'

'You could wait.' Evelyn looked down at the diary again but when she looked up the girl had knocked on the door and gone in.

'...or not,' said Evelyn. She glanced at Tamás. 'That's a pretty girl,' she said.

'You know Charlie,' he said very softly.

'We'll sort that later,' said Charlie into the phone and put it down. 'Well, Karen, honey, you look sweet enough to eat.' His tone was soft but his smile was tight.

'Charlie, I...' She stood in front of his desk, lost

142

for a second.

He moved round the desk, closed the door behind her and returned behind his desk. 'Great to see you, lover,' he drawled. 'But I think not here. Not in the office.'

She looked round. 'Why not? You come down and talk to me on the line.'

'That's to show my visitors what a whizz you and Patsy O'Hare are at what you do. It's different.'

'Because you're the boss?'

He lifted up a Biro and started to twiddle it. 'Because, quite rightly, you'll be in trouble with Stan Laverick. He even knows when you girls go to the toilet. And if he spots you up here, that'll be – wa-al – embarrassing for us both.'

She leaned forward, putting her hands on his desk. 'It's just I want to tell you something, Charlie...'

'You can tell me tonight, lover,' he said, keeping his voice low. 'I'll pick you up tonight, round the corner from the bus stop.'

'I tried to tell you last night, Charlie. But we didn't have no time to talk then, did we?' She giggled, her eyes too anxious. 'International love-making, Patsy calls it. *Roman hands and Russian fingers.*'

'Patsy O'Hare? I expect you didn't–'

'No. No. But Patsy's not daft. Shrewd as an old fox, that one.'

Charlie stood up and she took her hands from his desk, intimidated.

'Karen, honey, you've gotta get out of here,' he said. 'Say what you need to say and get back down the line.'

'Charlie, I love you.'

He moved round the desk and took her hands tightly in his.

'I know that, lover. Me too. Don't I tell you that every time we go out?'

'Go out?' she said shrilly. 'That's a new word for it.' She clutched his hands hard. 'Charlie, I'm expecting, well, pregnant.' She laughed wildly. 'My mother'll kill me. Kill me!'

He wrestled free from her hands and took a step back. 'Jesus Christ, Karen. You're on the Pill! You told me. You use the Pill. You've told me a dozen times. Otherwise I wouldn't have... You take the Pill, Karen. I asked you.'

It was true. Charlie always checked.

'I do use it,' she said. (It had taken all kinds of lies to get it from her reluctant doctor.) 'Like I say. But one night I forgot. Just forgot. I was tired after work and forgot. Just the once. I thought it would make no difference.' She touched his arm with her hand.

He flinched away from her. 'Thought? Thought? You stupid little bitch. You know very well what you were doing.' He had lost his American intonation. 'Things'r different these days with the Pill, didn't you notice? That's how...' He reached up and took his jacket from its peg on the door, pulled it on, straightened his tie and went back to sit behind the desk. 'You got yourself into this, Karen, you can bloody well get yourself out of it.'

Karen raised her beautiful black-rimmed eyes to his and stared at him for a very long moment. He looked uneasily at the door. 'I want you to do

144

one thing for me, Charlie,' she said.

'All depends, Karen, on just what you want. I'm promising nothing.'

'I just want one more lift. Not to the motel. No more *Roman hands and Russian fingers.* I want you to take me to this woman in Durham. Patsy let on about her a while back. She has some stuff. She can get rid of...'

Charlie came back round the desk and took her hand again. She could smell his familiar cologne, the rich scent of those cheroots he smoked. Stevie told her once that some of the men called Charlie a 'nancy boy' because of the cologne. Only behind his back of course. 'Yeah, yeah, lover. Of course I'll do that for you,' he drawled. 'Anything, lover. Anything to help. Money? You need money? A new dress to dance in?'

She snatched her hand away from his. 'I need money, all right. You get nothing you don't pay for.'

He got out his wallet. Took out a sheaf of notes and shoved then into the pocket of her overall, the action turning into a rough caress. 'There you are, lover. You see to it, this *expecting* thing. And the two of us can be like before.' He tried to kiss her. 'We can have fun again.'

She took a step away, put space between them. 'You won't forget? Tonight?'

He smiled at her. 'Cross my heart, lover. Cross my heart.'

She turned to leave, then turned back at the door and looked him in the eye. 'I always wanted to ask you about that Yankee twang, Charlie. Half the time you sound like you come from America

145

but I know you're from round here. Everyone knows that.'

He frowned. 'Not that it's anyone's business.' He paused. 'I was six months training in America when I was in the army. I liked the way they talked. It was easy to catch.'

'So you turned yourself into an American?'

'Well, I came back here and all I could hear in the streets and the factory was barks and quacks. Made me see that must be how I sounded. So I kept my Yankee twang, as you call it.'

She scowled at him. 'You're kidding yourself if you think you can be someone else, Charlie. You know what? You call me stupid. But they laugh at you down on the shop floor. Think you're bloody ridiculous.'

He shrugged and then grinned. 'That's their prerogative, lover. I'm honoured to be a passin' amusement in their tiny lives. But just remember. They're down there and I'm up here.' He sat back in his chair, lit a small cigar and looked at her through the rising smoke. 'Now then, lover, you run along. You take care of yourself, now! I'll look out for you tonight. Watch for the car.'

Karen banged the door behind her, muttering, 'Prerogative? Quack, quack, bloody quack quack.' She charged through the office and opened the door onto the gantry to the strains of Eddie Cochran moaning yet again about his 'Summertime Blues' wafting up from the shop floor.

Evelyn looked across at Tamás. 'That girl's in a state.'

He hunched his shoulders over his production sheets. 'Ours not to reason why. Linda Fox used

146

to say that to me when I was working down in stores. *Ours not to reason why.* You know Charlie.'

Charlie crashed through the middle door. 'Get me Stan Laverick, Evelyn. Pronto!'

She shook her head. 'Sorry, Mr Priest. Alan just rang. I took the call because I knew you were busy. He said Stan's gone off to see our prize-winner across at the coast.'

He scowled. 'Alan Cartwright wants his head examining, letting Stan go off today of all days.' He looked from her to Tamás and back again, then grinned. 'Make me a cup of coffee, will you, Evelyn? And get me one of those chocolate meringues from the canteen. For some reason I really need cheering up today. I love meringues. Melt in the mouth. Home baking just ain't the same, is it?'

Good Enough for the Man From Marvell's

Thursday

Mrs Mary McLochlan lived on Sea Drive in Hartlepool with her nephew, Alwyn: a thing of convenience since her widowhood and his divorce. In the two years since, they had lived together as much for his comfort as her benefit.

From the beginning Alwyn had made every effort to get his Auntie Mary to modernise her lifestyle. The issue of the cooker had been a case in point. They had gone to the store 'just looking',

147

and had come away with the promise of a free cooker. 'Karma!' he had told his auntie as they came away from the shop. (Alwyn did not see himself as one of those beatniks, but he had been reading about these things in the magazines he glanced at while queuing for his morning paper.) His auntie just gave him one of her exasperated looks and left it at that.

Mary had to admit that today the boy had been quite a help. Today they had worked together quite well: tidying up, cleaning windows, getting the house ready for the man from Marvell's, who was coming to visit. In his honour Mary had scrubbed her old Baby Belling cooker to within an inch of its life. Apart from a few scratches it was as good as new.

Alwyn, who was not above being jolly, teased his auntie, saying, 'Never mind about the cooker, old dear, how about a bit of spit and polish for you?'

She sniffed. 'Don't know what you're talking about, Alwyn. I've got my new Crimplene frock and best shoes. Good enough for our Lewis's wedding, good enough for you. And good enough for the man from Marvell's.'

'Ah, but is it good enough for Sandie Shaw?' he said.

She sniffed again. 'Who's she? She's just a girl who sings.'

'What she is, Auntie, is a gift horse.'

'A gift horse?'

'You don't look her in the mouth without a new frock on. Geddit?'

She scowled at him. 'You know, Alwyn, sometimes I don't understand a word you're saying.'

'Anyway, Auntie, whatever and whoever she is – just think! A brand-new cooker!'

'Don't get me started on that! Like I said in the shop – only you weren't listening – I *like* my Baby Belling. We were just there *enquiring* about a new one, and you got carried away. And, like I said then, I can't see why they couldn't have just given us the money.'

'That's not the point, Auntie. Not the point at all.'

So now she had to endure this man from Marvell's, who wanted to look her over, see if she suited. She knew that was what it was all about. So, one minute to the appointed time she made tea in her best teapot and place it on her papier-maché tray alongside her best cups and saucers.

Just then the door chimes played 'Morning Has Broken' and Alwyn stood up and looked in the mirror to straighten his tie. Then he sat down again and picked up his paper as though this were no great event. Mary took off her apron and touched her smooth grey hair. She had never gone in for perms. She always told her friends who succumbed that perms ruined the quality of your hair and made it go white as cauliflowers. She went to the door and opened it.

The couple standing there struck her as rather odd. The man was thin, with a head too big for his body. His slightly creased suit was grey and his tie was purple. In his hand he clutched a pork-pie hat. The woman beside him wore very high heels that made her taller than he. She had red frizzy hair and wore more make-up than was decent. Mary thought she looked vaguely familiar.

'Mrs McLochlan?' The man shook her hand enthusiastically and smiled a very nice smile. She warmed to him. 'I'm Stan Laverick,' he said, 'from Marvell's. You knew we were coming? We just came round to see you're comfortable about the do next week. This is Mrs Temple...'

Mary looked at the woman beside him, who smiled but didn't offer to shake hands. 'And you are...?'

'She's my ... assistant,' said Stan Laverick.

'Well, Mr Laverick, this here is my nephew, Alwyn. He lives here. Wife chucked him out, he got made redundant and the poor lad has nowhere else to go.'

'Auntie!' Alwyn scowled at her, stood up and shook hands with both the man and the woman. 'Pleased to meet you, Mr Laverick. Take no notice of Auntie. She has this sense of humour...'

'Alwyn,' said his aunt, 'go and get an extra cup for Mrs Temple. You'd better sit down,' she said to her visitors. Then she frowned down at the woman. 'I really feel I've seen you before. Have you worked for the council?'

Alwyn brought back another cup and saucer and started to pour out the tea. 'Me too, Auntie. I remember her. This lady was in the shop. When they told us about the prize.'

'That's it!' she said. 'You were in the queue.'

Leila Temple laughed. 'You spotted me!' She glanced at Stan.

'Mrs Temple was there to see that everything went smoothly,' he said. 'Reporting back to Marvell's, like.'

'Kind of an observer,' said Leila helpfully. 'To see fair play.'

Alwyn handed the visitors their tea. 'Well, everything did go smoothly. We're witness to that, aren't we, Auntie?'

She shrugged. 'I suppose so.'

Alwyn sat down and cradled his cup of tea in his hand. 'I have one question to ask you, Mr Laverick.'

'And what would that be?'

'Well, Mr Laverick. Will Sandie sing when she's there? Will we see her singing?'

Stan was already shaking his head. 'I'm told not. But I am also told on good authority she'll be taking off her shoes.'

'Bare feet? What a palaver,' said his aunt. 'Are you still sure I can't just have my money?'

Stan ignored that. 'You don't have to worry about finding your way to the factory. We'll send a car for you.'

She looked at him, a faint smile on her face. 'I'd have no problem finding my way, you know. I worked at Marvell's in Grafton once, in the war. Of course, we weren't making cookers then, were we? We were filling shells, that's what we were doing. Women died, you know.'

Stan's mind was racing. The newspapers would love that. '"Swords into plowshares,"' he murmured.

Mary beamed. 'You know your Bible all right, Mr Laverick.'

He smiled. 'You can put that down to chapel anniversaries. Forced work. Anyway, we'll have a car here for you at twelve,' he said. 'That'll get you there at one and we'll show you round the factory before Sandie Shaw arrives. Then there's a bit of a spread and a bit of a shindig and she presents you with the cooker.'

'So, no point in saying that the money would be just as useful?'

Stan grinned. 'Not a chance.'

Mary finally abandoned thoughts of getting the money. 'That'll be nice,' she said. 'I've gotta say I'm quite looking forward to it now.'

Leila put down her teacup and made a great show of looking at her watch. 'Mr Laverick,' she said primly, 'We're gonna be late for our next meeting.'

As they were driving away Leila said, 'Well, *they* were an odd couple all right.'

Stan pointed the nose of the car to the sea road and – more importantly – Leila's little bungalow. 'Hard to make out, really.'

'Yeah,' she said. 'The lad was thirty going on fifty. And the old girl was sixty going on ninety. Did you see that dress? And she could have done with a nice perm.'

'It takes all sorts. I thought her hair was nice. Anyway, they look respectable enough. Mr Priest wants no riffraff.'

'*Riffraff!* I bet your Mr Priest'd think I was riffraff.' She giggled and stretched her legs in front of her. 'D'you think they bought it?'

'Bought what?'

'About my being a kind of secret spy and your assistant?'

Stan laughed. 'Well, they wouldn't know any different, would they?'

He turned onto Leila's drive, sparkling in the afternoon light with bright bedding plants in military rows. She had laughed once when Stan expressed his admiration for her gardening skills. 'Me? Can you see me with a spade and fork? There's this very nice bloke out the back. He sets the garden and keeps it trim for me.'

Stan knew better than to ask anything further about the bloke out the back.

He took her keys from her and opened the door. 'Well, then!' he said heartily. 'What's on the agenda this afternoon, Leila?'

She closed the door behind them and leaned on it. 'Well, it's me. I *am* the agenda, Stan. Item one, a couple of glasses of my very nice port. Item two, a bottle of beer, if you want that. Item three, me and my couch. Item four, any other business. That would be me and my nice couch again.'

'You are a shameless woman,' he said, reaching out for her.

Stan got home at nine o'clock and had settled with the paper when Joanie came down from her bath. Her cosy housecoat was buttoned to the neck and her hair was up in a streaming topknot, making her look very young. 'What were they like, those people?' she said, leaning over the back of his chair.

'Nice enough. Respectable. She was a bit of an odd one. Seemed to think she could have the money instead.'

'Wants her head looking at,' said Joanie. Then

she did a strange thing. She kissed the side of his face. The scent of her special lavender bath salts invaded him. 'You coming to bed, Stan?' It was an invitation. A very rare invitation. No hope of *that*, he thought. He had as much life inside him as a deflated balloon.

He rattled his paper, 'Not just now, Joanie. It's been a long day and I have the paper to catch up with. And work tomorrow.'

He could feel her gaze on his cheek. 'What is it, Stan? Think you're a footballer or something? Saving yourself for tomorrow?' And she flounced off.

Stan took out his glasses so he could make out the smaller print of the back pages. Really, he thought, sometimes Joanie could be quite vulgar in the way she went about things. Still, like a miser, he focused on the secret pleasure of his time with Leila. That was worth even Joanie's wrath. Wasn't it?

The House With the Purple Door

Thursday

There was little conversation in the car on the way to Durham. Charlie did try to ease the atmosphere by saying how pleased he was with the car, now he had had the engine tuned and what a big deal this Sandie Shaw thing was for Marvell's. But Karen just grunted, keeping her face to the window, her eyes glued to the broad fields lit up by the bright afternoon sunshine and to the old heavy-laden trees that lined the road into the city.

Charlie was peeved. 'No need to be surly, lover. I'm doing what I can.'

She said something he couldn't hear.

'What was that?'

She turned to him. 'You did what you could. That's what I said.'

He shrugged. 'You're a volunteer in all this, lover. Not a victim. Nobody forced you.' He kept his eye on the road.

'I would not ... could not have...' She hesitated. 'Anyone else but you I'd have waited. Made them wait.'

'Like I said, lover, nobody forced you. As far as I could tell you were having fun. If you're waiting for me to say I feel guilty, you'll have to wait a long time, lover.'

She looked back out of the window at the sun glittering like diamonds in the spray of a fountain at one of the big new colleges. Charlie was right, of course. She had been a volunteer. Their relationship had always been on his terms and she'd accepted that. It was always a private, secret thing, the very privacy being part of its charm. Her mother didn't know, Patsy didn't know, his wife didn't know. For her and Charlie there was no past or future, merely a joyous present. They'd been like two kids playing truant.

Not kids now, though. This was a very grim, grown-up ride. She was frightened. Her insides felt like lead and she hated the slick, smooth man in whose car she was riding.

Silenced now, his face bleak, Charlie eased the car to a stop at the top of the steep street. Karen sat very still. He opened her bag and pushed a sealed envelope into it. 'Another fifty for you, lover. That should do the trick.' The tightness of his jaw wiped out all trace of his mid-Atlantic accent. Then his arm was heavy across her as he leaned over and opened the door, which swung open with a pricey clunk. 'Now then, lover, make sure that woman gives you the very best stuff. No funny business with needles, mind.'

She jumped out of the car into a street cut off entirely from the sun by the tall narrow houses and the looming viaduct overhead. She shivered, then made her way, teetering on her high heels, down the steep street to a house with a purple door and flower-painted panels. Despite its film of dust it was still the brightest door in a dingy street. She pressed the buzzer in the crosspiece of panels and heard a large click. Above her a window dragged open and a mellifluous voice bellied down.

'Come up, won't you?'

The door opened onto a narrow staircase drenched with the scent of dust and patchouli. Even in her numb panic every detail of this staircase chiselled itself into Karen's brain. This image of the staircase would always shape her memory of this visit. Its high walls were daubed with childlike flowers and random, scrawled words. The stairs themselves were uncarpeted, painted purple, with a central, worn-through patch where people had stepped. Towards the top of the stairs the daubings gave way to posters: The Animals with a vision of the House of the Rising Sun looming behind them: the dark visage of Manfred Mann and a formal pose of this new group called the Rolling Stones, who had wild faces. (Patsy had once commented that Rolling Stones was a stupid name and would never get them anywhere.) At the very top of the staircase, just before the door, was a poster of a man with wild hennaed eyes and Indian robes. Karen didn't recognise him.

Into Karen's mind jumped images from films she'd seen – mostly second features – where a fate worse than death met people in rooms at the top of creaking stairs. She made to go back down again.

'What is it, love?'

Karen turned to see a woman standing in the open doorway, her hands high on the doorjamb, her wide kaftan creating wings on either side of her, its silk fringes falling back over her arms. Her face was in shadow.

The voice went on, 'Maybe you're losing heart? Want to run away? Look, why don't you just come in for a chat?' The woman stepped back then and Karen could make out large eyes, a spade-shaped white face. There was no threat in it. The woman led the way into a room as crowded and exotic as the staircase. Two walls were filled with shelves of objects from glass balls to battered teddy bears, from books to bottles and phials. The summer evening light was filtered through sheer curtains to a kind of orange striped with blue. Under the window was a table covered with an embroidered cloth covered with stubby candles, some of them lit.

Karen thought of a storybook she'd had as a child, of a page showing the inside of the witch's cottage in *Hansel and Gretel.*

The woman, standing now before her, was less impressive than her lair. She was plump, of middle height. Her frizzy grey-brown hair was clipped back in wings on either side of her face. Her shape, beneath the flowing kaftan, was hard to make out.

'And what do we call you, pet?' The voice was local, comfortable.

'My name's Karen.'

'Well, pet, why don't we sit ourselves down and get started?' The woman nodded at a seat on one side of the table and sat down close by, on the end of a draped day bed. Karen stared at the bed, her heart suddenly in her throat. She sat down and put her clutch bag on the table.

'Now, pet. What can I do for you?'

'They said ... my friend said...'

The woman nodded, making her chin wobble slightly. 'In trouble, are you?'

Karen nodded.

The woman glanced at Karen's hands. She noted the rough patches on the index fingers and the lack of a ring on the left hand. 'Not married then?'

Karen shook her head.

'Bit of a surprise, was it?'

'A shock more like.' Karen got the words out. 'My mother'll kill me.'

'Couldn't you marry the lad? Make it legal?'

Karen laughed shrilly. 'He's not a *lad.* That's

158

not possible. It'd never be possible.'

The woman sniffed and nodded. 'Married already.' It was a statement, not a question.

Karen nodded, waiting for a disapproval that didn't come.

'Are you sure you couldn't just have this little 'un, pet? People do.'

Karen shook her head. 'Like I said, my mother'd kill me. She'd throw me out and never talk to me for the rest of my life. You should hear what she says about other girls when this happens to them. She can be right cruel.' Tears started to trickle from her eyes. 'You see, I love my mam. I do. She's ... well ... you know.'

'What about your doctor? Could you go to him?'

'Joking, aren't you? I got the Pill from my doctor and he took me through all this rigmarole. You'd'a thought I was asking for the keys to hell. He's dead old fashioned. And it didn't work anyway. The Pill.'

'Nothing's copper bottomed,' said the woman morosely.

Karen frowned at her.

The woman sighed. 'You'll get no guarantees even from me, pet.'

Karen looked around the room. 'I thought...'

'Nothing's copper bottomed,' the woman repeated.

Karen tried to sniff away the tears that were flowing even faster now. The woman gave her a clean tea towel to wipe them away. 'A handkerchief is never enough,' she said. Then she went on, as though it were an ordinary conversation, 'I

159

started out as a midwife, you know. Trained and everything. It's the most wonderful thing bringing these canny small people into the world...'

Karen looked at the door, wondering if she should just escape, run away.

'But then a woman would die giving birth to her seventh or eighth child. Another would look with loathing on a child just come out of her, thinking of the unbearable burden this extra one would bring... Do you know, love, the law says there can be no rape in marriage but I've seen it all my working life, and my sister midwives have seen it too, through the generations. Not just now in this misbegotten age...'

Karen put a hand up to stop the waterfall of talk. 'Could you... I want...'

'Oh, yes. You want it to be no more?'

Karen nodded vigorously. 'Yes, yes. Like you say. I want it to be no more. I want it to be like before.'

The woman shook her head. 'It'll never be like before, pet. That's the pity.' She looked Karen up and down. 'You can't be more than a few weeks on?'

Karen nodded.

'Well, pet, seeing as you're so early on we can try two stages. I'll give you something to take. That's the easy way. It might just work. Bring on your period and that.'

Karen's tears dried.

'But then if that doesn't work you must come back,' she glanced at the draped couch. 'There is another procedure. Another thing I can do. That makes it a certainty. Maybe that *is* copper bot-

160

tomed, except what you feel like, after.'

Karen frowned at her. 'Why can't you do that first? Now?'

'You really need to do it in this order, pet. And it gives you time to think.' She glanced at Karen's clutch bag. 'It'll be forty pounds for the medicine.' Her voice was cool now, businesslike.

'And what if it doesn't work?'

'Well, twenty-five pounds for the procedure.'

'Why's that cheaper?'

'Well, pet, that really makes it sixty-five pounds in all, doesn't it?' She paused. 'There are people who would do it much cheaper in one go. But they've not got my training and ... well...'

'Fine ... fine!' Karen scrabbled in her bag and took out forty pounds of Charlie's money. 'Here you are.'

The woman opened a shallow drawer at her side of the table and took out a small fat envelope. 'Here you are, love. Dissolve this in some tea, but don't put milk in it. Take it before you go to bed tonight. With a bit of luck your period'll come on tomorrow sometime.' She gave a very deep sigh. 'And if the little bugger still hangs on, get back to me after the weekend.'

'Do I make an appointment?'

The woman shook her head. 'I'm always here. I never go out.'

Despite herself and despite the envelope clutched in her hand, Karen was curious. 'You never go out?'

The woman shook her head. 'It's a sickness. Can't seem to make myself get over the doorstep. I have a friend who shops and a little lad who

161

runs other errands.'

Karen looked round the cluttered room, now turned into an exotic gaol for this strange woman. She put out her hand and shook the woman's. 'Thank you for talking to me,' she said hesitantly. 'For helping me.'

The woman smiled faintly. 'That's what I'm here for, love. That's why I'm here.'

Making her way back up the street Karen started crying again, but this time, for some strange reason they were tears for the woman locked up there in her room with only desperate women for company.

Charlie leaned over and the heavy door of the Volvo swung open. 'You all right, lover?' He frowned. 'You shouldn't cry, you know. You'll be all right.'

She jumped in and closed the door with a thud. Suddenly she felt much, much older than Charlie. Older than his mother, older than his grandmother.

'I'm all right, Charlie. And I'm not crying for me. I'm crying for that woman up there.'

He looked her up and down. 'Did she...? What happened?'

'She did nothing. She just gave me a powder to take. Now take me home, will you?' Her face was set, grim, her pretty mouth turned down at the corners.

He gunned the engine and put it into gear. 'You said it, lover,' he said. 'Home, James, and don't spare the horses.'

Past and Future

Evelyn Laing had been uncharacteristically annoyed with herself and, at one remove, with Tamás Kovacs. When she worked in the liberal Leavis household in London she had prided herself on having friends and lovers through the years while still keeping her working life and the life of her affections distinctly apart. In her time in London and further afield she'd made good friends and had some adventurous but ultimately short-lived affairs, and that was that. The one time her policy of separation had proved too much of a challenge was when Peter Mallory, Mrs Leavis's Irish-American cousin, turned up and fell for her. Perversely – because despite being a very attractive, funny man he *was* Mrs Leavis's cousin – Evelyn had kept him at arm's length.

So how could she have been so good at all that and get herself into this muddle with Tam Kovacs? She really liked Tamás. They shared confidences. He was good company. He occasionally came to tea on Sundays, a casual thing that started when she'd mentioned once how long Sundays seemed at home with her dad.

But now this week the plates had moved and she was beginning to feel over-self-conscious when he was around. He was beginning to watch her when he thought she wasn't looking and touch her in a more than a friendly way, like Monday after the party.

Now she had to work out a way to let him down lightly and still keep him as a friend. She was quite good at plain friendship, of course, these days. Her good friends had dispersed across the world like leaves in the wind, chasing their own destinies. They were alive for her on the page in their regular letters, but – being sprinkled about the globe – were short on bodily presence.

Working at Marvell's and taking care of her father had left Evelyn little time to find few friends. The only friend she managed to cultivate these days was Tamás. And now she was in danger of losing him. Since his attempt to kiss her, and his reference to a 'date' she had decided that something must be done. But how could she let him down so gently that they could keep their friendship? She knew that at Marvell's and in Grafton itself, the idea of mere friendship between a man and a woman was as likely as a fish walking or a pig flying. At best it was very suspect. At worst it was a cover for the man being a pansy, as they called it, or a woman being under her mother's thumb.

Her chance came on Thursday night when she was walking out of the factory into the sunlight with Tamás and he offered her a lift without the pretext of overtime. She grabbed her chance. As they settled into his little car she turned to him.

'This is good. I wanted to talk to you.'

He flushed and she remembered – as if she needed reminding – how young he was. 'Do you? Talk away.' He drove down the factory road and out through the big Marvell gates, still there from the factory's shell-making days in the war, and still locked securely at night.

She decided to start obliquely. 'How do you find it, living here, Tamás?'

'Where?'

'Here, here in Grafton.'

She could feel his shrug. 'I live here. It's my home.'

'Do you ever think about before? Before you came here?'

'When the Russians came to my city?'

'No. Before that.'

He was silent for a while. 'Well, things were different then.'

'How different?'

He took a breath. 'There was my mother. My brother, Anton...' His voice tailed away as he concentrated on the traffic.

'Tell me about your mother.'

'Why are you asking me these questions?' There was a rare note of anger in his voice.

She stayed silent.

'Well, my mother, she was tall and fair, like me. Not like my father and my brother, Anton.'

'Was she pretty?' she persisted.

'How would I know? She was my mother. She looked very beautiful to me. She always smelled so nice.' He paused. 'I think perhaps she was more elegant than beautiful. She always wore a jacket and skirt. Kind of dressed up, you know? Not like the women round here. And she smelled of jasmine. Not like Maria, who I live with. She smells of paprika. But that is a nice smell too. It

165

reminds me of home.'

'Home?'

'My home when I was a boy.'

'What did she do, your mother?'

'She taught in school. History.' His mouth turned up in a smile. 'She used to get very angry about what they made her teach. When the revolution came she wrote samizdat leaflets – you know, papers criticising the Soviets and planning our brave new world. The one that didn't happen. These papers were passed hand to hand.' He took a breath. 'Anyway, when everything turned on its head she was rounded up with my brother, who had done the cyclostyling with her and sometimes carried an extra satchel.'

Evelyn stayed silent.

'Then they came after my dad and me. But we were away – near the border making arrangements for them to follow on.'

'Didn't you...?'

He coughed. 'We got the news about the round-up at the same time as we got the news my mother and Anton had been shot. Summarily shot. That's what the telegram said. "Summarily shot."'

She pressed her lips together. 'I'm sorry about that, Tamás.'

He crashed the gears and the car bucked, then limped back again up to speed. 'We cannot be sorry about something we did not cause and about which we can do nothing. My father and I have decided that. We honour my mother and Anton alive. We do not imagine them dead, We look forward.'

She was shocked. 'That's very single minded of you. Of you both.'

He banged the wheel with the heel of his hand, then braked, pulled over to the side of the road, and stopped. 'I was fourteen years at that time, Evelyn. What other way is there? That was what my papa said then and he says now in his letters. "We can only look forward." That's why I like Marvell's. Here we look forwards. Simple universal things, cookers. Not guns or tanks. Swords into plowshares.'

'I know,' said Evelyn. ' *"They shall beat their swords into plowshares, and their spears into pruning-hooks: nation shall not lift up sword against nation, neither shall they learn war any more."* The Bible. We had a school pageant based on that. Just after the war.'

'Exactly,' he said. 'The plowshares are cookers, and all that kind of stuff is the future. I am living in my future and it is all right.'

She put a hand on his, where it was clutching the wheel too tight. 'I'm sorry, Tamás. It was crass of me to send you back to thinking all these things. I'm a crass simpleton. But now I know, I know what I want to do for you.'

He put the car in gear and set off again. 'And what might that be?'

'This is what I want to say to you, Tamás. I will be your mother, your brother, your friend. I'll always be here for you, now and for ever. But that is just what I'll be. A friend. Anything else would be disaster. For both of us.'

He drove on in silence, then pulled up in her back lane and turned to face her. 'And is that it?'

She took his angry face in her hands and kissed it. He grabbed her and pressed her to him, kissing her, forcing her mouth open with his, half moaning as he did so. She let him do that, stroking his face and threading her hands through his soft hair. Then she pulled away slightly, closed her mouth and kissed him again very lightly like a mother would, moving her lips to each cheek and his forehead. 'Like I say, Tamás. I will be your mother, your brother, your friend. I am always here for you.' She took out her handkerchief and dabbed her eyes. 'Look now, you've got me in tears!' She opened the door. 'See you tomorrow, Tamás.'

'And tea on Sunday? Is that still allowed?'

'Of course,' she sniffed. 'Like I said. We're friends, aren't we?'

She watched him back the car up the alleyway and made her way into the house.

From the front parlour came her father's plaintive voice. 'Is that you, Caroline? Were there many people at the shops?'

'No, Daddy. It's me. It's Evelyn.' She closed the door behind her and leaned on it. Now she was crying in earnest and dashed up to her bedroom to wipe her eyes and pull herself together before she would face her beloved father, who sometimes thought she was his beloved Caroline.

Night Caller

Thursday

There's this late night when Tamás Kovacs calls on my mother. Or me. My mother and I don't discuss it afterwards (when do we discuss anything?) but neither of us was sure whom he came to see.

At ten o'clock there's the click of a ring against the window. We don't take much notice. The window is right on to the pavement and men often rattle the letterbox or bang the window on their way back from the pub. A widow and her daughter are fair game, I suppose. They say that round here. 'I was only macken gam!' (It's in Chaucer, you know, that. The translation of 'makin gam' in the Middle English dictionary is 'having a joke'. When I told Emma they still said that round here she laughed, and nudged my knee with hers. 'Living language! I always thought you were out of the Dark Ages, Cass. Part of your charm.')

The clip on the window is succeeded by a crisp knock on the door. I'm in my pyjamas, just waiting for *Ready, Steady, Go.* to come on the TV. I pull on the cardigan that does service as a dressing gown. (At least my mother has her clothes on. She's never less than fully clothed, except in the front bedroom, which is her personal kingdom.)

169

I peer out of the window and there is Tamás Kovacs standing in the rain, which is also splashing onto his car, making it gleam like fractured glass in the light from the streetlamp. There must have been a storm. It's been sunny all day.

My mother opens the door. 'What? Oh! Tamás,' she says.

I lean over and turn off the television.

'Yes, I recognise you now. Is there something wrong?' There is surprise in her voice, as well as irritation. 'Oh, come in!'

And in a step – our house giving straight on to the street – Tamás Kovacs is in our living room, the rain standing in his hair and on his long fair eyelashes. He looks from my mother to me. 'Hello, Cassandra. I hope I do not disturb you, Linda.' His faint accent resonates in the little room, dwarfed now by him standing there on our battered hearthrug. I find myself biting the top button of my cardigan.

'I should not have come,' he says. 'I do disturb you.'

My mother shakes her head decisively. 'No, no. It's fine, Tamás. I'll make some tea.' But she pauses, staring at him. 'Your father used to say it was the English solution to everything. To make some tea.'

She vanishes into the back room, leaving me stranded. I can hear the pots clashing loudly – a sign of her volatile temper. Clashing pots. *Keep away from me. I am angry.* Late-night visitor, I suppose. But anything can trigger her temper, it's not that unusual.

He sits down opposite me. 'I was passing the

170

end of your street,' he said. 'I'm on my way back from the club.'

I realise now his voice is looser. Not quite slurring, but loose.

'I was talking to Stan Laverick in there and we mentioned Linda. Then I was passing the streets and...' He shrugs. 'I used to come here with my father when I was a young lad...'

My mother comes in with the tea on a tray. My God, there are saucers too. We're rocking.

He sips his tea. I sip mine. Silence. To break the silence I say, 'Tamás tells me he came here with his dad when he was young.'

'Yes,' she says. 'I remember. You were here with Constantin.'

I am puzzled about this. 'I can't remember them coming. I would be here, surely?'

She frowns. 'You'd be at the library, I think. Or maybe up there,' she nods at the ceiling, 'sleeping or reading. You only ever did one or the other.' She turns her gaze to Tamás. 'Proper bookworm. Always at the library. Stayed there till it was closed.'

'You never said anything about Tamás and his dad being here. I would have remembered.'

'Why would I say anything?'

Tamás looks in my direction. 'Me and my dad came here to talk to Linda about me and school. He respected her advice. She talked to my father about a lot of things. He translated for me. Between us we realised that school was not really on. Me, I was too old to start from scratch. My English was so very bad then. Very.'

Suddenly, incredibly, my mother is beaming at

171

him. 'Not so bad now, though, Tam?'

He grins at her. 'The only way was up, Linda. Charlie Priest often says that: "The only way is up!"'

She takes out a packet of cigarettes, offers him one and lights up her own. Her gestures are graceful, self contained. Very Katharine Hepburn. The pity of it is there's no Spencer Tracy around to get the benefit.

She picks up my thought. 'How *is* Constantin, Tam?' she says, the smoke rising like fine gauze around her face.

'Papa's very good now. He lives on this tall street where you can see Edinburgh Castle. He loves his job and is taking further examinations this year to complete his English architecture qualification.' He smiles. 'He says he's the oldest boy in his class.'

She concentrates on the cigarette for a few minutes. Then she says, 'And has he many friends there?' Her tone is very, very careful.

'He is married now. And he has a son. My half-brother Ernest. He's two.'

Another silence. Then she says, 'So he met someone?'

'He was on his own a long time, Linda. Erzsébet is from our country. She was sent up there to Edinburgh and met him at a friend's house. She had a son, Miklos. They call him Micky, so I have a stepbrother as well as a half-brother. It is all very complicated. For pure-bred Hungarians those boys are more Scots than the Scots.'

My mother leans forward and concentrates on the glowing tip of her cigarette. 'Sounds like

172

Constantin is happy?'

He looks closely at her before answering. 'I believe he is. He only talks of practicalities in his letters. But I visit him from time to time and he is – how would you put it? – serene. He loves the city of Edinburgh. I think it gives him great satisfaction to be living and working there.'

She nods. 'That's good. Will you tell him I'm asking after him?'

'Most certainly. He will be pleased to know you are well.' Then, at last he turns to me. 'Oh, Cassandra. One thing. I was wondering whether you're going to the Gaiety on Saturday?'

'The Gaiety?' I can't stop smiling broadly, thinking of Patsy and Karen's urging. 'I'm going all right. Patsy and Karen have got me in for that bopping competition.'

My mother's head kind of jerks up. 'Competition? The first thing I've heard of any competition. First time I knew you could even dance, never mind jitterbug.'

'*Jitterbug!*' says Tamás, relishing the sound. 'That *is* a word?'

'Well, Tam, you could say it's the grandfather of rock'n'roll,' says my mother, 'and the father of bebop, which I think is what Cassandra is talking about.' She turns back towards me and says, 'I didn't know you could dance. I never saw you dance.'

I hug my cardigan about me. 'Well, I can!'

Tamás eases the tension. 'I have learned this new saying,' he says. 'It's a wise parent who knows her own child.'

I think of Constantin Kovacs. 'And it's a wise

173

daughter who knows her own mother.'

Then, for no reason I can fathom, we all laugh and everything is all right. Then Tamás stands up. 'I have to go. Early start tomorrow.'

My mother stands up. 'You see Tamás to the door, Cassandra. I'll get these pots.'

I give her *a look,* stand up in my bare feet, hug my cardigan to me and follow him to the door. 'Thank you for calling,' I say. It sounds formal and stupid but I don't quite know what I should say.

He stands there and looks down at me. I breathe in his scent – some kind of lemon and spice. My senses swim for a moment but I stand quite steady.

'I am sorry,' he says. 'I intrude here at your house.'

'No, no,' I protest too loudly, clutching my cardigan even closer to me. 'Not at all.'

He smiles. 'Then I might call again? Can I call on Saturday to take you to the dance?'

Now I am scarlet. 'Yes. Yes, if you like.'

Then he does this curious thing. He rescues my hand from my cardigan, takes it in his and bends his head over it, at the same time bringing his heels together. 'That is good. I will call again.' He keeps my hand in his. 'My father was very fond of Linda, you know. She was his first friend in England, the first friendly face.'

When I turn back into the room my mother is back in her chair, cigarette in hand. There is the smallest glimmer of a smile in her eyes. 'What was that about?'

'It was about *you,*' I say. 'He just told me that

you were Constantin's first friend in England.'

'Funny, that. I've been here for the seven years since Constantin went off and Tamás has never called on me till now.'

I ignore the dig. 'Were you really his friend? Constantin Kovacs'?'

'It was very easy to be friends with Constantin. He had this thing – I suppose you'd call it charm. But it was genuine. He was very kind to me. Sometimes he brought me flowers.' Her voice is quiet. It's almost as though she's talking to herself.

'How come I never saw him?'

'Like I told the boy, you were always at the library, head in a book.'

'But why didn't you talk about it? About him? After? To me? When I came home?'

She shrugs in that irritating way of hers. 'Nothing to tell.' Then she nods towards the television. 'Your programme'll be finished.'

My turn to shrug. 'I can live without it.'

'You can put it on anyway. I want to catch *What the Papers Say.*'

I go to bed then, first cleaning my teeth at the kitchen sink. I leap into bed in my chilly back bedroom, snuggle down under my grandmother's green eiderdown and think for a while about Constantin Kovacs, struck now by the thought that my mother had fallen in and out of love without me ever noticing. Lying there waiting for the bed to warm up I work out, to my astonishment, that when Constantin visited her here with Tamás my mother would only be in her early thirties. Think of that.

I am just drifting off to sleep when I get this flashing insight that the best place to keep a secret is at the heart of the family. I wonder if it was *she* who sent Constantin away, or it was he who moved on and forgot about her? And then I wonder whether it makes my mother happy or sad to be told that Constantin Kovacs is content now in Edinburgh with his wife and his sons.

Ah, well, as Tamás says, early start tomorrow.

A Fruitful Man

Saturday

Charlie Priest could tell by the state of the house when his wife Millie was not happy. Flowers went unchanged and died in the glass. The barest film of dust was allowed to settle on her precious dining table and her teak cocktail cabinet.

Worst of all for Charlie was that she would skimp on his usual Saturday morning full English breakfast, with extra black pudding. He had this breakfast every Saturday before he went late to the factory to check on business and mop up any outstanding jobs when the production lines were silent, the place empty except for the clumping sounds of people in the stores with their check-lists, and old lads sweeping up about the place. This Saturday he would check that the squad of painters were there, repainting the main road entrance where Sandie's limousine would sweep in. He was glad he had thought of that. Couldn't have the place stinking of paint with the big event coming off next week.

As it was Saturday Charlie was wearing his casual clothes as though he weren't going to work. Usually Millie made Saturday breakfast complete with the orange juice freshly squeezed in the machine, a gift from an Italian manufacturer to back up an idea that Marvell's might produce it under licence in the UK. Millie loved that machine. But this morning there was no orange juice and no black pudding. There was only one sausage and his fried egg was cracked like a broken sun.

He could sense her rancour as she sniffed at her toast and he made the decision not to comment on her uncombed hair and the fact that she had covered her nightie with a cardigan rather than her usual elegant peacock-coloured kaftan.

He sighed. He had really had enough of sulky women this week. He finally looked at her over his copy of the *Daily Express*. 'You all right, lover?'

She sniffed. 'Why shouldn't I be?'

'You look a bit down, that's why.'

She munched on her dry toast. He noticed that today she had not even put out her honey and butter. She was punishing herself. That was a bad sign.

He persisted. 'Anything worrying you?'

'Why should there be?'

He ducked down over some account of a tunnel they were digging through the Alps and left it at that. He was planning his day. Golf clubs in the boot: a couple of hours at the factory, then across to the golf club for a game with Alan Cartwright, who, as well as being an excellent sales manager, was a half-decent golfer.

As it was, when he finally got to the golf club he realised he had left his putter by the back door. He raced back home to find Millie still in her nightie and cardigan, curled up like a sea creature on the sofa, an eiderdown over her feet.

'What is it, Mill? Shall I get a doctor?'

Her reply was muffled. 'Nothing he can do. Or you!'

He felt desperate. 'I need to do something, Mill. I can't leave you like this.'

'You go and play your golf. You should play golf after a hard week. Don't you say it unties the knots?'

Charlie pulled at his red jumper (a vivid tribute to his golfing hero, Brian Huggett). 'Are you sure, Mill? I can ring Cartwright, you know, and cry off.' He knew what her answer would be.

'No. You go,' she said.

'Wa-al, lover, we gotta talk about this.'

'Oh, we'll talk all right.' Then she pulled the eiderdown over her head and vanished from sight.

By the time he got to the end of their cul-de-sac Charlie had forgotten all about Millie, who did have her mad moments, and was concentrating on the sweet shot he could sometimes manage across the ravine, and the possibility that he might beat Cartwright, who had won their last two games by a squeak. He thought as well that he should call on the professional to iron out the shanks that had suddenly appeared in his drive and also consult him about the acquisition of a new driver.

Apart from his sheer passion for Marvell's, Charlie's ability to focus on the moment was one of the sources of success both at work and in the rest of his life. It allowed him to be in love with Millie as well as follow his fancy with the various women who were fortunate enough to cross his path. And at work when crises emerged, he used this ability to focus to resolve them without machine-gunning disaster all around him. He knew his way of focusing energetically on the people who worked for him somehow made them feel they would go to the ends of the earth for him, all for the benefit of Marvell's. He liked that.

With the men above him Charlie was another kind of man: always aiming to deliver, to please, to demonstrate his loyalty like a small boy showing off to his parents. This did not make him likeable to them but they had to admit he got the job done. The man had extraordinary energy and did deliver the goods. Who could argue with that?

This ability to focus had also led to success on the golf course, allowing him to drive down his handicap to nine – not bad for a weekend player. This Saturday Charlie beat Cartwright three–two and, forgetting about Millie, he stayed on for a beer and a bite in the clubhouse. He and Cartwright talked about work, and next week's Sandie Shaw shindig. Charlie allowed himself to gloat with Cartwright on the mere fact of the millionth cooker and luxuriate in his own role in that achievement. Cartwright did nothing to puncture his boss's pride.

When he got home Charlie put his clubs in their own special cupboard in the garage and went in through the kitchen. In there the breakfast dishes were still piled up unwashed and Millie was nowhere to be seen. He went upstairs to find her on the bed. The room smelled of sweat and old scent. Now he was really concerned. It was not like her. Not really like her at all. She wouldn't lift her head off the bed.

'Millie...'

'Go away!'

'Look, Mill–'

'Get lost!'

He opened the curtains, and the window, then he went into the bathroom and started the bath running. Then he pulled back the bedclothes. 'I've run you a bath, lover. A bath'll make you feel better.' The kindness of the words was belied by his grim tone. 'You just have yourself a bath, lover. Put on some decent clothes and come downstairs. If you're not down in half an hour I'll come up here and throw you in the bath myself. I promise you.' At the door he turned back. 'Listen to that. Both taps are on. If you leave them the bath water will overflow and your pricey shag-pile will be ruined.'

Millie was downstairs in twenty minutes, in neatly pressed trousers and grey sweater, with her wet hair scraped back in a ponytail.

Charlie turned off the television, smiled up at her and opened his arms. 'There, lover, what is it? You tell your Charles. You tell me what it is.'

She flopped down beside him on the long sofa

and burst into tears. He took her tenderly into his arms. 'There, baby. What is it? Tell me what it is.'

She put a hand over her face and mumbled something.

He pulled her hand away. 'Tell me. Tell me what it is.'

She took a lumpy, sobbing breath. 'I'm late. I'm sick. I'm pregnant. That's what it is.'

Charlie became very still. 'Pregnant?' His mind was racing. Married fifteen years and not a sign of progeny. In fact, this had given their love-making a hedonistic quality: a delightful game with no sheath, no Pill and no ultimate outcome: another thing of the moment that Charlie liked to focus on. Neither of them had been troubled at their childless state. He had never fancied kids. And Millie had her house, after all. 'Pregnant?' he repeated,

'Yes, you know. Expecting one of those small things that shits and bawls and spits sick.' She put her hand up in front of her face again, gave one loud shriek then stopped.

His quick brain turned all this over and he said, 'Well, lover, that's great news, ain't it?'

Her hand came down from her face. 'What? Aren't you going to tell me what a mess they make, how I'll lose my figure? About becoming one of those women you turn your nose up at?'

He stared at her. 'It's you who turn your nose up at them, Millie. Not me. All that talk about women who let themselves go and forget their husbands in a welter of Ostermilk and nappies. You're the one that says that.'

'But I'm thirty-seven, Charles. It would be silly.

181

Inconvenient. I can't do it.' She paused. 'This thing can't be too difficult to stop. People do it, don't they? Stop them.'

Something hit Charlie, then, in the solar plexus. He felt like laughing and crying at the same time. What a great thing this was! A boy in his image! A little girl with that same soft baby hair at the nape of her neck, just like Millie. It had been so easy to throw money at Karen and tell her to get rid of her troublesome burden. But this was different. So very different. This was his wife.

He kissed Millie on the cheek, on the brow, took a clean handkerchief from his pocket and dabbed her damp cheeks. 'This is great news, Millie. Wonderful. We're not stopping this. Never.'

She sniffed. 'You think so?'

'Never! I want this kid.'

Her face brightened and she touched her hair where it swept back behind her ear. 'We would have to make the back room into a nursery. There is this new shop specialising in just everything for babies...'

He grinned. 'There. You'll be a better mother than any of those other slack women. You're older, lover. You'll do it better. You'll see.' He pocketed his hankie and patted her cheek. 'Now, honey, why don't you clear the mess out there and I'll pour your G and T and tell you how I beat the chuff out of Alan Cartwright this afternoon?'

Her face brighter now, Millie stood up and bustled off to her glamorous kitchen. He could hear the breakfast dishes being washed and the

182

pleasant click of things being put into place.

Full of feelings he did not quite recognise, Charlie poured himself a whisky and lit one of his small cigars. He felt wonderful, powerful, full of future. He went across to the large starburst mirror over the faux marble fireplace. As he looked at himself the weird thought struck him that perhaps he should talk to young Karen. Perhaps seeing that woman in Durham was not such a good idea. Perhaps all was not lost. He could take care of Millie. And he could take care of Karen. It would need a bit of discretion but it was not impossible. It would be such a waste, wouldn't it, to get rid of something that had something of the surge of pure life that he felt inside himself at just this moment?

He would have to see Karen soon. That needed fixing.

Moving Like Two Sisters

The Gaiety Dance Hall is legendary in Grafton. It metamorphosed from a pre-war roller-skating rink to one of the best dance halls in the region, with dancers flocking to the Friday and Saturday night dances on special buses from as far away as the coast. There were special, straight-up dances – foxtrot and tango and all that – to famous bands such as Victor Silvester. Top hat and tails and all that. Then there were the swing bands – bands you hear on the wireless, like Ted Heath, and hot jazz bands like Eric Delaney. Karen told me that she once danced right through an Eric Delaney drum solo. 'Double time, Cassandra. They all stopped to watch, made a ring round me. When I'd finished even the lads in the band applauded.'

My mother and father, like many other Grafton couples, met at the Gaiety. One lonely Christmas Eve, after a single large glass of sherry, she told me that my dad did a great foxtrot and a wonderful tango (although that dance was banned for a time from the Gaiety for being indecent, being referred to as 'vertical sex'). Seems my dad was very light on his feet. Maybe that's where I get it from, why learning to bop in the common room with Emma and the others was such an easy thing for me.

I sometimes wish my mother had cultivated more the habit of drinking. The odd times she does indulge, the veil kind of lifts. But we are so stretched for money it's a habit she doesn't indulge. Maybe that's a good thing though. She might be the kind that likes it too much. Elaine – the one who knows John Lennon – has told Emma and me some hair-raising tales of having to rescue her alcoholic mother from the pub and put her to bed.

On the Saturday morning before the Gaiety competition there is clearly something different in the air in our house. At her urging, my mother and I clean right through the house, polishing furniture and lino, changing beds. She even digs into the bottom sideboard drawer and hooks out a chenille cloth to spread on the table under the window.

Into my mind seeps a memory of just such an unusual flurry of cleaning and polishing; another time when there was a chenille cloth on the table under the window. I would be about twelve at the time. Counting back now, that would take us to 1958. Of course now I know that this was the year Constantin Kovacs was in this house. He and Tamás had been here in my house and I hadn't known. I was at the library or upstairs reading with a torch under the covers. Just as misery had been my mother's retreat from our lives together, books were mine.

And now, because Tamás knocked on our door the other night we are both calling ourselves to order. Neither of us mentions the fact that our restoring the house to a semblance of unaccustomed order is down to the fact that Tamás is calling for me tonight to go to the Gaiety. My mother and I are both playing games, but that is nothing new.

She does reflect thoughtfully that it's odd that I've never been to the Gaiety before. 'Must be the only girl your age in Grafton who can say that, Cassandra.'

When he gets to our house Tamás is clutching a bottle of wine, wrapped in yesterday's *Daily Mail*. 'Linda!' He hands it over to my mother, bowing his head and bringing his heels together in that way he has. She protests, pushing it back at him but he insists she takes it. 'It is not from me. It is a present from my father. Tokay. Wine from home. You can't get it round here. I was talking to him on the telephone. About being here in this house again. And about taking Cassandra to the Gaiety.' He turns those eyes on me. His green tie makes them look quite green, not grey as I first thought. 'The wine came in the post yesterday. Two bottles in a wooden box. One for you and one for Maria, my landlady.'

She peers at the label. 'Tokay. I drank this with Constantin once.' She takes the bottle from him.

'It's very special,' he says. 'You can't get it round here. But my dad found this wine merchant in Edinburgh who has this in his old stock.'

'Wine merchant?' She stands the bottle carefully on the chenille cloth. 'You should thank him for it. It's a kind thought.'

He dips into his inside pocket. 'He sent this note for you. It was in the box.'

She lays the letter beside the bottle on the table but doesn't open it. She looks at us from one to the other, smiling slightly. 'Well, you two. Go off and enjoy yourselves.' She looks up at Tamás rather severely. 'Mind you don't keep her out *too late.*'

That means more than the words, of course. It is not just about being late that Tamás has to mind.

He opens the door of his little car for me. It will seem odd to you but I've never been in a car. Buses, even trains, yes. But never a car. No. I tell a lie! There is this boy from the university who has a battered, rather smelly van that they sometimes use for gigs. (Two or three of them are good guitar players but rubbish singers.) Now and then he gives us all a lift to the nearby beach where we walk in clusters, collect shells and skim flat stones on the waves. But no one before has ever opened a car door for me in quite this way.

It takes only a few minutes to get to the Gaiety. I could have walked there on my feet in five minutes. One part of me wishes I had done that. Actually going *with* Tamás Kovacs to the dance is a different kettle of fish from meeting him inside. I show my slight frustration at this by insisting on paying for myself as we go in. He gives me a quizzical look and just shrugs. Maybe he's used to girls letting him pay. How much do I know about him? Anyway, his shrug makes me feel gauche and petty. Not a good start to the night.

We are early. In the low lighting the mirror-ball spins, splashing fragments of light on the scattering of dancers: only a sprinkling of people in the vast hangar-like space. The band – a very tuneful five-man combo – is doing its best, but music echoes thinly with so few bodies to absorb it. We sit down on a row of seats by the door.

'Wait!' Tamás leaps up, vanishes and reappears with two glasses of diluted orange juice. He is grinning, his usually grave face alight. 'The woman behind the counter says we can only drink these at the tables.' He nods towards the far end of the hall where tables are clustered, café-style. It is not so different, when I think of it, from the factory canteen.

Obediently, I grab my clutch bag and stand up.

He's still smiling. 'We can always be rebels and drink them here. They may not execute us.'

I suppose when you've seen tanks in your streets a few canteen women are no problem.

'No, no,' I say. 'We'll make our way down there.

Patsy and Karen'll be here soon. They'll want a table.' I'm making it clear we're not here on our own.

We choose a table and I gather chairs around it for Patsy and Karen. And one for Steve, as he's sure to come. Tamás watches me with interest. 'All these people? You are trying to tell me something, Cassandra?'

I feel myself colouring. 'Patsy told me that whoever gets here first bags a table.'

'That's fine. So now...?' The music has come to a stop and the bandleader is asking us to take our partners for a foxtrot. 'Should we dance?'

I look at the dancers on the floor who are making flamboyant use of the space this early in the evening: the women in their wide skirts and the men in their decent suits dipping and diving. Suddenly I wish I could do this, I wish I could swish around this gleaming floor with Tamás's arm round me, my hand close in his, as we dip perilously towards the floor. It must be an easier way to get to know someone than this so stilted conversation.

'Sorry,' I say. 'I can't do this. All I can do is bop. Rock'n'roll. I never learned to dance properly.'

He laughs. 'To be honest, all I can do is the Viennese waltz. I just change it about, if it is a foxtrot or an ordinary waltz.'

'And you don't bop?'

'It always looks so strange to me. I have not the courage.'

'But still you come here?'

At that moment two girls come by, hand in hand. One of them, in a short black skirt and four-inch heels says, 'Hi, Tam!'

The other looks at me with open curiosity and giggles.

'Oh,' I say, stiffer than I intend to be. 'That's why.' Then I'm embarrassed at being so sniffy. Who do I think I am?

'It's not like that, Cassandra.' His unemphatic protest is a rebuke in itself. 'It's sociable. Everybody comes.'

I'm saved from having to apologise by the sight of Patsy and Karen coming down the wide staircase that leads from the ladies' powder room. I wave at them and they set off towards us. They make such an incongruous couple. Patsy is wearing a pale green bouclé wool suit with a boxy-cut semi-fitted jacket, fur trimmed at the neck. It strains a bit at the upper arms and over her breasts. Karen is wearing white boots and a really short, well-cut flared minidress. (Her clever mother must have been copying those *Vogue* patterns again.) Her hair is in a very high, pulled-back ponytail, which emphasises her cheekbones. Her black-lined eyes are modelled tonight on Elizabeth Taylor as Cleopatra rather than Sandie Shaw. She looks stunning and draws glances as she and Patsy make their way down the long hall.

As if their entrance is a signal, people start to pour, rather than trickle, through the big double doors. These are younger people – minidresses and skirts rather than ball gowns, wearing more rather than less make-up. The boys are less casual. No jeans is the rule here. They wear drainpipe trousers with their jackets, but unlike the older men they wear no ties.

189

The music stops, then starts again. The band-leader has observed the influx and the music starts to move up tempo, with the electric guitarist rather than the trumpeter up front. Soon, the margins of the hall are pulsing with boppers, some dancing together, some doing their own thing. But there is the oddest thing. In the centre of the hall, ringed by the boppers, the conventional dancers dance a restricted version of their conventional dance, their more extravagant moves curtailed now by the press of bodies. They step and weave to the music, responding (elbows held *in* now) to the strict tempo buried beneath the with-it melodies.

Karen flops down in the chair beside me while Patsy makes her way to the counter to buy a couple of Coca-Colas. There is this other thing about this place: no alcohol. But the wave of newcomers – many having started the evening in the pub – have brought a breath of alcohol with them. I can smell gin on Karen's breath.

Tamás stands up as Patsy brings the drinks and places them carefully on the table. She grins up at him. 'Well, look who's here! Tamás Kovacs, as I live and breathe. What an honour!'

He smiles sweetly at her and sits down again. 'The honour's all mine, Auntie Patsy.'

She gets him by the arm and shakes it. 'Stop it, you! You think you can charm the birds off the trees, you lot! Over-paid, over-sexed and over here. They said it about the Yanks and it applies to you lot.'

He puts his hand on hers and looks into her eyes. 'The charm is in telling the truth, dear beloved Patsy.'

She shakes off his hand. 'I said stop it! Do as you're told!' She looks at Karen, who is looking unusually glum. 'And who knocked your pint over? Cheer up! It might never happen!'

The bandleader goes to the microphone and makes an announcement. Karen's face clears and she turns to me. 'This is us. Are you up for it, Cassie, or what? A bit of a bop?'

'Am I?' I say. 'I'll say I am.'

So we set off, there by the table, on the edge of the dance floor. We are lucky that, at this moment, the saxophonist puts down his instrument and picks up a guitar. Now the band consists of only two boys on guitars and an older man on the drums. It is transformed. The beat is great. *Great!*

Now the flouncy – that is, 'proper' – dancers melt away and the boppers command the floor. Two thirds of them are women dancing together but this doesn't matter. Everyone moves to their own individual pattern. After a bit of a muddle between us, Karen takes over and we manage to dance together. Before long we are moving apart, coming together, allowing the beat to flow into our arms, our legs, our heads, passing the baton from one to the other. At this point everything I have learned from Elaine comes into its own. I am content now to lose myself in the beat.

All around us, on this perfectly sprung dance floor, boys are flicking girls into the air and girls are sliding on their bottoms through the legs of their partners. In contrast, Karen and I are neat and controlled, only occasionally flamboyant. Still, somehow we work out between us this

191

whole range of moves that joins us perfectly to the beat. My moves are always sub-Elaine, but Karen's are all her own.

I hardly know Karen. I don't even know whether I like her – of the two of them probably Patsy is my favourite. But here on the dance floor Karen and I are two parts of a whole. We read each other's minds and move like true sisters.

The set ends too soon and we return to flop down at the table. Tamás and Patsy are laughing and clapping. Steve, beside Tamás now with a glass of Coke beside him, is whistling through his fingers. Tamás has his eyes on me and is grinning from ear to ear. I glow with a kind of self-satisfaction I've never experienced in passing even the hardest of my exams.

'Great, that, lasses,' says Steve, lounging beside Patsy. 'Wouldn't'a thought you had it in you, Cassandra.'

Karen pushes his shoulder hard. 'Me! I was dancing too, Steve.'

'I know that,' he says, sucking at his straw. 'But I've already seen you, Karen. I already knew you were great. But tonight I thought you'd lose Cassandra off, but you didn't.'

She laughs. 'Nah. But then we're partners, ain't we, Cassandra?' Her face is flushed and her eyes as they meet mine are very bright.

Patsy beams at us both like a proud mother hen. 'I knew you'd be great, you two. Felt it in my bones.'

Tamás pushes a fresh glass of orange in front of me, 'Drink this. It certainly looks hot work.'

I put a hand on my burning cheek. 'Do I look

that bad?'

'No. No. You look different. So ... full of life.' His tone is urgent, conciliatory.

Patsy laughs. Stevie starts to sing along with the band, 'Stranger in Paradise'.

I'm saved from replying by a small man in a black suit and a dicky-bow, carrying a battered black notebook. He stops by our table. 'Right, you two,' he says. 'You're on the list. Second round's at ten o'clock. You two are number ten.' He hands over battered wristbands supporting discs, each scrawled with a big 10.

Steve meets my puzzled glance. 'You two're in the second round. The pick of the crop.'

'I didn't realise any competition had started,' I protest.

Tamás winks at me. 'Could you have tried harder?' He puts his hand on mine where it lies on the table. 'No! So it is good you didn't know. Isn't it?' I love the warm dry feel of his hand.

Patsy thrusts a ten-shilling note in Steve's hand. 'There, love, fill 'em up. All this dancing is making me thirsty.'

The dancing has started again and the spinning globe is spilling its light on all of us, the just and the unjust. The man in the band has exchanged his guitar for his trumpet and the music is more swinging than rocking and rolling.

Later the music changes again and I'm in this dreamy state when Karen and I get to dance in this final set. Now our style steps up a level and the others end up in a ring around us as we dance. It seems a foregone conclusion that we should bring our small shields and big boxes of chocolates back to the table, to the wild cheers of our friends.

I am experiencing a moment of true happiness with no past and no future. The music throbs in my ears. I am sitting at this table in the Gaiety Dance Hall, hand in hand with Tamás Kovacs, in the company of people who are truly, in this moment, my friends. I have never experienced this feeling of splendour, of success, even in college. Never at school. How the plates are changing in my world.

Patsy Has Her Say

I'm in this crowded place that smells of hairspray and scent and sweat, and I can't stop dancing. The dancing is making me buzz inside. I've been bopping with Karen and Steve, even waltzing with Tamás Kovacs. That of course, is something else: sweet and intimate. It feels like I'm drinking him in on a very slow pulse. When we get back to the table Steve tries to 'tice Tamás to have a try at the rock'n'roll but he's not having any. He just grins and says, 'I only dance if it's a waltz, Steve. Waltzes I can manage.'

'Out of the Dark Ages, you,' Karen shouts above the music.

He shakes his head. 'I come out of a place where they invented dancing in ballrooms.' He seems quite happy, lounging there beside Patsy, fixing us dancers with a close eye.

At one point, Patsy says in my ear, 'Canny mover, you.' She keeps her voice down under the clamour. Tamás can't hear.

I thank her and she shrugs, throwing off the gratitude. 'I speak as I find,' she says brusquely. She nods towards Karen, who's bopping away with Steve. They are flushed and bright eyed. 'That one's a canny mover too. Could always do it, even as a little 'un. Should'a seen her. She used to dance at the Grafton Galas in the "Go as You Please" competition. It was Irish dancing, then. Her dad's a Paddy.' Her still face moves to a scowl. 'Much good it's doing her now, though,' she says dourly.

'We won the competition.' I'm offended for myself as well as Karen. 'Me and Karen won the competition.'

'She's a silly lass,' said Patsy glumly, putting down her cigarette. 'You'd think she'd know better.'

'Better than what?'

She opens her mouth to say something, then shuts it. 'Like I say, she's a silly lass.'

Now I'm lost for something to say, but Patsy hangs on to my attention. 'She won't talk to me any more, you know.'

'She talks to you all the time, Patsy.'

She shakes her head. 'Not about owt that matters, believe me.'

Again I can only stay silent. Then I make a real effort. 'What is it, Patsy? What's it you're saying to me?'

'She's slithering about. She's telling lies these

days. There's no trusting her. You can't beat lies. Anything but that.' She sounds very miserable. Not like Patsy at all.

This is too maudlin for me. I get brisk. 'Patsy! She's there dancing with Steve! She's not telling any lies. She's happy dancing and we've just won the competition. That's the truth.'

Then Patsy does this strange thing. She leans over and puts her hand on my arm. 'See if you can talk to her, pet. She might talk to you, being younger, like. She won't talk to me, that's for sure.'

The bandleader flourishes his baton and the dance comes to an end. The dancers trickle away from the floor like melting ice. Steve strolls across with Karen, a delighted grin on his face, one arm around her waist.

Karen meets my glance, then nods towards the sweeping staircase. 'Gunna freshen my lipstick. You coming?'

I've seen but not participated in this before; this thing where two girls go to the toilet together like Siamese twins. Me and Emma laugh when our friends do it. 'Fancy, Cass,' she'll say. 'Can't even go to the bog on their own!'

I can feel Patsy's pressure on my arm. 'OK,' I say now to Karen, gathering up my bag. 'I could do to freshen up. Hot work, this dancing.' I feel rather than see Tamás's quizzical gaze. Maybe like Emma he thinks these joint toilet visits are all a bit comical.

I follow Karen down the edge of the dance floor, dodging the dancers who are coupling up for the next dance, a very upbeat mambo.

Karen turns towards me and shouts over the opening bars of the music, 'You and Patsy had your heads together, like.' It is more a question than a statement.

I catch up with her and take the plunge. 'We were talking about you,' I shout in her ear. We climb the shallow steps side by side, leaving the dancers below us twinkling in the fragmented light of the swirling globe.

At the top of the steps she says, 'There's not anything to say about me. Me, I'm one of those really boring people. Ask anybody.'

'Except Patsy?' I say.

Then, instead of going through the double doors of the powder room she turns left and pulls me along the balcony that runs the length of the ballroom, leading to more steps down at the other end, We walk along, stepping over the stretched legs of boys who are sitting smoking, crouched against the wall. We are forced to run the gauntlet. They whistle and jeer as we pass; some of them comment on Karen's legs. I am a bit relieved that mine are not worth commenting on.

At the very end there are these three banquette seats. She throws herself on one and says, 'Here! Sit here, Cassandra. And tell me just what the hell Patsy's been on about.'

I shake my head. 'She said nothing, Karen. Well, nothing bad. Just that you were a silly lass and should know better. Nothing else.'

Karen stares at me and then a fragment of the roaming silver light in her eye holds on to a tear. 'She's all right, Patsy. She watches out for you.'

197

Then, just for something to say, I say, 'She takes some getting to know, does Patsy.'

Karen dabs the underside of her eyes with her embroidered hankie. I wonder if her mother did that embroidery. Probably. She makes everything else. 'Good thing she's on my side,' she says. 'She'll do anything for you, will Patsy, if she has a fancy for you. She'll go all the way.'

'Seems like,' I say. Then I take the plunge. 'She says you're telling her lies. Is that true?'

She sniffs and returns her hankie to her little bag. 'She's as sharp as a tack, that one.' She takes a breath. 'You know that friend of mine, the one I got the name of that woman in Durham for? The women who could change things? Who could stop you ... well, stop a baby coming?'

'Yeah. I picked that up.' Even as I say this I know in a flash what's coming. I stare at her, not wanting her to go on. A tumble of consequences charge round my head. I don't want her to tell me her secret, a secret that I know now without her saying. But I convince myself that if she doesn't say the words, it will not happen.

'Well, it's not her, it's me needs to *get rid,*' she says simply. 'Cassandra, it's me that needed the address of the woman.'

I can't bear it. I think I said that Emma's sister went through this 'getting rid' thing. She went riding on a wild horse and drank a bottle of gin to get rid of the baby. And she did *get rid* in the end. There'd not even been a romance: some horrible thing about an uncle just back from the army. 'The rotter,' Emma said to me when she told me, banging one hand into another. 'We thought he was nice, kind. You know? But he was a real *rotter!*' There were big tears in her eyes.

'You don't believe me, do you?' says Karen now. 'It's me! Not some girl on the bus.'

The dancers and the clicking mambo music down below seem to fade away from us, to go into the distance, like when a film is coming to its end.

'I do. I do believe you!' The words tumble out of my mouth but one part of me doesn't want this confidence. *Go away, Karen, go away.* 'Oh, Karen, what'll you do?'

'I went to the woman. The woman in Durham.'

A pain like a knife hits my solar plexus. 'Did she ... are you ... are...?' The words dry in my mouth.

'She gave me some stuff. To take. To start the curse.'

Now I am looking very closely at her. She looks very young, glowing and fit. When I have my period I'm like death for three days. 'And what happens?' I am blushing at my own ignorance.

'I took the stuff like she said. But nothing's happened. No curse.'

'So that's it? It didn't work?' I have only a sketchy idea of the mechanics. I have a hard time getting hold of the fact that sex happens with the man right on top of the woman. I laughed when I first heard that. But Jeanette laughed at my ignorance. Then she said it can happen in a hundred different ways. Hadn't I heard of the *Karma Sutra?* Of course, Jeanette is a bit of a fantasist.

'Well,' says Karen, 'if nothing happens by tomorrow I have to go back to her. Then she'll do something herself. Bring it away.'

I have this nightmare image of a big tool, like tweezers the size of a carving knife. I take a very deep breath. 'Don't do it, Karen. Please don't do it!' Inside I'm thinking there is no need for this now. Pills, sheaths, coils, diaphragms – Jeanette has educated us all about ways *not* to get into this state but still be able do The Thing. She's a temptress, that one.

Karen puts one hand on her broad brow just under her long fringe and drags it right down her face, making it a gargoyle where beauty had been. 'What can I do? If my mother finds out she'll kill me, then die of a broken heart. I'll lose my job,' she wails through sobs and hiccoughs. 'Anyway,' she sniffs, 'I don't want no baby. It'd be mad to have one. Not me, not now. It's not right.'

I take her hand hard in mine. 'Karen, I have this friend at college, see?' I take a huge breath. 'We're kind of best friends. We tell each other everything.'

Karen's head goes up. 'She lives round here?'

'No. She's from Newark, near Nottingham. In France just now. Picking grapes.'

'I bet you wish you were with her.'

A day or so ago that would have been true. But I think of Tamás Kovacs and I think of winning the dance competition just now with Karen. 'No,' I said. 'It's all right here. I like it. I belong…'

She sniffs. 'Belong? You? Well… So what about this friend?'

'Her sister got pregnant.'

'Lucky her!' says Karen gloomily.

'She'd been attacked, raped. Not so lucky at all. She tried all ways to *get rid*. Gin. She rode a half-tame horse. Tried wild bike-riding down hills.' I pause. 'Then...'

'Then, what?'

I grip Karen's hand tighter. 'Karen, she died. Emma's sister died! Emma says that now *she* has to live for the two of them. It's real hard on her.'

'Died,' Karen wrestles her hand free of mine. *'Died?'*

'They rushed her to hospital and she died there. She was just twenty, Karen, like you.'

'Bloody horrible, that.' She falls silent.

I touch her hand again. 'That thing, Karen. That horrible thing. Don't do it.'

She shakes her head so sadly my heart aches for her. 'There's nothing else. No other bloody thing I can do.'

Downstairs there is more drumming, more electric guitaring, more rock and roll. I suddenly have to shout. 'There's living. There's choosing to live!'

She laughs hysterically now. 'With a kid in tow? You're bloody joking. You're making game!'

'The father? What about the father?'

She's already shaking her head. 'Wants nothing to do with me. I embarrass him.'

I think of Mr Priest's car slowing down by the bus stop. 'You didn't embarrass him when it happened, did you?'

'That's what I said to him. Makes no difference. Like Patsy says, men are bloody selfish bastards. That's what Patsy says.'

'But think on, Karen. Think on. Before you do anything. Promise me!'

She's already shaking her head.

201

That's when I see Tamás, a glass of orange in each hand, weaving his way through the stretched legs on the balcony. He grins down at us and my heart lurches. Here's one who's no bastard. I'm sure of that. I look at his face afresh. His nose is that bit too long and his eyes that bit too large but somehow put together they make a perfect whole.

'Patsy asks, where have you gone?' So very good to hear his voice. 'She sends me to you bearing gifts.'

Karen treats him to a watery smile. 'We're coming. Thought we'd come the long way round and got chatting.' She stands up. 'You hang on to those drinks. We'll follow you.'

Downstairs Patsy looks at Karen and then at me. 'All OK then?'

Karen picks up her shield and her box of chocolates from the table. 'I'm off. I told our Tony I'd meet him outside the Lord Raglan. You comin', Pats?'

Patsy hauls herself to her feet. 'Might as well. All over bar the shouting, here.' The two of them look across at me, their eyes neutral, neither welcoming nor rejecting.

Tamás saves me the trouble of answering. 'I am taking Cassandra back to her house.'

Patsy shrugs. 'That's all right then.' Still, she looks at me, her eyes full of questions.

We all look across at Steve, but he is already shaking his head. 'Not me,' he says. 'I'm on a promise.' He nods across at a short dark girl who is dancing with her taller friend. 'She's from Meadowfield. Went to school with her. She's *saving the last dance for me.'* He grins and dances a few steps. 'Geddit?'

'Steve, you're a bastard,' says Patsy genially, and leads the way down the dance floor.

Karen, Patsy and I collect our coats from the powder room. Karen goes into the toilet and Patsy grabs my arm. 'Well?' she says.

I wait one second before shaking my head. 'We just talked about ... things, Patsy.' I can't break Karen's confidence.

She buttons up her Dannimac and peers at herself in the mirror. 'Liars,' she says fiercely to her reflection. 'I am surrounded by liars.' Then she stalks out of the double doors.

I wait for Karen coming out of the toilet. 'Look!' I say. 'Tell your mother. Please tell your mother!' She looks at me like I am a stranger and shakes her head and hurries after Patsy.

I stay in the powder room and take down my ponytail, then put it up again. I stroke on another layer of eyeshadow and pat my face with my Coty powder. Around me girls are renewing their heavy eye-lines, back-combing their hair like eighteenth-century courtesans and preparing for the last event of the evening. Beside them I look like I'm going to a Sunday school anniversary.

Tamás is waiting at the bottom of the stairs alongside the other lucky boys who are waiting for their partners for the last ritual of the evening.

'It's a nice night,' he says. 'I thought I might walk you home and come back for the car.' So, side by side, we go through the big double doors with all the other couples, and out into the night.

'Walking home' is an important part of the Gaiety experience. This is where love – or something like it – blossoms, where marriages take their first step. It was on just such a 'walking home' that my mother embarked on her affair with my father, which led to their hurried marriage because I was on the way.

I know from girls I went to school with that 'walking home' is a euphemism for zigzagging home by the back lanes, being kissed and fondled, sometimes even underneath your clothes. Sometimes – according to Jeanette – people actually do the full thing, actually make love in these dark corners. According to her it's possible to do it standing up. Just how that is achieved baffles me.

I only once experienced the walking home thing, with this boy who was in the sixth form at school. It was the end of the last term at school and I had been enticed to a church social by a couple of friends who were in my English group. Sam was the brother of one of them – smooth faced and dark – handsome in a Tony Curtis kind of way. I thought then that 'walking home' meant just that. So I was taken by surprise when he pulled me into the back doorway of the barber's shop and covered my face with kisses, his hands grasping at my barely existent breasts. I laughed, pulled myself away and ran all the way home. Thinking of that now, Patsy's *Russian hands and Roman fingers* is not a bad description.

Tonight, though, I am keyed up to tolerate a bit of that, just so I can get closer to Tam Kovacs. In fact, I might experiment with a bit of kissing and fondling myself. After all, he's volunteered to be here with me tonight. He's a big reason why the thought of Emma and Jeanette in those French vineyards is suddenly less appealing. France may have its charms but tonight I'm very content to be walking home from the Gaiety Dance Hall with Tamás Kovacs, clutching my Best Dancer shield and my box of chocolates.

The Way Home

Dealing with *Russian hands and Roman fingers* does not seem an option on the way home. As Tamás and I walk along the pavement he carefully maintains a distance between us; there is no convenient bumping of hands that could turn into a friendly clasp.

We talk a bit about Patsy and Karen, and he asks politely about my mother. Then, as we make our way through the streets we become more and more silent. The dark back entry of the barber's shop seems to hold no charms for Tamás. We glimpse a couple engaged in a friendly wrestle down a back alley and that makes it even harder to walk shoulder to shoulder with a gap between us.

We come to a stop outside my front door. I look up into his face, hoping at least for a chaste kiss, to feel his skin against mine. He stops this by taking my hand in his. 'You danced great, Cassandra. I never thought you could dance. Does not seem like you. How surprising to see you move just so. You're a surprising girl.'

I try an enigmatic smile. 'What's so surprising about that?'

'Well.' He pauses. 'You seemed to me very composed. I had not thought you could be so wild.' Then he takes my hand and squeezes it, and the thrill goes right down to my heels. Not quite *Russian hands and Roman fingers*. An improvement on that, in fact.

'Was my dancing that awful?' I pull my hand away from his.

He grasps it again. 'It was great, Cassandra. Fantastic!' Then he kisses my hand. Again, that electric charge right down to my heels. *Crikey. Hormones raging. Leaping. Jumping. Sizzling.* I get myself under control and leave my hand where it is.

'Will you walk with me tomorrow in the park?'

I have to take a very deep breath. 'Well...'

'Two o'clock. The park gates.' It is a statement, not a question.

'Yes. Right.'

And he turns on his heel and marches away.

I fumble for my key, open the door and shoot straight into the living room. My mother looks up from her book. 'Nice evening?'

I stand in the kitchen doorway, poised to flee upstairs. 'It was all right.' I put the chocolates and shield on the table.

'What's this, then?'

'I won them dancing with Karen.' I open the chocolates and offer her one.

She takes one and pops in it her mouth. 'I heard voices,' she mumbles.

'Tamás Kovacs walked me home from the dance.'

'Did he, now?'

'It's not like that. Really.'

'Like what? Of course not.' Her eyes stray back to her book and I go into the kitchen to boil a kettle so I can have a wash. Her voice follows me. 'That Tam Kovacs is a nice boy, you know.'

I don't answer her. I just stand watching the blue flame lick around the battered aluminium kettle and relive that burning kiss on my hand. *Yes he is,* I say to myself. *He's a very nice boy. No ... a very nice man.* The thing is, I really wish he *had* dragged me down the alleyway and played Roman hands and Russian fingers. All over me.

Suddenly Patsy comes into my mind. What would she say about all this? I laugh out loud.

'What's that?' My mother's voice comes through the door. 'What are you laughing at?'

'Nothing,' I say. 'Nothing at all.'

'Doesn't sound like that. Can I have another chocolate?'

'Help yourself.'

Later, in my cold bedroom, I lie there hugging myself, letting my own fingers roam around my own body. (Jeanette has this theory that some women can do *It* to themselves but that is obviously another of her fantasies.) I have to say it takes a long time for all the bubbling and buzzing I feel inside to subside.

It is only when I'm just about to drop off to sleep that Karen comes back into my mind, dragging her hand down her beautiful face and making it look so ugly. And I feel a leaden guilt at being so happy that Tamás Kovacs has kissed my hand. I should be thinking how I can help Karen. I try to think about her, then I give up. Think about it! How can a girl who is not totally sure of the mechanics of getting pregnant help somebody who actually is in that state?

Dinner With the Wife

Sunday Morning

Charlie Priest liked Sundays even better than Saturdays. They always had several treats in store. Now, friends again, he and Millie had a lie-in followed by what (after last year's holiday in Florida) Millie had started to call 'brunch' in the dining room, with all the trimmings. Not only was there an egg and bacon breakfast, there was fruit juice and yoghurt, flapjacks and muffins. It was one of Charlie's regular jokes that he was forced to play golf on Sunday afternoons to shift the weight of Millie's brunches.

Today they munched their brunch and read the papers – the *Mail* for Millie and the *Express* for Charlie. Yesterday's *Financial Times* lay unopened on the table. He always kept that for Sunday nights so he could pore over it in his little study off the hall, making notes to discuss with his broker on Monday. Charlie was the only person among his friends or his extended family either to have a study or to 'make investments'. This all started ten years ago when Mr Owen advised him to buy Marvell shares. He bought a block of them then, and more as Marvell shares went up and up. He learned more about Marvell's from the annual shareholders' meeting than he'd ever known striding the Marvell factory floor. After that he had studied the market and got the knack of buying other shares that were improving. When Millie complained about him spending all his bonuses with nothing to see, he told her it was his hobby, growing money without working for it. It was one of his secret pleasures, making money out of money with no work involved. Here, he knew, was power.

Millie was quiet as she turned the pages of her paper. He touched her shoulder. 'How are you this morning, lover?' he said tenderly. 'How's my little momma?'

She smiled her watery smile. 'I'm pregnant, not ill, Charles.'

'Well, you take it easy today. Rest up.' He stood up and touched his mouth with the rayon napkin. 'Well, I'm off, lover.'

She barely looked up, just murmured something, her head still over her paper. He kissed the top of her head and went off whistling. He put his golf gear in the boot. He was wearing his snazzy golf clothes, but he didn't go directly to the golf club. Another part of his Sunday ritual was to call in at Marvell's to check up on the Sunday overtimers, the maintenance men and cleaners who were happy to exchange church, chapel and Sunday pub for the triple-rate overtime. Of course, there was no need at all for

Charlie to be there, but he liked to be at the factory when it was virtually at rest, to walk the empty gangways and have a think. He got some of his best ideas on Sundays.

Today he arrived at a quarter to twelve in time to talk to the women in Packing, who were preparing a rush order, and to confirm with the maintenance crew that they were up to scratch with the electricity checks for Wednesday's presentation. His next call was at Goods Inwards to check the overnight delivery of crucial parts from Inverness; then to the stores to check that the mid-month stock check was a reality not a figment of the sly storekeeper's imagination. He was always genial with the people who worked Sunday overtime – patted them on the shoulder, shook them by the hand. He knew that then they would spread the word. 'You can say what you like about Charlie Priest, he has his finger on the pulse. Nothing goes on here he doesn't know about.' These small touches were another part of Charlie's particular genius. He knew the right questions to ask the maintenance men and the stock clerks, the right phrases to use with the women workers. He knew how to keep them up to the mark.

And this week his Sunday morning tour furnished him with sharp comments to make in the following week to the shop-floor managers like Stan Laverick, to show *them* he had his finger on the pulse.

On his way to the office he came across someone in the progress office. 'What's this, Tam? Sunday working?' Unlike the other people Charlie had seen, Tamás Kovacs would not be paid for his Sunday overtime.

Tam shut the ledger in front of him. 'Just a final check on some parts for this special cooker for the presentation. I've been down to stores and there's nothing missing.'

Charlie put a hand on his shoulder. 'Good man. Now you get yourself away, son. The sun's shining out there. You're only young once.' He paused. 'Got anything on today?'

Tamás stood up. 'Well, I'm going for a walk in the park. Then I'm going out to tea.'

Charlie grinned. 'Who's the lucky girl then?'

'It's not a girl. There are two of them. And no, Mr Priest, you don't know them.' He coloured. 'It's complicated.'

'That's what they all say, son. I've even said it myself from time to time.' He watched as Tam almost ran out of the office. Strange lad, that. Clever, hardworking. In here on Sunday when he didn't need to be. The workers liked him. He got things done. But he wasn't like the other young line-leaders and managers. And this wasn't down to his foreign accent or unforced manners. There was something deep about him. You couldn't get at him, somehow.

Charlie let himself into his office, sat down and dialled the number of his friend Claire Boustead. He often rang her from work on Sundays. Her husband would be on some Surrey golf course and she would be curled up in bed wearing one of those kaftan things, drinking filtered coffee. They were old friends, he and Claire. They'd met at a Marvell's sale conference where she was demonstrating a three-course meal in forty minutes on the Marvell Duchess cooker. It was sex at first sight for both of them. It was quite a time ago and now they rarely saw each other. But these days they didn't even need to see each other for the old magic to work. Claire certainly lit up his Sunday mornings with a few fireworks. Today he would talk to her about the demonstrators she was sending up this week to make the spread for the shindig. Then they would talk about sex. The telephone was a wonderful thing.

'Claire?' he drawled. 'And how are you this sunny morning?'

It was two thirty before Charlie got down to the golf course, a substantial and challenging course in the picturesque grounds of Masterson Hall, whose former gatehouse was the Grafton clubhouse. He found his Sunday partner, Felix, striding up and down outside the clubhouse.

'Missed our two o'clock slot, Charlie,' he blustered.

Charlie grinned at him and patted his arm. 'Well, then, let's just go and have a drink and wait for the next slot, shall we? Come on, Felix, you wouldn't deny a man his Sunday morning conjugal comforts, would you?' Then he winked to let Felix in on the secret of his happy marriage.

Felix, whose company supplied Marvell's with packing cases, was forced to relax. This man was not only his bread and butter, he was the jam as well. He grinned broadly. 'Well then, Charlie. What is it? G and T?'

They got onto the course at three and took

their time around the eighteen holes, talking in a desultory fashion. Felix, a big Tory, was certain Reggie Maudling would be made Tory leader, ahead of Ted Heath. Charlie favoured Maudling, who was a businessman, after all, but thought Heath, as Shadow Chancellor, might have something to offer. But by the time they got to the ninth they had progressed to Marvell's and Charlie enjoyed letting Felix into the secret of the PR benefits of the Sandie Shaw shindig and told him he was welcome to attend if he was free on Wednesday. But then Felix beat him roundly and was rather too jaunty for Charlie's taste as they walked back up to the clubhouse.

Coming through the carved wooden doors Charlie blinked to see Millie sitting there in the lounge, very trim in her white flared trousers, fitted red jacket and very high-heeled white shoes, her make-up a little too thick even for his taste. He hadn't noticed her Capri in the car park but then he hadn't been looking. He leaned down to kiss her on the cheek. 'This is a surprise, lover.'

Her eyes glittered up at him. 'Do I need a reason to have dinner with my husband?'

He glanced at the clock. 'No way. You've made my day, honey.' He nodded across at Felix, who was hovering in the door to the men's bar, wondering whether to stay or go. 'Look at me, Felix, old boy! One look from this one and I'm smitten all over again. Next Sunday, same time?'

Felix gave him the old thumbs-up and vanished through the bar door.

Nick Barnes, the steward, showed Charlie and

Millie to the best table overlooking the eighteenth green, Charlie ordered a bottle of Nick's best Côtes du Rhône and turned the beam of his attention on Millie.

'What is it, lover? I thought you'd be having a nice easy day, taking it steady.'

She scowled at him. 'I thought I'd come and surprise you. Nick Barnes said you didn't tee off till three.'

Gently, gently, he thought. Millie occasionally had these mad bouts but he could handle her. It ran in the family. Her mother and aunt were as mad as hatters. Thank God they were at the other end of England in Torquay. He smiled easily and touched her hand. 'Lots to do at the factory, lover. This presentation thing and all that. Old Felix was put out, but like I said to him, Marvell's gotta come first.'

They ordered steak and chips from Nick's wife, Beattie, who had worked for Mr Charles Forte and thought Grafton Golf Club was a step down in the world. Still, the food had improved since her arrival.

They ate in silence. At last Millie put down her fork. 'I thought it would be nice for us to talk outside the house, Charles. On neutral ground, so to speak.'

'Neutral ground? We don't need neutral ground, lover.' He smiled at her. 'We can talk all we want at home.'

She banged the table with the flat of her hand and the other diners looked round. 'But you don't concentrate, Charles! You smile and walk off into another room. Or bury your head in that pink paper of yours. You find a job to do. Or you turn up too late from work for anything but eat and sleep. I wait for you, I make everything nice, I dress for you...' Her voice tailed off.

He stared at her, his glance hardening. Brave men at Marvell's had quailed at that look. She didn't flinch. He leaned over and filled her glass nearly to the top. 'Well, now you've got me, lover. I am all ears. Who's perfect?' he laughed. 'What is it?'

'Not like that, Charles! Don't fill the glass full! It should be no more than half full. It said so in this article in the *Mail*. You don't get the *bouquet* if you fill it right up. I read it out to you. But like I say, you weren't really there.'

He poured a third of her glass into his. 'Is that all right?'

She raised the glass to her face, swilled the wine round, breathed in and closed her eyes. She opened her eyes. 'It will have to do. Not the same, though,' she said sulkily.

He took another look at her mutinous face and went into management mode. 'What the hell's biting you, Millie? Out with it!' he whispered fiercely. 'What is it? We're pleased about this baby thing, we've been through that. We're pleased!'

She scowled at him and her face seemed to fill with air. Then the words burst out. 'You're seeing someone! I know it! You're seeing another woman.' Her voice rang across the dining room. People who knew Charlie exchanged glances that said, *only a matter of time.*

Charlie grabbed her hand and held it painfully tight and they waited while Nick's wife came to

215

collect their plates and enquire about sweets. Millie ordered Black Forest gâteau and Charlie ordered crème caramel.

After watching her bustle away Charlie turned to his wife. 'Here we go again, Mill! You're mad. I keep telling you, it's all in your head, every bit of it. Apart from anything else where would I get the time? I'm at the factory all hours that God sends. When do I have time for extra-mural activities? It's work or home or something to do with Marvell's.'

She flushed a bright, ugly red. 'That's what I'm on about, Charles. That's it! I finally worked it out. Something to do with Marvell's. It can only be that.'

He had a blinding vision of Karen sitting on the other side of his desk, her big, dark eyes full of unshed tears. He took a sip of his wine and stayed steady. 'What's that word they use now? Paranoid? Another word for bonkers. That's you, Millie. Something to do with Marvell's? Can't think what you're talking about, lover. It's where I work, that's all.'

She pulled her arm out of his hard grip and knocked the nearly empty wine bottle off the table. He caught it and replaced it carefully on the table. 'I tell you what I'm talking about, Charles,' she said. 'I'm talking about that blonde tart in the office. The air hostess. That snooty woman who thinks she's too good for anybody.'

Charlie breathed out lightly through his mouth, trying not to show his relief. 'Well, Mill, like I say you're bonkers or wandering round in fairyland. She's just a secretary. Good one at that.'

She scowled. 'I saw her! I saw the way she looked at you at my birthday party. Eating you up with those eyes of hers. At *my* party! Sashaying in like she's a model or something. I *saw* the way she simpered at you. I saw it!'

He tried to take her hand again but she wriggled out of his grasp. 'Listen, Millie!' he said quietly. 'The girl was saying "thank you for having me"! That's all. She was only there because young Tam Kovacs brought her.'

'Ah! There you are! Poor lad. Young enough to be her son.'

'Hardly, Millie. To be honest I thought they made quite a nice couple.'

'See? See? She's a schemer. Sucking up to a young lad so she can worm her way into my house. And drink my cocktails. From my new cabinet.' She pushed away her glass. 'I can't drink this.'

'Good! Now you stop this, Millie!' The conciliatory note had gone from his voice. 'Stop it! You're working yourself up over nothing. That girl works in the progress office and it looks like she's going out with young Kovacs. He might be a bit young for her, but...'

'Ah! You really mean she's more your age, your type, don't you?' Her voice was very loud.

'Shut up, Millie,' he said quietly. 'Shut up! Or I'll do something you won't like.'

She stood up then and stormed past him, pushing his shoulder so that he fell right back in the chair, and stalked out of the dining room. The other diners followed her progress and then turned their attention back to Charlie. He smiled helplessly and shrugged his shoulders and they turned back to their food. At that point Nick's wife came with their sweets. She looked at Millie's empty chair.

'Just put them down, lover,' Charlie said, smiling. 'No good letting your wonderful food go to waste, is there?'

He set to work on the Black Forest gâteau with a will. He'd just deal with all this and go through to the bar and join Felix. Give Millie time to cool off. It usually worked. She was a funny old thing but her instinct was right. Luckily she'd homed in on the wrong target. Close call, that.

He was just spooning up the crème caramel when it occurred to him it might not be so easy this time, with Millie being pregnant. He might even have to give the innocent Evelyn Laing the sack, to placate Millie. Still, anything for a quiet life.

Another Part of Me

The Victoria Park was given to the town of Grafton in 1897, by the Mastersons who have the local big house. It's a very nice place, a bit of a surprise in a town like this. It has extensive, well-flowered leisure gardens to walk in, tennis courts and a velvet bowling green for the adults to play on, and swings and slides and a teapot lid roundabout for the children. On the downside the public toilets placed discreetly on the perimeter are inscribed by scabrous statements and crude poems illustrated by equally crude drawings of various body parts: a bit like the toilets at the factory, when I come to think of it.

On this fine summer Sunday the people of Grafton are making full use of the Mastersons' gift. Teenage boys stride across the tennis court like kings (I recognise one of them from the grammar school). There are two full teams playing bowls. A boy and his little sister are reaching for the sky on the swings.

When I arrive at the gates I can hear the band tuning up for their two o'clock concert on the bandstand. At ten minutes past I am still standing listening to them play a very full-blown brass version of 'Roses of Picardy'.

I am fuming, seething, cursing myself for an idiot when Tamás Kovacs finally runs up, breathing hard, beads of sweat on his long upper lip.

'So sorry, Cassandra. I had this thing to do at the factory. Then my father has turned up here, out of the blue. Then my car wouldn't start. This day is cursed.' (No English boy would have put it that way. I rather like all this drama.)

'You shouldn't have left your father,' I protest very faintly, 'if he's just arrived.'

'He's all right. He's drinking French coffee with Maria, my landlady.' He looks me up and down. (Why is this all right with some people and not with others?) 'You look very nice today.'

Well, I have made an effort. I am wearing this spotted dress with a boat neckline that my mother bought for me on a club. And white sandals. And I've let down my ponytail and swept up my hair at the sides with combs, more Rebecca of Sunnybrook Farm than rock'n'roll, you might say. But that's another part of me, as I think you know.

Tamás catches my thought. 'You look like something out of a storybook,' he says.

I glare at him. 'Like something out of the ark, you mean!'

He takes my hand. 'Not at all. You look lovely.'

We make our way along the crisscrossing paths, past the two old men, sitting on a seat, their faces mapped like underground tunnels. We pass a couple trailing behind two girls and a toddler in one of those pedal cars. Men and women, boys and girls walk in pairs off the paths among the trees and shrubs.

Under one wide-spreading tree a family sit around a blanket scattered with plates and sandwiches and home-made cakes: three boys and two girls. The father and mother sit on folding chairs reading papers that rustle in the light breeze. An older girl is sitting leaning with her back against a tree, her full skirt spread around her, her dark hair in a simple ponytail.

For a second I am pure envy. My mother is so much better now but when I was the age of these children she was in some dark place where I could not reach out to her. Picnics in the park were as far away as a dream life on Mars.

Then with a jolt I realise that the girl leaning against the tree is Karen. I nod and smile but she looks through me as though I were glass.

'Is your dance partner not speaking to you?' says Tamás when we get out of earshot. 'The one you danced with? Not so much Sandie Shaw today, hey? More Debbie Reynolds?'

'It was Karen. Yes.' I am put out that she didn't greet me. Maybe she was worried I'll say something to her mother.

'Perhaps she didn't recognise you with your hair down.' He senses my unease. 'You look different.'

'She certainly looked different,' I say. Then I turn and march back to where she is sitting. 'Hi, Karen!' I say.

She looks me in the eye. 'Oh. It's you!'

'You having a picnic?'

She glances at the laden plates. Her parents watch us. 'What does it look like?' she says.

Her mother nods at me over her *News of the World*. 'This a friend of yours, Karen?'

'It's Cassandra Fox. The new lass at work.'

'That's nice.' She returns to her paper. Probably some spicy tale of a vicar and his choir mistress.

I shoot Tamás a telling look and he strolls off in the direction of the bowling green.

'Have you told her?' I whisper fiercely to Karen.

'What do you think?' she hisses. 'No.'

'Nothing?'

'Don't need to. I'm still waiting. There's no sign, no show yet.'

'So it hasn't worked, that powder?'

'No!'

'You need to tell her.'

'You mind your own business.'

'But...' I search in my mind for something strong enough to say. 'You *have* to do something.'

The tragedy of Emma's friend is pouring through my mind like salt. I go across to Karen's mother. 'Hello, Mrs Duncan. I work with Karen...'

Karen is on her feet now and is dragging me towards the bowling green. Her grip on my arm hurts. She is hissing with anger. 'What the bloody hell d'you think you're doing?'

'I was talking to your mother until you pounced on me.'

We stop by the bowling hut, six feet from Tamás, who is keeping a steady eye on the old men on the green.

'You! You have no bloody right to talk to my mother,' she hisses. 'You should mind your own bloody business.'

I shake off her hard grip and say, 'I'm going right back to talk to her if you don't promise me.'

'If I don't promise you what?'

'Promise me you'll tell her. You can't, *can't* do this thing without telling her!'

She grabs me again. 'Listen, you toffee-nosed, pompous bitch! You don't know me. You don't know her. Who do you think you are, prancing in telling us all what to do?'

'Promise!' I shake off her hand again and look her in the eye.

She holds my gaze a second, then looks away, towards the bowlers. Then she pushes my shoulder, laughing shrilly. 'Why don't you just go off with your fancy lad and get some nous yourself before you start telling other people what they should do with their lives? Get away with you.' She gives me another hard push and stalks away.

Tamás is beside me. 'Are you all right, Cassandra? What is the matter with Karen?'

Karen's anger had rubbed itself into me. 'Oh, shut up, will you!' I say, and it's my turn to stalk off right across to the back exit of the park.

He catches me up by the gate. 'Stop, Cassandra!' He has angry pink patches on his pale cheeks. 'What is it?'

I look up into his troubled face and all my anger, even my concern for Karen, trickles away. 'It's nothing, Tamás. Just something.... Well ... that needs sorting out. Nothing.' I take his hand. 'Let's just walk on.'

We make our way through the narrow gate on to the path that leads past Masterson pit, long derelict now, and down towards the wood. If you turn right there it leads to a dammed beck called The Ponds, where people swim in fine weather. My mother swam there with my father; Patsy swam there with her truanting friends; even I swam there once with a girl from school. It is a surprising place. But today Tamás and I walk in the shade of the trees that dip and spread over the park wall. To our left the abandoned brick footings, the derelict buildings and the cast-down wheel tell their own dark story.

Tam catches my glance. 'Once you get through all these ruins there are woods, very pretty woods.'

'I know,' I say. 'You forget. I was born here. I live here.'

He laughs. 'I forget this. You are like a creature from another place.'

I groan. 'The Creature from the Black Lagoon.'

'Not quite that. But strange.'

'Strange? Why, thank you.'

'Strange but nice.'

So we walk on until the pit buildings are left behind and the woodland thickens up and swallows us. The tangle of trees shuts us in and shuts the world out. Shuts everyone out: my mother and her ironies; Patsy and her admonitions of care; Karen with her confusions of despair. But here there is just me and Tamás Kovacs; trees and bushes; birds and scurrying creatures; the smell of the recent rain on the leaves. This, I feel, I can handle. Compared with Karen – whether she's being Debbie Reynolds or Sandie Shaw – this I can handle.

So I can. We hold hands at last. We laugh. Tamás climbs up a tree and makes like a monkey. I laugh till my sides ache and he comes down and kisses my hot cheek. Too soon we emerge from the woods into the streets at the top end of the town. Now we become more sedate, more wary of each other.

We stop at the end of my street. He doesn't offer to walk me to my door. 'That was very nice, Cassandra,' he says. 'We have to walk again. Another day.'

I want to invite him to walk down my street, to come into my house, even if my mother is there. But my tongue is tied and he seems to have other plans. He glances at his watch. 'I need to be somewhere at five. That's if I can get my car to start.'

'Well?' I say, looking up at him in what I think is an appealing manner.

He glances around the deserted street, then

dips his head to kiss me lightly on the lips. 'We will walk again,' he says. 'Next week.'

I plod on home, suddenly very depressed about Karen, about Tamás, about everything. The house is empty and cold. My mother must have gone to bed to read. She does this when she feels extra gloomy.

I light the gas fire and curl up on the sofa with *The Second Sex,* an impenetrable book about the suppression of women that Emma lent me in our third week in college. I am on page seventeen. It's about women but it seems to have little to do with Patsy or Karen. Or Karen's mother. Or my mother. Or me. I think I'm reading it to punish myself because Tam Kovacs has not kissed me. Well, not *properly,* whatever that means. I'll know it when it happens, I'm sure.

Sunday Customs

On Sundays Evelyn always made a traditional midday dinner because this is what her father most wanted. He called her Caroline more on Sundays than any other day. He would say, 'Caroline, only you can make Yorkshire puddings the way I like them.'

The truth was that when Evelyn came from abroad she had to dig out her mother's old Be-Ro cookbook to: a) find out how to make these Yorkshire puddings and, b) how to cook a joint without drying it to a crisp.

Still, no matter how burned or unappetising her food, when it came out of the oven, her father would say, 'I always say, Caroline, that no one can make a Sunday dinner like you.'

After they had eaten their dinner she would settle him down in his chair, a cushion behind his head, turn the Home Service on low and talk to him until he went to sleep. Then she would go back into the kitchen, clean up the Sunday chaos, put away the Be-Ro cookbook, then spread one of her mother's embroidered cloths on the tray, and lay out shop cakes and scones for tea.

Then she would take out her writing case and catch up with her letters. Today it was to Laura, the first friend she made in her flying job.

Dear Laura,

It is absolutely wonderful to hear all your news from New Zealand. To be honest it's really hard to picture you on this farm of yours, complete with gumboots. (I bet you still wear high heels on high days and holidays.) Thank you for the photos. It's amazing how much Nicky and Ben have grown in six months.

I have to say I envy you all that Antipodean sunshine. We've had a few fine days here, it being July. But I think nostalgically about Florida and the Leavises' house by the ocean. (I think of them very often, and miss the busy life I had with them. And the people.)

My father is well. Thank you for asking. That is to say, he is well in body, although sometimes is very forgetful and strange. This can sometimes be hilarious as he tends to think I am my mother.

He loved her dearly so this is not entirely unpleasant. But to be truthful he is not his old self at all and that is heartbreaking.

My work goes quite well. It's never less than interesting at Marvell's. All different sorts of people turn up there. This week's big news is the presentation of the millionth cooker to a Mrs McLochlan. Just think, in this little town they've actually made a million cookers! (I told my friend Tamás about you seeing an advert for a Marvell cooker in Auckland!)

Anyway this cooker's being presented by Sandie Shaw, who's quite a big thing here. She's a jolly good singer although not as sophisticated as the Beatles, nor so cool as those Rolling Stones. The whole thing is a gold tick for me because I helped to fix it up through Mr Leavis! I think it'll be quite a good day for the company and a celebration for the workers too, which is only fair.

In answer to another of your questions, no, Tamás Kovacs is not a *bel-ami* nor anything like that. For one thing, he's nine years younger than me. For another I think it would spoil everything. Tamás is the only real friend I've made since I came home. Don't think I'm not tempted. If things changed between us and it all went wrong (which it probably would) then I'd lose my dear friend and get what? A brief affair? A doomed relationship? To be honest I want neither of these just now. Anyway I have my dad to think about and, quite truthfully, things won't get better there.

And as you well know after the doom of Peter Mallory everything pales by comparison. As I told you at the time, 'Follow that!' Truthfully, if I ever met anyone who had that impact on me even here and now, I would jump at it. I was stupid not to jump at it at the time. But Tamás Kovacs is no Peter Mallory.

Anyway, dearest Laura, keep the letters and photos coming as they are the breath of the outside world for me.

Much love to you, Dean and the little ones.

Evie

PS. Thank you for persisting in your kind invitations, One day I *will* come to New Zealand I am sure. The photos are so enticing (and it would be good to do another long-haul flight). How lucky you are to have that cottage by the ocean! Looks like a storybook house.

One day ... one day I'll join you there!

Evie x

'Evie? Evie? Are you writing letters?'

She looked up to see her father smiling at her, to feel his hand tight on her shoulder. The face that looked down at her was filled with a familiar cheerful radiance. It was his old face, the face of the man she'd always adored.

'Daddy?' She felt she was calling to him through a long tunnel.

'How do you stand this, Evie?'

'What? Writing letters?'

'This awful thing. Me?' A spasm crossed his face like the shadow of a cloud on a sunny day. 'I keep forgetting, I know I forget. There is blank. Then there's Caroline. Then there's you. Then I forget.' He paused. 'I look at myself in the mirror, and wonder, who is he, that man? It's bloody awful, Evie. Bloody awful for you. Awful for me.'

'Daddy!'

'What?'

'You never swear, never!'

He frowned. 'Don't I?'

She tried to breathe easily, naturally. 'Would you like a cup of tea? Coffee?'

He stared at her. 'What?'

'Tea. Coffee? It's a bit early for our proper tea.'

'Shall we have our dinner? Nobody makes Sunday dinner like you, Caroline.' He put his face close to hers. 'You're crying. Why are you crying?'

'We've had our dinner, Daddy,' she sniffed. Then very deliberately she licked an envelope and addressed it to Laura. 'And I'm not crying. I think I might have an eye infection. I used to have it when I was away. Remember?' It was easy to lie when she knew he wouldn't remember.

He did not seem to hear her. 'Why are you crying, Caroline? I don't like it when you cry.'

She shoved her writing things into their box and stood up. She took his arm. 'Come on, Daddy, come through and sit on your chair. I'll tune in the wireless for you. It loses the signal so easily, doesn't it?'

Her tears dried completely as she tucked his rug around him. When she retuned the radio she kissed the silver top of his head and went back into the kitchen. Deliberately she made her mind a blank. She stopped herself from thinking about her mother and father, the past and the future. She started to think about the itinerary she had made for Mr Priest about the plans for the presentation. She would probably get it back from Mr Priest tomorrow with lots of changes. He liked to think he was laid-back but he could be a real nit-picker, sometimes.

Just then there was the click of a ring on the window followed by a rattle on the door. She ran her fingers through her hair and bit her lips to make them red. No time to refresh her lipstick.

She opened the door. 'Tamás Kovacs! You're a sight for sore eyes!' She beamed at him.

Tam had thought that this weekend of all weekends he should call on Evelyn.

He'd had a long lie-in, a goulash with Maria and the kids for lunch. Then the factory. Then his father bursting in on them like the sun. Then the fiasco with the car. But today as well he'd had the walk with Cassandra Fox in the park. He'd enjoyed that but still couldn't break his word to Evelyn. She always made him welcome, went to some trouble. The old man could be welcoming if he were on form. Tamás liked to watch the relationship between them – father and daughter – a delicate thing. The boys in the factory called fragile things *femmer*. For all her glamour and self-control, at home he knew that Evelyn was *femmer*.

He watched as Evelyn uncovered the tea tray, lifted the cups and saucers and set them out. Every movement was graceful. The china rattled thinly on the Formica kitchen table. She put on the kettle and went in to check on her father. 'He's asleep. Let's just sit here.'

From the first day Evelyn had fascinated him,

with her slender good looks and her gentle style. Beside her the other women he had met – despite being jolly and very friendly – had begun to seem trite and kind of *everyday*. The road between feeling like that and falling for Evelyn had been a short one. For months he looked forward to her daily arrival in the office at the start of the working day, even while he feigned disinterest. Then they started sharing their packed lunches and he was in Heaven.

All that was at an end now, of course, but he had been touched when she'd said to still call for tea on Sunday. It was a proper affirmation of their friendship and he couldn't let her down.

And, strangely, now he had no desire to get past that point with Evelyn. Two days can make quite a difference. All he wanted now was to be her friend.

'So,' he nodded at her writing box, 'writing letters?'

'Just one. To my friend Laura in New Zealand. The one who married the pilot and emigrated. Now instead of nurturing a plane full of passengers she nurtures a thousand sheep.' She handed him a plate and he forked a piece of layered cream cake.

'Do you ever wish–'

'That I was a world away, nurturing a thousand sheep? No, thank you!'

'Not really that. That you had settled for something more ... exciting than all this.' He glanced round the small neat kitchen.

She glanced at the door through to the front room. 'What choice have I, Tamás?'

'But there must have been someone who wanted to ... give you a different life. You're so ... well ... very beautiful... And kind,' he added hurriedly.

She smiled at his earnestness. No man from around here would have been so direct, even in such a polite way. It took a foreigner. 'To be honest there have been two *someones*. One was an American who came here to study painting. And the other was a musician who lived in Somerset.'

'They didn't work out?'

'Well, the American was related to my boss, so it was difficult. The musician went to live in Mexico. But I liked my job with the Leavises too much to follow him as he wanted. The children I took care of were too precious to me. But of course they started to grow up. Nothing stays the same.'

'Do you regret all that? Not having all those things? The things you were used to?'

She stared at him over the top of her tea cup. For the first time he noticed the fine lines around her eyes. 'Isn't there a French song? "Je ne regrette rien". Isn't that it?'

He smiled. 'This is quite a philosophy.'

'You have to treasure the moment. The experience. The friendship. The taste. The smell.'

He left that for a second. 'I treasure each moment of our friendship, Evelyn. You know that.'

'And I yours. That's why–'

He hurried on, 'And I like it as it is. Spending this time with you. This is OK. Nothing further. We will be friends in old age, you and I. This way I'll last longer in your life than the American or the artist. I know it.'

She took a deep breath and relaxed. 'Yes, we will visit each other in wheelchairs, you and I, and exchange pictures of our grandchildren...'

'Caroline? Caroline? Are you there?' Her father's plaintive, feminised voice came through the door. 'I'm hungry. Have you got the dinner on yet? I do like your Sunday dinners, Caroline.'

Tamás stood up. 'I will go. My father has turned up on my doorstep and I have some figures to work on. Sometimes I wonder if this presentation will be worth all the work.'

'You know it is.' Evelyn stood up and kissed him on the cheek. 'You must go out and find a really nice girl, Tamás. Waste no time. Find a girl who will be the mother of your children, the grandmother of your grandchildren. Get started on the bit of your life that's not all Grafton.'

'Caroline! Where are you! The wireless has gone funny.'

Tam saw the tears standing in her eyes and felt helpless. Then she turned. 'Coming, Daddy. And it's Evie, not Caroline. Try to remember. Why don't you try? I really want you to try and remember.'

A Chosen Life

For the last ten years Patsy O'Hare had lived with her black cat, Pearl, in a small flat on a battered estate behind Grafton High Street. The estate was built after the war to house the influx of new Marvell workers, as well as the more aspirational miners who'd had enough of the low pit rows and were willing to pay higher rents.

Patsy had reached thirty-eight by the time she escaped the heavy-duty clasp of her father and brothers in their pit house. She finally got to the top of the housing list by dint of her key-worker status at Marvell's. The first thing she did was to get a kitten, which she called Pearl, after her mother's sister who had been a bright light in her childhood.

Since her mother's death her father and her last two remaining brothers had got used to her fettling for them and missed her sorely when she went. For the first few weeks they brought her their washing in a big canvas flour sack. That stopped the day her brother Ike brought the usual sack and she shoved it back into his arms. 'Here, do your own washing,' she said. 'I'm doing it no longer.'

He looked down at her, his heavy brow bristling with disbelief. 'Me? I canna wash clothes!'

'Neither could I when I was thirteen and Mam died. But I learned. You're thirty-six. It shouldn't be beyond you.'

'Our da'll play war.'

'You just tell him to get another wife and work her to death like he did our mam,' she said. Then she shut the door in his face.

An hour later her father was there, sack in hand, hammering on her door, asking her what she thought she was about. She opened the door and faced him. 'Me? I'm about going to work every day from half-past seven till five. I'm about doing my job at Marvell's, earning my money, keeping it for myself instead of tipping up to you. I'm about minding my own bloody business. That's what I'm about. I'm about me!' It was the longest speech she'd ever had with him and it came out very sweetly.

'Bloody unnatural, you are. I always said that. Mouth like a sewer, no natural feelings.'

She grasped the lapel of his best suit, the one he always went to the club in on a Sunday, and the sack fell from his hands. 'That's a bloody fine thing coming from you. How many nights did I have to fight you off when you came in from the pub? Unnatural? I'm not the one that's unnatural.'

He pushed at her so hard that she fell into her own hallway. 'Like I say, bloody unnatural. Ugly as sin. I was doing you a favour. What feller would ever look at you?' He picked up the sack. 'I wouldn't want your filthy talons on my things anyway. You're a bloody witch, livin' here with your cat. Nothing but a witch.'

Patsy had not spoken to him or her brothers from that day to this. She felt no loss. Marvell's had become her family, people like Karen her young sisters. Her little flat became her private kingdom. She had it arranged to be the very antithesis of the larger pit house, that crucible of endless labour involved in keeping three grown men clean, fed and afloat. Her flat was neat and sparely furnished, easily maintained by a one-hour flick round on a Sunday morning. She had almost stopped cooking: cornflakes for breakfast: cheese or sandwich-spread sandwich for packed lunch; tinned beans or spaghetti on toast for adequate after-work suppers. On Saturdays she treated herself to bought high teas in Carricks in Durham City. On Sundays she no longer made the heavy-duty traditional Sunday dinners. Instead she would fry a *nice* piece of steak or a *nice* New Zealand chop with chips, fried *nice* and crisp in her deep pan, and eaten with tinned marrowfat peas. Delicious!

On the Sunday after the rock'n'roll competition she had chosen the chop option. She made her dinner about five in the afternoon and ate at the kitchen table with the *News of the World* spread out in front of her. She was just reading about a vicar who had been up to no good with his choir mistress when there was a knock on the door.

She dismissed the thought that it might be one of her brothers or her father, wiped her hand on a tea towel and opened the door a crack.

Stevie Hunter was standing there in cavalry twills and a check shirt. He was swaying very slightly.

Patsy opened the door a bit further. 'Stevie, what's up?'

He grinned. ''Lo, Patsy. Surprise!'

No trouble then. 'What is it, Steve? What do you want?'

He glanced at the door, then past her into the hallway. 'I was at the club then when I got home my ma sent me across here with a set of curtains for my auntie.' He giggled. 'She likes me out of the house of a Sunday afternoon. She and my dad–'

'Shut your mouth, Steve.'

He stared at her. 'Well, anyway, my mam's got new curtains and my Auntie Renee fancied our old ones. She lives in the flat downstairs from you.'

'I know where your Auntie Renee lives!' she said crossly.

'I've just told her I'd pop up and see you.'

'Well, then. Now you've seen me.' She made to shut the door.

He leaned against the doorjamb, his foot casually on her threshold. 'Don't be narky, Patsy!'

A note in his voice made her open the door wider again. 'I want to know just what it is you're after. No bullshit, Steve!'

'What I want to know is what's the matter with Karen?'

'Don't know what you mean.'

'Look! Me and Karen started Marvell's the same day. We go back. I know her. And I know she was right off form last night.'

'She won the competition,' Patsy defended her friend.

'Nah. That was down to that Cassandra. Now that was a surprise. Nice little mover. Thought she'd be too toffee-beaked for that.'

'Karen always puts on a good show.'

'But not last night.'

'So, why are you so interested in Karen all of a sudden?'

'Like I say, we go back. And then Stan Laverick and me–'

'Not one of those bloody bets, Stevie! I'd'a thought better of you. Not him, like.'

'That's just a bit of fun, Pats. You know what the lads are like.' He paused. 'Seriously, I really think she was a bit ... well ... funny last night. Not the usual ... well, you know. Then, when I was having a drink today, I thought about her and Charlie Priest. He's got an eye for her. Everybody knows that. Is he coming on too strong, like? Is all this about him?'

Patsy sniffed. 'I don't know nothing about any Charlie Priest. I tell you what, Stevie. It looks to me like you've got a bit of an eye for our Karen yourself.'

His head went down. 'Wouldn't get a look in, me,' he muttered morosely. 'It'd take more than a bet with Stan to make anything happen.'

'You're right there, son. Now, will you go home and sleep it off or are you going to stay there all day and let my dinner get clay cold?'

'You're right. Pats. I might be just a bit the worse for... But you just tell that Karen, if she needs owt – anything at all – just tell her Steve's around. Tell her that. Hard for me to say it to her face, like. She'd laugh.'

She looked him up and down. 'I can tell you're the strong, silent type. Come to think of it, you look a bit like Rock Hudson.'

'You'll tell her?'

'I'll do that. Now – get yourself away home.'

She closed the door with a click and turned the key in the lock. She wondered how she had missed this thing that Steve clearly had for Karen. Too bothered, of course about the thing Karen had for Charlie Priest. An earthquake waiting to happen, that.

She sat back down in front of her chop and chips and looked around her neat spare kitchen. She was pleased she'd resisted inviting Steve inside. He was a nice enough lad. But no one had crossed her threshold since she moved in. And that was the way she liked it.

Golfing Rage for the Under-Twenties

I don't know why I'm so angry when I get home from the park but I am.

Tam Kovacs asks me to go for this walk and I do. We have this nice walk. We have this civilised talk. He holds my hand. He kisses me on the mouth. I feel really comfortable and think the two of us might go on to the Roma Café, put some music on the juke box, have some coffee and keep on talking. Then we might go across to the Odeon and watch a Sunday film. These are usually black-and-white war epics, cheap for Sunday showing. Sunday night at the Odeon is famous for its courting couples. The fact that the back two rows of seats are doubles is a big attraction. They facilitate the heavy petting and more. Don't get me wrong, I'm not speaking from experience. I went there once with my mother (to see *Captain Horatio Hornblower* for the third time – she's a big fan of Gregory Peck). The scuffles and low moans from the back row penetrated even the loudest of the French naval guns. Surprisingly my mother, far from being disgusted, was quite amused by this. I wondered some time later whether she and my dad made me on those back seats. I do know I was born only four months after their wedding. I've seen the certificates.

But of course all this is theory. Tamás Kovacs never asked me to sit on a park bench, much less in the Roma Café or the back row of the Odeon.

'Nice afternoon?' says my mother, looking up from her crossword.

I throw myself on the hard leather sofa. 'All right.'

'Where d'you go?'

'To the park. I went for a walk in the park with Tamás Kovacs.'

'Nice day for it.' Her eye wanders back to her crossword. 'Nice boy that.' She nods towards the mantelpiece. 'I had a card from Constantin, his dad. Dinnertime post yesterday. Seems he's around this week.'

I pick it up.

Dear Linda.
My Tamás tells me he visited you. I hope you keep well. I am here in Grafton this next week and will call.
Your grateful friend,
Constantin Kovacs

On the other side is a picture of Edinburgh Castle and a man in a kilt playing the bagpipes.

'Nice,' I say.

'He's a nice man.'

She peers at the paper. '*Greek starter.* Five letters. Any idea?'

'*Alpha.*' The word fell out of my mouth without me even thinking.

'Ooh. Clever girl.' She scribbles the letters in the squares. 'It fits. Now...' Her eye wanders down her list of clues.

She's not really interested in any of my tales about the park or anything else. I can't blame her. I have nothing to tell.

She looks up again. 'A card came for you as well. Did you see it? I put it into your book. Inside, so it wouldn't float away.'

The postcard is tucked into *The Second Sex.* I'm still not past page thirty-one. The existential musings of some Frenchwoman are fading into insignificance beside the reality of Marvell's and Tam. And Karen. And Patsy. They exist all right.

The card is filled with Emma's tiny writing.

Dearest Cass (*she's the only one I let call me that*), This place is utterly gorgeous. I have blisters on my fingers and raging pokers on my back. But it's worth it, believe me. There's this nice Cirencester boy here, who's at King's. We walked hand in hand to the *auberge* and drank new wine together. Not sufficient privacy for much else here. Although Jeanette keeps managing with various Frenchmen. I have to console myself with reading the steamy bits in Françoise Sagan. Do you know she wrote *Bonjour Tristesse* when she was just our age? I can tell you, we are way behind her in the s** stakes. Way behind. I do so wish you were here. It's all a great laugh but we do miss you.

Em xx

My mother looks up again. 'Now then! *Golfing rage for under-twenties.* What do you think?'

'Will you bloody well shut up?' I scream the words at her and race up the stairs. I tear off my clothes and leap into bed, pulling the quilt over my head to muffle the sobbing. When that subsides I am still buzzing. My body's aching right to the core. I want to touch myself but I resist. I know Jeanette probably does it but me and Emma think it's a sad sign of desperation in a woman. She calls it self-abuse.

I jump out of bed, put on the dim overhead light, and look at myself in the dressing-table mirror: eyes wide, staring; hair lumpy and unkempt, unconfined by its usual bedtime plait. My brow is too wide, too big. I root around in my still half-unpacked college trunk and find my sharp fabric scissors. Then I part my hair, comb down the front hair and start to chop away. In ten minutes I have a pretty reasonable long fringe hanging down over my eyes. The buzzing feeling in my body has fizzled away, as though the scissors have cut that away too.

Yawning, I plait up my back hair and jump into bed. I go on to have the best night's sleep I've had since I got home.

The next day I get up earlier than usual for

work and make the tea before my mother appears. On the kitchen table is her crossword, completely filled in. I check the *Golfing rage for the under-twenties* clue and see she has pencilled in the answer: *T-e-e-n-a-g-e-r.* In the white margin she has put three exclamation marks.

I laugh out loud at this. I laugh so much that my sides hurt.

'What's so funny?' My mother comes down the back stairs fully dressed for work. Right down to her lipstick. She blinks at me. 'What in grief have you done to yourself?'

I touch my fringe. 'I'm changing my style.'

She laughs at this, and I laugh too. We don't pat each other or hug each other as would have happened with Emma. But we laugh till we cry. Together. That really is quite nice.

Not Quite Grace Kelly

Millie Priest was getting really, really mad. The feeling crawled through her like snakes. Normally she knew she was a kind sweet person; a loving wife. But there were times when the iniquity of others just made her so mad. This feeling had come over her a couple of times when she was young: once when her aunt had refused her the money for a school trip to Norway; the other when her mother said she wasn't quite sure about Charlie – 'I don't know, Millie. Perhaps he's a touch too common?'

243

Those times, respectively, she had slashed the tyres of her aunt's little delivery van with the carving knife and vandalised the shop, setting a very small fire in the storage room. The police were called but they all pretended it was soldiers from the local barracks playing havoc. Nothing was done.

The Sunday when she got back from the golf club she went straight upstairs, took all Charlie's suits out of the wardrobe and threw them into the corner of the spare bedroom. She took all his shoes from their boxes, put them in the bath and then covered them with water from the hot tap.

She looked on her work and it was not enough.

She picked up the phone and rang Stan Laverick's number. 'Stan?' she said sweetly. 'I wonder if you could help me?'

Later she felt like purring with pleasure when she saw the smallness and meanness of the row where Evelyn Laing lived. Catch her living in a street like that! Even the flat above the shop, where she had lived before she was married, had more style than this.

She'd had to be quite cunning with Stan Laverick but he had swallowed the tale about Charles needing papers that Evelyn had brought home to work on, and coughed up the address. 'I wouldn't a' known,' he said. 'But my cousin lives down the road from her. Number ten. She'll be number six.' He paused. 'Charlie all right, then?'

'Charles is fine, Stan. Down the golf club. Preoccupied at the nineteenth hole with his cigar and whisky. You know what he's like. Asked me to run this errand for him.'

Made bold by the drabness of the street she knocked hard on the door, tapping her foot impatiently until it creaked open. A silver-haired man in his sixties stood there and looked down at her. He was good looking, but he had to be too old for a husband or fancy man unless Evelyn *Miss Snooty* Laing was even weirder than Millie had thought.

The man's pale, frowning face broke into a smile like sunlight striking water. 'Caroline! At last! I've been waiting for those Penguin biscuits.' His eye dropped to her hand, empty save for car keys. 'Oh,' he said sadly. 'You forgot! I was sure you'd remember?

Millie blinked. 'You must be mistaken. Mr er... I'm Mrs Priest. I don't know any Caroline.'

His face fell. 'I was sure you were Caroline.'

She peered past him. 'I've come to see Evelyn Laing. Is she in?'

He put his finger to his lips. 'Shshsh! She's asleep. She had this visitor who came and went rather faster than usual. I heard his voice. Then she sat with me to listen to the wireless and then she went to sleep. My Caroline went to sleep, you know.' His eyes filled with tears. 'Evie left me to go to her place called sleep, so I had to watch for Caroline.' He put his head on one side. 'But you don't seem to be her. You don't have any Penguin biscuits, do you? Do you?'

Irritated by his quavering voice Millie pushed past him into a narrow kitchen that was barely more than a corridor. She glanced sourly at the march of fine china in a display shelf by the window. How out of place was that, in a hovel

245

like this?

She went through to the front room to find Evelyn Laing pulling herself up on the sofa, still looking elegant even though her fine hair was awry. Millie furiously blanked out an image of Grace Kelly in *Rear Window*. This stuck-up cow living in this hovel was no film star.

Evelyn frowned. 'Mrs Priest? What is it? Is something wrong?'

Millie glanced around the small room, cluttered with the dainty detritus of a forty-year marriage. The most modern things here were a miserable little television and a Bakelite wireless: not a single piece of teak in sight. Like something out of the Dark Ages.

Evelyn stood up. She was taller than Millie. 'What is it, Mrs Priest? What's the matter? Is something wrong with Ch– with Mr Priest?'

Millie pulled herself up to her full height. 'You're the matter, lady. You're what's wrong!' She was seething. Behind her she could hear Evelyn's father start to mumble, 'No! No!'

Evelyn said, 'Daddy, you go in the kitchen and sit by the table. Everything is fine here.'

Daddy! Like the woman was in some play or film. Nobody round here called their father *Daddy!* Not even in Millie's family, and *they* were a cut above most people in Grafton.

Evelyn shut the door behind her father. 'Now, Mrs Priest. How dare you – how dare you come to my house and distress my father like this?'

Millie cast an eye round the room. 'House? And if I may say, the old man's easily distressed.'

That was when Evelyn got hold of her arm in a

vice-like grip and made for the door. 'Out! Get out of my house!'

Millie wriggled hard. 'I just wanted to know the style of the woman who's got her claws into my Charles.'

Evelyn let her go. She grinned. 'Charlie? Me? You must be joking.'

Millie looked up at her. 'Don't you laugh at me, lady!' Then she slapped Evelyn really hard. When she brought her hand away there was a red patch on Evelyn Laing's white cheek. Millie felt a surge of satisfaction.

Evelyn rubbed her cheek. 'You mean it,' she said soberly. 'You really think Charlie and I...?'

'You bet I mean it!' said Millie. Suddenly tears welled up in her eyes and started dripping down her cheeks.

Evelyn stared at her. Then, 'Look, Mrs Priest. Millie, isn't it? Why don't you sit down and we can talk?' She backed Millie into her father's big cushioned chair by the gas fire and sat her down. Then she herself sat on the small footstool. 'I wasn't laughing at you, Millie. I promise you. I was laughing at the mere idea of me being like that about Mr Priest. He's a good boss. Kind enough in his own way. Makes you want to work your socks off for him. But no, I'm not carrying a torch for him, nor him for me! I promise you.'

Carrying a torch! Listen to the woman! Millie glanced around the room. A little flame under that pile of newspapers would make quite a torch.

'Millie! Are you listening?' Evelyn touched the forearm she had so recently gripped hard. 'There is nothing happening with me and Charlie, I'm telling you.'

'Well,' Millie sniffed, 'who was that bloke who was here today? The old man said there was a man here today.'

Evelyn raised her eyebrows. 'He remembered my visitor? He doesn't remember much these days.'

'That was my Charlie, wasn't it? I know it.'

Evelyn laughed then put a manicured hand to her still red face. 'Oops! Sorry for laughing. But no. It wasn't Charlie.'

'I bet it was,' said Millie sulkily.

'It was Tam Kovacs. The one who was with me at the party.'

Millie raised her eyebrows. 'That one? I thought he was far too–'

'Young for me? Well, you and I might agree on that. We're just good friends, honestly, me and Tam.'

Millie stared at her. 'A man and a woman can't be just good friends, There has to be something in it.'

'D'you think so? To be honest, I've had some great women friends when I was travelling round. But most of the good friends I've had in my life have been men.'

'I bet! You're just the type.'

Evelyn stared at her. 'Do you have to be so very...'

Millie scowled. 'So very ... what?' She mimicked Evelyn's accent.

'So very small minded ... so very Grafton?'

'Ha! D'you know what, lady? You're a snob, just

a bloody old snob.' Then the tears started to flow again.

Evelyn shook her head, stood up and handed Millie a white handkerchief from the sideboard drawer, then waited for her to mop up the fresh flood of tears. 'Now then, come out with it. What on earth's the matter with you? Tell me! You've burst into my home. I have a right to know.'

Millie sniffed. 'My Charlie's distracted. Something's going on. I feel it. Here.' Millie touched herself on her breastbone. She wondered why she was telling this not-quite-Grace Kelly stranger things she wouldn't tell her best friend. But then she didn't have friends really. Just family at the other end of England, and the wives of Charlie's colleagues, who were too busy minding their own and their husbands' backs to be friends.

'Millie! You've got to realise he's distracted by all this stuff going on at Marvell's. It's a big week, this week, with this Sandie Shaw thing. It's taken a lot of fixing, believe me. He's had us all run off our feet.'

Millie pouted. 'It's not just that, I can tell.' Feeling suddenly very tired she searched round in her head. 'There is somebody around. Somebody in his head. I can feel it. Don't you look at me like I'm an idiot! I can smell it on his breath, see it in the shade of his eyes.'

Evelyn was very still for a moment. 'You really *do* love him, don't you?'

'Love him? Course I do.' Millie gazed at her. 'Look! I know women like my Charles. Course they do. He's an attractive man and he has a say in things. Women like that in a man. And I know

249

he can be a flirt. That's his way. Some women think that's it. But they don't know him. There was this woman a couple of years ago – I had to make him sack her.'

Evelyn frowned. 'So you came here on a Sunday night to threaten me with the sack?'

Millie looked round the cluttered room. 'I made a mistake, now I come to think of it. You're not his type. Too classy ... too old, to be honest. I've always felt safe with my Charles, if you want to know. Whoever he has his bit of a flirt with. He never chooses anyone with class, 'cos he's got me. He likes his flings young and tasty. Easy to drink up, just like a cocktail.' She laughed a bit too loudly. 'But this time I thought it had to be you and that got to me. You're like me, you see? Got a bit of class. He likes that best of all, does Charles, but he's got that in me. But if you'd got to him I wouldn't be safe. See?'

Evelyn stayed silent.

Millie went on, 'And it's important for me to be safe just now because I'm expecting, see? Having a baby? My Charles seems thrilled, really thrilled. But you can never tell with Charles, can you?' She stood up and put her clasp bag under her arm. She sniffed. 'You won't tell him I came, will you? Or that I told you about me being in the club?'

Evelyn shook her head.

Millie smiled too brightly, 'Good. That's all right then. Cleared the air, haven't we, Evelyn?'

They made their way past Evelyn's father, who had tipped out the knife drawer and was placing the cutlery in size order on the table. At the gate

Millie looked up at Evelyn. 'What's up with him, your *daddy*, then?'

Evelyn shrugged. 'Don't know really. He gets confused. He was heartbroken when my mother died.'

'Men!' Millie said briskly. 'Never even knew nothing about them till I met my Charles. All aunties and grandmas in the shop where I grew up. Charles was a revelation, I can tell you.'

Evelyn watched her get into the low-slung Capri. 'I bet he was,' she murmured. As she walked back down the yard, for the first time ever she felt sorry for Charlie Priest. It looked like he had quite a bit to put up with. Then for a second she was angry with herself for allowing that irredeemable woman to harangue her in her own home.

She went into the kitchen. 'Now then, Daddy. Let's get these knives back into the drawer, shall we?'

He looked up at her, grasping the small sharp vegetable knife in his hand. 'She didn't bring me Penguin biscuits,' he said. 'I was mad at Caroline because she didn't bring biscuits.'

She unpeeled his fingers from the knife. 'But it wasn't Caroline, Daddy. Our visitor was not Caroline. I keep telling you she has gone, don't I? I keep telling you! That woman was just some stranger. Just some mad, bewildered stranger. A bit like you.'

251

Fringe Benefits

Monday

It's only when I am clocking in at seven twenty-five on Monday morning that I start to worry about what I'll say when I see Tamás Kovacs again. It seems a world of time since I parted from him after our walk in the park, since I flared up at my mother and inspired her crossword solution.

I spent much of the night dreaming up conversations with Tamás, where, as he makes his abrupt departure, I casually say to him some witty thing about whoever the woman he was meeting, such a woman couldn't touch me. Then there was this scene where I forestall him and ask him to take me for coffee at the Roma café, then to the pictures to see Paul Newman in *The Silver Chalice*. (It's on. I checked that out this morning, from the bus.) Then in my dream Tamás says OK, that would be nice, he can easily put off his urgent appointment. Then I ask him about the appointment he's willing to miss and it's some harmless thing about his father. Then of course we kiss. I can feel his lips on my jaw-line, on my brow.

Emma says that when someone gets into your dreams it shows they're significant in your life. I dream all the time about my mother, so that might be proof of something.

So, after all those dream conversations how can I be ordinary with him today? I am now quite, quite mortified at the reality: that yesterday he went off at five o'clock because I was so plain boring he couldn't bear to waste any more of his time on me. I am also mortified by my dreaming and feel he'll take one look at me and know. He'll be able to tell, I'm sure.

These dismal thoughts are smashed to pieces by the whooping and whistling (Karen former, Patsy latter) as I take my seat on the line.

Patsy grins. 'Been at your hair with a knife and fork, honey?' She's busy stowing her bags under the bench. All along the line women of all ages and sizes are doing the same. I do the same myself. We're like a line of Tiller girls going through their motions.

'So who did that? Cut your hair with a knife and fork?'

Karen's smile is not so broad. And she has tried to cover the shadows under her eyes with make-up.

'I did it myself last night.'

The conveyor starts to hum, gearing itself up for the day.

'That explains it,' says Patsy. 'Did you know it's lopsided?'

I put my hand on it to touch it. 'It feels straight.'

'It's crooked. I'll fix it at dinnertime in the lav,' says Karen. 'I've got my scissors here. I'm not saying you suit it, mind. We got used to you looking like Dorothy on the Yellow Brick Road. And now you're looking like ... well, Lassie.'

'Ha!' laughs Patsy. 'That's it. You're more like Lassie now. Wait till young Stevie sees it. He'll have your life.'

Me, I'm now thinking wait till Tamás Kovacs sees it. He'll be really, *really* pleased he didn't take me to the Roma Café last night. In my head I start to write a letter to Emma describing all these disasters but making them funnier than they really are.

'O-oh! Clickety-click! Someone's gunna be late,' says Patsy gleefully, nodding along the line.

The tall blonde woman from the production office is tip-tapping on high heels along the gangway, in a hurry to get to work. Her fair hair is piled smoothly on her head and she's wearing a green straight skirt that just reaches her knees and a pale green blouse with oversize sleeves. She's very elegant.

'See that handbag?' says Karen. 'Cost a month's wages, that.'

'A woman on the bus says that lass is Tamás Kovacs fancy bit and, like I said to her, if that's the case she must enjoy a bit of cradle-snatching.' Patsy's round flat eyes gleam in my direction. 'But I told her she's got duff information as our Tam O'Shanter was dancing attendance on our Cassandra here all Saturday night. Wasn't he? Walked her home, didn't he?'

I shake my head. 'Me? I know nothing about anything, Patsy.'

I'm rescued from further interrogation by the long, nerve-jangling whine of the buzzer. Now we're all part of the machine and for a while we don't have to speak, we don't even have to think.

254

Penance

Charlie Priest came to work in dark glasses. He'd worn them from time to time before, after watching *The James Dean Story*, and any Elvis Presley film. He occasionally wore them when he had a hangover. This Monday morning he did not have a hangover but he had endured a bad night. He'd walked on eggshells through the darkened house, said a humble, 'Well, good night, lover,' as he climbed onto his side of the bed. Then when, after five minutes he put a tentative hand on Millie's thigh (their old signal), she'd kicked him. Kicked him! That was new.

That was when he slipped out of bed, and into the back room, disturbing the pristine purity of the all-white decor with his green silk pyjamas. He tossed and turned, and on the fifteenth turn he was aware of a figure at the door watching him. 'What the...?' For a split second he thought it was his mother but then he realised it was Millie in a strange candlewick dressing gown.

He sat up groggily and clicked on the bedside light. 'What is it? What's that you're wearing?'

'What're you doing in here? I'll have to wash all that bedding now,' she said.

He put out his bottom lip. (It usually worked.) 'You didn't want me in there with you, lover. You kicked me!'

She came to sit beside him. 'You're a big baby,

you know that.'

'I don't like it when you kick me,' he whined.

She put a hand on his cheek. 'You're a very naughty boy. D'you know that?'

He put a hand on her sturdy candlewicked waist. 'I'm sorry. But really, Mill, I don't know what I've done. I'm pleased about our baby. We'll be a family now.' He put his head on her candlewicked bosom and she leaned down and kissed it, just where the hair was beginning to thin.

'Whatever it is I'm sorry.' His voice was muffled.

'You're a naughty boy, you know that?'

He sat up and began to unbutton the candlewick, exposing the vista of the naked bosom beneath. He nuzzled her and kissed each breast separately, running his tongue over its large erect nipple. 'Oh, Millie!' he groaned.

That was when she slipped out of the dressing gown and allowed him to make love to her right there on the pristine white cover. With a true sense of occasion he put on a great performance. He was newly moved and entranced with her flesh, her body. Inside there somewhere was his future, his immortality. Time seemed to expand as Millie teased him, enticed him and kept him waiting in her familiar, skilful way so that when he came it was fireworks: it was a rocket to Mars.

He rolled away. 'That was the best ever, Mill. The best ever,' he gasped. 'You, me and our babe all one.'

She sat above him and pushed his hair from his sweating brow. He looked sleepily into her eyes, which were very bright, her pupils still dilated with passion.

'This is your last, your very last, warning, Charles. No more. From now on it's just you, me and this baby. That's it. No more women.' She paused. 'I went and sorted that Evelyn woman tonight.'

'The post-coital drowsiness left him like a receding tide. He sat up. 'You what?'

'I saw Evelyn Laing and warned her off.'

'Evelyn? There's nothing, I swear...'

'I believe you now I've talked to her.'

'What did she...?'

'She didn't say much, matter of fact.' She paused. 'Well, not after I gave her a crack.' She tapped him on the cheek to demonstrate.

'You hit her? Millie...'

'She was all right, really. That's when I knew it wasn't her,' said Millie calmly. 'But I'm telling you if there is ever another fling, encounter, whatever you call it, I'll not just kick you out of my bed, I'll kick you out of this house and let the world know just how strange you really are.' She stood up and got into the all-enfolding candle-wick. 'Just you think about that, *lover!*'

He made to get off the bed with her.

'No. You sleep it off here. I'll have the bedding to do anyway. You just think on. No more girls. No more anything. Just me and you and the baby. The Family.' She glided out of the room and the door clicked behind her.

That was when he saw the pile of suits in the corner. He leaped up and put them back on their coat-hangers and, swearing out loud, hung them in the spare-room wardrobe.

So Charlie had spent the night in the white bed robbed of his post-coital torpor, tossing and turning, thinking of Millie transformed by motherhood into an intoxicating Boadicea protecting her young, into a madwoman who was not quite recognisable. His passion for her had gone sky high tonight. He had a second and third erection just thinking of her in her rage. Then he thought about her going to see Evelyn. That would have repercussions. He'd have to sort that out. Then there was Karen. Poor little Karen. She didn't stand a chance beside his Millie. Poor little thing.

He was not so enamoured when he saw his shoes floating in the bath the next morning. But Millie eyed them calmly and said it was not her fault. She had started to clean them and got distracted.

So it was a sleep-deprived Charlie who marched through the production office disguised in his sunglasses.

'Evelyn!' he rapped out. 'Can you come in?'

She picked up her notebook and exchanged glances with Tam Kovacs, who was just going out of the office. She followed Charlie into his office and sat down, pencil and pad at the ready.

Charlie took off his sunglasses and looked at her with tired eyes. 'I understand my fool of a wife came to see you last night,' he said.

She lowered her pencil. 'Yes, she did call on me.'

'She tells me she did more than that.'

Evelyn touched her cheek briefly. 'We did talk. She seemed to be under the apprehension–'

'Yes. But we both know she was wrong, don't we?'

Evelyn laughed. 'I certainly do.'

'Well, I've gotta tell you that Millie's pregnant. Not quite herself, you know? Hormones. Is that what they call them? Drive a woman crazy?'

'She seemed really upset.'

'Upset?' Charlie sighed. 'To be honest she's gone a bit crackers, you know? It's in the family. Her auntie was as mad as a hatter.'

'Well, Mr Priest, I promise you I'll say nothing. Nothing. I wouldn't embarrass you.'

He let out a long breath. 'Thank you for that, Evelyn. I appreciate it. You're a lady.' He hesitated. 'I thought perhaps you might be due to move up to the next scale. I can check with personnel…'

'There is no need for that, Mr Priest. No need at all.' She stood up, holding her notebook close to her chest. He noticed, not for the first time, what a fine figure she had: not showy, just short of voluptuous, in fact, but it looked first rate under that pale green blouse that was reflected in the colour of her eyes.

She caught his eye and he had the grace to blush.

He coughed and put on his dark glasses again. 'Thanks for that, Evelyn. Now would you mind getting hold of Stan Laverick for me?'

Time Out

Stan Laverick stood on the unloading bay at Goods Inwards, thinking back on his wonderful weekend. On Saturday he'd watched his son Clyde's team play cricket against Evenwood Juniors and saw him bowl 3 for 20, and score a very creditable 19 not out. Joanie liked the cricket. She took her knitting, sat on the boundary with three of the other mothers and talked away the afternoon.

Stan had watched the match, walked the boundary and chatted to men he knew, most of whom worked at Marvell's. He had laughed and joked with them. ('Joe Harvey'll make a difference for the Magpies. You mark me. At last we're on the up.') He enjoyed all this chat but as he talked, in another part of his mind, he was gloating over just one thing: the fact that he would spend all of Sunday in the Lake District with his friend Leila. It had taken some fixing: a well bedded-in tale to Joanie about this bloke at the club wanting to go sea-fishing at Seaham; borrowing fishing gear and discussing techniques with his brother-in-law; talking Joanie into going off for the day with her mother on a bus trip to Whitby; arranging for Joanie's younger brother to take Clyde to his Sunday cricket match and to mind young Joe: all this so he could go off for the day with Leila in her friend's caravan near

Ambleside. He couldn't wait.

On Sunday his family were still asleep when he got up at six and set off on his adventure. The arrangement was to meet up with Leila in a village off the A68, where they would leave her car among a few others parked outside a garage, waiting for their Monday service. No one would notice an extra car. He had done his research.

He was barely out of Grafton when it started to pour that straight-down, persistent, soft rain so familiar in midsummer. It crossed his mind that Clyde and Joe might not go to the cricket and that Joanie would have a bit of a wet time in Whitby. Never mind. She would do the cafés and the fish-and-chip shops and play a bit of bingo. Joanie wasn't one to complain.

Leila was there sitting in her car when he arrived. At least he thought she was. The rain streaming down the windows made it difficult to tell. He parked in front of her and watched through his wing mirror as her car door opened and a red umbrella poked out, opening like a flower to allow her to get out of the car without getting soaked. The first part of her body he saw was her legs, and her very high-heeled shoes. So, he thought, they wouldn't be tramping the fells. Then he just caught sight of a wide-skirted green dress before she vanished behind the car. Then she was opening the door on the passenger side, backing into the car, closing the umbrella and shaking it before throwing it into the back seat and closing the door with a bang.

Coming into the car out of the fresh rain she brought a breath of carnation, vanilla and

261

orange: a perfume called Habit Rouge, which he'd bought for her on the six-month anniversary of their first meeting. Now she turned to him and his heart lurched at the teardrops of rain on her tightly permed hair. She smiled.

'Well, hello, my pet!' she said. 'We made it!'

'You look really nice,' he said humbly. 'You smell really nice.'

'I have to, don't I, for you?' She leaned across and kissed him on his cheek. He was drowning in her perfume.

'Oh, Leila!' He put a hand up to her face.

She placed it back on the steering wheel. 'Drive! We can't sit here in an alley necking like a couple of teenagers. We have all day, after all.'

He grinned. 'So we do.' He turned the key, put the car in gear, gunned the car and it lurched forward like a kangaroo. She roared with laughter and they were away.

The rain had eased off by the time they had breakfast in a café in Kendal. By the time they were on the Ambleside road the cloud ceiling had lifted and they could see the tops. Stan felt his heart swelling to bursting point at the sights of the mantles of greens and purple on the high plains, the great reaches of stone and shale on the tops. This was all new to him. Holidays for Stan had always been Whitby or Scarborough; Blackpool in the autumn for the Illuminations. Anywhere for a crowd. Joanie was like his mother in her eagerness for being in the bustle of a crowd. Last year's ground-breaking trip to the Costa Brava had been deemed a great success by Joanie, who had said with delight that it was like

Blackpool with the sun. There was even a fish-and-chip shop. He'd enjoyed it all himself. He couldn't deny that.

But this was different.

Leila talked away about things in her life – settling a quarrel over a glass of wine with her neighbour, going to see *The Sound of Music* at Newcastle with her best friend; this brilliant new purple dress she had bought at a bargain price in Fenwick's; this good crack with the boiler man when he fitted a new boiler in her bungalow.

As she talked Leila would touch his knee or thigh to make some comic point or other. This excited him rather too much and he forced himself to cool down, to keep his eye on the road. He loved her chatter, her liveliness, the way she lived in the world like nobody else he had ever met. He could have listened to her all day.

She directed him off the road into a woodland wilderness where there seemed to be hundreds of caravans nestling beneath the trees. They pulled up at a caravan near the edge of the site, over-looked by only two others. She unlocked the door and led him into a well-ordered, well-fitted space that was nearly as big as her bungalow.

She showed him round. 'And here,' she slid open the door, 'here is the bedroom.' The space seemed filled by the bed, its cover crowded with geraniums like his father's perennial garden border. The light in there, filtered through the drawn curtains, was dim and kind.

Leila turned then, and kissed him, drowning him again in the scent of carnation and vanilla. 'You know what I thought, Stan? I thought it would be great to make love on a bed for a change. And take our time.' In her bungalow they always made love on her chaise longue – always in so much of a hurry.

He couldn't help glancing at his watch. It was still only ten o'clock in the morning. She laughed again and touched his face. 'It's allowed, pet. We're outside time here, you and me. We've got all day.'

He pulled her to him hard, then, and kissed her. His fumbling fingers went to the buttons of her dress. She stopped him. 'Wait!' Then she stood on the other side of the bed, unbuttoned her dress herself, stepped out of it and he could see the pull of flesh under her arm as she reached into the wardrobe for a coat-hanger. Her hand went beneath her slip to unclip her stockings from her suspender belt and take them off, followed by her suspender belt and her bra, somehow undone and threaded out of her slip like a frilly snake.

Then she came and stood before him in just her slip, her freed breasts straining against the silk. She grinned at him with some anticipation.

'Now, my treasure, we'd better get you out of yours before you explode.'

Afterwards they went down to Ambleside for their lunch, bought vodka and beer in the off-licence to take back with them. His delirium was sustained on the drive back. For him the sky was extra blue, the lake glittered silver in the sunlight, and the unfolding mountains were ancient and full of wisdom.

At the caravan site families were coming and

going. They passed children in the playground, playing on the swings and shrieking wildly as they went higher and higher. They could have sat outside in the dappled shade but they could not wait to hurry inside, into the dim privacy of the caravan.

They spent the afternoon laughing, talking, drinking and making love. When in the end he couldn't quite manage it she showed him other things that pleased her, all new to Stan. And he loved her then so much that he entered into this kind of play and there was pleasure for him in the giving.

Then at five o'clock she went to the camp shop and brought bread and coffee, and they ate and drank themselves sober so he could drive home.

At the garage where her car was parked he kissed her hand and clung to it, before she wrestled it free to get out of the car. She leaned in at the car window.

'Aren't I a lucky girl? On Wednesday I'll get to see you and Sandie Shaw at the same time!' She winked at him. 'We'll have something to think about then, won't we, you and me? Oh. I had this thought. Maybe you could take another trip over to the coast. Check on the old dear. Or say you are. What about Tuesday?'

He watched her drive away in the cool evening sunshine and tooted back when she tooted her horn at him. Then he drove off with the window open to get rid of the Habit Rouge smell of carnation, vanilla and orange. He was halfway home when he remembered her red umbrella on the back seat, so he pulled in at a lay-by and moved the umbrella into the boot, tucking it away in his fishing bag. Joanie would never look there.

He started to worry just a bit about what he would say to Joanie about the absence of fish. But he needn't have worried. Joanie had just got in herself and was full of the dramas of her day. It seemed there was this old dear who had died on the tour bus and had been taken off by ambulance. Of course, the bus passengers had voted to carry on, as after all they had paid. And as the old dear's friend said, her friend would have liked it that way.

Joanie stopped mid-sentence and sniffed the air. 'What's that?'

Stan waited.

'Beer!' she had said then. 'Stan Laverick! You said you were going fishing, not drinking!'

He had picked up the Sunday paper, still in its morning folds. 'Well, love,' he said, 'let's just say I was doing a bit of both. You know me.'

'Stan! Stan! Are you listening? Mr Priest wants you.' Evelyn Laing shook his arm. 'You're miles away.'

He was still standing on the loading bay at Goods Inward, watching some Italian parts being unloaded. He put his clipboard under his arm and stubbed out his cigarette. 'Tell him not to get his knickers in a twist. I'm on my way.'

Say It With Flowers

At last I'm quick enough with the wiring and don't have to think about it. So I have some space in my head to think about what Patsy just said about the blonde woman and Tamás Kovacs. Since I've been here at Marvell's I've seen this blonde woman a few times: in the office on that first day; passing to and fro on the gangway with a ledger or a sheaf of papers in her hands. She draws lots of attention from the women on the line, but she seems not to notice. She always looks as though she's in some other place. And the men like her. That's clear. She's very smart. There are plenty of smart and pretty women in the factory but then she's taller than most and has that blonde hair. It's not yellowy or peroxide but silvery and soft looking. It reminds me of photographs that Emma has on her desk, of herself when she was a little girl. These days Emma's hair's no longer blonde, just mousy fair. That Evelyn Laing must have some magic potion to keep her hair that way.

I'm certain now in my heart that it was Evelyn Laing who Tamás was rushing off to yesterday when he ran away from me. And I don't blame him. Taking a walk with me must have been like coming back to the infants' class when you're in the juniors'. He must have thought me very quaint and bumbling, beside this Evelyn Laing.

And now, from out of the corner of my eye, I can see the subject of my thoughts strolling down the gangway. I don't need to see Tamás's face; that easy loose walk is now printed on my consciousness. I keep my eyes down on the wiring job, shutting him out of my vision till he gets past. I know he's looking at me. I know he's willing me to look up at him but I don't raise my head. Then he has passed and I allow myself to look at his receding back and the nape of his neck, just where his hair stops.

On the other side of the line Patsy whistles, then lets out a cackle and shouts above the hum of the conveyor belt, 'That's quite a blow-off! Has our lovely lad been wrestling you for your cherry, pet?' She winks at me.

I scowl at her, suddenly hating her for the crude mind that up till now I've quite relished.

Karen saves me from responding. 'Leave off, Patsy,' she snaps. 'You can't let things alone, can you?'

The merriment drains from Patsy's face and I feel sorry that somehow I've caused a rift between these two friends.

'It doesn't matter, really,' I say. 'He never tried anything, Patsy. Maybe I wish he had. Maybe that's the problem.'

This makes Patsy laugh again. Even Karen's hard face softens.

All is saved when Stan Laverick comes bustling up to us, Steve at his elbow. He nods at Karen. 'Charlie Priest wants to see you, lass. Sommat about the flowers for Wednesday.'

'What?' says Patsy, outraged. 'Leave her be! It'll

stop the line!'

Stan sniggers. 'No worries, Patsy. Got my secret weapon here. Stevie'll do a stint. Then Karen'll make up later.'

'How'll I stand it?' Patsy groans. 'Not just one ham-fisted orang-utan but two!'

'Patsy!' I protest, still wiring like crazy. I'm used now to working continuously, no matter who's talking, no matter what's happening. 'That's not fair.'

'All right, pet, you're not so bad now. Quick learner,' she concedes, her hands, too, moving swiftly as she speaks. She throws a glance at Stan. 'If this affects my bonus I'll have that bloody Charlie Priest.'

He grins. 'I'm sure he's shaking in his shoes, Pats. Come on, lass,' he says to Karen. 'We can't keep the great man waiting.'

Without hurrying Karen finishes the jacket she's wiring, puts it onto the conveyor and slips off her seat. She smiles faintly at Steve. 'Don't be slow, or Patsy'll have your guts for garters.'

Steve climbs onto Karen's stool and sets to work. He knows the job but is even slower than me, making me feel smug as well as competent.

Pasty nods at the receding backs of Karen and Stan. 'Wonder what buggerlugs wants with her,' she says sourly. 'Why would he need to talk to her about flowers? What's wrong with bloody Stan Laverick handing down the great man's orders with a few bob to buy these flowers?'

'Sit down, lover,' said Charlie to Karen. 'Help yourself!' He nodded at the tray on his desk, set with two china cups of coffee and a plate of chocolate biscuits. He relished the style of things now in his office: Evelyn Laing had certainly brought a touch of class to his rough-and-ready workplace. She was worth promoting.

Karen sat down but left the tray untouched. 'Stan said something about flowers,' she said. 'For Sandie Shaw.'

'Yeah, we said you'd present them, didn't we?' He pushed an envelope across the desk to her. 'They're ordered. The money for them is in there, lover. Go to the Silver Vase on the High Street. I rang them. They're sourcing some decent flowers from Holland as we speak. You can go off tomorrow at three to pick them up. And put them in a bucket overnight. No loss of pay. I'll sort Stan over that.'

Charlie could have sent the Marvell driver to pick up the flowers. But it kind of tickled his fancy to get Karen to collect them as well as present them. It would be a treat for her. She really was a nice enough kid.

He went on, 'Then on Wednesday, when Sandie gets here, you can present her with the flowers. Best bib and tucker, mind!' He paused. 'There's a bit more in there for your own special expenses.'

He looked at her, feeling some regret that the dark rings under her eyes spoiled her looks today. That was only to be expected, under the circumstances. She'd recover. She was a pretty thing, with her glossy hair and that long black fringe. He had toyed with the idea of telling her to go ahead with the baby. He quite liked the idea of siring two offspring. But then with Millie in such a mad state the situation was far too incendiary even for his delight in taking risks. He had to think of the big picture. That was his job, after all. Thinking of the Big Picture.

'How is it?' he said. 'How are you?'

The words hung in the air between them.

Finally she said, 'It's still there. The powder didn't work.'

He took out a cheroot and lit it. '*So...*'

'So I'm going back tonight. To see the woman in Durham.'

He definitely couldn't make that journey. Millie would be operating a three-line whip into the foreseeable future. 'Tonight? I don't know that I can–'

'Don't worry. I'll make my own way. I wouldn't want you to put yourself out.'

He took a drag of his cigar and let the smoke trickle from his mouth, a trick he'd acquired from watching Humphrey Bogart on the screen. 'Wa-al, lover, I think this is really all for the best. We don't want...' He stopped as she grabbed the envelope and opened it.

She laid out twenty-five pounds. 'That'll do for the flowers.' Another twenty-five pounds. 'That'll do for the woman in Durham.' Another ten. 'That'll do for the taxi home. I'll make me own way there.' She pushed the torn envelope full of notes back at him. 'I'll not be paid off, Charlie.'

Even he flushed then. 'Well, Karen, you know it's difficult, I...'

She stood up and pushed the notes deep into the pocket of her overall. 'Shut up, Charlie. Just bloody well shut up, will you?' The quiet words were drenched with anger. Then she went, leaving the door wide open.

'Evelyn!' he roared.

Evelyn appeared with her notebook.

'Let's get on with some work, for God's sake,' he said. 'This Sandie Shaw thing is getting on my nerves.'

The Arrangement

Karen is very quiet when she gets back to the line and slips into the seat vacated by Steve.

He looks at her quite anxiously. 'You all right, kidder?'

She smiles this empty smile up at him. 'Why shouldn't I be? I got money for those flowers and the afternoon off tomorrow on full pay to go and get them.'

'Right,' he says uncertainly. 'Lucky for some.' And he slopes off.

Then Karen sets away with her work with the energy of a fury. I've never even seen Patsy work that fast. The conveyor can't move fast enough for Karen's done work.

In the end Patsy speaks. 'Hey, slow down, pet,' she says softly. 'Or you'll leave us all behind.'

Karen slows down and up till lunchtime she works at a more normal rate. Then, before we settle down with our sandwiches, she looks directly at me, keeping Patsy out of her eyeline.

'Let's go down the lav now, Cassandra. Make sommat of that haystack of a fringe. It's getting on my nerves looking at you.'

I glance at Patsy, who just shrugs and concentrates on laying out the contents of her plastic box on the bench. 'Yeah,' I say. 'Good of you, Karen.'

In two minutes we are there in the deserted toilet. 'Never anybody here straight off,' Karen says. 'Too busy scrannin' their grub.'

I sit down on the broken chair and she gets out her comb and scissors, moving around me silently, like a professional, cutting very small strands until the shape is absolutely right.

'You should be a hairdresser, Karen,' I say, just for something to say. 'You're good at this.'

'I fancied that when I was at school,' she said. 'But you had to pay to do it. And my mam said there was more money in the factory. Right too, I think. I like it here.' She looks at me through the cracked mirror. 'Would you do me a favour, Cassandra?'

'Yes. Anything. What is it?'

'I need to go somewhere tonight and I need somebody to go with us.'

'Course I will. So where's that? Where do you want to go?'

'It's this woman in Durham. She takes care of things.'

'What things?'

'You know. I told you: babies and all that. Sees them off. Gets rid.'

In this single split second I am enlightened, horrified, scared, sympathetic, frightened. All of

273

those things. In that second I enter the real world at last. I grab her hand, nearly cutting myself on the scissors. 'Karen. You! It's you. The baby is you. You can't see it off.'

She rescues her hand and starts cutting again. 'Will you come with us, then? Straight from work? Or not?'

'Course I will. But,' I hesitate, 'I would have thought Patsy's the one. She's your mate...' I stop when I see the tight fold of her lips.

'I don't want Patsy anywhere near. Not her.' She combs my fringe, lifting it with a bit of back-combing, then combs my hair right through before tying up my ponytail again, loosening the sides for a softer effect. 'There!' she says. 'That's better. You don't look so much like a drowned rat any more.'

I have to say I look pretty good. The long fringe is soft and fine and the general effect is looser, much more attractive. 'Thanks, Karen,' I say. 'That's great.' I look different and now I feel different. And that's not just about the hair.

She tucks her scissors and comb into her overall pocket. 'Well, then. Favour for favour. You'll come with us tonight? Right from work?'

'Sure,' I say. 'Right from work.'

We go back and eat our sandwiches with a very quiet Patsy. Steve, finding us all unresponsive to his jokes, wanders off. It's a relief when the buzzer goes again.

It turns out to be a quiet afternoon altogether. Patsy keeps her head down, Karen works on at breakneck speed, coming round from time to time to supplement my slower efforts. I'm better, but not that good. Stan comes with his clipboard to tell us we are on a production record. Steve lopes by now and then, and stares a bit at Karen, then wanders off. Tamás Kovacs passes our place on the line three times, but I keep my head down.

Just now I am not so bothered about him. I can't think of anything at present except Karen and me going with her to this place, to this woman in Durham. I can't think what will happen. I know my yawning innocence – more properly ignorance – will be no help to Karen at all. I can't for the life of me think why she's asked me and not Patsy to go with her. But in my heart of hearts I'm honoured that she has asked me and I'm determined to be a good friend to her today. I can't fail her. I can't.

Mothering

Karen and I have to walk across to the big outer car park to catch the special Durham factory bus after work. Seems like there are hundreds of these buses, many so old and battered they're more museum pieces than transport, hauled out of their nests for these two lucrative runs of the day: to and fro from Marvell's to all four corners of the county.

There are hundreds of us streaming towards the buses, hurrying to get good seats. 'All these people!' I say to Karen. 'You don't realise...'

She grabs my arm and hurries me on. 'Marvell's not just the lines, you know. Paint shop, tool room, injection moulding, packing, warehouse, plating shop.' We get a front seat in the bus and flop down. The bus is full in minutes.

A spiky-haired girl sitting on the other side of the aisle knows Karen. 'Slummin' it, are you, Karen? Honourin' us with yer company?'

Karen laughs. 'Not bloody likely. Me, I get the service bus home every day. No cheap Marvell buses into Grafton for us.'

'Where you off to now then?'

'Down Durham.' She nods towards me. 'Me friend here has an auntie there and we're going to tea.'

Pleased to have donated a convenient lie, I sit back and listen while they reminisce about starting at Marvell's together at sixteen, and people whom they knew then. Patsy is not the only bit of a character. Marvell's is full of them. The girl knew Patsy, of course.

'Me, I was scared stiff of Patsy O'Hare when I started. Glad to be out of her sight, I'm telling yer. That one could cast you down with an eye. Witchy, I always say.'

Karen laughs. 'She's all right, is Patsy. Bark's worse than her bite, our Patsy.'

It's nice to see her laugh. I've been worried about what we would talk about on this journey, Karen and me. Then a thought of my mother creeps into my mind. Crikey. I haven't let her know I'm not coming straight home. Never mind. She'll hardly notice.

Now they are talking about Sandie Shaw.

''S not right,' the girl is saying. 'We've cleaned

our whole section. There's white paint every-where. Billy, our foreman, says she won't be coming down packing, nor any of the other shops. Just down your end, he says. Seeing as you're on the way to the offices. Billy says Sandie'll only be here a single hour, top whack. Hop off the plane, do the deed. Hop back on. He says Priest says there's no need to shut down things altogether. Says mebbe they might per-suade her to come down our end, but. So we've cleaned all our shop just on the off chance. Wouldn't care, I don't even like Sandie Shaw. The Animals, Herman's Hermits is more my cup of tea. There's no real beat to her. Hers is a cheeky kind of beat.'

'I hadn't heard that,' said Karen. 'That she was only coming down near our line.'

'Yeah, well, Billy says Mr Priest says we can't lose so much work. Not fair, I say.'

'I thought you said you didn't like her.'

'Well, the only time somebody famous comes here and we miss it. Not fair.'

Then they move on to other mutual acquain-tances, name-checking their lives from when they were sixteen. I check my life since I was sixteen. Moira, my now not-so-close friend from school, who has vanished into the army. Then Emma. And Elaine. Then there's Jeanette, though you can hardly call her a friend. My mother. Ditto. That's about it. But now – just maybe – I can count Karen as a friend. She's asked me to do this thing for her, after all. And Patsy, who has showed me peculiar kindnesss. And Tamás Kovacs. I wish I could call him *friend* even to

277

myself. But I can't. Even now he's probably calling on blonde Evelyn. Even now he's probably got his feet under her table. I bet she lives in a smart house, all G Plan and white paint, like you see in the magazines.

'Here we are.' Karen clutches my arm.

The bus is pulling in by the station. I know Durham: the narrow streets, the huge viaduct rearing above us, the castle and cathedral invisible from here but defining the city. The bus station itself is dreary, even though when you look up you can see the viaduct, when you walk right you can see the castle and the cathedral.

We're first off the bus and, still clutching my arm, Karen marches me up through the streets behind the station and stops at a purple door painted with flowers. It's very different from other doors in the street: they are all peeling or painted a glutinous dark green and brown.

We stand looking at the door.

'Is this it?' What a stupid thing to say. Of course it's it. I thought it might look like – what? A cave at the mouth of hell?

'It's a flat.' Karen nods up to a window hanging with crystals that catch the afternoon light. 'Upstairs.'

I shiver. 'What's she like? The woman?'

'She's all right, considering.'

My turn to clutch Karen. 'D'you really want to do this? Really?'

She looks at me in pure misery.

We haven't knocked but a head pops out of the window and a voice shouts for us to come up. We climb these narrow stairs. The room, when we

278

get there, is quite something. Intricate. The woman matches it. A bit ordinary. A bit extraordinary. A bit normal. A bit hippie, maybe. She sits us both down but talks only to Karen.

'How's it been, love?'

'Nothing happened,' says Karen. Her voice is desolate.

The woman glances at me, then back at Karen. 'So-o.'

'What's the next thing?'

'Well, I can do ... the next thing. Only if you're sure.'

Karen looks at her. 'Do you think I should?'

''S not down to me to say yay or nay, sweetheart. But if you're *asking* whether you should, mebbe you shouldn't do it at all. That's why I like to give the powder first. To see if a girl really wants to do this.'

Now Karen starts to cry. 'It's my mother! She'll kill me! Honest she will.'

The woman takes Karen's hands in her own, which are large and unblemished. 'Look, sweetheart. Having a baby isn't a thing you "can't do" 'cos you're scared of somebody. You have to do it 'cos you need to do it for *you!* No other reason.'

Karen just sobs. I hear the sound of her heart breaking. I have tears in my own eyes.

The woman glances at me. 'Look. Cassandra, did you say your name was? Pretty name, that. Why don't you take your friend here and go and see her mother? Talk to her.' She turns to Karen. 'Your friend will help you explain, won't you, Cassandra?'

I'm like a rabbit frozen in the beam of her eyes. 'Yes. Yes,' I stutter. 'I'll do that, Karen. I'll come with you.'

The woman stands up. She's made her mind up even if Karen hasn't. 'That's it then. You go and talk to your ma, love. And if you want to come back again, mind properly made up, then you can.'

Karen cries all the way home. This time we are on the service bus, which seems to take ages. People look at us with curiosity as Karen sniffs and sobs all the way back to Grafton. Me, I keep thinking of those lunch boxes Karen brings to work, carefully packed with exquisite home-made cakes and pies; in my mind's eye I can see the blouses and skirts sewn to order with a tailoress's finish. Surely this woman will fold her daughter in her arms and rescue her from all this worry and pain?

I'm wrong, of course. When we get to the house, after an initial fuss about whether the weeping Karen has been in a road accident or not, her mother clears the immaculate sitting room of all the children, leaving just us and Karen's father and the television with the sound down.

I try to tell her what this is about. Karen can't get it out for sobs.

'She *what?*' the woman shouts at me, her round eyes staring.

'She's pregnant!' I shout back and my voice fills the whole house. The clicking noise of children playing in the kitchen stops. The house is heavy with silence.

'Sure, there's no need to shout,' grunts Mr

Duncan, pulling up a newspaper in front of him.

'Karen's pregnant,' I whisper. 'And I came here with her because she's too frightened to tell you herself.'

Mrs Duncan, a neat plump woman with powdered cheeks, is breathing very hard. 'What?' She grabs Karen's arm. "What have you been up to, you dirty little–'

'Ma-am!' Karen cries the word, mouth wide open like a little girl. 'Ma-am!' she wails.

Mrs Duncan shakes her. 'Who is it? Tell us who it is an' I'll give him...' She glanced across at her husband, still invisible behind his paper.

Karen shuts her mouth tight and shakes her head.

Mrs Duncan pushes her away so hard that she overbalances and falls into a chair. I rush to her and put my arm around her, looking up at Mrs Duncan. I have to admit I'm puzzled. Where's this loving mother who bakes the pies and stitches the buttonholes? My own mother, the inadequate housewife, the depressive crossword obsessive, would never do this. I know that like I know the sun shines.

'And you, lady!' Mrs Duncan turns her ire on me. 'You! The cheek of you! Leading my Karen on like this. I always tell her you sink to the level of the company you keep. She wouldn't be in this state if it weren't for you!'

This even brings Karen out of her storm of tears. 'Mam, it's not like that. Cassandra just–'

'And you, lady! You can get out of this house. I'm not having any bas–'

Mr Duncan's newspaper rattles.

'...I'm not having someone in your state in my house. What about the bairns? What will they make of it?' She reaches down and hauls Karen to her feet. 'Out! Get out!'

I stand up and the woman manhandles us both out of the room and down the hallway to the front door. I glance back and see two little girls and a boy in matching hand-knit jumpers sitting on the stairs watching goggle-eyed as their big sister is thrown out of the house. Mr Duncan is back in the sitting room, lying doggo behind his newspaper.

On the pavement Karen turns to me, her tears drying. 'See? See what I mean?'

Oddly enough I can see that at this moment she's relieved: homeless on the pavement and strangely relieved.

'What now?' I say.

She sniffs. 'Dunno. Not back in there, for sure.'

'You could come to mine,' I say, doubting my own words. 'There's not much room but...'

'Your mother won't want me there.'

I have to smile at this. 'We'll be lucky if she notices.' It's not my mother I'm worried about. It's the house. Our house is a kennel compared with Karen's immaculate place.

Somehow, through her misery, Karen senses my hesitation. 'I tell you what,' she links my arm. 'We'll call round at Patsy's. She might have some idea.'

As we set off through the neat council estate I glance back to see the net curtains twitch in the Duncans' downstairs window. Stupid woman. I'd rather have my mother and my house than

Karen's any day. In fact I'd rather have that abortionist for my mother than her, and that's saying something.

Elements of Love

Although she would never admit it, Linda Fox was enjoying having her daughter at home for her college vacation. She had sensed a sea change in Cassandra after her year away. The child had grown. She was less enclosed now, and had put on some weight, even though she still had her boyish figure. And here she was, making a very decent fist of the factory! Linda knew for herself that was not easy. She'd seen a number of people engulfed and spat out by the unassailable compulsion that was the machine of production.

And hadn't their laughter this morning over the ridiculous fringe been a bit of a breakthrough? Cassandra was altogether too serious for a girl of nineteen. When she was that age Linda had been anything but serious: living in lodgings with no family of her own, she was free to go dancing three nights a week at the Gaiety, and the pictures on Sundays and Tuesdays. She'd encountered a range of boys, who all tried their luck in vain. Of course, most of the boys one met then were either soldiers from one of the camps in the region, or miners, who had been conscripted to be miners during the war. Young Linda, like many of the girls, was drawn to the soldiers because they came from far away and were usually taller and somehow exotic.

Oddly enough the same thing had happened in 1956 when the Hungarian boys came and, with their unusual looks and good manners, stole the girls from the local boys. There had been a few fights in pubs and streets over that. Of course in Linda's time it was the exigencies of the recent war, not revolution, that delivered these good-looking boys to Grafton, into the laps of the Grafton girls.

Erik, Cassandra's father, was a soldier. The son of a solicitor from Barnstaple in Devon, he'd gone straight into the army from school. A wild, funny boy, he'd fallen hook, line and sinker for Linda when they met one night at the Gaiety. After his demob he bought a motor-bike, got a job in the Co-op offices, and stayed on in Grafton to be with her. They married when Linda was four months pregnant and then – just after Cassandra was born – Erik died when his friend's motor-bike crashed into a motor transporter on the Great North Road. They were returning from a visit to Erik's father's house in Devon.

The police – who tutted to Linda about the boys undertaking such a long journey on a small motor-bike – returned to her Erik's wallet, which contained fifty pounds and photos of Linda with Cassandra. There was blood on the money and on the photos. But no matter how broke she had been since – and she had been very broke before she got the factory job – she never spent the money. It was in a box in her bedroom alongside the postcard from Barnstaple from where Erik

284

had written, telling her that his father loved the photos, was now quite reconciled, and would visit them on the train in June. 'Love Erik.' Those last words on the card were blurred now with so much touching.

She had known Erik little more than a year when she lost him. He was a vivid, optimistic boy, confident that they were on their way up. And he loved her. But his love and his loss in that single year had defined and confined Linda's life ever since. In those early years after he died her world was drenched with shades of black and, although she fed and watered the child, they lived a quiet, drab life in this awful house. It was already dreadful when they bought it (Erik had gaily called it a stop-gap) and it deteriorated in tune with her own misery, living with a child on a tiny widow's pension.

Then, reduced to living on toast, she had fainted in the street. The doctor had prescribed a tonic and his receptionist had told her they were taking on unskilled women at Marvell's. The work would be a tonic in itself and the wage would rescue her and her child from starvation. Linda protested that her little girl was only eight and the woman had said airily, 'Give her a key, love. I had my own house key from when I was seven years old.'

So Cassandra became a latchkey kid and Linda went to work at Marvell's, which for the most part she loathed. Funnily enough Cassandra had always seemed proud of the house-key on a string round her neck and each day would come in and light the gas fire so the room was warm when Linda got in from the factory.

In the years since she'd started at Marvell's Linda's world turned back from black to grey and the house was retrieved from the brink. And the child came to no harm. She got into this valuable habit of reading and doing her homework to the last full stop to fill in the time until her mother came home from Marvell's. So, quiet little Cassandra had done well at school and now she was reading herself out of the sink of a life into which her mother had been cast by an incident on the Great North Road in 1946. Linda thought that Erik would be pleased at his daughter growing up so well in her own peculiar way.

After work that night Linda bought fish and chips for both of them on her way home from the factory. She put Cassandra's package to keep warm on a plate over a pan of simmering water on the gas stove. She ate her meal, read the paper, listened to the news and finally washed up her plate and cup and put them away. At six thirty she turned off the gas under Cassandra's tea and turned on the television to watch a new science programme she'd felt attracted to.

At seven there was a knock on the door. She turned off the television and went to the door, regretting the day Cassandra took the key off the string round her neck. 'Drat the girl!'

It wasn't Cassandra.

Linda smiled slightly. 'Tamás! Constantin! How nice.'

'Linda!' Constantin Kovacs smiled his delight.

Father and son were standing there, side by side and peculiarly unalike: one dark and one fair. Hiding her reluctance, she invited them in, conscious of the cluttered room and the fact that her hands and face still had the glaze of the factory on them. She had not even taken off her overall. 'Sit down. Sit down, won't you?' She decided it was rude, really, people calling without notice.

Tamás sat down and looked round. 'Cassandra is not here?'

She shrugged. 'That girl! Not in from work and no sight nor sign of her. Dinner's burned to a crisp. She lives in a world of her own, that one.'

They stood there and looked at each other and then Constantin put a bottle of wine on the table. He looked intently at her. 'You look well, Linda! Better.'

He should know. He had seen her at her worst. She pushed her hands down her overall, whipped it off and folded it over the back of a chair. 'You look very well yourself, Constantin. Blooming.' He did. His grey three-piece suit was well cut. His dark moustache was luxurious. She reached into the sideboard for glasses. 'Would you like to drink your wine?'

'Why not?' he beamed.

The three of them sat down with their glasses of Tokay and talked about Edinburgh, about Marvell's, about all the fanfare of the Sandie Shaw event.

'I hear about this. And my Tamás fixed up for me to attend!' said Constantin. 'The great occasion for Marvell's!' Tamás had very little accent now, but Constantin's English, though perfect, was strongly accented. 'Is that not so, Linda?' he beamed.

It had been Constantin's unremitting good humour that first broke down the distrustful barrier Linda had set up around herself in her early days at the factory. Here was this man, chucked out of his own country, his wife shot, his small son in tow, in a land where he couldn't speak the language and the only job he could find was sweeping up in a factory. And then, when she had started to help him with his English he had laughed and shrugged at his own poor tries to get his tongue round the language. 'Thees wonderful language that says everything and means two things at once. No?' He would click his heels to thank her for helping him. Then, when he began to talk to her about Khrushchev taking over in Russia and the need to break the ice round the Soviet Union, she bought a paper and read about it in preparation for their next conversation. Linda marvelled at Constantin's lack of bitterness as they talked about his changing world. In their lunchtimes they pored over articles about Khrushchev coming to power and the miracle of the Russian sputnik circling the earth. He collected English words like glittering beads and threaded sentences together like exotic necklaces.

As time went on, Linda began again to take care of herself. She had her hair cut at the hairdresser's and began to put Pond's Cold Cream on her face at night.

When – brushing aside her protests – Constantin Kovacs began to call on her at home she tidied the house and put flowers in a jar. One Friday he invited himself to supper at her house. When she protested that she couldn't cook he turned up at eight o'clock with goulash in a Kilner jar in one hand and a bottle of wine in the other. He held them up like victory trophies. 'To thank you for help, Linda!'

That night he had kissed her with some passion and she'd fought him off, confused and peculiarly angry. He never tried that again and things were never again the same between them. He was embarrassed and she was mortified at her own gaucheness and full of regret at a missed chance. Such moments change lives. She saw that now. When, furnished with a reference from Mr Owen, he got an office job in Edinburgh, she wished him well and the tide went out again in her life.

Now Constantin stopped talking about these amazing pictures of Mars that he'd seen in a magazine and was looking at her more closely. 'You seem to be many miles away, dear Linda.'

The small carriage clock on the mantelpiece – a present from Erik's father that arrived by post the week after their marriage; it was the only valuable thing in the house – struck nine. 'Oh?' she said. 'Sorry, Constantin. I was thinking where our Cassandra might be.'

Tamás said quickly, 'Where did she go, after work?'

Linda shrugged. 'I can't say. She said nothing to me.' She paused. 'It's unusual; to be honest. She would normally come straight from the factory. On the other hand, she's her own woman. She

289

doesn't like to be told...'

The men exchanged glances. Tamás stood up. 'I'll go and take a walk around. Walk across to the factory. See...'

'No...' she hesitated, full of fear now. 'She'll be in soon.'

'No harm to take a look, Linda,' said Constantin quietly. 'Let the boy look.'

She shrugged. 'No harm, I suppose.' Her heart was racing.

Then the door clicked behind Tamás, and now it was just her and Constantin, and now she could feel a dull ache just below her ribs where her heart must be. For Cassandra. And for herself.

Constantin came to sit beside her and took her hand. 'Don't worry, Linda. The boy will find her.' She looked at him, tears in her eyes. He took her hand and kissed it, then put his arm round her and drew her close. She breathed out a deep sigh and relaxed, just enjoying the closeness: the rare feel and scent of him. In the circle of his arms she ached with a deep obscure pleasure, as one part of her recognised that, dragged to powerful feeling by her worry for Cassandra, she was free to show herself to Constantin Kovacs in a way that had been impossible all those years ago.

Too late, of course. But just for now she felt very good: even happy.

No Resting Place

Karen tells me Patsy lives in an upstairs flat on the old council estate behind the Victoria Park. We climb up to an outside walkway lit every twelve yards by a dim light behind a security grille. We knock on the door and Patsy answers, keeping us there on the doorstep.

'What is it?' Patsy frowns, and looks first at Karen and then at me. 'What's up?' Patsy glances behind her and I have the feeling someone is in there. I can smell tinned beans and bleach. 'It's late.'

I can feel Karen wanting to turn away but I hang on to her arm. 'We need to see you, Patsy. Karen's in trouble. We can't talk about this on the doorstep. It's personal.'

A man walks along the walkway and lets himself in the next-door flat.

'Patsy!' I say.

She opens the door wider. 'I suppose you'd better come in.'

There is no one in the flat except a small black cat, which looks up from where it is sitting, on top of a television with the smallest of screens. The room is very orderly. Apart from a neat pile of *Woman's Weeklys* on the Formica coffee table, there is nothing here that is more than functional.

'You'd better sit down. What is it?' She directs

her question at Karen, not me.

'Me mam's thrown us out, Pats,' says Karen, looking away from Patsy at the drawn curtains. 'Chucked us out. Says I can't be there at home with them. Because I...'

Now Patsy does look at me. 'Only one reason for that, I suppose. Must be up the...'

I manage to nod slightly.

'Karen, you're a bloody fool.' She actually prods Karen with her finger. 'A bloody little fool. And we all know what kind of fool.' She keeps prodding. Karen keeps her face turned away.

'Don't do that, Patsy,' I blurt out. 'No need to push Karen like that. She's upset.'

She turns on me then. 'What business is it of yours, you smart-arse? Johnnie-come-lately. I can do what I want in my own house. See? It was you knocked on my door, wasn't it? And if I want to make a point to a lass who's stupid enough to get herself knocked up by a slimy smooth-talking snake then I can, and you can keep your bloody snooty nose out of it.'

But at least she stops prodding.

At last Karen lifts her head. 'Don't get at Cassandra, Pats,' she says. 'She's helped me. She came...'

'You went to the woman in Durham?' Patsy looks her up and down. 'So you've had an–'

'No I haven't. I didn't go through with it. The women said I had to talk to my mam. So me and Cassandra, we went home to tell her. And now my mam's thrown us out. Wants nothing to do with us.'

Patsy sits back in her chair like a collapsed

balloon. 'I suspected, you know,' she says in a low voice, almost like a moan. 'I suspected as much but I didn't want to think ... not you, Karen, not you!'

The cat jumps down from the television into her lap and she begins to stroke it. Head to tail. Head to tail.

I break the silence. 'The thing is, Patsy, Karen needs somewhere to stay until she gets herself organised. Somewhere to lay her head.'

Patsy sits up straight and looks around the small room. 'Here? Oh, no. I couldn't have nobody here. That's a rule I made when I came here. No more living with anybody. No more taking care of anybody. I can't do it, Karen. Can't do it. Even for you.' Her voice thins out. 'I can't, even for you,' she repeats.

Karen sits there looking bewildered, her smudged mascara making her a clown's face.

'Right!' I say. 'That's it then. We won't bother you, Patsy. Karen'll have to come to mine.' My heart is sinking as I say the words, but what else can I do?

Patsy stands up and the cat scatters. 'Well, if you think so, Cassie. Karen can come to yours just till she gets things sorted. Take no notice of me. You're a good mate to Karen. True.'

Karen is already at the door. She nods at Patsy and sets off along the landing.

'I'm sorry,' says Patsy to me. 'You see, I–'

I put my hand on her arm, which is taut like whipcord beneath my fingers. 'Don't worry, Patsy,' I say. 'I'll take care of her.'

And when we get to my house the whole thing,

unbelievably, gets worse. I use my key to let myself into my house and there is my mother, all flushed, sitting on the sofa with a man with a moustache. She jumps up.

'Cassandra! Who's this?'

I can feel Karen move closer to my side. I look at the man, who has also leaped to his feet. 'Who's this?' I say.

She puts a hand on my arm. 'This is my friend Constantin Kovacs. You know, Tamás's father. We knew each other. Know...'

'Knew? Know!'

Constantin Kovacs takes my hand in his and shakes it heartily, with that half-bow that reminds me of Tamás. 'I am delighted at last to meet Linda's daughter. At last.' He smells of paprika and his hand is very warm. He looks nothing like Tamás and his accent is really heavy.

I rescue my hand and look around.

'Tamás went to look for you,' says my mother. 'I thought something had happened to you. We stayed, in case...'

'Well, you shouldn't have sent him.' I'm annoyed. 'What on earth did you do that for? I'm not some kid to be chased after.'

Karen is pulling at the back of my jacket, muttering something.

'Well, Linda!' Constantin Kovacs turns, picks up my mother's hand and kisses it. 'I will go and find my Tamás. Head him off at the pass, you might say, like Gary Cooper!' He smiles at me, clicks his heels, bows his head. 'So good to meet you, Cassandra. And your friend.' And he is gone, the front door clicking shut behind him.

294

I see my mother's chest rise and fall with one very big sigh. 'Well, then. That's that. Now then, Cassandra. Back to the beginning.' There is a very hard glint in her eye.

To my surprise it's Karen who speaks. 'Don't get on at her, Mrs Fox. She came to Durham with me to see this woman who gets rid of babies, like. Then I didn't want to do it and she took me home and my mam chucked me out. Then we went to Patsy's and she didn't want to know.' She paused. 'Seems like you're our last port of call.'

'Ah-oh-oh,' my mother speaks the word over the sigh. 'You'd better sit down, love. It's been a long night. Look! There's the last of Constantin's wine. What if I pour you two a drink?'

I could really hug her. I could hug her for ten years. These are the first kind words we've heard since the abortionist wished Karen well. Later I sit with my glass in my hand and look up at her. 'She needs to sleep here tonight and then tomorrow...'

My mother holds up her hand. 'You sort it out, love. One on the bed and one on the couch. Blankets in the understairs cupboard. Only one more glass in the bottle, so no worries that you'll drink too much.' She half closes her eyes. Perhaps she's a little drunk herself. 'I'm gonna have to go to bed myself, love. Can't tell you how tired I am. You just make your friend welcome, Cassandra. I'm pleased at least that we're someone's last port of call.'

She drifts upstairs and I look around the room which, after Mrs Duncan's, and even Patsy's, sitting rooms, is frankly scruffy; the walls not painted or papered for years; piles of books and newspapers everywhere; two empty wine bottles and five wine glasses. One of the glasses must have been Tamás's. He was here when I thought he was with blonde Evelyn. But he's here with his father and my mother. Without me.

Karen has drunk half her wine and is reaching for her cigarettes. 'I wish I didn't have to do this, Cassandra. Honest I do.'

I'm thinking wildly about my bedroom that's scruffier and even more strewn about than the front room. Maybe I should have Karen sleep down here. Then my mother can take the blame for the house, not me.

Karen goes on, 'It's only for tonight, mind. Tomorrow I'll find some lodgings somewhere.' She sounds quite steady; better than she's sounded all day. She'll have to have the bed. You can't put a pregnant woman on a leather couch with wooden ends.

To thin down the tension I turn on the television to the portly sight of Maigret puffing his pipe over some French *crime passionnel*. 'Look, love, you just sit there and I'll sort the beds.'

Karen takes a deep breath and sips her wine. She looks more relaxed now, easy in herself. I race upstairs and shake the mattress, straighten the covers, scoop up all the stuff lying around and throw it into my college trunk. I leave on only the little bedside light, so that shadows will disguise how lost the room really is. Then I shake up one of the pillows and take the other for myself.

I tap on my mother's door as I pass but there's no answer. She must be asleep, exhausted after a more eventful evening than usual.

Karen herself is asleep when I get back downstairs, her head thrown back on the sofa and a smouldering cigarette in her hand. I make the cigarette safe, sit in the chair and watch Maigret solve the crime with the sound down. There is no tension in the story. I know, after all, that Maigret will solve the crime. I know Karen will wake up soon but for the minute I relish the quiet. I know she'll ask for the bathroom, but there is none. I know she'll look askance at my weird bedroom. But just for now she's asleep and somehow I drift off too.

I'm dreaming of walking up the stone steps at college, arguing about something with Emma, when I am woken by a great battering on the door, Karen leaping up and screaming, and the thump of my mother's feet overhead. I rush to the door and in tumbles Karen's mother, followed too closely by Patsy, with Karen's father bringing up the rear.

Patsy stands at Mrs Duncan's shoulder. 'Go on, Sarah. Say what you've got to say to your lass.'

Mrs Duncan has been crying. 'Patsy came to our house, Karen. She said ... well, anyway, I think you should come home.' She glances round. I can see her making an effort not to wrinkle her nose. 'You should be in your own house.'

Karen folds her arms. 'I'm not coming. You'll only shout.'

'I have a right to shout,' said Mrs Duncan. 'Me, I have a right to shout.'

'That's why I'm not coming,' says Karen, jutting out her bottom lip. Now she really doesn't look old enough to be having a baby.

'What's all this?' My mother is standing in the doorway between the front room and the kitchen, wearing her threadbare dressing gown and with Kirbigrip pin curls all over her head. Even I never see her like this. 'What's this?' she says quietly.

'Our Karen's coming back to her own house, her home.' Mrs Duncan's voice sounds loud. Her glance drops to the two wine bottles on the table. 'This is not our kind of place.'

'You watch your mouth, Sarah,' says Patsy grimly. 'Linda Fox had just put a roof over your daughter's head. A thing neither you nor I had the guts to do.'

Karen sits back on the couch and folds her arms. 'I'm not coming home,' she says, picking up her half-filled glass. 'I'm staying here with Cassandra. I don't want to come and you can't make me.'

'You're coming!' says Mrs Duncan sourly.

'The girl can stay here as long as she wants,' says my mother. And she too folds her arms. It's like the battle of the Titans.

Then at last Patsy breaks the silence. 'Look, you two! How about if Karen comes to stay with me? It's just round the corner from you, Sarah. And,' she sits down at last beside Karen, 'you won't be under your ma's feet. What d'you think?'

'You've changed your tune,' says Karen, a bit ungraciously in my view.

'You just caught me on the hop, flower. No-body's ever been in my flat. Not one step across the threshold. But you and me's old mates,

Karen. I should help you. Like I say, you caught me on the hop. And I have this spare bedroom going to waste.'

'You can always stay here, Karen,' my mother joins in. 'As long as you like.'

I'm staying silent. One part of me wants this whole circus out of my house and my own private life back. Another part of me knows that after today me and Karen have something between us. A comradeship like I've never felt before, even with Emma. I've never helped someone not to have an abortion before. Perhaps that's what sisters would do.

Karen raises her eyes to mine. 'D'you mind, Cassandra? If Pats has a spare bedroom?' I can sense her relief. There's a kind of fit about this arrangement. After all, she hardly knows me. It's Patsy and Karen who are the real friends.

I manage a very careless shrug. 'Whatever you want, Karen. It's your affair.'

Karen stands up and looks at Patsy, carefully avoiding her mother's gaze. 'That's good of you, Patsy. If you don't mind. It'll only be for a few days.'

Patsy nods. 'It can be as long as it needs to be, flower. My door's been shut too long, if you ask me.'

Suddenly Mrs Duncan is wailing. 'You can't live with strangers, Karen! What will people say?'

Then the rather large hands of Karen's father descend on her shoulders. 'Come on with you, girl,' he grunts. 'You want nothing making more of a fool of yourself than you already have.' Then he kind of pulls her out of the room into the street and we can hear their voices rattling past our window.

Patsy gazes around. 'Now, flower, where's your bag?' She looks across at my mother. 'Very good of you to offer the lass shelter, Linda. Many wouldn't.'

My mother smiles a rare open smile. 'The least I could do, Patsy. I would always hope that people would give my Cassandra a roof, should the need arise. Like you are now for Karen. A bargain offered is a bargain returned later from another place.'

My Cassandra! That's a turn-up for the books.

Patsy and Karen move to the door and suddenly they are mere voices in the street outside. Now I can relax. My mother is still smiling. She seems looser now. Different. Something about Constantin Kovacs. It has to be.

'Well then, love,' she says, 'there's clay-cold fish and chips on the stove, or toast. Apart from that, the cupboard is bare.'

Suddenly I am very hungry. 'Toast!' I say.

As I pass through to the kitchen to light the grill she catches my arm. 'That was a good thing you did, love. You were a good friend to that girl today.' Then she is off up the back stairs. I would swear she is singing under her breath. Like I say, I'd rather have her than Karen's mother any day of the week.

And when I finally get to sleep who do I dream about? I dream that Tamás Kovacs comes back to the house and there's only me in the front room. We drink the rest of the wine and then make mad, passionate love on the sofa with the wooden arms. But beyond the touching of lips and the opening of mouths the details of the making love were kind of fuzzy. Can you really dream what you have never experienced? Reading's no help there. Even for a dream.

A Bit of Old Budapest

Maria and her children were in bed when Constantin and Tamás got back home. Constantin had bumped into Tamás at the end of Linda's Street, explained the search was over and that they could go home. Now Constantin hung his coat, jacket and cap on a hook behind the door. As usual, he was overdressed for the summer but he was always cold in England.

Maria had left coffee keeping warm on an electric hotplate beside the fire. Constantin smiled at his son and the light glittered on his golden tooth.

'When I enter Maria's house I am always reminded of coming into her father's little back room on the Fortuna utca in Buda.' He spoke in Hungarian. Tamás had to pick his way through the words but managed to make out the meaning as it tumbled through echoes of his childhood. 'The way this room smells, these wall hangings. The small things on every surface. The icons.'

Tamás poured out two tiny cups of strong coffee, handed one to his father and went to sit opposite him at the carved table that stood at the centre of the room. He smiled faintly. 'Some-times I sit here and imagine Mama and Anton in those other chairs. But sometimes it is hard to see their faces.' His tongue stumbled a bit with the language. He and Maria always spoke English. She always insisted on it because of her children, determined that English would be their first, not their second language. Now, of course, they could speak very little Hungarian.

Constantin shook his head. 'Your mama would want you to look forward, beloved son, not back-ward. She used to rage against our nostalgia for the romance of the past, said it delivered us into the grasp of tyrants. The tragedy of cavaliers against tanks. She fought for change and was a valiant soul. But she would not want you to conjure her from the past.'

'Do you never think of her, Papa? Do you never conjure her up?'

Constantin tapped his chest. 'I do not need to. She is sewn here into my heart, my beloved son, just as she is sewn into yours. We need not think of her face to know this.'

Then Tamás slipped into English. 'Linda was pleased to see you. I did not realise...'

'Ah, Le-enda!' Constantin grinned, flashing his gold tooth. 'I was pleased to see her also. We are old friends, Linda and I.' His English was still quaint.

'Tonight I had – have – the feeling you two are more than just friends.'

'We were. We are.' Constantin heaved a sigh. 'You are a man of the world now, dearest Tamás. I will tell you the truth. There was one time, when I first came to England, that I was obsessed with Linda. I clung to her like a man clings to the edge of a boat to save him from drowning. I think she rescued me from all those terrible events at home, from my despair at losing your mother and Anton in that way, from the dark pit of always being the stranger. I can't say whether it was love but it was like love.'

Tamás was watching his father intently. 'So what happened?'

His father shrugged. 'Nothing happened. I did try my luck, as the English would say. But Linda was in some dark pit of her own, still mourning her husband. It was all embarrassing in a very English way. I tried to change things and spoiled the friendship that had sustained me. So I went to Edinburgh. If Linda had welcomed me I think I would have stayed. But I obtained this chance of the opening in Edinburgh and I went.'

'And met Erzsébet.'

'Eventually.' He tapped his chest again. 'But Linda also is sewn into my heart.'

Tamás shook his head. 'Papa! You must have a very big heart.'

Constantin flashed his youthful grin. 'History has taught us that this is necessary for our survival, dearest son. The big heart, not the vengeful spirit.'

'And you are now friends with Linda again?'

'Still friends,' Constantin said complacently. 'The barrier is broken.'

It suddenly struck Tamás what his father meant. 'Papa! You didn't—'

Constantin put his finger to his lips. 'Shsh! There

303

is enough said. Now, you must tell me about your life. Have you inherited this large heart of mine?'

Tamás shook his head vigorously and smiled as he said, 'I'm not telling you anything. My life is my own.' He thought of Evelyn. And of Cassandra. Perhaps he was too like his father.

'Aha! I see the heart is at work in the English way. All closed up. Perhaps this Cassandra?'

'I'm not saying anything.' The humour was replaced now with stubborn will, determination.

Constantin stared at him, then came round the table, took him by the shoulders and raised him to his feet. 'Come, come!' He dragged him across the floor to the mirror. 'Look! Look!'

Tamás looked into the mirror at their two faces, so very different: his father dark visaged with springing black hair that seemed to have a life of its own, like an image from an Hungarian story-book; Tamás himself clean shaven, finer boned, fairer skinned, his fair hair flopping over his brow.

'Look!' repeated Constantin. 'Never fear that you will forget your mother's face. It is there before you in the mirror in the morning when you clean your teeth.'

And they embraced in the Hungarian fashion, in a way that would be viewed askance here in the North of England. Tamás knew now how much he had missed that energy of touching without realising it. And as they stood there before Maria's mirror, they both wept, one for his lost mother, the other for his brave, beloved wife.

Then Constantin pushed Tamás away, took out a snowy handkerchief and blew his nose. 'Now then, these English would say we are a pair of nancy boys, hugging and crying like this.' He smiled then and said in Hungarian, 'I am pleased, beloved son, that you do not have too much of the "stiff upper lip".'

Tamás coughed. 'Am I really like Mama?'

'More so each time I see you. I had not realised this. But you have her face, the set of her head. And like her you are true and quiet and brave.'

'Brave?' Tamás sat down again at the table. 'There are not the causes nor the opportunities here to be brave in the way Mama was.'

'But you have lived here on your own. You have become a man, made a career among strangers. That, my beloved son, is a very special thing.' Using a cloth to protect his hand he picked up the coffee pot. 'Now we drink more coffee and I tell you all about the magnificent Edinburgh and you may tell me all about this party at the factory with the barefoot singer.'

'It's not a party. It's a kind of event. Mr Priest and Mr Owen are keen to celebrate this millionth cooker.'

'Ah. Mr Owen! Such a fine man. He made space in his works for us when we came here. He came to the camp to search for us.' Constantin beamed. 'And then he wrote to Edinburgh about me and called me a fine man.'

'Like I said, you should come to the event. Talk to him.'

'And I will do that. I will come to Marvell's marvellous party. Will Linda be there?'

'I don't think so. That section will be working.'

Constantin smoothed his moustache with his

305

forefinger. 'Now that is a great pity.'

Tamás grinned at his father and shook his head. 'You are incorrigible, Papa.'

'*Incorrigible?* I will look that word up in my *Oxford English Dictionary.* I know many English words now but they are all to do with building and architecture. "Baluster" and "balustrade". You know? And "incorrigible" is not one of those!'

Refuge

Tuesday

Karen forced her eyes open, glimpsed the strange room, and closed them again to reach back into sleep. Then she opened them really wide, wondering for a split second where she was. She wasn't in her own pink bedroom with its rose-scattered bedspread and its posters of Elvis and James Dean. This place was painted bright white and the curtains and bedspread were scarlet, scrawled with black and white sunbursts.

Then she remembered what had happened, flopped back again and pulled the sunburst bed-cover over her head. Christ! It all rolled before her like a comic silent film. The bus-rides to Durham and back. Cassandra Fox, with her wide, scared eyes, her firm reassuring touch. Then the two of them in that scruffy Fox house with that weird, nice woman, Cassandra's mother.

Karen sat up, the bedcover falling away. Her

eye fell on the small suitcase on a chair under the window. It was stencilled with a string of numbers and 'Cpl S.S. Duncan': her father's army case, the one that had been to Korea and back. He had filled it with her clothes and brought it here to Patsy's flat. Her father who always hid behind newspapers brought it here. Himself.

Patsy. Christ! She leaped out of bed.

A knock on the door. 'Breakfast on the table, flower. Time for off.' It was Patsy's voice, furred up with yesterday's cigarettes and recent sleep.

Karen raked in the case for clean clothes, pulled them on and grabbed her toilet bag. Then she found the bathroom, took off all of her clothes again and had a very thorough wash, scrubbing her skin hard. She looked at her stomach through the mirror, wondering how another human being could be in there, tucked away, magicked into being by making love to Charlie Priest in an hotel where the sheets were hard nylon. A wave of strong feeling rippled through her, almost like the intoxication she felt at the height of making love to Charlie, the thing that made the scrabbling about worthwhile. She held onto the basin for a moment to steady herself. She forced herself to concentrate hard. This thing inside her was hers, hers alone. *This ... human being.* Bloody hell.

A knock on the door, 'You all right, flower?'

Karen stood up straight and started to pull on her clothes. 'I'm all right, Patsy. I'll be out.'

The two of them were silent over their breakfast of cornflakes, toast and Co-op cherry jam. Patsy gruffly told Karen there was no need, when she

307

got up to wash the few dishes, but still she washed them. As she rinsed the dishes Karen marvelled how clean and plain Patsy's flat was, but didn't say anything.

Patsy busied herself making two packs of sandwich-spread sandwiches for what she called their 'bait', and tucked an extra apple into Karen's work bag. As she unhooked the cat-flap and threaded the cat through it, Patsy looked up at Karen.

'You can stay here at the flat as long as you like, flower. We can arrange things between us. No need to worry about that.'

When they got to work, Cassandra Fox was already there, tucking her bag beneath the line. Karen smiled at her. 'All right, Cassandra?'

'Yeah.' Cassandra glanced at Patsy and back at Karen. 'You? You all right?'

'Yeah. I'm fine.'

'Don't know about that,' said Patsy 'The lass is gunna eat us out of house and home. You should'a seen the breakfast she put away. The lass eats like a horse.'

The buzzer went then and they slipped onto the stools.

Steve stopped his trolley by Patsy and lifted bundles of wires and a box of screws onto the end of the line. 'You all right, Karen?' he said.

Karen pouted. 'Why's everyone asking me if I'm all right?'

'Stoppin' the job, you,' said Patsy. 'You're losin' us our bonus, Steve. Get lost.'

Then, as the conveyor hummed and they started work they watched the blonde woman from the production office as she clipped past in the high heels clutching her electric kettle. 'Tea run, is it?' Patsy called across.

Evelyn Laing smiled. 'That's it. They like their cups of tea.'

''S not all they like!' said Patsy, her hands busy. 'You watch those men don't catch something from that water, Evelyn. No saying what that Mrs Mundy puts on her taps. More to her than curse pills and plasters, you know.' She turned to Cassandra. 'All right, that Evelyn. Gives respect where it's due.'

In twenty minutes I am working quite easily and can let my mind wander back to the events of last night. What a relevation Patsy's house was! Kind of cold and spare. And how she protected it! Hardly wanted us inside. And then how generous she was, coming back to my house for Karen. And how relieved I was when my own citadel wasn't breached and I didn't have to give up my bed. And how rumpled and odd my mother was when I met her with Constantin Kovacs. What was that about?

But that Patsy! Up to now I've just thought of her at work, as though she's part of the fabric of Marvell's and has no life apart from it. Up till yesterday I just saw her as kind of up-front, occasionally coarse, and often really witty. So it was interesting to see her there on home ground. But her bare flat told me nothing about her. It was like an illustration in one of those articles on compact living in *Woman's Own*. Clean. Shiny. Featureless.

I think now perhaps that the factory is the very best of Patsy's life. Despite all her shouting about not being done out of her bonus, for her the factory is not about earning a living, but is life itself. She is part of the fabric of the place in a good way, when you come to think of it.

This morning we work on in relative silence and have worked up a good head of steam by the mid-morning break. Stan Laverick strolls up as we sit over our flasks and biscuits. He nods approvingly at the stacked work. 'Getting ahead, then? Good thing too. Charlie Priest says you can go off at two thirty, Karen, and get them flowers for Sandie Shaw. And you're to take this one,' he nods at me. 'Charlie seems to think she might have a bit of taste. With all that education, like.'

'Sarky bugger,' says Patsy. 'And what are we to do about the bonus, with two of them off with the fairies?'

'Steve's gunna fill in again.'

'That one,' she grumbles. 'He has hands like some bloody panda from the zoo.'

'It'll take us all afternoon, bussing into Grafton and back,' says Karen.

'Ah. There you're wrong, flower. Mr Priest says he'll get one of the lads from the garage to drive you. Company car and all that.'

'Ooh! Get you two!' says Patsy 'Company car! It'll be a butler next.'

The buzzer goes and Patsy stands up, brushing the crumbs from her lap. 'No rest for the wicked. Pity we all can't have drivers and butlers.'

I feel a bit embarrassed. 'Why don't you go,

310

Patsy? Go with Karen for the flowers? It's a look out.'

She laughs out loud at this. 'What? You must be joking. Do that and we won't get a cooker off the line the rest of the day, will we, Cassandra? You go, love, and get the two of you a cream cake while you're out. Keep that bloody driver waiting.'

The three of us work on very quickly. I keep my head down and work as fast as I can, conscious of Patsy having to carry the dead weight of Steve this afternoon. Secretly I'm pleased with myself for being considered the insider and not having the hands of a panda like Steve. Interesting how Patsy has me caring about all this now, as more than just a job. Part of her Marvell magic, I suppose.

By the time the big clock at the end of the line is ticking round to twelve, the line is clogged up with done jobs and I have to slow down. I lift my head to see Tamás Kovacs descending from the gantry and strolling along the line towards us inside the newly painted white lines. My head goes down again, but he stops beside me and I have to look up. I feel rather than see Karen and Patsy exchanging glances. Patsy actually mutters under her breath, 'Here we go!'

He smiles. 'Hello, Cassandra.'

'Hello.'

Patsy looks up. 'And is it "Hello, Patsy!" and "Hello, Karen!" Tam?'

He winks at her. 'Sure it is, Auntie Pat. Hello, Patsy and hello, Karen.'

'Bloody Hungarians!' she says. 'Good-lookin'

nowts! Fickle!'

'Ah, but I'll always love you, Patsy.'

'So you say.'

The buzzer goes and we all breathe out as the conveyor grinds to a halt. He turns to me. 'You coming down the canteen, Cassandra?' He looks at me quite seriously. 'I could buy you coffee? Just a cup of coffee?'

'You'd better go, lass. Or he'll be haunting the line for ever.'

'If you say so.' I jump off my stool and root around under the bench for my bag.

Karen dips into her bag and pulls out a brush. 'Here, love. Sit down. You look like you've been pulled through a hedge backwards.' She runs the brush through my hair and attends to my fringe, back-combing it a bit then smoothing it down. 'There,' she says. 'That's pretty canny.'

'Thanks, Karen,' I say submissively.

'Bring us back a Mars bar, anyway.'

'I will.'

Tamás and I walk shoulder to shoulder down the now-pristine gangway. He says, 'Well, I think we've got their blessing.'

'What? *We...*'

'I said, "I think–"'

'I heard what you said.'

We get to the great exit door and the blast of fresh summer air hits us after the dry, used air of the factory.

He tries again. 'What was it, last night, when you went missing? We came to your house and you weren't there. Your mother was–'

'My mother seemed pleased to see your father.'

312

'They are old friends from long ago. But where were you?'

'No business of yours.' I pause. 'I was with Karen. We were at her house. And her mother threw her out. Then we went to mine, but you were gone by then. Then she went to Patsy's. She stayed there.'

'You had a busy evening.' He slows down. 'I thought you'd been...'

I can feel him searching for a word.

'...waylaid.'

I have to laugh at this. 'Waylaid? It's not Robin Hood country, you know.'

He moves closer. I can feel the heat of his shoulder near mine. The other workers stream round us like water round a pair of stones. One or two people stare at us. One man grunts, 'Now, Tam!' as he brushes past.

Tamás puts an arm through mine and urges me along. 'Now, coffee! And I will persuade you to come out with me tonight and we will forget me running away from you at the park.'

'And will you tell me about Evelyn Laing?'

'And sure, I will tell you all about my friend Evelyn.'

Mr Owen Expects

At one o'clock on Tuesday Mr Owen's big Humber purred onto the site and Goods Inwards got onto the phone to Charlie to warn him. He caught up with Mr Owen at the big warehouse doors, where they shook hands and strolled through the immaculate factory together.

Mr Owen looked around him. 'Been cracking the whip, I see, Charlie. Never seen it better.'

'Marvell people can be a handful, Mr Owen, but when called on they'll step up to the plate.'

'So you say. I tell you, Charlie, Marvell workers are pretty up to the mark all over the country. But here at Grafton there's something extra...'

They stopped by the wiring jackets. Patsy O'Hare's hands didn't stop moving. 'All right, Mr Owen?' she said.

'I'm fine, Patsy. And you?'

She allowed a slight smile. 'Still slaving away for you, Mr Owen. A martyr for Marvell's, that's me.'

'How about this shindig then, Patsy? A million cookers? We've seen them come and we've seen them go, you and I. Think of it! A million cookers. And you and I have seen them all come down the line.'

She lifted a bunch of wires and examined them carefully 'Like you say, Mr Owen. But me, I was skinnier and you, you had more hair when we

314

started. Isn't that so, Mr Owen?'

Charlie coughed.

Mr Owen laughed out loud. 'That's *quite* so, Patsy. And what do you think about tomorrow's celebrations. This presentation?'

Patsy shrugged. 'Me? I can take it or leave it. Means nowt to me unless it cuts my bonus. And Mr Priest here says it won't, so, that said, I'm not bothered about no barefoot contessa.'

He considered her for a minute, turned to the other girls on her section. 'And this is our new generation?'

'Well, that one is.' She nodded at Karen. 'Thinks she's Sandie Shaw's double but she's as good a worker as me when I was her age. And that's sayin' sommat. But that one, hiding behind the fringe...' She nodded at Cassandra. 'That one's a bird of flight, taking a break from a real hard life at college.' She sniffed. 'She's not bad, like. Give her a year and she'd catch up with Karen. Not me, like.'

Mr Owen shook his head. 'You know what, Patsy? Marvell's would be nowhere without old hands like you and me. There'd be no million cookers. No nothing. Just closed-down mines round here.'

Then a strange thing happened. Patsy blushed, red patches staining her solid cheeks. 'Wouldn't say that, Mr Owen. Don't flatter yourself, or me. Nobody's that important.'

The two men walked on. 'That's me put in my place,' said Mr Owen.

'I wouldn't take Patsy too hard, Mr Owen. She has a mouth like Tynemouth.'

315

'Me? Don't worry, Charlie. Patsy and I go back to the beginning, when Mr Abrahams set up here. We have each other's measure, Patsy and I.'

Then, with his eagle eye, Mr Owen went on to examine every area of the shop floor, even the parts Sandie Shaw would never see. Charlie breathed out when there were no criticisms. One of Mr Owen's obsessions was what he called 'good housekeeping'. This meant, as he often explained, that no part of a factory should be less congenial to work in than a laboratory, or even your own kitchen. He was aware that each time he entered any of the Marvell factories there would have been a scurrying around to fulfil this expectation but that, as he saw it, was part of his strategy of keeping tabs on factories that were outside his day-to-day control.

They made for the boardroom where Charlie had quickly organised a sandwich lunch with the other senior managers. The main item on the agenda was to discuss tomorrow's presentation and tick last-minute boxes. Evelyn was already there, laying out sandwiches and stirring the tea in the teapot. Charlie popped back to his office to take a phone call from his wife and Mr Owen took the seat at the head of the table.

He said quietly to Evelyn, 'It was very nice to see you the other evening, Evelyn. My wife seems to have enjoyed the conversation. She said you had travelled very widely. To be honest she's a bit of a frustrated traveller herself. Marvell's prevents us from travelling as much as we'd like to.'

Evelyn smiled. 'I enjoyed talking to her. Mrs Owen was very kind.'

He glanced at the door. 'She did say the ladies were less than kind. Bit like being thrown to the crocodiles?'

She smiled at him. 'I'm a big girl, Mr Owen. I've been in more dangerous swamps than that.'

He was just laughing at this when Charlie came in clutching a folder, followed by his senior men, including Alan Cartwright and Tamás Kovacs. Mr Owen greeted Tamás and asked about his father and whether things were going well in Edinburgh.

'He's here in Grafton, Mr Owen. Coming to the do tomorrow.'

'I'll have a word with him. Your father was always an impressive man, Tamás. I saw that from that first time I saw him at the resettlement centre in '57. He and his compatriots were a godsend to us then, we were so short of labour on the big expansion. He's an architect now, I believe?'

'Not quite. On the last step towards that. He's taken lots of exams. He says he'll be the oldest apprentice architect in the world.'

'Well,' Mr Owen turned to Charlie, 'lucky we hung on to Tamás, isn't it, Charlie?'

'So it is, Mr Owen. He's a good chap.' Charlie took a seat beside Mr Owens. Evelyn distributed the teas and everyone sat back expectantly.

'So, I suppose Evelyn will take the minutes for us?' Mr Owen asked.

Charlie frowned. 'Well, usually Tamás here takes the minutes, Mr Owen. Then Evelyn types them.'

'Well, Charlie, I'm sure Evelyn is more than capable of doing the minutes herself. Tamás'll

317

need to make his contribution to the meeting, without the distraction of minutes, surely?'

At that these experienced senior Marvell men sat back, knowing they had witnessed Mr Owen's particular gift of promoting people who would be of benefit to Marvell's. His very successful habit through the years had been to do this disregarding the impedimenta of qualification or hierarchy. He had done this with Charlie Priest and many others, and had never been wrong. And he wouldn't be wrong either, in the case of Evelyn Laing or Tamás Kovacs.

Millie Priest Betrays a Secret

Millie opened the door and ushered her windswept visitor into the kitchen, 'Sit down! Sit down! Must be windy out there. Your hair's all over.'

Joanie put her hand to her hair. She'd done it specially, carefully, knowing she was coming here. She had brushed it a hundred times before she pinned it up and thought it was quite nice. Now it felt like barbed wire under her hands. 'Yes. It was a bit of a walk. The bus doesn't come out this far out.'

She had been busy when Millie phoned. But Charlie's wife had sounded shrill, frantic. She had demanded that Joanie come this minute. And Joanie had come. Millie was Charlie Priest's wife, after all. Joanie had to think of Stan and his job at Marvell's. No point in stirring the pot. Millie could be unpredictable but she had never sounded this strange.

Millie busied herself with the kettle, cups and napkins. 'Sorry about that, Joanie,' she said sweetly over her shoulder. 'I didn't think, when I rang. Forgot you didn't have a car.'

Despite her humble nature, this annoyed Joanie. 'Me and Stan do have a car, of course.'

'Oh, yes, I remember. Charlie's–'

'Old one. Yes.' Then in her embarrassment Joanie told a lie. 'Stan's getting me lessons for my birthday. Then I'll have the car and drop him off at the factory. That way I'll have the car all day.'

Joanie decided then that it needn't be a lie. That's what she'd do. She would learn how to drive. She would have lessons and then keep the car herself in the day. What a good idea. Millie always gave her good ideas. That's how they got to replace her grandmother's old elm dresser for a nice teak sideboard like Millie's.

Millie led the way through to the lounge, placed the tray on the long john table and perched on the puffy sofa. She poured them both tea and sat back. 'Now then, how are you, Joanie?' she said brightly.

Joanie noticed that Millie's lipstick was very thick, taken right to the corners of her mouth. 'I'm very well,' she said. 'Me and Stan really enjoyed your party.' She thought that's what Millie had invited her for, to gloat about the party. Millie never invited you for no reason.

Millie sat up very straight and sipped her tea. 'I say it myself but I really thought it went well. I had this very nice note from Mrs Owen saying it was the best party she'd ever been to. *Ever,* she said!'

Even the faithful Joanie thought this might be an exaggeration.

'But,' Millie went on, 'don't get me on about that Evelyn Laing!' She tucked bunny-rabbit-slippered feet underneath her. 'Flaunting herself about! Vulgar, I call it. And as for her making an exhibition of herself with that Kovacs boy. She's far too old...' She frowned at the thick lipstick mark on her china cup, picked up her napkin and rubbed it vigorously.

Joanie frowned. 'Me, I thought she was a bit quiet. Kind of watchful. Except when she was talking to Mrs Owen.'

'See?' said Millie victoriously. 'Flaunting herself to the boss's wife! Not that any man'd really take a second look at her. Did you know she lives in this pit hovel down in Brigg village? And her father's as mad as a hatter.' She rubbed the cup so hard that the tea spilled on her slacks and she started to rub away at that.

Joanie decided to be honest. 'What's wrong, Millie? Is there something wrong?'

Millie threw the napkin down in disgust and glared at her.

Joanie persisted. 'It was nice, you ringing and asking me over for coffee...' She looked down at her cup and laughed. 'Well, tea, isn't it? Don't get invited out much in the day. Then, with working in the evenings, not much at night either.'

Millie sniffed. 'Yes, I remember. The twilight shift. Sounds romantic in a way. But it must be very difficult for you, Joanie. *Must* cut back your social life!'

Maybe it was being nearly blown off her feet by the wind, but Joanie got really mad at this. She sat up straight. 'Well, I took a night off to come to your party, didn't I? Even though they docked my pay for it.'

Millie laughed shrilly. 'A person hardly needs paying for going to a party!'

'I never said that.'

Millie shook her head. 'Pity, though. Pity you have to work nights, I mean.'

Joanie tossed her head. 'Don't you waste your pity on me, Millie. The girls on the twilight shift are a bit of a laugh. We work hard but the time passes that quickly. And they're pretty decent lasses, too. All of us are the same, doing the house in the day and working for our families at night.'

Millie wasn't used to seeing Joanie on the offensive. 'I didn't mean–' she began sulkily.

Joanie drove on. 'I'm just like them meself. I wash, clean and cook for Stan and the lads in the day. I work evenings so I can get extra things for my boys. Our Clyde's into men's clothes now, you know. And school says he's good enough to go to university, so I have to save for that.'

'Well, I suppose it must be worth it or you wouldn't do it,' said Millie in a smaller, more neutral voice.

Joanie looked at her, her eyes very bright. 'It is worth it. Really. Twenty times over.'

Millie sighed dramatically. 'Funny thing is, that's what I asked you over for.'

'To listen to me go on about the twilight shift?

321

You're starting work?'

Millie shook her head. 'Not that. I wanted to tell you something. It's just that I think – I know now – I've just found out that I'm expecting myself. A baby. And I wanted to ask you about it.' She paused. 'There's nobody in my family, just the old aunts from the shop, and they're in Torquay. And what would they know about having babies? I've no one to ask what it's like, having babies.'

Joanie looked blank. With another woman she would have gone across, hugged her and said well done. But not with Millie. She had experienced Millie's hidden talons before. She shrugged. 'It's what all women do, isn't it? Have babies. The great and the not so great. The queen and the beggar lass. No point in asking what it's like. It just something that happens and you endure it.'

Millie's face wrinkled with distaste. 'It sounds awful, what happens. I read this leaflet.'

Joanie shrugged. 'It's bloody hard. Excuse my French. But whichever way you look at it, Millie, it's only twenty-four hours of your life. It's what happens after they come out that's a bit of a bugger. Losing sleep, losing your waistline, endless washing with all those dirty nappies. Your husband running away to the club when he gets sick of the smell and the wailing. And sick of you.'

Millie groaned. 'Joanie! Stop!'

Joanie looked Millie in the eye. 'It's not so bad now, like. Clyde and Joe are fit and well. All they do is play football and eat you out of house and home.' She sat back and glanced round the room. 'But mebbe Charlie's not like other men. And mebbe – placed as you are – you can get some help, Millie. Money talks, even about being a mother. But not the having of them, like. No difference there. We all have to go through that no matter how much there is in the bank.'

Millie stared at her, furious with Joanie for letting her down. What she had wanted to hear was how delightful and romantic motherhood was, that even though having them was a bit painful it was a wonderful bonding between man and wife. Joanie was stupid. She should have known that she should help Millie by saying it all in that way. But here this stupid woman was describing the whole thing like it was a sentence in the coal mines. How rude! Yes, above all Joanie was being rude, sitting there on Millie's own sofa, drinking her tea and frightening her about the most important thing in her life. Stupid woman.

Millie drew her slippered feet from under her and placed them flat on the floor. Then she learned forward. 'And how is your Stan, Joanie?'

Joanie frowned. 'He's ... well, he's Stan, isn't he? Living for Marvell's and boring for England. Mind you, he's been quite chirpy lately. Something must be going right at Marvell's.'

'Ah!' Millie smirked.

'What do you mean, Millie, *ah?*'

'Well, perhaps I shouldn't say this as I was told it in confidence. Horse's mouth. Alan Cartwright's wife, had it on good authority, told to her in confidence...'

'Told *what* in confidence?'

Millie looked at Joanie, her face smooth, her

lipstick just a bit smudged. 'Well, she told me that Stan was ... well ... seeing someone. A woman.'

Joanie's laughter rang out like a bell. 'Somebody's having you on, Millie. Stan'd never have time to ... well ... see someone. Unless it's Miss *Marvell!* He's been going steady with her for years.'

Millie kept her face very concerned. 'Well, they do say needs must when the devil drives, Joanie. I was told about this in good faith, dear. You know factories. No secrets there. Being your friend, Joanie, I felt I had to ... well ... let you in on the secret. Forewarned is forearmed, they say.'

Joanie felt sick, bile rising in her throat. She swallowed the bitterness and stared at Millie for a full minute, thinking how she had kept all the seedy secrets she'd known through the years about Charlie Priest, one of which was the time he made a heavy pass at Joanie herself at her own engagement party long ago. This woman in front of her was a fool and the truth was Joanie had never thought Charlie was really a bad sort. Why should she upset his applecart just to get back at this mad woman? She stood up and looked down steadily at Millie. 'I should go now. I know you're wrong, Millie, so if you don't mind, please don't spread this stupid tale any further. You know there are tales I could tell.' She put down her cup and somehow it missed the table and spilled all over the white shag-pile carpet. 'Oh, I am sorry,' she said, not looking in the least bit sorry. 'Have you got a cloth?'

'Leave it!' said Millie through gritted teeth. 'I'll see to it. You can see yourself out, can't you?'

At the door she looked back. 'And, Millie. Take a look in the mirror. Your lipstick's smudged.'

She stayed long enough to see Millie pick up a cup to throw, then fled. Buzzing through her mind was the thought that it was the last time she'd enter that door. Thank God for that. The woman was a cow anyway. Just some jumped-up shopkeeper's daughter. Who did she think she was, acting like the lady of the manor? The girls on the twilight shift were real ladies compared with her.

She ran through the estate and the park, then down the main street, her brain streaming with those nasty things Millie had said about Stan, and the things she could have said about Charlie if she'd been as bitchy as Millie. Then, just by Woolworths, blinded by tears, she bumped into two girls who were carrying a huge bunch of yellow lilies and white roses. One was tall and glamorous in a common kind of way. The other was smaller, more nondescript. The bouquet shot out of the tall girl's hand, only to be saved by the other. The girls shrieked with laughter and asked Joanie if she were all right, but she just charged on.

By the time she got home she had calmed down. She took off her coat and surveyed herself in the hall mirror with unusual closeness. Her hair was like a wild hedge, her eyes red, wild and staring. Bugger Millie Priest! She took out her pins and reached for her brush. What did Millie Priest know about anything? She was mad, vicious. Stan was not like that. Ask anyone.

Cakes

After recovering from some wild woman in the high street, who barges into us and knocks the flowers out of Karen's hand, we take refuge in the Roma Café and treat ourselves to a cup of frothy coffee and a cake that the boy behind the counter calls 'Siena honey cake'. I can't taste honey, just almonds, candied fruit and bits of dark chocolate. Something to write to my friend Emma about, this cake. *Very exotic for Grafton, this cake, Emma.*

Karen grins at me. ''S like playing the nick from school, isn't it? Everything tastes better, looks better, when you play the nick.'

I shrug, which makes her laugh more. 'You never did it, did you, Cassandra? You never bloody played the nick! I'm telling you, if you never played the nick you never lived!'

My glance falls on the bouquet, stuck there on a chair like the third person at the table. 'Brilliant flowers. I hope Sandie appreciates them.'

Karen shrugs. 'She'll not notice, will she? I bet she gets flowers like this every day. Do you know she gets hundreds of marriage proposals every day?'

My mouth is full of cake. The lemon tastes tart against the chocolate. 'You said. Lucky her.'

Karen sits back, her eyes sharp. 'So, what about Tamás Kovacs, Cassandra? Are you striking lucky with him? Is he trying it on?'

My mind goes back to lunchtime. There in the canteen I was conscious of people looking at us. Another story to run around Marvell's like an infection. Tamás was well known about the place but I wasn't, so I suppose that might make us interesting. Any change of routine is exciting in a place that depends on routine. We sat there looking at each other as the canteen rattled with footsteps on the hard floor, with knives and forks on the Formica tables; it hummed with talk and laughter, straining above the echoing music on the Tannoy: Frankie Laine, Guy Mitchell, Tab Hunter. All old stuff. A group of women by the plate-glass window joined in 'Young Love'. Then one broke off and shouted across, 'Isn't that right, Tam?'

He just ignored them, drank his coffee and watched me, waiting. I waited as long as I could, but I broke first. 'So! Is your dad here for a long time?'

'A few days. He's coming into the factory for what Charlie calls "the shindig" tomorrow. He said at breakfast that he's calling on your mother again tonight. He told me that. And I wanted to tell you that on Tuesday nights Maria takes her kids with her when she plays cards with her friend. The kids all stay over and go to school from her friend's house because it is nearer. Sometimes Maria stays as well.'

'That's nice. Nice for her. To have such a friend.'

It was that kind of conversation where one thing was being said and another being meant.

We were holding each other's gaze. He was looking at me over the rim of his cup, those bright pale eyes watchful.

'I bet you have lots of friends,' he said.

I shook my head. 'Not here in Grafton. I wasn't very sociable at school. Too busy working.'

'At your college, then? It can't all be work. You must have friends there.'

I have to laugh. 'Patsy and Steve think it's all sex and drugs and rock'n'roll in my college.'

'And is it?'

I shake my head. 'Nah. But I've learned quite a bit since I got there, about enjoying myself, relaxing. I've learned lots about what friends are.'

'So tell me what you have learned?' He was watching me very intently.

So I told him what I felt about the grape-picking and Emma and the others, and about Jeanette and her strange ways, aware all the time that as I did this I was offering him little bits of myself, trusting him in a way I'd never trusted anyone.

'I'd like to meet this Emma,' he said in the end. 'She sounds kind of funny but full of proper feeling. You know?'

And it dawned on me that the message underneath all this was that there was not only a *present* between us, there was this future where he would meet my friend Emma. Maybe.

Around us in the canteen people were scraping their chairs back, getting ready to return for the afternoon shift. I moved to stand up but he put his hand on mine. 'I tell you what, Cassandra. Come up to the prefabs and see me tonight. I'll give you some of Maria's goulash. A bit of old Budapest. She has some records from the Hungarian gypsies. It will amuse you. You can make a study of it and go back and tell your friend Emma all about us Hungarians.' His hand squeezed mine tight. 'Come!'

I stood up and the scrape of the chair made an ugly sound. 'I can't do that. I don't know where to come!' It was a very weak protest.

He hung on to my hand. 'She lives in the prefabs behind the church, number seventeen.'

I wrestled my hand away. 'All right then, I'll do that.' I thought of my mother, in disarray when I got home last night. 'If your father's coming to my house to see my mother I'll only be playing gooseberry.'

As we walked out of the canteen he took hold of my hand.

'Gooseberry? What does that mean?'

Now, in the café, Karen is waving her hand before my eyes. 'Hello? Hello? Anyone there? Come on, Cassandra. Did you click? Is it on? You and Tam Kovacs?'

I laugh. 'I thought I might give him a try.'

'Attagirl! Show the lad what for. Class to class, that's what I say.' Karen smiles broadly. She seems her usual self this afternoon; her eye-lines are perfect, her make-up is in place and her dark hair, with its long fringe and loose locks, is immaculate. She seems quite recovered from those events of yesterday that started with the woman in Durham and ended with Patsy rescuing her from my house, and from her own parents.

I spoon up the froth from the coffee and lick the spoon clean. 'What about you, Karen? Are you OK?'

'OK?' She coughs over swallowed coffee. 'Well, flower, I'm pregnant, sleeping on somebody's spare bed and will lose my job when I start to show. If that's OK, well, I'm OK!'

'So you've made your mind up about it? You sound chirpy enough.'

'Well, it's not quite that I'm *having* this baby, but that I'm not *not* having this baby. If you see what I mean.' She pauses. 'It's like, this morning I began to think of it, well, as this *baby thingy inside*. Not *getting pregnant*. D'you see what I mean? Once I'd thought of it as a *baby thingy*, I could never go back to the woman in Durham.' She sounds quite tranquil.

'Will you manage? How will you manage?'

She lights a cigarette and lets the smoke rise in the air before she answers. 'Well, Patsy's cool with things as they are. But to be honest, I think my mother'll come round. My dad said as much when he brought my case. "Give her time," he said. "She'll come round."'

'Then?'

'Then I'll have the baby, my mother'll mind it, and I'll go back to Marvell's and keep the both of us. Patsy says she'll make sure they keep my job on at the factory. And we all know that what she says there goes.'

I watch Karen stub out her cigarette, half smoked, in the ashtray. I think how lovely she is, how she's still kind of unbroken. But even in my ignorance I know that this is the end of something bright and good. We think nowadays we're all so advanced, that things are moving on, but being an unmarried mother is no more of a picnic than it was twenty years ago. Look at my mother. Bringing up me, a child without a father, has just about done for her. It strikes me now that my mother at the same age would have been like this, bright and unbroken, before I came along. This makes me feel so very sad for her. And for me too.

Karen dips in her bag and brings out a clean embroidered handkerchief. 'Here! Mop them up. You've got it wrong. It's *me* that should be crying, not you!' She stands up. 'We gotta go. That Patsy'll be murdering Stevie Hunter by now and mithering on about her bonus.'

In the road outside, the Marvell driver puts away his *Playboy* magazine and stubs out his cigarette. 'Took your time, dincha?' He screws round in his seat and surveys us. 'Thought you were supposed to be gettin' flowers?'

'Crikey! Hold your horses, will you?' I scramble back out of the car and back into the café, to rescue the beautiful bouquet, which is still sitting there like an unwanted guest. I carry it carefully to the car, almost swooning with the perfume of lilies. Sandie Shaw will surely like them, even if she does get hundreds of proposals a week.

Joanie

Joanie went about her Tuesday jobs in the house still jumpy from her morning visit to Millie Priest. Her feelings were hurt. What had she done to Millie, for her to be spiteful like that? She had always tried to be helpful to Charlie's wife. She had patently admired her house and her car. She had cooed with her over Charlie's magnificent successes. Then there was the golf weekend in Scarborough. Hadn't she gone along with Lynne Cartwright to keep Millie company while the men played golf? Hadn't she endured the way the other men smirked over Stan's fumbling efforts with the knives and forks? Hadn't she gone to a fortune-teller with Millie and Lynne, only for him to paint far shinier futures for them than for her? Now today again, Millie, far from sharing her delight about expecting a baby, had sunk to sneering at Joanie and being catty about Stan. How could she? It was lies. Evil tales. Everyone knew Stan was not a lady's man. Not like Charlie. Her Stan was a proper man's man. Work. The club. Home. That was Stan. Everyone knew that. But what was it that *everyone knew* now? What was Millie on about?

Joanie's tumbling thoughts generated so much energy that afternoon that not only did she do her Tuesday jobs – the boys' room, the ironing, the daily once-over for the kitchen – she did

Wednesday's jobs too – the hall and landing, the front and back doorsteps, the pictures and mirrors.

Finally she sat down for a cup of tea, only to leap up again, throw on her coat, pick up her purse and run to the butcher's to get best steak and kidney. Jack the butcher wrapped the meat up carefully in yesterday's *Daily Mirror*.

'Not mince, Joanie? You usually get mince on Tuesdays.'

'Stan really likes steak and kidney pudding. Thought I'd treat him.'

'Lucky man.' He handed the parcel order. 'Pudding! My wife just throws a couple of chops in the pan.'

'Lucky you!' said Joanie. 'That's a step up from mince.'

When the boys came in she gave them boiled egg sandwiches for their teas before they went out to kick a ball on the rec. Later, on her way to work, she called round to her mother's to say that she'd left steak and kidney pudding in the steamer for Stan, and that the boys would be in soon to do their homework. Could Ma make sure the boys hit their beds after *The Man From U.N.C.L.E.* on TV? As she walked to the factory with her hair neat and her overall in her bag she felt glad that the wind had dropped. No good turning up at the factory looking like she'd been hauled through a hedge backwards. The girls would be more kind about that than Millie Priest had that morning, but they would still laugh.

None of it made sense. Unless being pregnant had made Millie Priest madder than she usually was. Joanie's heart eased and her step lightened. That was it. Millie Priest had turned the corner. Now she truly was bonkers.

Later, when she arrived to check on the boys, Joanie's mother turned off the steamer thinking it odd that Stan had left his dinner when he'd gone off to the club. A few minutes later she was surprised when Stan arrived home in his best work suit, saying no, he'd not come in and gone out again, that he was just in from work. He'd been to the coast to check again on arrangements for the ceremony tomorrow and, no, he hadn't had his tea. She told him to go and get changed and she'd warm it through.

'Steak and kidney pudding!' she grunted. 'The lass spoils you.'

He grinned. 'She knows what I like. Just leave that and get home, Ma. I'll put the lads to bed. I'll not bother with the club.'

She reached for her hat. 'Wonders never cease! Stan Laverick misses a night at the club!'

After changing into an old jersey and slacks he called on the boys in their rooms. They had their heads down over their homework, sitting side by side on a long workshelf that Stan had rigged up. Clyde was working on something about the sputnik and Joe was drawing his version of the water table.

'All right, lads?' he said.

'You're early,' said the Clyde.

'I wondered what you two were up to,' said Stan, admitting and denying nothing. He looked at Joe's neat diagram of the water table. 'Didn't know you could draw,' he said.

Joe looked him in the eye. 'Well, I *can* draw.'

'Well,' said Stan helplessly, 'I'll just go down to get my dinner.'

The boys were tucked up and asleep when Joanie got home. Stan had cleared the table and stashed the dishes. 'You're early,' she said.

He put down the paper. 'Late, really. I had to go across to the coast to check again on this couple for tomorrow. That woman who is getting the cooker. That she wasn't sick or anything. Then I got home pretty late. But that steak and kidney pie, Joanie! Bloody good. Only you can make it that way. Wolfed every scrap, I did. Nice surprise. I thought we always had mince on Tuesdays.'

Joanie took off her overall and laid it neatly on the back of the couch. She smiled slightly. 'No law saying we have to have mince on Tuesdays. You didn't go to the club?'

'Nah. Long day. And a long day tomorrow. Thought I'd have an early night.' He needed it. Charging across to the coast to check on that Mrs McLochlan. Then down to see Leila for an hour. It wore a man out.

Joanie vanished into the kitchen and returned with two mugs of Horlicks. 'I made you one. Looks like you need it. You look worn out.'

She sat with him on the sofa shoulder to shoulder. She had that special smell, Joanie. A mixture between roses, Fairy Liquid, and a kind of sweet sweat. He turned to look at her. 'Your hair's different,' he said.

She touched the soft hair above her ear. 'One of the girls at work did it for me in the break. She said it would look better pinned up higher and these sides looser.'

'She's right. You look like ... you look like that day we went to Keswick before we got married. You remember?' That was the first time they had made love properly, in a bed, not in an alleyway. Almost without thinking he reached across and kissed her cheek. 'We had a good time, didn't we, lass?'

She turned her head and they were kissing, holding each other tightly like two drowning people. He groaned and squirmed until they were full length on the couch, pulling at each other's clothes. She giggled her pleasure and egged him on. One edge of Stan's brain cursed himself for his stupidity. He couldn't – *could not* – do this! Not twice in one evening.

But he did do it. And it was absolutely great. She was above him. Her eyes gleaming. 'You're great!' he mumbled through her falling hair. 'Bloody great!'

She laughed. 'You'd better believe it, Stan Laverick!'

Later, properly in bed, with Joanie snuffling and snoring beside him, he wondered how he had pulled it off, where the strength to do that had come from. Then it occurred to him that it was probably the steak and kidney pudding. Long time since he'd had one of them. He pulled Joanie closer too him, tucked his arm around her, and slept.

Ringing True

It's Wednesday night and I am lying here on the bed thinking about Jeanette, that time she held us spellbound one night in the junior common room, claiming that after the first time you did *IT* you were never the same. I remember Emma challenged her, saying that she was making a sweeping statement. Exactly *how* were you different?

Jeanette regarded her scornfully. 'Look at it this way, Em. You have this china cup. Perfect in every way. You drop it and it cracks. Then you mend it with the finest glue. Nobody can see the join. But then, ever after, whenever you flick it, it never rings true, does it. See? You're never the same!'

Well. I have to tell you I don't feel like a cracked cup. And I hope I'll always ring true. But I don't think I ever will be the same. In the event, the mechanics of making love were odd but kind of expected, as was the fumbling, the pleasure of touching, the incredible, almost unendurably sharp pain. But what was the biggest surprise was the feeling of benign helplessness towards the end *and calm of mind all passion spent*. The most enormous revelation was not the panting and the wrestling, not the pain nor the passion, but this heart-rending feeling of helplessness at the end: he helpless in my arms, me helpless in his. After recognising that exchange of power I know

Jeanette is right. You are never the same. But it's nothing to do with cracked teacups.

This strange evening started oddly, with me and my mother walking round each other like cats in a cage. Because Karen and I had coffee with Steve at the Roma (our second that day), I get in later than usual from work to find my mother at the scullery sink, stripped down to her bra. The place smells all flowery: the body lotion I bought her for Christmas is on the draining board. I see she has broken the seal at last. She doesn't look round. We are both embarrassed. It is so rare to see her without her top layer of clothes. I feel like a voyeur.

'I'll just get changed.' I leap up the back stairs and just sit on the edge of my bed giggling about the strangeness of it all. Like father like son. Like mother like daughter. How strange is that? I hear her padding up to her bedroom and I take my turn at the sink washing as far up as possible and as far down. Baths can only happen on Saturdays in this house. We have time then to fill the boiler by hand, light it, bring the bath into the scullery, wait for the water to heat, then take turns jumping in to have our baths. One of the undisclosed delights of college has been the hot gushing water and the daily bath in a room designated for that purpose.

But tonight I am clean enough, and when I've finished I dip into my mother's body lotion and rub it all over. (Later, when we are in the middle of *IT,* Tamás will tell me I smell nice, I will tell him the perfume is called Y, after Yves St Laurent. I will not tell him it's my mother's...)

'*You* look nice!' she says when I get downstairs.

I am wearing the blue polka-dot cotton dress with the boat neck that she bought for me on tick, as part of my college trousseau. I have never worn it at college. We mostly wear jumpers with jeans or leggings, and I didn't go to the college Formal at Christmas, as the blue cotton, was not sufficiently formal. But still, it's a very nice dress.

My mother is looking pretty nice herself in a straight brown skirt, white ruffled shirt, and Cuban-heeled shoes. She is wearing lipstick and holding herself straighter than usual. I broach the subject.

'Are you going out with Constantin, then?'

She glances round the front room, which tonight, like her, has had a wash and brush-up. 'No,' she says. 'I thought we'd have a cup of tea here.' She nods at the tray of glasses and short-bread on the table. 'Or some of his blessed Tokay. He's an ambassador for that drink.' Then she finally looks me in the eye. 'But it's talking between old friends. That's all. Nothing more.'

And I am blushing. I don't want her to tell me that. Or say anything about what goes on between her and Constantin Kovacs. She's thirty-nine, for goodness' sake. And he's even older. It doesn't bear thinking about.

'Are you going out, then?' she says.

'I don't know. I said I'd just call up there for him. We might go out.' I am pulling on my coat, dying to get away.

She nods, loses interest. She straightens the cushions on the settee. 'You have a nice time then.'

339

The road up to the prefabs is the road I used to walk every school day for seven years. I know every house, every alleyway, every dusty front garden. Tonight, instead of walking past the church, I turn right and find my way to the Toytown squares of the prefab estate. I can't miss the house, because Tamás's little car is parked outside. A woman two doors down stands blatantly at her window and watches my progress. A boy's bike painted in bright red leans drunkenly beside the door of number seventeen.

Tamás is at the door before I knock, looking unfamiliar in jeans and a white open-necked shirt. He smiles, a touch of colour on his high cheekbones. 'You came,' he says, opening the door wide to let me in.

'I didn't know you rode a bike,' I say, instantly regretting saying such a stupid thing.

'It's not mine,' he says over his shoulder, leading the way into the small sitting room. 'I'd need shorter legs to ride that. It's Maria's boy's bike.'

The room is crowded with furniture, the walls covered with pictures in dense reds and ochres. In the centre is a small table, covered with a white cloth, set for two, flanked by two carved chairs.

'Maria made us some of her goulash,' he says. 'Special version. It's very good.'

Our embarrassment is alleviated by the business of serving the goulash and pouring the wine, the process of eating and talking of neutral things: Tamás's life at the factory, about how sharp Mr Priest really was, despite being a bit of a character; how Tamás has grown up among

340

Stan and women like Patsy O'Hare. How much he likes my mother, although we skirt round any mention of my mother and his father, at this minute drinking Tokay and eating shortbread.

As we clear the table I ask him about his mother and he doesn't tell me directly. But he tells me this story about something that happened last year, when he saw this weird thing in Grafton. He leads me across and we sit on the high-backed over-stuffed sofa. 'There was this time I saw my brother Anton who is dead, here in Grafton. I shouldn't have seen him but I did.

'I stopped off at Rollisons, you know, that decrepit garage at the bottom of the High Street? Well, this scruffy oil-spattered old man fills up my car. I had this old Ford then. It doesn't take long to fill it: two panfuls will do. The old man pats the top of the car lovingly like you would of a rather large dog, the glowing end of his cigarette splashing onto the bonnet. "Nice little movers, these. Good runners."'

Tamás takes my hand in his. 'Me, I can only see the rust on the wheel-rims, the worn upholstery. But that night I agree with him. It's easier to agree with some people than get into a hassle. Especially with old men with such sharp eyes and hands like talons.

'So there I am, Cassandra. As I close the petrol cap I raise my eyes to the edge of the sliproad that leads to the garage. And – I'm telling you the truth here – there on the road is this boy with a shock of black hair; his white shirt a bit too big and his corduroy pants dipping over his boots. And I have no doubt at all that it is Anton, my little brother. But I also have no doubt that I *shouldn't* see him. This is impossible. My little brother Anton is dead.

'You need to know, Cassandra, that I last saw Anton on our narrow street in Budapest, hand in hand with my mother, the day they both died. She had her canvas bag over her shoulder, stuffed with leaflets as usual. She turned and waved, the dip in her felt hat hiding her eyes. And that was the last time I saw her. And him.

'I must tell you, my mother had no fear. She was always passionate, very active. And these new events in our city fired her up even more. She argued with my father just that day, that the Uprising was working. The Russian tanks had withdrawn. We had secured international interest in our fight. There was to be a great conference. The leaflets she was showering around her would turn the last doubters. She was a great campaigner, my mother.

'So, Cassandra. How do you think I can see Anton here, a thousand miles away, nine years later, still wearing the same sagging corduroys? I'm telling you I blinked so hard, so very hard, to get rid of that image. When I opened my eyes again I could see Anton still, standing there, smiling straight at me. And then I realised that I could see a green van passing behind him. I could see that green van *through* him. Through him!

'Listen, I know he shouldn't be there, couldn't be there, but still, I rush towards him, to embrace him. I move right away from the car.' Tamás is breathing heavily now, clutching my hand really hard. 'And then behind me there is this great

342

crack and *booo-om* and I am thrown onto my face in the mud. When I haul myself to my feet Anton has gone. And I turn back round to see great licks of flame shooting up around my car. Beside it is the old man in a crumpled heap.' He paused. 'I kept quiet about it. I never told anyone that before. Not my father. It is far too weird,' he said.

'Not even Evelyn! You didn't even tell Evelyn?'

He turned to face me, his gaze locked with mine. 'Not even Evelyn. But I have told you about Evelyn.'

That was when he took my face in his hands and kissed it, and I experimented in kissing him back. I was surprised at how smooth his skin was. I thought it might be rough, with all that shaving business. He muttered something in Hungarian.

I drew back. 'What was that? What does that mean?'

He pulled me to him again. 'It means that you are extraordinary.'

And then it happened, like I said. All that stuff about pain and powerlessness, joy and resolution. And now, here I am, lying on my bed, luxuriating in the feeling of being a total part of Tamás's life for those long exulting minutes, knowing that I would never be the same again. And I am thinking of the gift he gave me: the untold story of how his brother Anton came from the dead to save his life.

Now below me I can hear the rumble of voices. Constantin and my mother were still at it when I arrived home. Talking, I mean. The room was untouched: not a hair or a cushion out of place.

Not quite like mother like daughter, after all.

A Note for Caroline

Tamás hadn't been around on Tuesday lunch-time so Evelyn had her sandwiches on her own. Perversely now, she was surprised that Tamás had not been more cast down by her rejection. She had been prepared to be kind and supportive, even apologetic. But Tamás had been cheerfully busy when he came back from lunch, winking at her one time when he caught her staring at him. She thought she might catch him at the end of the day, perhaps accept his inevitable offer of a lift home. Then they would have been able to talk about the future and how good it would be that they would always be friends without the threat of a doomed relationship always about them. But this opportunity was denied Evelyn as, at the end of the day, Tamás was nowhere to be found.

She asked Stan Laverick (ready to go off himself in an unusually smart suit), whether he had seen Tamás.

'The lad lit off ten minutes ago, Evie. Said he had to go and make himself beautiful. I had the feeling he was on a promise. You know!' He winked and pulled his head to one side.

'Tamás wouldn't say such a thing, Stan,' she said severely. 'If I didn't know you better, Stan, I'd call you a dirty old man.' She looked him up and down. 'You look very smart yourself. Are there promises out there for you?'

He went red. 'Nothing of the sort,' he said gruffly. 'Going out to check on that old dear across at the coast, who's getting the cooker tomorrow. See if she's still standing and breathing. There can't be any hitches.' He pulled down his cuffs so that they were visible. 'Gotta put a good face on for Marvell's, haven't we? No good turning up in overalls.' And he stalked off.

It was a slow journey home to Brigg. The Marvell factory workers that packed Evelyn's bus seemed to take extra time to get off at the many stops. The bus took ages to trundle its way, just about empty now, to her village. So she had lots of time to think about Tamás Kovacs. Perhaps she had cut her nose off to spite her face, in being so honest with him. If she lost him as a friend the drabness of her life would really start to show through. Just now the thought of a life stretching before her, alternating between the factory and the narrow house she shared with her father, made her feel uncharacteristically wretched. She stared out of the window as the narrow streets broadened out into fields and villages, and wondered if this really was *it*. In her mind she began to go over the cities, the countries she had seen; the wonderful houses in which she had stayed; the colourful people she had met; the clever attractive men with whom she'd had more than a passing acquaintance. Was that really over? Was this really *it?*

Then she blinked and rubbed her eyes to stall the embryonic tears lurking there. She told herself not to be silly, that she had been lucky to have those years, those experiences. And at this point in her life there were other priorities. She had worked that out very well at the beginning, and she should keep it at the front of her mind. This thing with Tamás would find its new place in her life.

When she finally alighted from the bus the wind was stirring, as it always did on this narrowing part of the valley, and rain was drizzling down. She put her best foot forward, picking her way down the back lane in her high-heeled shoes. She passed a girl playing two-ball up against a wall, and a man grooming his dog up on an old table in his back yard: both of them were oblivious to the rain.

When she arrived at her house she looked up at it and, even although it was broad daylight, she saw that all the lights were on, upstairs and down. Then she saw the open door and began to run.

Her father was lying on his face at the bottom of the stairs, one hand under his head as though he'd fallen to sleep naturally there. She kneeled down and turned him over so that his head was on her lap. She felt for a pulse in his hand, then his neck and was rewarded with a faint fluttering.

'Daddy!' she whispered in his ear. 'What have you done?'

His eyes flickered and he made a faint humming sound and then was silent. She looked round wildly, then leaned across to the small table and picked up the phone, blessing the day when she insisted they should have one, despite being so stretched for money. Theirs was the only telephone in the row and neighbours often came here to use it in emergencies. Well, this was her emergency. She dialled the number and spoke into the handset. 'I need an ambulance,' she said. 'Rather urgently.'

Later, looking at her father's narrow, still body in his Durham hospital bed, she wondered whether it was her fault; whether she had caused his accident by thinking those treacherous, selfish thoughts on the bus. The fall could have happened just then, just as she was moaning to herself about being stuck here with him, in this place. She listened numbly as the doctor told her they suspected some kind of bleeding into the brain. It had probably caused the fall rather than was the consequence of it. No, they didn't know whether it had been caused by the dementia. The doctor speculated that perhaps the symptoms of dementia had been caused some time ago by the beginning of such bleeding.

He was a quiet, young, man and seemed detached from her pain. He told her she should go home, get some rest. Was she on the telephone? He would take her number and would telephone her if there were any change. He promised he would do that.

It took two connecting buses to get home and she was trembling with exhaustion as she finally sat down at the kitchen table. She raised her eyes to the enamel clock ticking away on the kitchen shelf. It was ten o'clock. She had neither eaten nor drunk anything since her lone lunchtime sandwiches in the office. She breathed in very deeply, let the breath slowly exhale, then stood up to put on the kettle. As she did so she noticed scraps of newspaper on the table, and on the surface of the kitchen cabinet. What had he been doing, tearing up bits of newspaper? She picked up one piece and peered at it. There were words in the blank margins. 'Caroline.' He had scrawled her mother's name three times. 'Caroline. Caroline. Caroline.' She picked up another and it too was scrawled with her mother's name. Her eye dropped to another piece of paper by the front-room door. There were three in the front room. Two on the stairs. Two in her bedroom. In his bedroom there was one on the bed and two on the bedside table.

The picture of her mother that always sat there was missing. She looked around, then saw it on the floor by the window with the glass cracked and crazed, obscuring her mother's smiling face. He must have ground his heel in it. She sat down hard on the bed, fell awkwardly sideways and drew her knees up, coiling herself inwards like a spring. She put her thumbs under her chin and cupped her face in the way her mother used to. 'Nothing to worry about, Evie, love. Nothing to worry your pretty head.' Evelyn said the words herself but it was her mother's voice she heard. It seemed then that her mother was there in the room with her. Evelyn closed her eyes tight, just in case she might see her. If she opened them her mother might be there. That she couldn't bear. She just couldn't bear that...

Later, she woke with a start and sat up, rubbing her cold arms. The bedroom light was on and the night outside was very dark. The telephone! She had to be downstairs for the telephone. The hospital might ring. She rooted in the drawer and found one of her father's big pullovers: one that her mother had knitted for him, years ago. It smelled faintly of lavender. She pulled it on and was warmed by it.

She went downstairs then, made herself a strong cup of tea, a tomato sandwich and went to sit in the hall beside the telephone.

Making Up

Patsy and Karen, in bed that night by nine thirty, both heard the knock on the door but it was Patsy who put on her quilted nylon housecoat and padded to answer it.

'Oh, it's you!' she said sourly. 'I suppose you'd better come in.' She led the way in and turned to face her visitors. 'I expect you've not come here to cause trouble.'

'No, no. Not at all,' said Karen's father.

'It's not right,' began Mrs Duncan. 'My Karen not being in her own home.'

'Nobody's forcing her,' said Patsy.

Mrs Duncan looked round. 'If she hadn't here to come to, she'd have to come home, to us.'

'No she wouldn't,' said Patsy. 'Linda Fox would have had her. Karen's good friends with that Cassandra. You saw that.'

Mrs Duncan peered behind Patsy as though she were hiding Karen behind her skirts. Then she called out, 'Karen!'

Karen appeared in the doorway in her baby-doll pyjamas, her hair mussed up. 'Mam! What're you doing here?'

'You don't know what you've done to me, Karen. Couldn't rest, couldn't settle...'

'Sure, the woman's been prowling round like a caged lion, she has,' growled Karen's father, peering at Karen over his wife's shoulder.

Mrs Duncan shook her head. ''S not right, our Karen, you not being at home. That you're sleeping under someone else's roof. They're all asking for you at home. The little 'uns. Our Eric asked me if you had died and gone to heaven. 'S not right.'

'That's not fair, Mam. I don't know why you're saying that. You don't want me there. You said so.'

Mrs Duncan went bright red. 'What was I supposed to do? You come home, lady, you throw this baby thing in my lap, and you expect me to just go along with it? To say nothing?'

'Listen, Mam! This is about me, not you. Me, I've no choice but to go along with it. You said as much to me. "You make your bed and you lie on it." That's what you said. That's what I've done. Only it's Patsy's spare bed that I'm lying on.' She looked across at Patsy, who had thrown herself into a seat and was concentrating on lighting a cigarette.

Karen's mother examined her from head to toe. 'You don't have to ... well ... accept what's happening to you. There's ways...'

Patsy sat up straight and grunted.

'You what?' Karen raised her voice. 'You'd rather have me do *something?* Go through God knows what?'

'Well,' her mother hesitated, 'people do it. People always have. I knew–'

Karen interrupted her. 'Cassandra, this friend of mine from work, her friend's sister did just that. She did *something*. And, you know what happened? She died!'

Her mother stared at her for a minute. Then she folded her arms. 'Anyway! What would you know about taking care of any baby? Can barely take care of yourself, you.'

Patsy drew on her cigarette. 'Aren't you supposed to be good at all that stuff? Mother of the Year and that? You can teach her,' she said through the smoke.

'Her? Teach me?' exploded Karen. 'Let me tell you something, Patsy. She won't even let you fold towels. You're not good enough. You do it all wrong. This one time I pegged the washing out and she took it all down and pegged it again because it wasn't in the right order.'

Patsy sniffed. 'Well, pet, it's gunna be your baby. Up to you to learn. You can peg the washing which way you like, seems to me. If it was your own washing, your own baby.'

Karen's father moved so he was shoulder to shoulder with his wife. 'Your mate's right, darlin'. You would learn. You're sharp. Always been sharp.' Then he moved right in front of his wife so her mother was blocked from Karen's view. 'And your mother's right, love. The kids are mooning about the house with long faces. Sure, the house isn't the same without you. We should all stick together, whatever happens. I told your mam that. I made her come here for you.'

Karen folded her arms tight around herself. 'She'd get on to me. I'd have a dog's life. You know what she's like.'

'That's what families are for, love. To get on to each other. To give each other a dog's life. Only they have the right to do that. That's one of the binds that tie. Painful, like, I'll admit.' He shrugged.

Mrs Duncan came round her husband to get closer to Karen. 'We have all this stuff, love!' Her voice was much softer now. 'In the loft. Stuff from our Eric. Pram, pushchair, all those jumpers I knitted. No good letting them go to waste, is there?'

Karen's arms dropped to her sides. 'You wouldn't get on to me?'

Her mother shrugged. 'What's done's done, love. The bairn's innocent, no matter what. And it's blood of our blood. I wouldn't get on to you more than usual, I promise that.'

Karen took a step back to look at her mother more clearly.

Her father spoke up. 'I tell you what, flower. You sleep on it. I'll come back half-six in the morning and, if you're ready I'll pick up your stuff and you can pop home and pick up your lunch box. Big day, tomorrow, eh? With that singer coming?'

Karen looked from one to the other and retreated into the bedroom, closing the door behind her.

The couple turned towards Patsy. She waved her cigarette at them. 'Don't you two look at me! None of this is my doing. Me, I was her very last resort.'

Mrs Duncan looked at her. 'You won't persuade her to stay?'

'Why would I? Karen's my workmate and she needed a hand. That's it. If you think I'm coming between a lass and her family you think wrong.'

Mr Duncan said, 'Thank you for helping our girl, Patsy...'

'She had no need–' began Mrs Duncan.

He took her arm. 'Now, Sarah. No need to be ungracious.' He turned back to Patsy. 'Like I said, if she wants to come home I'll be here at half-six and we can drop her stuff at our place before she goes to work. Then they'll both have all day to simmer down. Just you watch. Tomorrow night it'll be like nothing's happened.'

Patsy stood up, grinning. 'Like nothing's happened but there's this elephant in the corner of the kitchen?'

Mrs Duncan would have said something then, but her husband hustled her out of the room.

Patsy closed the door behind them with a satisfying click and stood with her back to it. *Families!* You could keep them! And please God, though she was a great kid, Karen would have to decide to go back there tomorrow, because more of this clatter Patsy could not stand.

She took her time finishing her cigarette, then put out the lights. The door to Karen's door was ajar so she went in to have a word. The low bedside light was on but Karen was fast asleep, her black hair spread across the pillow, her hand under her ear like a child. Patsy turned off the light and tiptoed out, shutting the door behind her.

As she settled herself back in her bed the thought occurred to her that it was not only the unborn baby that was an innocent in all this. Karen too had been an innocent but now she was learning fast.

Patsy pulled the blanket up to her neck and thought how nice it would be to get her flat back to herself. She would have to give it a good bottoming at the weekend to clear out all this stuff in the air. But after that it would be as though all these shenanigans had never happened. She hoped.

The Italian Suit

Wednesday Morning

Millie Priest couldn't sleep. She woke up at one o'clock, then two. At two forty-five she went downstairs and made herself a cup of tea in her new mesh-interior teapot. She sat under a single spotlight in her lounge and turned the pages of a new book she had bought by Dr Spock. She looked up hiccoughs and learned that it was quite normal for a new baby to hiccough as long as it was warm, secure and well fed. It seemed they grew out of them in time.

Well, that's a relief, she thought, closing the book. She herself had suffered from hiccoughs as a baby. Her mother had rushed her to the hospital four times with hiccoughs. In the shop where she grew up, hiccoughs were keenly discussed when the subject of Millie's babyhood came up, as it did time and again. They were like a record with the needle stuck, her mother and her aunts. The three of them had always babied her, right up to her wedding. Then Charlie took over, treating her like bone china, indulging her to keep her sweet. That, she had to admit, was the way she liked it. But now that would stop. She knew that. You can't baby a woman who has a baby of her own. Things were about to change. She put her hand flat on her flat stomach. Impossible really, a baby in there. Wasn't it?

Then the spotlight seemed to dim as the morning light began to penetrate her curtains and illuminate the room. She took her cup into the kitchen and left it on the stainless-steel draining board. When she got back upstairs Charlie was still asleep, half the covers thrown off and his hand flung out, palm upwards. He looked boyish and young. She suddenly hoped that the baby would be a boy. Then she'd have two men to spoil her.

Charlie's best suit – a grey Italian job bought on a trip to an appliance factory near Milan – was hanging outside the wardrobe. It had survived her vengeance by living in a special plastic hanger in the third bedroom. The Italian suit! Only the best was good enough for Miss Sandie Shaw. Millie slipped into bed beside Charlie, curled up and went to sleep. She was just dreaming of a teenage girl with bows in her hair trying to sell her cakes at a ridiculous price, when she woke up to Charlie shaking her.

She sat up.

'Cup of tea for you, baby,' he said. He put a mug of tea on the bedside table. He looked glamorous in the impeccable grey suit.

She smiled sleepily at him. 'All dressed up for Sandie Shaw, I see,' she said. She watched him adjust his tie in the dressing-table mirror. 'Big day, for you, Charlie.'

'You bet your bottom dollar, lover. Factory's looking good. Mr Owen's here already. Rumour's that Mr Abrahams's flying up too. The mayor and his minions. The press'll be there. Even telly. This thing was a bloody good idea. Never happened before in any of the Marvell factories you know. They'll all be rushing to copy us.'

Millie yawned. She had heard this so many times in the last week. She took a sip of her tea. Charlie glanced at her through the mirror. 'You won't like it when I tell you, lover. It was Evelyn Laing's idea, you know. Well, her and Tamás Kovacs. They cooked it up between them. It was her contact that made it all possible.'

She smiled sweetly at him. 'I don't have any-thing in particular against Evelyn Laing, Charlie. Not now. As long as she doesn't want to get her talons into you.'

He sat down on the bed. 'No chance. There is this film star who says: Why go out for burger when you've got prime steak at home?'

She grimaced. 'What a horrible thing to say.'

'Makes his point, though.'

She looked at him. 'What is it that you want, Charlie?'

'I want Mr Abrahams to be so chuffed with this

356

that he'll double the size of the Grafton factory. Start to make fridges. All kinds of things.'

'No, silly. I want to know what you want! Boy or girl?'

'Oh, that?' He paused for quite a long time. 'I think I'd probably like a son. Son and heir and all that.'

She smiled. 'That's what I was thinking. A boy would be nice.'

'Good!' He stared down at her fondly. 'Well, lover, another day, another dollar, as they say.' He leaned down to kiss her. 'Be there in that gorgeous frock. Twelve o'clock. Come and flaunt yourself for the telly.'

'It's not a frock,' she said to the closing door. 'It's a suit.'

She went back to sleep for another hour, then got up and had a leisurely bath before going to the hairdresser's for a quick wash and dry. Then she took time putting on her make-up and slipping into her pale blue shantung suit. She stood in front of her cheval mirror and knew she would do Charlie proud. Behind her the shades of her aunties and her mother were nodding in agreement. You had to put on a good show, no matter what.

She considered giving Joanie Laverick a ring to offer her a lift to the factory, but decided against it. Joanie would surely have made her own arrangements by now. She was a strange one, Joanie. Pretty ungrateful, when you came to think of it.

So she would go on her own.

Millie was suddenly sorry her mother and

aunties were not here to share this moment of Charlie's glory, and her own special news. When they finally sold the shop, the little bungalow in Torquay had been their chosen option. They had spent so many happy holidays there and the climate was so much better than the cold North. And you got such a nice class of person in Torquay. Millie had been quite happy once they went. After she got married she only wanted to concentrate on Charlie. Her mother and aunts faded into the deep background of her life.

But this morning Millie was thinking about her mother. Things were different now. She dialled the number. Her mother answered in her slightly raised, clipped telephone voice, which she dropped when she realised it was Millie.

'Oh, hello, dear. Are you well?' The faintest thread of anxiety; a Wednesday morning phone call must surely mean trouble.

'Very well, Mother. Extremely well, in fact. Charlie has this big do on today at the factory and I'm to be guest of honour.' She told her mother about the presentation, but the impact of her announcement was somewhat reduced because her mother had no idea who Sandie Shaw was.

'And there's something else. About me. Well. About Charlie and me. We're expecting.'

'Expecting? Expecting what?'

Millie was annoyed at the bewilderment in her mother's voice. What did she think they were expecting? A car, a boat, a cruise? 'A baby, silly! I'm pregnant.'

There was a silence at the other end. Millie imagined her mother putting her hand on the mouthpiece and relaying the news to the aunties. 'Well,' said her mother a little breathlessly, 'that's a surprise. I thought you and Charlie ... well ... that kind of thing wasn't for you.' She paused. 'You have been married a long time.'

'Well, we *are* doing this kind of thing. Aren't you pleased?'

'Of course I am, if you are.'

Millie put down the phone with a click. She shouldn't have bothered. Her mother and aunts had never really been interested in her, once she was married. Oh yes, they had spoiled her as she grew up, buying her clothes, patent shoes and ribbons for her hair, keeping her younger than her age so they could still dote on her like some dolly. But once Charlie came along and she moved into the world of grown-ups they seemed to lose interest, closing in on each other into a simpering maidenly trio, her mother's brief fling of a marriage dissolved into history and Millie along with it. Decamping to Torquay was the natural consequence of all that.

The phone rang again and she thought it might be her mother, ringing up to apologise. But it was Charlie, asking her if she would pick up Joanie Laverick.

'I told Stan you'd be happy to. Told him we don't want poor Joanie in her glad rags on the bus, do we?'

'I thought of that myself,' she said. 'I'll give her a ring.'

So, after her less than satisfactory call to her mother, Millie quite enjoyed ringing Joanie to tell her she would give her a lift to the factory in her

Capri. Joanie's thanks were not exactly gushing but this did not trouble Millie. She knew deep inside by now how important she was to Charlie's career and his important role in Grafton.

And now here she was giving him a son and heir. Surely she was the best wife ever?

Best Bib and Tucker

The factory today is a different place, a special place. It's not just the newly painted gates or the brand-new magenta hoarding, celebrating Marvell's new Empress Cooker. It's not just the white painted lines or the tidy gangways. It's the people, all in their best bib and tucker. There is a rash of brand-new smocks and not a single hair roller or turban in sight. Most of the younger women have their hair elaborately swept up or down, fixed hard by generous hairspray. Some older women, their hair neat like vari-coloured cauliflowers, must have spent last night in perm curlers. This has gone wrong in the case of one woman, who has had to shove her alarming frizz under a kerchief. Even my mother has pin-curled her hair in Kirbigrips and now, combed out, it looks soft and pretty. She's wearing the skirt and ruffled blouse she wore last night to entertain Constantin Kovacs, and over it, like everyone else, she's wearing a new smock.

Karen is looking fabulous in full Sandie Shaw mode. Her hair is sleek, shining like tar, and her eye-lines make her eyes look huge and full of glamour. She smiles easily as she slips onto her stool. You wouldn't know that yesterday's dramas had happened.

Of all the women on our line, only Patsy looks no different. Her lipstick is just as red, her hair just as tight and tidy as ever, and she's wearing her usual smock. I remember this thing my friend Emma once said, when we were discussing social class after an English Culture lecture. 'The thing is, Cassie, it's a known fact. The working classes dress up for big occasions, the upper class dresses down for big occasions, and the middle classes dress up all the time.' She then told a tale of her grandfather who had entertained the local mayoress and her friend for tea in his jodhpurs and old, mended jacket. 'I heard them muttering about him in our lavatory. She said *she* had worn her rust brocade specially and you'd think the old boy would have some respect.'

Much as I like Emma, this irritated me. 'Well, then,' I said, 'does that make your mayoress working class or middle class?'

She laughed then, and tucked her arm in mine. 'I don't know, darling, but it certainly makes *him* upper class!'

Well, today I must be a true working-class girl because I am definitely dressed up in my best skirt and blouse, my bobbin-heeled shoes and my Pretty Polly nylons. To be honest I'm not just dressing up for Sandie Shaw. If Tamás drops by the line I certainly want to look my best. I hardly slept last night, thinking of him, and how different I am now. Perhaps he is different as well.

361

I'm not sure of that.

The factory and its people may have been changed for the day but at seven thirty sharp the conveyor grinds to a start as usual, and we all set to. Steve is hovering around, looking very smart in new slacks and a shirt and tie. Patsy is not saying too much but Karen is going on about presenting the flowers – which she had left in the care of Mrs Mundy in the toilets – to Sandie this afternoon.

'What should I say?' she says. '"Hello, welcome to Marvell's" or "Hello, I'm Karen"?'

Steve is in helpful mode. 'Should definitely say you're a big fan. Although, looking at you, she couldn't doubt that.' He smiles at her very fondly and it strikes me that he really has a thing for her. That hasn't struck me before. Perhaps last night has made a difference to how I see things.

My hands are working in a pleasing rhythm and I am quite relaxed. 'You could tell her which song you like best,' I offer.

'Easy, that,' Karen says. '"Always Something There to Remind Me". I love that song.'

'Very ironic, that!' grunts Patsy.

Steve drags his eyes away from Karen and looks at Patsy. 'You all right, Pats?'

Her work rate doesn't flag. 'Me? I'm fine. Nothing a good night's sleep wouldn't solve.'

Steve looks at each of us in turn, knowing he's missing something. Then Stan's voice roars down the gangway and he hurries off.

I look from Patsy to Karen. 'How's things then?' If they are rowing today after two nights together, Karen will be back to my house like a boomerang. My heart sinks.

'Things're fine,' says Karen. 'Mam and Dad came over to Patsy's and we've patched things up.'

'Oh, good!' I say, relieved. 'It is good, isn't it?' I look at each of them again. 'You're pleased?'

'Well, I know Mam'll take over. But that's OK. I can get back to work in no time. I'll need the money more than ever.'

'If you imagine everything can carry on the same you're a fool,' said Patsy. She is screwing in the wires with a kind of fury that's hard to pin down. Surely she must be pleased that Karen has sorted things out?

Karen puts down her screwdriver. 'Don't take on, Patsy,' she says quietly. 'I have to take things as they are, or go back to that woman in Durham. And I can't do that.' Then she picks up her screwdriver again.

Patsy's work rate begins to slow and I relax. She sighs. 'I would have wished better for you, flower,' she says. And now I see how much she loves Karen, as a daughter, as a sister, or something I can't quite put my finger on.

We are saved from any more of this deep stuff by a kind of procession coming down the gangway towards us. Stan Laverick, his flapping white coat over a very smart suit, is leading a group headed by Mr Priest, and the burly man who talked to Patsy yesterday, and a much smaller man with large features, who is carrying a homburg hat.

'That's a turn-up,' says Patsy.

'Who are they?' I hiss.

'Well, thank you, Sandie Shaw! You saw big feller Mr Owen yesterday, Cassandra. He's Marvell's God Almighty in the North. The little one is Mr Abrahams, Marvell's God Almighty in the country. In fact he's *Mr* Marvell! Started the whole shebang.'

The procession stops by our bench and Mr Abraham nods at Patsy. 'Hello, Patsy. Still here?'

'They'll have to shoot us, Mr Abrahams, to get rid of us. Like I said to Mr Owen, me and Marvell's go back a long way.'

He laughs at this, showing a gold tooth. I think of Constantin Kovacs. 'Well, you know, Patsy, you could say the same for me. You and me and Marvel's go back a long way.'

The procession moves on, but not before Mr Priest, with a peculiar sidelong glance, has winked at Karen.

'Cheeky bugger,' says Patsy.

'Leave it, Pats,' says Karen. 'What happens to me now has nothing to do with him. It's my own business.'

I can hear this going on but I am now pre-occupied with Tamás, who is bringing up the end of the procession behind the two men with big leather camera bags. Tamás stops by my bench. He looks very smart in what must be his best suit (makes him working class, that!) and a dark green silk tie. He comes quite close to me.

'Cassandra! How are you this morning?' he says in a low voice in my ear. 'You look very nice.'

I keep my hands busy and my head down. 'I am very well, and you look nice yourself.'

'Would you like to come out with me tonight?'

he says. 'To the pictures?'

We're both aware of the very close interest of Patsy and Karen. 'Talk afterwards,' I hiss.

He raises his voice. 'Stan Laverick asked me if you would do something for us, Cassandra. At about twelve.'

'What's that?' I say, clearly now.

'He wants you to take care of Mrs McLochlan, to ride shotgun on her, so to speak. That's the lady who's getting the cooker. We're sending a car for her and she will be here just before twelve. We had Evelyn lined up to take care of her but she's not in today.'

'Is she sick?' says Karen.

'No. Something about her father being rushed to hospital. Pity. He is a very nice man.' He pauses. 'So Stan thought you might do it, Cassandra.'

'Typical!' grunts Patsy.

'What's that, Patsy?' says Tamás.

'Look at these two!' she says. 'One bowing and scraping with a bunch of flowers. One squiring the guest of honour. And here's me, I'll be flogging myself here making up the shortfall.'

'Ah,' grins Tamás. 'But where would any of these grand people be without you making the cookers? This is the most important thing! It was you that Mr Abrahams greeted. Not anyone else.'

'You!' she growls. 'You Hungarians can charm the birds off the trees. I've always said that.' But you can see she's mollified.

His smile broadens. 'You are always saying that, Patsy. And you're not the only one.'

Then Stan Laverick's roar resounds again

down the gangway above the hum of the conveyor and Tamás, like Steve, obeys.

Patsy is suddenly in a good mood. 'You've caught that one there, Cassandra. Hook, line and sinker!'

Karen smiles and takes a hand off the job to punch me in the shoulder. 'Look at her! Red as a beetroot! What have you been up to?'

'Karen!' I am flustered. Now I'm convinced that last night's events are showing on my face, in my voice.

'Leave the bairn alone,' says Patsy, grinning. 'You've got to admit, though, that she's on a better wicket than you, kidder.'

At last I'm relieved of their forensic attention by the buzzer for morning break and we relax and open our flasks. Karen opens one of her Tupperware boxes to reveal her mother's immaculate queen cakes. I rush to change the subject.

'So things are sorted, Karen? It's all right at home?'

She smiles wryly. 'The kids welcomed me back like I'd been away for weeks. My dad pretends nothing has happened. He's back behind his newspaper. Worst thing is, my mam's out to fatten me up like a Christmas turkey.'

'So it's all OK?'

She shrugs. 'Not really. Patsy here's not wrong there. But I'm gunna pretend this thing's not happening till it's too big to ignore. And I'll think about things then. I know my mam'll treat it like her kid and mebbe I won't like that. But something might turn up. You never know.'

Patsy bites into her sandwich-spread sandwich.

'Our little Steve carries a torch for you, you know,' she says with her mouth full.

Karen's eyes fill with tears and she takes a brave bite of her queen cake. 'Just wait till he finds out,' she says. 'Wait till they all find out. Then nobody'll want to know me.'

Patsy scowls. 'Anybody funny with you, love, and they'll have me to deal with.'

Karen sniffs back her tears and we both laugh at this. 'Oh, Patsy,' she says. 'You are a one-off.'

The buzzer goes and we get back to work. With my hands flying over the wiring jackets I think again of Patsy, fierce, protective and somehow vulnerable in the way she cares. I also think she might have got it right about Steve. Baby or no baby, I think he'll still be waiting in the wings.

Leaving

Despite being so worried, Evelyn Laing, on the phone to Charlie, had tried to state the situation calmly. 'It's my father, Mr Priest. He was rushed to the hospital last night. He's there now and I have to be with him. So I'm afraid I can't be at the factory today.'

'Bad news about your dad, Evelyn.'

'So I can't be there today. You see?'

There was silence on the line and she thought they had been cut off. 'Mr Priest? You understand? My father's in hospital and I have to go to him.'

He coughed 'Well, Evelyn, I *understand* your father's in hospital. I do indeed. But he's in the *best* place there, isn't he? He's in good hands. He's being taken care of. So surely you *still* can make it into work? You're badly needed here, today of all days. Don't you realise what an *important* day this is?'

'Mr Priest...'

He interrupted here. 'You *have* to be here, Evelyn. You just *have to,* to support me, to support Marvell's. You minuted it, didn't you? You're down to take care of the winner, whatever her name is. And to check the demonstrators are on time with the food, to make sure things are OK there. And to check on the special guests. Don't you realise what a special day this is? Evelyn? Evelyn?'

She looked at her watch. She had twenty minutes before the bus. She should make herself breakfast. She'd almost forgotten about breakfast as she screwed herself up to make this call to Mr Priest. She'd been quite hesitant about making the call, just because she *did* know what day it was and she was quite aware that she would be missed.

But now, with Charlie Priest storming at her, raving on, she began to care much less about this special day. If one took Mr Priest's words at face value, this special day was much more important than her father, who was probably dying.

If she needed a signal, this was it. What on earth was she doing there among these people? You had no value to them unless you fed their machine. With the exception of Tamás, they had no experience of the world. Their horizons were set by Marvell's. The job she did there was intricate and interesting, but – she decided now – was not worth selling your soul for.

'Evelyn?' he was shouting into the phone.

'Oh, will you just shut up, you silly man!' she said. And she cut him off..

When she got to the hospital she was kept waiting in the waiting room for an hour, only to be told by a young, fresh-faced doctor just what she had been told on the phone: that her father had not regained consciousness and there was no point of her being in attendance.

She stood up to her full height and looked the young doctor in the eye. 'It seems to me, Doctor, that you're really telling me that I may not sit with my father while he is ill unto death?' She sharpened her accent, losing the local intonation she had first discarded when she went abroad. It had been useful, since she'd been home, to let it slip in again.

He was flustered. 'No one mentioned death, Miss Laing...'

'Well, he has been unconscious for ... what? Eighteen hours? For me that is a kind of death, Doctor.'

He looked round the narrow reception corridor, as though help would come from the painted walls. 'Er ... I'll go down to the ward and see if Sister...' His voice tailed away and he turned on his heel and almost ran down the ward. He was back in three minutes. 'Sister says that, as your father is in a side ward, you could ... er ... go and see … sit with him.'

On the ward the Sister, an immaculate, heavy woman with starched ribbons to her cap, was quite welcoming. 'We have turned him every hour, and dribbled some water into him but to be honest, Miss Laing, there is no reaction. I looked at his notes. Apparently there is dementia?'

Evelyn nodded.

The sister shook her head. 'A sad thing. It happened to my mother. She left us in mind years before she left us in body. It was all very sad.' She settled Evelyn by the bed and returned three minutes later with a cup of tea. 'You stay here as long as you want, dear. Call us if you need us.' She glanced at the bed. 'Or if he seems disturbed, or wakes.' Her tone suggested that *this* was very unlikely. She left the door very slightly ajar behind her.

Evelyn put the tea on the windowsill, drew her chair closer, took her father's hand, and started to talk: first about the day she was missing at Marvell's and about how angry Mr Priest was now, and how she didn't care. She told him about how the people at the factory loved it, lived for it, with as powerful a vocation as any doctor or priest. 'I suppose it's like soldiers being loyal to their regiment, Dad, sacrificing their all in the name of their regiment. Well, I'm afraid I've proved today I'm not such a good soldier. So I think I'll have to leave that place now. Or I'll be cashiered. They'd see that as deserting the cause, wouldn't they? But I've decided that I'm ready to leave now. And it's a bit of a relief, to be honest.'

370

She got up to peer through the window at the old trees and the city beyond, then came and sat with him again. She took his hand and squeezed it, imagining that she felt pressure back in return. He stirred and his eyelids flickered.

'I'm not an envious person, Dad. You know that. And working at Marvell's has shown me in a way how wonderful my life was before. But I'm envious of the way you and Mum were. How much you really loved each other. All my travels have taught me how very rare that is, the love you shared. Me? I was merely the beloved outsider. Don't worry. I was happy to be launched into the outside world, the love you two had for each other behind me. I have tried loving people, you know. There have been a couple of very special men who loved me. I loved each of them for a time. But that love didn't match up to what I knew, to the way you and Caroline loved each other. So always I moved on.' She sighed.

Then she felt it. A distinct pressure on her hand. She did not imagine it. She leaned towards her father. 'What is it, Daddy?'

His eyelids flickered very slightly. The words came from him like ripped paper. 'Evie, dear Evie.'

She put her face close to his. 'Daddy?'

He mumbled something.

'What? What is it?' she whispered, tears falling unchecked.

His hand grasped hers with surprising strength. 'Go on your travels, Evie. Time now. Promise me.' The hoarse whisper impelled itself from his throat. 'Promise.'

She kissed him, wetting his cooling cheek with hers. 'I will. I promise.'

He half sat then, coughing, and she held on to him. 'Evie,' he whispered. Then: 'Caroline ... Caroline.'

And that was it. His grip slackened, his head fell slightly to one side, his eyes wide. She sat there with him in her arms as the life went from him. Then very gently she lowered him back onto the pillow and closed his eyes.

She sat back in the chair, her closed eyes brimming with tears. She took out a handkerchief and dabbed her eyes, blew her nose. Then she went across to the window and took a sip of the cool tea. When she went back again to touch her father's hand it was already clay cold.

She went to the door and called for the sister, then stood in the corner as the checks were done. The sister looked across at Evelyn and nodded. Evelyn swallowed hard to stop the tears and the sister stood back while she kissed her father for the last time. Then the nurse gently drew the sheet over his head, tucking it in at the sides. She looked at Evelyn, who was still trying to control her tears.

'I heard you talking with him. That was a very loving thing to do. And now you can remember the man you knew, before all this. That's the best thing.' Then she glided out of the room and left Evelyn alone with her father.

She stood there with her eyes closed for a long time. Then very oddly she could feel them both, her mother and her father, standing either side of her, joining their hands behind her back – the heavier muscled weight of her father and the scented softness of her mother's shoulder. She opened her eyes and the feeling left her.

She turned away from the shrouded body on the bed and made her way out of the room. The sister asked was she all right and she said that she was. She had to get home to see to things.

The sister nodded. 'Well, dear,' she said quietly, 'just be gentle with yourself, won't you?'

It was only when she was standing at the bus-stop that it occurred to her that she didn't know the name of the sister who had been so kind to her. That was a pity. She would have liked to thank her.

All History Now

At eleven o'clock we are all working away when the visitors start to drift in: the mayor in his chain, and a small, Mrs Tiggy-Winkle kind of woman who must be his wife; two men in crumpled sports jackets who have 'PRESS' printed through them like Blackpool rock; a middle-aged woman in very high heels and a tight suit, with alarming bushy hair and a nice, relaxed smile; a tall man in a three-piece suit, shepherding a little old woman with a cap of smooth silver hair and a nervous-looking man in his thirties. Then there is Constantin Kovacs, who beams at me in recognition. Last to come are two women in their thirties. One, dressed in a shirt-waister dress and a blazer jacket, nods at Patsy, who nods back. The woman with her is wearing a cocktail suit in pale lilac slubbed silk.

'Shantung, that. Nice bit of stuff,' comments Karen. 'My mum would give her eyes to get her hands on a nice bit of stuff like that.'

Patsy's eyes gleam. 'That, flower, is Charlie Priest's wife.'

Karen's hands stop moving.

'Yeah,' said Patsy. 'If you ask me that's the poor bugger you've gotta be sorry for.'

Karen starts working again, her hands moving to a blur.

'Who's the other one?' I say, to break up the atmosphere a bit.

'That's Joanie Laverick, Stan's wife. Nice enough lass. Started with me on the lines twenty years ago. Daughter to Clive Jones that worked in the plating shop. Marvell's marvellous family policy, see?'

Just down the gangway we can see one of the reporters pull a microphone out of a big leather shoulder bag and try to interview one of the women on the lines. He tries twice, puts his hands to his ears, then throws up his hands and rejoins the procession.

'Mebbe he thinks we should stop the line so he can get the interview,' says Patsy. 'Fat chance.'

She looks across at me. 'You should get down the toilets and put on some lipstick, love. Stan's not around with his clipboard and they'll be down soon for you to ride shotgun on the old lady.'

'Old lady?'

374

'Tam said, before. Too busy staring into those big green eyes to listen. You're to take care of the prizewinner. Gettit? You saw her. She just went down the gangway before your very eyes. Go get some lipstick on.'

I don't need encouraging twice.

The toilets, smelling strongly of ripe disinfectant and new paint, are the cleanest I've ever seen them. The mirror is gleaming, there is not a broken chair in sight, the floor has been scrubbed and the graffiti on the walls has been painted out with thick paint the colour of camomile lotion. 'Somebody's been hard at work,' I say to Mrs Mundy, who is sitting beside her little cabinet in a brand-new white overall.

She flicks the ash on her cigarette in the floor. 'Painters in here overnight, flower. Charlie Priest did a round last night and had a dicky fit when he saw in here.' She sniffs. 'He's never had cause to look in before. They have their executive toilet on that top corridor. Men only, like. But I'm sure they'll make an exception for her. Miss Sandie Shaw.'

'Isn't there a lady's toilet up there?'

'Nah. The girls up there have to come down here. Come down here to wash their dishes and fill their kettles as well.' She laughs. 'What d'they says? "Colonel's lady and Rosie O'Grady are sisters under the skin!" True, believe me. Anyway, what-for are you gettin' all glammed up at this time of day?'

'They asked me to take care of the lady that has won the cooker. That secretary Evelyn Laing was gunna do it and she's off.'

'Ah, Evie! Now there you have a real lady. Even washes Charlie's cups and saucers with her little finger cocked.'

I look hard at her through the mirror but still can't make up my mind whether she's being sarcastic. My ears prick up at the mention of Evelyn Laing because of Tamás. I have to say it's a bit frustrating because I've heard nothing wrong about her so far. She's a bit too much of an angel for me.

I put on more lipstick, take down my ponytail, put it up again and tease down the sides. I can't think of anything else to do. Mrs Mundy reads my thoughts. 'That's enough. You've got youth on your side, pet. No point in gilding the lily, eh?' She winks and I think that down here, guarding the toilets like Cerberus on the Styx, she must know a lot about all of us, especially the women.

When I get back to my place on the line, Tamás is there. He grins and my heart lurches. 'There you are! Patsy here said you had run away.'

Patsy sniffs. 'Didn't say where to, like.'

So here am I walking down the gangway with Tamás Kovacs by my side, his hand very lightly on my elbow. I can feel the envious eyes of the women, especially the young ones, and it is hard to gulp down a grin. Tamás is explaining to me that there has been a delay as Sandie Shaw has missed the first plane at Luton and will get the next one. 'In fact our guy went to pick her up and there was a delay at the house. So we need to stall a bit. This Mrs McLochlan, who you're taking care of, worked here years ago and has asked to take a look round the factory. No one wants to leave the party, so Mr Priest thought you could show her round and take her down to the canteen for a cup of tea. She's a bit uneasy up there in the boardroom. Or to be honest, I think they might be a bit uneasy with her.'

The boardroom – a big square room beyond the progress office – is teaming with people. A conference table, pushed against the wall, is laden with pork pies and quiches and quarter sandwiches. A smaller table, tended by some kind of waiter, is doing service as a bar. Mr Owen and Mr Abrahams are deep in conversation with the man in the three-piece suit. Tamás whispers to me that he's the retailer who sold Mrs McLochlan the cooker: a valued customer. Charlie Priest is close by, with the mayor and his wife, who is talking to the woman in the lilac suit, Charlie's wife. Beside her is Stan's wife, talking to Constantin Kovacs, who is laughing and waving his hands around. Stan himself is in the corner, deep in conversation with the woman with bushy hair and one of the reporters. Tamás whispers that she's something to do with the shop at the coast and has come across to join in the fun. It's great. I feel part of it all now, recognising so many people in this crowd.

The only people sitting down are the little old woman with smooth grey hair, and a younger man, who, Tamás tells me, are Mrs McLochlan and her nephew, Alwyn.

'This is Cassandra, Mrs McLochlan. She's going to take you and your nephew down to show you the lines and to the canteen for a cup of tea. You said you'd like to stretch your legs.'

The old lady hauls herself to her feet and shakes me firmly by the hand. 'Everyone's been very kind, love, but I'm getting choked up in here. All this smoke!' It's true. Everyone except Mr Owen is smoking. Charlie Priest and the mayor are even smoking cigars. 'Anyway, I said to Mr Laverick that I'd like to take a look round. I worked here myself once before, you know.' She lowers her voice and whispers in my ear. 'And to be honest love, I wouldn't mind a visit to the lav.'

So, the three of us make our way down the gantry. Then, after a brief visit to the toilet, we walk along the lines, passing the dais with the prize cooker draped in a red velvet cloth, and then down the gangway along the red carpet to the big exit doors.

Mrs McLochlan doesn't say much about it all and I can't think of anything to say. But once we're in the canteen she seems to relax. She overcomes my insistence on paying, sends Alwyn to buy tea and scones, and settles in her seat beside me. 'You're giving me a cooker, pet. Surely I can buy you a cup of tea?' She looks round. 'This place is all new-built, isn't it?'

This place, empty now, smells of cigarette smoke and warmed-over vegetables. It has plate-glass windows, panelled walls in a kind of scrubby yellow Formica, and metal swing doors. The light, filtered through the steamed-up windows, is dim for midday. Alwyn, across at the counter, is chatting animatedly with the woman serving. It strikes me that he must be used to older women, living with his auntie.

'I think this is pretty new,' I say to Mrs Mc-

Lochlan. 'I'm new here myself. Only been in the canteen twice.' Once with Tamás Kovacs, I want to say to her, the man I made love to just last night.

She stirs three sugars into her tea. 'There was a warehouse on this site when I was first here, you know. It was kind of a big barn left over from the farm buildings that were here originally. When I was here they kept explosives here, under lock and key.'

'You were here in the war?' I look at her again: pink hat, smooth white hair, Dannimac (stone grey) over pink Crimplene frock. Her age is hard to tell. She could be anything from old-fashioned fifty to spring-chicken seventy. 'You were here?'

'Oh, yes. I worked here during the war. It was munitions then. Filling shells. Really dangerous work. We had to be very careful.' She dips into her handbag. 'I brought this. Thought they might be interested.'

This is a photograph of a group of women, some in dungarees, some with turbans on their heads. They look beefy and bold. 'This is me.' She points at a slighter woman in dungarees at the end of the row with her dark hair swept up in wings on either side of her head. She is very good looking. I try and fail, to see that young woman today under the Crimplene and the white hair.

'It must have been hard work.' Stupid words.

'Hard enough, love. But there were girls here from all over, all doing their bit. And there was plenty laughs, I can tell you.'

Alwyn comes across and arranges our tea and scones before us as though we are both decrepit old dears. He peers across the table. 'Never seen that photo, Auntie.'

'I was just telling this girl – Cassandra, was it? – I was just telling Cassandra about working here during the war.'

He sits down and sips his coffee. Then he frowns. 'Mebbe you shouldn't say, Auntie. If they know that, maybe you won't qualify for the cooker.' His tone is quite severe.

'Don't be soft, Alwyn.' She looks at him quite fondly. 'They've committed themselves, haven't they? I'm here. Sandie Shaw's on her way. What can they do?'

No flies on her, as my mother would say.

She goes on. 'Best time of my life, just then, love. All bed and work and Saturday dances with the soldiers. But so many laughs. Such great girls. Like I say, it was the best time of my life, out from under my mother's feet. Away from the post and the papers, you could forget about people being bombed in London and what your Uncle Ernie was up to with Monty in North Africa.' She nods at her nephew, who is now making a picnic of buttering his crumbling scone. 'That's his dad, my brother Ernie. Died at Tobruk.'

She stands up, turns right round, looks around across at the window, then sits down. 'Yes. New-built, this! I was thinking about all that in the car on our way here. It must have happened just here, that big bang! Tessa, Madge, Big Nora and little Laura. *Pouf!* Up in smoke. Wasn't even in the papers. *Careless talk cost lives.* That's what they said. Things like that explosion showed you what you were up to, laughs or no laughs.' She smiles at me warmly and takes up her cup. 'No danger for you now, pet. Not much harm in cookers. No young girls dying these days for nowt.'

I close my eyes and see Karen, and think of Emma's sister. When I open them Mrs Mc-Lochlan is frowning at me. 'You all right, pet?'

I shake my head, then nod. 'Fine. I'm fine.'

'My little friend Laura would be just your age, pet. But she looked so much younger. She had this big blonde plait down her back, like some German kid. She got teased for that, called a Nazi woman. Look!' And there in the photo beside the young Mrs McLochlan, is young Laura, her blonde plait over her shoulder like a silvery snake. 'I was real fond of her.' She glanced at Alwyn. 'She called me Auntie even though I was no relation. Then *pouf!* Up in smoke.' She sighs. 'It's all history now, like. All history.'

Then she busies herself with her scone and butter and the only thing we can hear is the clattering of pans behind the kitchen screen.

She finishes her scone, removes a couple of crumbs from the corner of her lips and looks at me. 'So you work on the lines do you, love?'

'Yes. But I just started this week.'

'Are you good at it?'

'No. Not much good. But there are two girls I work with. They're brilliant. They carry me along.'

'I bet you're popular!' She is being ironic.

I match her tone. 'Oh yeah, they really *love* me, those two.'

She stares at me a second, then sighs very deeply. 'Poor scrap. She was blown to smithereens, you know, young Laura. Just across there where the door was. They never found a single bit of her, poor bairn. Not a fingernail. Not a golden hair from her little head.' She nods towards a trolley full of dirty stacked plates. 'There. Just there. You can't tell me nothing about factory life, pet.'

The Tannoy crackles and her head shoots up at the syrupy tones of Tab Hunter singing 'Young Love'. 'We had that, you know, as well. Called *Workers' Playtime*, then.'

Desperately I stand up and look at my watch. 'Mr Kovacs said he wanted you back in the office by twelve. And this place'll fill up with bodies soon. We'd better make our way.'

Tamás is waiting for us at the top of the gantry steps. 'Thank you for that, Cassandra.'

'Is she here?' says Alwyn, his voice squeaking slightly. 'Is she here? Sandie Shaw?'

'Not quite,' says Tamás. 'Like I said, there's been a little hiccough. Seems that she is catching a later plane. She won't be here till one fifteen. They are starting to eat in there. He says to take you into the boardroom, Mrs McLochlan.' He turns to me and smiles. 'You too. You are to join us to eat, Cassandra. I'm instructed by Mr Priest.'

Mrs McLochlan smiles vigorously. 'It'll be nice to have a friendly face in there.' As Tamás and I walk in behind Mrs McLochlan his hand touches my elbow. 'So, tonight? To the pictures? Or a pub or something?'

I nod slightly

'Right. I will pick you up at seven.'

So with Mrs McLochlan and her Alwyn, I join the bosses at their party, which is starting without its guest of honour. The first thing I do is take Mrs McLochlan across to the reporter and tell her to show him the photograph and tell him the story behind it. He gets quite excited and says that's a very good angle. Mr Priest, who has obviously been listening, butts in. 'Now, now, Mrs McLochlan, we can't have you upstaging our guest of honour, can we?'

Mrs McLochlan looks up at him and then around the crowded chattering room. 'Sorry, Mr Priest, but I can't see no guest of honour here.'

I fight back the desire to applaud, then flinch as Charlie Priest throws an arm round me and laughs. 'I can see we have quite a character here, Cassandra!'

I am just fuming at the over-intimate hug, and the sheer patronage of the man when I look up to catch a look of loathing in his wife's eyes, directed straight at me. It is so black that for a second the lights in the room seem to dim. I wriggle out of his grasp and take Mrs McLochlan's arm. 'Now, then, let's fill a plate, shall we? Before it all gets eaten up?'

Behind me I can hear Mrs Priest's plaintive voice. 'Get me a G and T, Charles, will you? A woman could die of thirst in here and no one would notice. Joanie, tell Charles I need another drink, will you?'

Share and Share Alike

Joanie Laverick left Millie plaguing Charlie for a third G and T, gathered a plate of food to go with her orange juice and drifted across to the corner where Stan, beer in hand, was talking to a woman with a very pale face and bushy red hair, wearing high stiletto heels. She was clutching a schooner of sherry.

'Oh, Joanie,' Stan said, touching his tie as though reassuring himself it was still there. 'This is Leila Temple. She's from the coast, was next in line in the store on the appointed day when Mrs McLochlan won the cooker. Anyway the manager asked her to come along to the party in compensation.'

Joanie grinned. 'Bad luck, that!'

Leila smiled back. 'I'll survive.'

There was a little silence, and then Stan said, by way of conversation, 'Leila was asking about Millie Priest.'

'Very spectacular suit, that,' said Leila dryly.

Joanie rolled her eyes and allowed herself to be disloyal. 'Yes. Millie's very ... flamboyant.' Privately she thought that the woman in front of her was a bit on the flamboyant side herself.

'Must have cost a packet, the shantung suit,' said Leila.

'Well, between them, her and Charlie have quite a few packets,' said Joanie. They laughed at

384

this. After that business yesterday and a car-ride with the insufferable gloating Millie, Joanie was having fun.

'Mind you. Even she's knocking them back more than usual,' Stan observed.

'Don't tell me,' said Joanie. 'Her fourth gin and tonic. Silly, considering...' She stopped, remembering only she knew about the baby.

'Considering what?' said Stan.

Joanie stared at him for a moment. 'Boss's wife. Middle of the day.' She held up her glass of orange. 'Always a mistake, middle of the day. Specially if you're a boss's wife.'

Leila giggled and held up her schooner of sherry. 'Oh, Joanie, you make sinners of us all.'

Stan looked from one to the other and relaxed. 'Millie might be enjoying a drink, like, but she doesn't look that pleased.'

'You know Charlie, Stan. Likes being cock of the walk and makes up to anything in skirts. Not surprising that Millie can't stand it. Any of us would kick up about that, wouldn't we?'

Leila nodded wisely and took a large sip of sherry.

'It's Charlie's habit,' explained Stan. 'Can't help himself. It's like a twitch or a tic.'

'Lord save us from men like Charlie Priest,' said Joanie. 'That's what I say.'

'Amen to that,' said Leila.

Joanie held out the plate to Leila. 'Try this quiche, love. It's not half bad.'

'Oh, I can't take your quiche!' said Leila.

'Share and share alike, that's what I always say,' said Joanie.

'Oh, well, if you insist. To be honest I *am* a bit peckish.'

Across the room Millie felt herself observed and thought darkly about Joanie standing there with Stan and that woman with the ridiculous hair. Charlie had turned away and was sucking up to Mr Abrahams now, with that Tamás Kovacs and his father hanging on his every word. They were jawing on about fridges and the need to extend the Grafton plant, going on about the pool of skilled labour in the district and the Canadian market expanding. No one today, not even Charlie, had so much as mentioned her nice suit, and everyone here, except herself, seemed to be having a good time, even that wretched little prize winner who had the mayor and his wife laughing their heads off.

Millie suddenly felt very dizzy and sat down heavily on a chair.

At last Charlie looked down at her. 'You all right, lover?'

She made a great effort to get the words out. 'No,' she said. Her lips felt like rubber bands. 'I don't feel all right. I feel like a bloody spare part and my head really, really aches.'

Charlie glanced round the room and beckoned across Cassandra Fox, who was standing behind Mrs McLochlan's shoulder. 'Cassandra, I wonder if you'd take my wife home? She's not feeling too well. I'll get the driver to bring the car by the big door. You just take her home and get her comfortable.'

Millie slumped back. '...Not going with one of

your fancy bits...' she muttered.

He leaned down and muttered in her ear. His tone was vicious. 'You behave yourself, Millie, or that's you and me finished. I'm telling you. I won't forgive you.'Then, very gently, he drew her to her feet and handed her over. 'The driver knows our house, Cassandra. Just see that my wife is comfortable, will you?'

The people in the room watched as Cassandra guided Millie out of the room, then, when the door shut behind her, returned to their conversations.

Charlie made his phone call to the driver then turned back to Mr Abrahams. '...and young Tamás here, he's a man of the future, key to these new developments.'

The little man looked up from Tamás to Constantin. 'Mr Owen tells me that, like myself, you are an incomer here, Mr Kovacs? The boy flourishes here at Marvell's and you are an architect? A son is a fine thing.'

Constantin smiled. 'Not yet an architect here in Britain, Mr Abrahams. One examination to go.'

'I tell you, Mr Kovacs, this is a great country for incomers. Thirty years since I come with nothing. And look now. They have their ways, the British, but they will let you work and flourish. It is all a man can want.'

'Yes, sir, that's the truth,' said Charlie, brimming with pure happiness. 'Yes, sir, that's the truth. It's all a man wants, to work and flourish.'

The Map of Africa

So here I am, going down the gangway on the red carpet as yet untouched by the bare feet of Sandie Shaw, my arm around the boss's wife, who's had a couple too many. Not surprisingly we get a few amused glances from the women, still busy on the lines.

As we pass Patsy and Karen I raise my brows and shrug my shoulders and carry on. Then Karen comes racing after me with what looks like Patsy's work mac over her arm. She thrusts it at Mrs Priest. 'Here,' she says, 'get this round you.'

Mrs Priest looks puzzled. 'I don't need a coat,' she slurs.

Karen looks at me. 'She must have the curse. Her skirt...' Our eyes drop to the back of the blue shantung skirt, now sporting a bloodstain the shape of Africa.

Crikey! No wonder the women were staring at us.

'What's the matter?' says Mrs Priest.

I just pull the coat around her. 'Come on, Mrs Priest, let's get you home. The car'll be at the door.' I turn to Karen. 'Thank you for that. The others just stared.'

She shrugged, 'Patsy's idea,' and loped off to her bench in her very high heels.

The car driver greets Mrs Priest politely and she mumbles a reply.

'She's not very well,' I say, very defensively.

'Dinnet worry, flower. We'll get youse home in no time.'

I settle Mrs Priest in the back, making sure Patsy's coat is pulled down behind her so she doesn't stain the seat. She looks at me and frowns, her voice suddenly very sharp.

'Who are you? What are you doing?'

'I'm Cassandra. I was helping in the board-room and Mr Priest asked me to help you to get home.'

She picks up on my different accent. 'Oh, *Cassandra!*' she says. 'And is *Cassandra* a secretary, like the *Evelyn* woman?'

'No, I'm not. I work on the lines. I came up to the office to help because Evelyn was off today.'

'On the lines? Don't be silly, dear. You don't sound like that trash on the lines.'

I move away from her. 'Don't talk like that. These women are brilliant. I–'

Suddenly she's clutching her fist to her mouth. 'Ough! I feel sick. Oh! Oh!'

I nudge the driver. 'Stop! Mrs Priest feels sick.'

So there, on the edge of the road leading to the new estate, I get to hold Mrs Priest's head while she is sick as a dog into the grass. I mop her up with a pristine hankie out of her bag and we get back into the car. In two minutes we are at the house, a big showy place with double gates. The driver helps her out of the car with a blank face and I hustle her up the drive, get her keys from her bag and open the door. I look round the big bright hall. 'We need to get you to your bedroom to change your clothes.'

'Change? Why should I change? Do you know this suit cost two hundred pounds? Why would I change it? I'm not not ... taking it off.'

'I think you've had an accident, Mrs Priest. There's a mark on the back.'

She twists round to try to look at it but nearly falls over.

'Look,' I said sternly, 'Just let's get you upstairs and get you out of that skirt.' I almost drag her upstairs, into the largest bedroom, and stand her with her back to the cheval mirror. The stain has increased. 'Do you see? We need to get you to the bathroom, Mrs Priest.'

'Bathrooms!' she says, flailing her arm around. 'Bathrooms! Plenty bathrooms here!' Then she takes a closer look in the mirror. 'Christ! What's happening?' She rips off her jacket and her skirt and holds it up to take a closer look. There is an even bigger stain on her silk petticoat. 'Oh, no!' she moans. 'Oh! Ouch!' She clutches her stomach, stumbles from the room to the toilet and I follow her. In there, oblivious of me, she rips off the slip and the matching panties and collapses onto the toilet, moaning and crying at the same time.

Now I am panicking, tears in my own eyes. This is like no period I have ever known. 'What's happening? What can I do, Mrs Priest? What do you want me to do?'

She scowls up at me and then suddenly stops moaning. She shakes her head. 'You're very young, dear, aren't you?' She doesn't sound drunk any more. 'I'm losing a baby, love, that's what's happening. Pass me that towelling bathrobe from the door. Go in my bedroom, top drawer, left-hand side. Cotton interlock knickers. I keep them for my period. Two pairs, please. And bottom drawer right side. STs. Two of those please. Then you can ring the doctor and get him here. McDonald. Name's on the pad. Hurry, will you? I can't sit here all day.'

I hover. 'And shall I ring Mr Priest?'

'You shall *not*. Charles is where he wants to be, where he should be. I'm not having him here when I'm in this state. Oh! When you've rung the doctor take my skirt and put it in the sink in the washhouse. Cold water. I'm not losing that, as well as everything else.'

I obey her to the letter, impressed by the transformation from lurching, mumbling drunk to this organised, efficient creature. This woman who lost her dignity has retrieved it. I admire her.

By the time the doctor comes she's sitting in a chair in her bedroom, her make-up creamed off, her hair tied neatly back in an Alice band. He confirms that it has been a miscarriage, gives her a small bottle of pills, makes some kind of set speech about it being nature's way, and bustles off.

I still don't know what to do. 'I'm really sorry, Mrs Priest,' I say. 'About all this.'

'You?' She looks at me soberly. 'Me too. I had great hopes, you know about this baby.'

'How do you feel?'

'Sore, like I've been through the mill. And sorry for myself. And this head of mine is whirling. Maybe I'll know tomorrow what I really feel.' She stands up. 'Come on, love. I'd rather be downstairs than sticking up here like an invalid. I need to put my undies through the washer ... see to that skirt...'

Watching her carefully as she comes downstairs I reflect that I've not liked her very much today. I specially hated her crack about the factory girls. But at this minute I admire her. She's a brave woman. Unflinching.

She stops in the hall and picks up the phone. 'I'll get you a taxi. You need to get back to the factory.'

She brushes away my protestations that I can walk. 'No. I don't want you here and you should get back to the factory. Charlie has an account with this taxi firm, so you won't have to pay.' She has spotted my worry. I certainly can't afford a taxi.

As I make my way out of the house with Patsy's mac over my arm, Mrs Priest stops me. 'You say nothing about this to Charlie, Cassandra. Nothing! Just let him think you put me to bed the worse for wear. I don't want him charging home. There'll be time enough for explanations.'

Like I say, I might not like Mrs Priest but now I do admire her.

It is only in the taxi that the thought strikes me. I am so dumb. Charlie Priest and Karen! Charlie Priest and his blue shantung wife! I wonder what Karen will think. One baby kept, one baby lost. All due to that man. Not nice at all, when you think about it. I check my watch. Three thirty. It'll probably all be over now anyway. I can't say I'm sorry. I've had too much excitement for one day anyway.

Then, for the first time in days, I think about Emma. I wonder whether she's still having a good time picking her grapes and hanging about with those clever boys. I suppose I'm reminding myself that there is a world out there, a world away from Grafton and Marvell's Domestic Appliances, where the people are stranger than you think.

The Red Carpet

Well, I'm wrong, after all. I don't miss the big event. I just catch it.

As my battered taxi pulls through the gateway we are followed by a big limousine, which waits while my taxi parks and I leap out. I scuttle past Mr Priest, Stan Laverick and Mr Owen, who are clustered inside the big doors.

Mr Priest glances in my direction. 'Everything OK, Cassandra?'

'Yes, fine,' I say. I want to tell him all about Mrs Priest and to ask whether he wants me back up in the boardroom but his eyes shoot back to the big limousine that is sitting there like a crouching black cat. I scuttle up the red carpet and back through the lines, which are busy and clattering as usual, but different. Some of the women have even taken off their smocks. Not Patsy. She is exactly the same: smock on, hair over-neat and as usual just a bit too much make-up. Of course, Steve is there on the opposite side of the gangway, trying to look casual, but pink with excitement.

I thrust Patsy's mac into her hands and she shoves it under the counter without a glance. I'll have to tell her about the small stain on the back.

'She's here!' That's a bit redundant. The news is buzzing across the whole shop floor like a swarm of bees.

Karen slips out of her seat and takes out the big bouquet from under the bench. 'You do my set, will you, Cassandra? Patsy says we're not stopping the line even for Sandie Shaw. Mr Priest says she has to see us in action.'

Of course, Karen has changed out of her smock. She's wearing an A-line minidress in swirling blues and reds that makes her legs look really long; even longer with those high heels. No bare feet for her. And she has redone her hair: full fringe pinned to one side, glossy locks to her shoulders, eye-black heavy, eyes sparkling. She looks gorgeous.

Steve whistled. 'You look really something, Karen.'

She looks at Patsy. 'Do I curtsy or something?'

Patsy's hands are flying over the wiring jackets. 'Nah. You only do that for the Queen. Just say welcome to Marvell's Domestic Appliances.' But she has that secret smile on her face and you can't tell whether she's kidding or not.

I slip onto Karen's stool and pick up her screwdriver. Along at the big door there is all this murmuring clatter. Now the party is setting off down the red carpet, with photographers fluttering round them like moths to a flame. The Tannoy booms out '(There's) Always Something There to Remind Me' and even I am thrilled with the thought that the singer of that song, the *actual* singer, is walking down the gangway in Marvell's factory in Grafton amongst us more ordinary mortals. In *my* factory. I would not be anywhere else at this moment. Not even picking grapes in France.

Sandie Shaw's wearing these patent pumps with tiny heels and is certainly tall, taller than Mr Cartwright, the sales manager, and as tall as Mr Priest, who is hovering at her elbow with a grin on his face as wide as Tynemouth She looks young, younger than Karen, even. Like Karen she's wearing an A-line dress but hers is in swirling greens and blacks. Her hair is down, her fringe too is swept to one side and pinned with a slide. She has these enormous eyes in a pale face that is pretty and strong at the same time. Strange, though, there is this aura around her, like she is in the spotlight, although there isn't one here on the factory floor. The women applaud as she passes. Some of them shout out, 'Hey, Sandie!' 'Take off your shoes, Sandie!' And, 'Give us a song, Sandie.' It's as though they all know her personally.

It's really weird.

The entourage slows down when it reaches us and Karen steps up to hand Sandie Shaw her bouquet. Sandie passes the bouquet to the smartly dressed woman beside her, shakes Karen by the hand and asks her name. Then she looks her up and down and says with a warm, broad smile, 'For a minute I thought you were me!'

Some people clap and everyone laughs at this, Mr Priest most of all, who beams proudly at the pair of them. A good thing, I suppose, that I didn't tell him about his wife. This really is his finest hour.

The entourage moves on and Karen, still smiling her pleasure, says, 'Here, Cassandra, give us me screwdriver.' She is buzzing like a helicopter, full of energy. 'Patsy'll have me, wasting all this time. Just look at this backlog!'

'Get away with you,' says Patsy, hard at work herself.

I stand there, looking along the red carpet, feeling a bit lost.

The Tannoy has changed now to Roy Orbison singing 'Oh, Pretty Woman'. All along the lines the women join in the songs. It's true. Sandie Shaw is a very pretty woman. Really, really pretty. Aren't songs amazing? Songs for all seasons, all reasons.

'What're you waiting for, Cassandra?' says Patsy. 'You get yourself away with that Tam and those other nobs. You've been running around for them. You deserve the party.'

I take another look at the receding figures on the red carpet, then back at Patsy, and know exactly where I want to be. I pull out my own stool on the opposite side of the line and pick up my own screwdriver. Karen and Patsy exchange glances.

'Better party down here, eh, pet?' says Patsy.

We work on for a while, then Patsy says. 'So, was Madame Priest three sheets to the wind as well as caught short?'

I remember. 'Oh, Patsy! I forgot to tell you. There's this mark on the back of your mac.'

'I noticed. So, was she drunk, then?'

'I don't think it was just that.' I glance across at Karen, who still has her head down over the job. I whisper. 'It was a miscarriage. I had to get the doctor and everything.'

Karen's hands stop moving. We all stop working.

'Poor lass,' said Patsy slowly. 'Not a nice thing, that, to happen to any woman, is it?'

Karen jumps off her stool and does this funny thing. She pulls back all her hair into a plastic band, making the thick black kohl round her eyes look odd now. Then she puts on her smock over her dress and jumps back on the stool. 'Well, lasses,' she says, 'this won't get the job done, will it? Haven't we got jackets to wire, cookers to make?'

But now Tamás is loping towards us down the gangway. 'Cassandra, Mr Priest says you've gotta come. Mrs McLochlan asked where you were. At the presentation. Her nephew's drunk and she's on her own.' So we hurry back down the carpet towards the big dais that's standing at the bottom of Line Two like some kind of altar, with the velvet-covered cooker as an offering. The bigwigs are crowding at its foot; Sandie's gleaming head is waving like a tulip above the shorter men. Mr Priest is introducing her to the mayor. Flashbulbs are cracking as the photographers edge forward for the best shot. Then, with a grind and a moan, the conveyor belt comes to a stop. Now we can hear the crackles as an engineer links the microphone on the dais to the Tannoy.

The relative quiet is ripped by a spontaneous

cheer that rolls across the shop floor in a sound wave. Mr Owen, Mr Priest, the mayor and Sandie Shaw mount the dais. When Sandie climbs up the steps everyone claps and cheers.

I stop beside Mrs McLochlan and she clutches my arm whispering, 'This is a big to-do, isn't it, pet? I never thought it would be a big to-do like this. All this fuss. Me, I just thought I was coming to collect my cooker.'

Tamás's quiet voice comes from behind us. 'It's a big day for Marvell's, Mrs McLochlan. A celebration.' I can feel the heat of his body behind me, smell his special lemon-and-almond smell.

Now Mr Owen is at the microphone, talking about Marvell's and its expansion in recent years. Then the mayor talks about Marvell's effect on the Grafton economy after the loss of the mines. Then it's Mr Priest's turn, which evokes big cheers down the lines as the workers recognise their own man. He quietens them down with a wave of the hand, and says this is the happiest day of his life; how proud he is of his factory, how glad he is to be here in a fine town like Grafton, and what an honour it is to have a great star like Miss Sandie Shaw come here to present the millionth cooker. Now the workers are cheering Sandie to the skies, which makes her smile broadly and wave cheerfully at them, which generates another cheer.

When all this quietens down Mr Priest introduces Mrs McLochlan as the lucky winner and she mounts the dais with a little help from me. She smiles weakly when they all cheer her. Then she shakes hands with Sandie and, at a signal from Mr Priest, the red velvet cloth is pulled away to reveal our magnificent Empress Cooker, gleaming white under the strip lighting, inspiring yet another great cheer around the shop floor.

Sandie shakes Mrs McLochlan's hand again and whispers her congratulations. Charlie drags Mrs McLochlan to the microphone and asks her if she has anything to say. She puts her mouth too close to the mike so her voice is distorted, and her very loud, raw 'Thank you!' seems to scrape off the iron girders. But we clap her, we keep clapping, we all clap till our hands are raw.

And then it's over. Mr Priest is hustling Sandie and her party up onto the gantry as, with a grind, the conveyor starts again. The workers groan and catcall, but drift back to their stations cheerfully enough.

Stan Laverick comes across to escort Mrs McLochlan back to the boardroom but she shakes her head. 'I don't think so, son. Our Alwyn's had enough, don't you think?' She nods across to her nephew, who is on the edge of the crowd with his arm round the bushy-haired woman whom I last saw talking to Stan's wife. The woman is laughing. They seem to be having a great time.

'So I think me and our Alwyn'll get on home, son,' says Mrs McLochlan. 'No need for a car. That nice Mrs Temple says she'll give us a lift home as she lives down our way. To tell you the truth I'm whacked.'

Stan scowls and makes his way towards Alwyn and the woman.

'What's the matter with him?' I ask Tamás.

He looks at me for a second. 'Well, the word is

that there's a thing on there.'

I frown. 'A thing? Where?'

'With Stan and the Temple woman.'

I laugh at this and he shrugs. 'Only gossip,' he says. Then, 'So, are you coming back up the boardroom to rub shoulders with Sandie?'

'Nah. I'm going back down to Karen and Patsy. The line'll be backed up.'

He smiles such a nice smile at this, and I am remembering last night again, my night in old Budapest. 'Anyway, we're on for tonight. Is that right?' he says, touching, just touching, my forearm.

I nod, and turn to go. He puts a hand on my shoulder so I have to turn back. 'Would you mind if we went to see Evelyn first? Her father is in hospital so she might like to see a friendly face. Or two friendly faces. Please?' He smiles.

I smile back at him. It's all right now, this thing with Evelyn. Everything, simply everything, has changed. I'll go quite happily to see Evelyn Laing, because I know for a fact that she, unlike me, was never in Budapest.

Aftermath

The nightly production meeting on the day of the Sandie Shaw event was unusually short and self-congratulatory, with Charlie handing out cigars as though there had been a christening. Stan was glum and surly but he was like that sometimes, so no one took any notice. His day had been ruined by the sight of that stringy nephew of Mrs Mc-Lochlan hanging around Leila. The worst thing about that, as far as Stan could see, was that Leila was lapping it up. She was clearly on to the next game. He knew it. He knew that he was yesterday's news. His mood had not been helped by Joanie buttonholing him at the party and wanting to gloat about Millie Priest making such a show of herself. Then she started to go on about wanting driving lessons and Stan couldn't get rid of her fast enough. He even got the Marvell driver to take her home without checking it out with Charlie.

After they had all gone Charlie sat in his empty office and rang Millie, but there was no answer. She must be spark out. His euphoria at the day suddenly leaked away, replaced by anger at Millie, who, without his quick thinking, would have ruined his special day. As he drove away he realised he couldn't face her. It was easy – sometimes too easy – for him to bawl out the men who worked for him. But he had never found it easy to be angry with Millie. It was she who usually became cross with him over some slight thing or other, but that was like a feather in the wind. It was easy enough to buy Millie off, with cars or cocktail cabinets.

Charlie decided to call at the golf club to dilute his anger with a Scotch or two before he confronted Millie. At the bar he fell into conversations with a few acquaintances who had seen the segment about Sandie Shaw on local television and were keen to buy him a drink and let

401

him tell his story. Charlie Priest was always good value.

So, by the time he was turning into the estate Charlie was quite mellow, thinking tenderly about his poor Millie having a few too many. After all, that wouldn't have happened if Sandie Shaw had not been delayed. He would go home, and tell her his tales of Sandie Shaw, and how pleased Mr Own and Mr Abrahams were about it all.

When he got to the house, all the lights in the house were blazing and the door was half open. He walked a little unsteadily through the rooms, turning off lights as he went. Inside the laundry room, hanging from the window frame, he found the blue suit Millie had worn today, dripping into the sink. She must have been sick on it. Really!

He went upstairs to storm into the bedroom to confront her but could not open the door. He hammered on it, roaring, 'Millie, what the hell are you playing at? Open this door.'

He heard her muffled voice from inside.

'Open this bloody door or I'll tear it down.'

Silence. Then the key turned in the lock.

By the time he got into the bedroom she was back inside, the bedspread up to her neck. Her face was scrubbed clean and her hair held back with a wide Alice band. She looked about thirteen. Standing by the bed, Charlie's anger drained away again. 'What's happened, Millie? What's this about? What was all that in the boardroom?'

'This is what it's about, Charles.' She scowled at him. 'There you were at the party, fingering the girls, as usual. You didn't even say you liked my suit.'

He sat on the bed. 'It was a beautiful suit, lover,' he said softly. Now, buzzed up by the success of his day he wanted to stroke her, make love to her. 'I saw it in the laundry.'

'I've been waiting for you, Charles. I've been waiting all night.'

'I rang and there was no answer so I called at the golf club. I thought you must still be sleeping it off.'

She said nothing. He moved around the room, taking off the Italian suit and hanging it up carefully. He went to clean his teeth and have a shower and came back into the bedroom with a towel round him. He lifted the pillow and looked around. 'Where's my pyjamas, lover.'

She was watching him, her eyes suddenly quite beady. 'They're in the spare bedroom.'

His anger came flooding back. 'What? What're you playing at, Millie? It was you that got so pissed you couldn't stand. It was you that made a show of yourself at the do.'

'Do you want to know what happened to me today, Charles?'

'Yeah. You got drunk, you got taken home, you slept it off.'

'Not quite. I got drunk. I got taken home by the girl you'd been fingering. I lost our baby and ruined my blue shantung suit. The doctor came. And I waited for you. I waited and waited.'

'Lost...' Charlie collapsed, half sitting on the bed, half kneeling on the floor. 'Lover!' he reached for her. She flinched and shook him off.

'It's not so bad, lover, We can try–'

'No more! No more of that. No babies, no blood, no nothing. Don't you kid yourself, Charles.'

'Millie...' he tried again, but she wouldn't let him touch her.

'Your pyjamas are in the spare bedroom, Charles. They and you can stay there. For good. I don't want you in here again. Ever.' She snuggled down and her face was lost from sight. Her voice was muffled. 'Put the light off when you go out, Charles.'

In the bedroom next door he pulled on the pyjamas and paced the room. How could she? How could she ruin his day like this? And how could she ruin his dreams of a son to follow him, his investment in the future. Really, Millie had shot her bolt now. He'd taken all her nonsense but that was it. He would finish with this nonsense for good.

He threw himself into the bed and just as he was pulling the pure white covers under his chin he had this very comforting thought. There was always young Karen. *She* could be his investment in the future. Changing partners was not so hard these days. People did it all the time.

There He Blows

On Sandie Shaw Day Tamás and I went straight to Evelyn Laing's after work. No, I tell a lie. First I go down to circuit breakers to tell my mother where I was going. She's still working with her friend Marje, both of them purring with the extra inspiration of newly granted overtime. My mother looks less tired than usual, her white ruffled blouse emphasising her rosy cheeks. The reason for her flushed demeanour is leaning against her bench like an advertisement for Dunhill suits: Constantin Kovacs. He straightens up and smiles when he sees me.

'Cassandra! And how did you enjoy the festive day?' he says.

'It's been interesting,' I say. 'Did you see Sandie down this end?'

'We did,' says my mother, her hands busy. I think of Patsy O'Hare. 'Charlie Priest walked her right through the whole factory floor so everybody got a look. She had this very nice smile. That's when Constantin dropped off here. I've been trying to get rid of him ever since.' But my mother smiles, not meaning it.

'He's a proper stop-work,' says Marje from her side of the bench. 'We were just packing up when Stan Laverick was down here with a face like a mile of bad road, saying the numbers were down. Looked like he's lost a bob and found sixpence.'

'You're not telling me, Marje,' says my mother, 'that you won't want the overtime.'

Constantin beams at me. 'I am trying to persuade Linda to come out with me tonight, for a drink.'

'And I've told him I don't drink in pubs,' says my mother, in a bantering tone I hardly recognise.

'First time for everything,' grunts Marje.

'You should go,' I say. Then I tell them I am going off straight away with Tamás, '...first to see Evelyn Laing, you know, the secretary? Then me and Tamás are going out. I don't know where.'

Marje cracks a smile. 'Like mother like daughter.'

'It's not like that, and you know it, Marje,' says my mother sharply.

I turn away, wondering whether it is really 'like that' with her and Constantin. She can't have forgotten he's married. Then I smile at the thought that I'm acting as though she were the daughter and I the mother.

Tamás is waiting for me by the buses and I get in the car in front of the watching queue of women, feeling now as though he really is my boyfriend. Boyfriend! Crikey. At first the conversation is quite cheery, with him going on about the success of the presentation, how pleased Mr Owen was and how very pleasant Sandie Shaw was, even though she didn't eat or drink anything.

'Not surprising, really,' he says. 'By the time she got there the boardroom was like a bombsite and the shop manager and the mayor's friend were drunk.'

I don't mention the drama with Mrs Priest; I can't talk about things like that to Tamás.

We drive right out of Grafton and at the road sign for the village of Brigg we finally get down to the subject of Evelyn. Tamás talks again about Evelyn telephoning the office after the meeting to say her father has died. 'He was a bit confused when I met him but he had been a great man, I think. Evelyn was very fond of him.'

My heart aches at this, not really because of my sympathy for Evelyn or her father, but because of the affection and sympathy in Tamás voice. 'Poor thing,' I say, floundering.

As we turn into the narrow back street and Tamás puts on the brakes I am intrigued at the sight of the house. I thought it would be quite smart but this is only a little pit house. It's even smaller than ours and the street is even meaner.

When Evelyn comes to the door she is wearing a silver-grey top and a straight black skirt. Her blond hair is swept up neatly as usual, but her face is pale and she's wearing no make-up. She's older than I thought.

She steps aside and we squeeze down a narrow hall and through a tiny kitchen into a small sitting room. It's half the size of mine but much daintier and better kept. By a fireside chair with a rug over it is a small table on which stands a radio, an alarm clock, and a plate with a half-eaten sandwich. On the mantelpiece are several glamorous photographs of Evelyn and a studio study of a very formally dressed, handsome couple.

We stand there awkwardly for a moment, then Tamás just takes her in his arms. 'I am so sorry,

Evelyn. He was a fine man.' He kisses her cheek and she clutches him tight. I have this cruel rush that makes my skin prickle: I am jealous of their friendship and their intimacy. I feel clumsy and in the way.

'You know my good friend Cassandra,' he says.

She pulls away from him and glances at me. 'I have seen you,' she says. 'You work with Patsy O'Hare.'

'I'm sorry for your loss,' I mumble.

'They say he didn't suffer. And he recognised me at the end.' She looks up at him. 'I am fine, Tamás. Really.'

He stands there awkwardly now, her hand still in his. 'Can I do something, Evelyn? Can we do something?'

She looks around the room. 'My father spent most of his time here. Do you know this is the first time I've been in here since, he ... since it happened.'

'We can help you clear up,' I said desperately, too eagerly.

She shakes her head. 'No. Thank you, Cassandra. It'll get done in time.'

'What will you do?' he says. 'What will you do now, Evelyn?'

'Well, the funeral will be on Saturday. Would you come?'

He takes her hand. 'Of course. Of course I'll come.'

She turns to me. 'And you – Cassandra, isn't it? Will you come?'

I can only nod. I am scarlet, astonished to be included.

'So what will you do, Evelyn?' he repeats.

'I'll be back at work tomorrow.'

'You shouldn't, Evelyn.' At last he lets go of her hand. 'You shouldn't come to work.'

'I should and I will. Where else would I go? There are the schedules to do, and there will be work to catch up from today. Charlie was really annoyed when he heard I wasn't coming in today.'

'Charlie's mad. You know Charlie. The sun rises and sets on Marvell's.'

'Anyway, I'm coming in to work tomorrow and I'll give two weeks' notice.'

'And then?'

She smiles slightly and her drawn face lights up. 'And then I'll clear this house. That done, I'm going to New Zealand to see an old friend, and then back to my old employer in London. He'll have some work for me. After that, who knows?'

We're still standing there awkwardly. She hasn't invited us to sit down. She laughs thinly. 'It's odd, you know. We've had to live so carefully, but my father's insurance was set up when he had the shop. Now that will free me to do just what I want. Otherwise I might have been working at Marvell's for ever.'

Then the silence weighs heavily in the room. There is nothing to say. Evelyn seems relieved when Tamás kisses her cheek again and says goodbye.

She shakes hands with me. 'Take care of him, Cassandra. He's a great person, this Tamás Kovacs.'

Then we are back in the car and driving to

Grafton in silence. It is only when we are in the Roma drinking frothy coffee that Tamás starts to relax and we become ourselves again, separate from Evelyn, thinking about the future, not the past.

The morning after Sandie Shaw Day, just before the first break, Charlie Priest stops by the wiring jacket line.

'Mornin', Karen,' he says. 'You seen the pictures in today's papers? You and Sandie Shaw? All over the front page. You look a million dollars. You did a great job for us with those flowers, lover. So, how are you this lovely mornin'?'

Karen doesn't look up.

'I said, "Hello, Karen".'

Patsy eyes him. 'Seems like the lass doesn't want to say nowt, Mr Priest. Must've had a bad night. Not surprisin' really, in her cond–'

'You mind your own business, Patsy,' he growls. 'Karen...'

Then, unable to resist it, I pipe up, 'So how's your wife today, Mr Priest? She seemed very poorly yesterday.' I wait, then, 'I am really so very sorry for your ... loss.'

He turns and scowls at me.

At last Karen looks up. 'Get lost, Charlie, will you?' she says. 'I want nothing to do with you. *Ever.*'

Charlie looks at us, one to the other: from Patsy, to Karen, to me. We can barely contain our laughter. He turns on his heels and strides down the gangway, our chuckles raining on his head like thrown flowers. He catches up with Stan Laverick

410

and we can hear him right down the line, berating Stan loudly about a threatened strike in the paint shop that might still affect this week's production.

'There he blows!' said Patsy, and we laugh so much we have to stop work all together.

Funny, isn't it, how one thing leads to another? Like I said in the beginning, all this was a long time ago. But for me that week in the 1960s was the beginning of the life I have now. My friend Karen went on to have the baby called Cassie (after me, because Karen always says without me Cassie wouldn't have been on this earth). Young Cassie is the oldest of a large brood: Karen is as dedicated as her own mother when it comes to family, although Steve is what they call now a more 'hands-on' father than Mr Duncan.

Being a working mother, still with my head in books, I've never matched Karen at all that. Even so, I have quite a brood myself. My Emma and Constantin have only a smattering of Hungarian but their children, my grandchildren, have still been brought up on Hungarian fairy tales. But my youngest, Patricia, is a great linguist: her brilliant diplomatic career began with a Doctorate in Eastern European Studies that sprang out of her fascination with the homeland of her father and grandfather. My late friend Patsy O'Hare always took pride in the career of her namesake. She used to call her a 'lass after my own heart'.

Our good friend Evelyn Laing is now Evelyn Mallory. She lives in America, but has visited us many times here through the years. Her son, like his father, is a well-known painter of peculiarly

American landscapes. Patricia stayed with them during her year at Harvard. At one time I thought she would marry Evelyn's son, but that didn't come off. It was Patricia who was always closest to Linda, my mother, who wakened up somehow during that Sandie Shaw summer and began to live.

My beautiful Tamás is retired now and although Marvell's no longer exists, he and I often talk with great affection about the old place and particularly the unique people who made it. And I blush to admit it, but *old Budapest* still retains the attraction for us both that it held in that week when Sandie Shaw came to Grafton to present the millionth Marvell cooker.

The publishers hope that this book has given you enjoyable reading. Large Print Books are especially designed to be as easy to see and hold as possible. If you wish a complete list of our books please ask at your local library or write directly to:

Magna Large Print Books
Magna House, Long Preston,
Skipton, North Yorkshire.
BD23 4ND

This Large Print Book for the partially sighted, who cannot read normal print, is published under the auspices of

THE ULVERSCROFT FOUNDATION